"I DON'T LIKE THIS."

And then Rab[...] danc-
ing wildly a[...] t up
and soon s[...]

The body wa[...] one eye
was closed, [...] destroyed, bulged
milkily from th[...] socket. There was a blood-
rimmed hole in the poncho. The bullet had
broken his back, and death had no doubt
been instantaneous.

This gave little sense to the second wound
she discovered.

He had been shot in the back of the skull as
well. The scalp around the entry hole
showed tattooing, stippling from tiny hemorrhages caused by the discharge of burned
powder. The victim had taken this second
bullet from only inches away.

Dee knelt over him. She made a fist to stop
her fingers from trembling.

This was her first homicide.

HIGH DESERT MALICE

KIRK MITCHELL

AVON BOOKS ◆ NEW YORK

HIGH DESERT MALICE is an original publication of Avon Books. This work has never before appeared in book form. This work is a novel. Any similarity to actual persons or events is purely coincidental.

AVON BOOKS
A division of
The Hearst Corporation
1350 Avenue of the Americas
New York, New York 10019

Copyright © 1995 by Kirk Mitchell
Published by arrangement with the author
Library of Congress Catalog Card Number: 94-96861
ISBN: 0-380-77661-8

First Avon Books Printing: August 1995

AVON TRADEMARK REG. U.S. PAT. OFF. AND IN OTHER COUNTRIES, MARCA REGISTRADA, HECHO EN U.S.A.

Printed in the U.S.A.

RA   10 9 8 7 6 5 4 3 2 1

ACKNOWLEDGMENTS

I thank the Basque Studies Program of the University of Nevada, Reno, and the Nevada Office of the U.S. Bureau of Land Management.

HIGH
DESERT
MALICE

CHAPTER**ONE**

The sun broke over Cayuse Mountain in an eye-watering burst of gold.

"*Merde,*" Dee Laguerre said.

Keeping one hand on the steering wheel, she threw open the glove box and sifted through several inches of loose shotgun shells. Something rubbery and vaguely penile mystified her until she realized that it was the case to her snakebite kit. Pulled apart, it became two suction cups used to suck out venom. Snakebit was one thing she hadn't been these past nine months. Reviled, spat upon, even shot at from a darkened alfalfa field while on patrol. But not snakebit.

At last she found her sunglasses, but the lenses were covered with alkali dust. It was like looking through frosted windows.

"*Merde,*" she said again, whipping out the handkerchief she kept in the right rear pocket of her chocolate-brown trousers. "Come on, rain."

Nearly every August, a hurricane slowly dying off the coast of Baja California would spin bands of moisture-laden clouds into the Great Basin, that drainless sink between the Sierra Nevada and the Rocky Mountains. Then it would rain more in a few days than it did over all the rest of the year. But until that time, the summer dust off the dry lake beds was everywhere. Even in Dee's mouth, coating her teeth like talcum powder. Each night before bed, she spent ten minutes going over her

.357 magnum revolver with a felt cloth. The interior of her Ford Bronco was so drenched in dust it looked as if it'd been sculpted in clay, and the engine's air cleaner had to be replaced every week or the cruiser ran like a carnival bumper car.

At long last, the weatherman in Reno was talking about some low pressure on the way. There was no sign of the front yet, but she could feel the humidity in the air. Her hands were sweaty this morning, and ordinarily perspiration in the high desert evaporated like breath mist on a mirror.

She could see again. *"Bon,"* she said, putting away her handkerchief.

This stretch of Highway 95 cut across open range. Empty, flat land that had been the bottom of a huge freshwater lake when woolly mammoths roamed west central Nevada. The two-lane road ran perfectly straight for ten more miles before curving up out of Cayuse Valley and on into the next parched basin. Endless ranges and basins—this was the Nevada most tourists never saw, America's back forty, where the military bombed and strafed in complete privacy, where the Department of Energy hoped to salt away enough nuclear waste to make a smaller state, like Delaware, glow in the dark. Cayuse Valley was precisely in the middle of this wind-scoured nowhere. A three-and-a-half-hour drive north to Reno, and the same south to Las Vegas.

Dee adjusted the dusty rearview mirror for a glance back at Holland Station.

It had once been Holland Way Station, a stagecoach stop between Virginia City and Tucson. A century and a quarter later, it was still a cluster of weathered shanties, a pit stop between far-flung destinations. The biggest building was throwing a forlorn shadow across the surrounding sagebrush. It was the Pyrennes Hotel, a Basque island in a sea of hostile Anglo cattlemen. Here, in the lobby, her father had courted her mother, and here Dee now rented a room. The concrete walls were a pretty saffron color in the dawn light, instead of their usual scabby gray.

Yawning, Dee nudged her glasses back up onto the bridge of her nose. The hum of the mud tires against the pavement was making her drowsy again. Her need for coffee was bordering on addiction.

Suddenly, she smiled at a road sign. It was meant to warn motorists to watch for cattle on the highway. The black silhouette of a steer. Except the illustration was too muscular to be a testosteroneless steer, so some local wag had drawn in an enormous pizzle.

Maybe that's why she'd come back home after the divorce. San Francisco had no idea what was genuine.

Any cattle were staying clear of the highway this morning. She could see them scattered out across the range, dots of black and brown, doing what they'd been doing for more than a century: turning the Great Basin into an unbroken carpet of sagebrush. Nobody really knew what this country had looked like before the pioneers put their livestock on it, but the best guess was that it had hosted a wide variety of plants. Most of these, the grasses and the wildflowers, wound up as cud. Cattle and sheep usually don't care for sagebrush, so it flourished, spreading like a gray-green stain across ten western states.

The shadow of an airplane flitted across the Bronco's hood.

Dee rolled down her side window for a look overhead. A small Cessna. The pilot was banking westward, toward California, after taking off from Jewell Farley's dirt airstrip. Climbing a bit unsteadily, Dee thought.

No wonder.

A night of drinking and whoring at Jewell Farley's Guest Ranch would make even Chuck Yeager look like he was on his first solo.

She left the window open. The air was still velvety and cool, although in another hour the sunlight would feel like fire on her exposed skin. Cayuse Valley was almost a mile high, but from May to October that only made it seem closer to the sun.

She slowed, then turned off the highway onto a gravel lane flanked by whitewashed stones. The Bronco's tires kicked up a floury roostertail that blotted out her view to the rear. But ahead she could see Jewell's aluminum compound, a jury-rigged affair of old mobile homes grafted onto one another. Jewell had started with one small, single-wide trailer, but "the beast with two backs" had made it prosper even beyond her most optimistic hopes, and now the hodgepodge of a structure contained over three thousand square feet of air-conditioned space.

A red beacon flashed day and night atop a steel tower alongside the landing strip. The light was to mark the radio antenna, not advertise Jewell's trade. She'd been among the first brothel operators with the foresight to realize that business could drop right out of the sky, and now most of the houses had airfields.

Dee parked between two tractor-trailer rigs. Both drivers had left their diesels purring while they ducked inside.

"How romantic," she muttered.

She got out and slid her nightstick into the ring on her Sam Browne belt. Then, stretching and yawning once more, she studied the sign attached to the ten-foot-high chain-link fence:

JEWELL'S GUEST RANCH
Miss Jewell Farley, Proprietress
—Men Only—
—No Iraqis—

The first restriction had always been there. A Pinyon County ordinance mandated it, as women loving women ran counter to everything rural Nevada stood for. Jewell had tagged on the second proviso in a fit of patriotism during the Gulf War, and once she made an enemy it was for good. The same was true of her friendships, and Dee had been Jewell's best friend ever since the two of them had first boarded that yellow bus in pigtails for the 120-mile roundtrip to school in Tonopah, the largest town between Reno and Las Vegas.

Last night, Jewell had phoned, inviting Dee for morning coffee—adding matter-of-factly that she'd better come unless she wanted another bullet whistling at her. Dee had asked her what she meant, but Jewell wouldn't say over the line.

Dee pressed the button on the intercom box that hung next to the electronically activated gate.

"What's your pleasure?" Jewell's tobacco-raspy voice asked.

"Coffee," Dee said urgently.

"Already brewed, Baa." It was a nickname, affectionate now, that had come from the cattlemen's kids baa-baaing at her and the other Basque children on the bus. Dee and the Arrache boys retaliated by depositing fresh cow flops in the lunch pails of their taunters.

The lock buzzed open, and Dee pushed her way through the gate. She paused a moment on the front steps and scanned the southwest horizon. The creamy tops of some cumulus were just starting to poke over the mountains in the distance. It'd be like Christmas to have rain after all these months.

So fresh.

But the air in the foyer of Jewell's place was anything but fresh. Mingled odors of stale cigarette smoke, beer, and unwashed bodies. The girls were scrupulously clean, but the steady clientele were a different story. Jewell's chief complaint about the buckaroos, or Nevada cowboys, was that they left a fine manure dust in the beds.

Dee met a customer heading out the front door, a trucker with a company logo on his baseball cap and a T-shirt too short to cover the sway of his belly. His amphetamine grin told her that he wasn't about to just pass by.

"Christ awmighty," he exclaimed admiringly, "I didn't know this was a place where the girls costume up. Where you been all night, darlin'?"

Dee wanted to retch. "Out on calls."

"That legal?"

"More than legal," she said icily. Someday, she'd go an entire week and not be subjected to this crap.

Finally, his pinkish eyes fastened on her holstered revolver. "That real?"

She gave him a wilting glare.

It must have worked, for he backed up, brushing the wall. A framed photograph fell to the carpet, glass shattering.

"You a deputy sheriff or somethin'?" he asked, ignoring the damage he'd done.

"Ranger, Bureau of Land Management. U.S. Department of the Interior."

He shook his head at her uniform. "Shit, you ain't like no forest ranger I ever met."

"Things get rough out in the forest."

"You some kind of *cop*?"

"What d'you think?"

"If you is, you're the sexiest damn little cop I ever seen."

She inflicted *the look* on him again.

"Wrong thing to say?" the trucker asked.

Dee nodded. "Give me five bucks."

"What for?"

She pointed at the broken picture.

He fumbled in his wallet and came out with a twenty.

"Have anything smaller?"

"Nope. Sorry, ma'am."

Dee said, "Jewell will give you the change your next time through." She raised an eyebrow. "Or you can take it out in merchandise."

Quickly, he made his escape.

Dee stooped and began gathering the shards of broken glass onto the photograph. Hated this kind of foolishness. At first, it had really rattled her, just the disbelief that a grown man would treat her this way. But now it was only mildly annoying. And *the look* worked wonders. To conjure it, she recalled the hard immigrant eyes of an old woman in a portrait on the wall of a Basque restaurant in Reno. A woman who'd suffered too much in the New World's deserts to back down over anything.

Dee glanced at the photo in her hands.

It was of Jewell and the Little League team she sponsored. Jewell's Gems. She stood behind the boys with the coach, beaming, although her cathouse pallor made her look like an owl caught out in the daylight. It wasn't often that she left her place unattended, even for a few minutes. As far as Dee knew, Jewell had never even gone to a game. But there she was for posterity. With her boys. Dee had seen out-of-staters gawk at this photograph, dumbstruck that a brothel, even a legalized one, had the brass to sponsor a Little League team as openly and proudly as a plumbing supply company. But rural Nevada had made its peace with prostitution long ago, and this sagebrush offshoot of the profession was far less brutal than what Dee had seen on the streets of San Francisco.

The parlor was empty, dimly lit by neon beer signs. Dee passed between the ottomans in the middle of the room. Here the girls could sit without being groped while the patrons mulled over their choices from the greasy couches set against the walls.

As expected, Jewell was in the kitchen, lighting what was probably already her tenth Winston of the morning. The skin around her mouth broke into tiny wrinkles as she sucked the cigarette to life. She was just twenty-eight, like Dee, but looked forty. The chain-smoking more than the job, Dee suspected. Jewell had started at age twelve, always taking a seat at the rear of the bus so she could light up without the driver's smelling it.

"Mornin', Baa," Jewell said, pouring Dee a cup of coffee. Turning from the sinkboard, she noticed the damaged frame and the twenty-dollar bill. "What happened?"

"Somebody thought for a minute I work here."

"Meet the nicest goddamn people in this business." But then Jewell gave a phlegmy chuckle. "And you're the last girl in the world I'd ever hire, Dominica Laguerre."

"Why—too skinny?"

"Not that. Some men prefer it. 'The closer the bone, the sweeter the meat.' It's just that you'd make a lousy actress. You say every damn thing you think."

"Actress?"

"Sure. What d'you think we do here?"

"Well, correct me if I'm wrong—"

"A brothel crib is a stage," Jewell interrupted, referring to one of the small rooms, "and, believe me, there's more actin' talent in a dump like this than you'll ever find in Hollywood. I got me a new colored gal who could put Meryl Streep out of work if she wanted all the attention. But she don't. We're all sick to death of attention." Jewell set the photograph on the sinkboard, then sat. She was a short woman with stubby legs, which she hid under long skirts, always black or dark gray. From time to time, usually in shifting light, Dee suddenly realized that she was pretty in a coarse sort of way.

Then Jewell swiftly changed the subject from whoring, as was her habit. "How's Gabrielle?" Dee's landlady, the hunchbacked owner of the Pyrennes Hotel.

"Tired of Japanese and Germans." They arrived by the busloads for lunch, having breakfasted in Yosemite and scheduled for a dinner show in Las Vegas. Once the hotel had been an authentic Basque refuge, the heart of a sheep grazier community that had largely moved on since. Dee could remember going there with her parents for Saturday supper in the last of that heydey, the dining room filled with a burble of French, Spanish, and—of course—the oldest, most mysterious of European languages, Basque. But no more. Just krauts demanding coffee as thick as mud, and Japanese taking flash pictures of Gabby's hump as if the old woman had no more feelings than a wildebeest.

"Wouldn't mind a few buses of those foreign boys stoppin' by here," Jewell said. "But they always travel with their goddamn wives." She paused, looking at Dee as if for the first time that morning. "How's my Baa doin'?"

"All right."

"That's not what I hear," Jewell said, then took a sip of coffee.

"Says who?"

"I got my sources. Why you stirrin' up that wilderness thing again?"

"I'm not."

"Bullshit."

"I mean, I've never stopped supporting the idea. And it's not just me behind it, Jewell. A lot of people all over the country want to see Congress designate Cayuse Mountain a wilderness area."

"Tree-huggers and granola-eaters," Jewell said contemptuously. "Lot of 'em pasty-faced Easterners who'll never set foot west of the Mississippi but wanna lock up our lands."

Dee guarded against a flash of anger. Jewell, despite their long-standing friendship, was a typical product of Pinyon County. "Honey," Dee said carefully, "those people may never make it here to Cayuse, but these lands still belong to them. *All* the American people own them, not just the folks living closest to them."

Jewell, clearly unconvinced, took a languid puff off her Winston. "Your ex-hubby's group in on this?"

"Yes," Dee said, "the Wilderness Conservancy Alliance is on board."

"You talk with him lately?"

"We're discussing Cayuse Mountain."

"Boring," Jewell said. But Tyler Ravenshaw was of immense interest to her. A handsome attorney with political clout. Her own ex-spouses—two or three, depending on how she told it—were admittedly no-'counts. The most violently alcoholic of the lot had sliced off the tips of two of her fingers with a hunting knife. T.R. had used more subtle means to pare Dee down to size. "Anyways," Jewell went on, "I thought the mountain was already some kind of wilderness."

"No, the legislation is hanging in the balance," Dee said. "At this point, the mountain's just a wilderness study area."

"What's there to study?" Jewell asked.

"Some of the last old-growth juniper-pinyon forest in the state. Shoshone nut-gathering camps. Petroglyphs. And there's bristlecone pine up near the summit. Oldest living things on earth. As old as the Pyramids, some of those trees.''

''I don't know, Baa,'' Jewell said suspiciously. But then she asked, ''You get your car back yet?''

Dee sighed. ''No, dammit.'' Her personal car, a twenty-year-old Fiat, was once again in the shop at Gold Mountain, the county seat, which lay forty miles to the northeast. ''They're still waiting on the part, which is fine with me—because I'm still waiting on the money.''

''Why don't you borrow some from your ex?''

''Sure.''

Jewell took another long puff, then exhaled. Through the smoke, her gaze fixed thoughtfully on Dee. ''I never seen Cayuse folks so pissed as they are now, Baa.''

''About what?''

''They say that if Congress gives the word, there'll be no more grazin' up there on the mountain. No firewood gatherin' or prospectin' either. No nothin' on hundreds of square miles of gov'mint land. That true?''

''Yes,'' Dee said flatly.

''And jobs'll be lost.''

''That too. How many, I don't know.''

Jewell took the cigarette from the corner of her mouth and leaned forward. ''Then what's the good of it? And why're you puttin' your neck on the block for it?''

Dee closed her eyes for an instant. She'd already been through the first public meetings on the issue. People she'd gone to school with screaming at her as if she were some faceless robot from Washington. She'd told Tyler in the weeks before she had finally made up her mind to leave him and San Francisco, ''If you really want to find out what kind of environmentalist you are, go home to practice what you preach.'' Well, she'd done just that—but had underestimated what it felt like to cross swords with people she'd known all her life.

''You've got a point, Jewell,'' Dee began slowly, quietly. ''It's easy to talk about job loss when yours isn't at stake.''

''Tell me about it.'' After high school, Jewell had

been the receptionist for a lithium-mining company that went belly-up.

"I'll be the first to say that it's complicated," Dee continued. "But in the long term something terrible is happening all over the Southwest. Something we'll never be able to undo. Desertification."

"What?"

"The range is turning into desert. A wasteland."

"Shit, Baa—it's always been desert. Open your blinds, lady."

"Not this severe, this barren," Dee said. "There are examples all over the world of what can happen here. Northern China and Mongolia, for instance. They've been overgrazed, and now dust storms bury Beijing for weeks on end. That will be Las Vegas or even Southern California one of these days. And if the land goes up in dust, Jewell, the watershed is right behind it. Nobody can live in the West unless there's a steady supply of pure water, and that's what wilderness does better than anything. It secures watershed. Forever." Dee paused to calm down; she'd raised her voice. "Jewell, I was born in the shadow of that old mountain, just like you. I'd like to save it for those coming after us ... wouldn't you?"

Jewell yawned widely, then said, "Who's gonna be here if there ain't no work in Cayuse Valley?"

A few pat answers sprang to Dee's mind, but they seemed hollow at the moment. Jewell knew what she was talking about. If mining and livestock went, she'd have to move on. And this valley was her home as much as anybody's, a rare place where she was accepted, respected even—thanks to the spirit of the frontier that lived on with spurs and Stetson hats. In Los Angeles or New York, Jewell would just be another whoremonger tussling with the justice system.

So talk of Chinese dust storms wasn't likely to make a big impression.

Sitting back, Dee asked, "Is this what you wanted to tell me?"

"Hell no," Jewell said, looking a bit hurt. "I don't

give a damn what trouble you make for yourself.'' But then she tossed a glance over her shoulder to make sure they were still alone in the kitchen. ''Last night, some dribbler told one of the girls—'' A squawking from the radio atop the refrigerator made her rise heavily: a pilot asking for landing instructions.

Jewell divided all men into two categories. Dribblers and squirters. Dee idly began applying the distinction to the two men who'd been closest to her, Tyler and Cinch Holland. But then she made herself stop. Too crass.

Jewell advised the pilot of wind direction and speed—and told him to keep an eye out for wild horses on the runway. Then she sat again and closed her hands around her coffee cup. ''Some dribbler,'' she continued in the same low tone, ''said him and his pards are goin' up on the mountain tonight. Had to break a date 'cause of it. Sounds serious to me.''

''What do these buckaroos have in mind?'' Dee asked. She knew Jewell would divulge no names, and it'd violate an understanding between them to ask. Still, by saying ''buckaroos'' she was fishing to find out if they were ranchers.

''Din't say. But it was definitely goin' down after dark. The date wasn't scheduled till midnight.'' Then Jewell added, ''Don't go up there, Baa. Steer clear.''

''Oh, I'm going.''

''Damn, then I shoulda shut up 'bout this, you pig-headed Basco.''

''No, I appreciate it, Jewell. Honestly.''

''Then show it by not goin' alone. Promise me now.''

''Why?''

''Girl,'' Jewell said, her mascara-lined eyes crinkling with exasperation, ''you gotta stop kiddin' yourself that that first bullet was just a potshot fired by some toasted cowpuncher. It was a warnin' to you and the gov'mint from every rancher in the county. A hun'erd different fingers pulled that trigger, Baa . . . don't you *see*?''

gave a damn what trouble you made for yourself. But

CHAPTER**TWO**

Cinch Holland took his wife, Rowena, down to the gravel pit with him. That way, she could drive the old GMC pickup back up the winding lane to the ranch house. Two nights ago, he'd left his tractor down there after suddenly realizing that it was too dark to drive the lightless rig home. Time seemed forever to be sneaking up on him. Luckily, he'd caught a ride back up the hill with his hired hand, who was returning from Gold Mountain with the freshly sharpened blades for the mower. Now he needed the tractor to cut the alfalfa. Even though it might rain today.

Far off in the southwest, heavy clouds were piling up against the mountains there.

Rowena and he rode in silence.

She stared out across the range, the loose flesh on the backs of her arms jiggling as the truck vibrated down the washboard road. Her face was puffy, her expression blank. He had no idea what she was seeing, certainly not what he was: a sunburned land covered this late in the season with only tall sage and cheatgrass. Both largely useless to stock.

The hooves of his cattle had scooped out a dust wallow in the brush around the salt blocks he'd set just inside the fence line. The BLM would get on him about that. Jack Reckling, the range conservationist, would give him holy hell. Must remember to move the blocks away from the road and out of sight before some environmental snoop reported him.

This was government land, and he played by its rules on the 5,000 acres he leased to graze his cattle. He owned only the original Holland homestead, 160 acres, plus some 40-acre plots around springs his ancestors had bought back in a time when simple ownership of the water gave a livestock operator the run of the surrounding countryside. Much of this acreage was irrigated meadow with lush grass, but still it could never support his entire herd.

"Doublin'," he murmured, not realizing for a few seconds that he'd spoken out loud. Next year the government was doubling the rate for each cow the Hollands put on federal land.

Rowena, no doubt, knew what he was thinking about. She didn't ask him to repeat himself.

He took his father's pocket watch from his Levi's and was disappointed to see that it was only eight-thirty. He was already noon-tired. A dull, smoldering headache. And he might not get to bed until long after midnight.

"Feels like rain, Row," he said, just to break the silence.

"Don't it though?" she said pleasantly enough.

"I mean, I may not get to the alfalfa today."

"That's fine."

It wasn't fine, not with some parts of the field already turning purple with blossom, slowly ruining the value of the crop as feed. But he hoped that he was beyond lashing out at her. It'd done nothing except frighten their son, Cody. All the fear under their roof was turning the ten-year-old timid, clinging.

Still, Cinch no longer trusted in Rowena's optimism. She'd always been religious, but it was almost spooky now, her faith that things would turn out fine. He supposed that he believed in God for a different reason than she did. He was in hell, and some power had to have put him here. A man just didn't drift into straits like these on his own.

Suddenly, he hit the brake pedal and bailed out.

"Cinch . . . what is it? Cinch . . . ?"

He broke into a run as he rounded the front of the pickup, then stopped beside the fence. He was angry for a moment, angrier than he'd been in months, but then an exhausted, sinking feeling took over. He eased down so that he was sitting on the heels of his boots.

"What's wrong?" Rowena asked from the pickup.

My God, he thought, *is she that blind to what's destroying us?*

But again, he told himself that he was finished pitching into her. It wasn't her fault. Not any of it. She was just within reach. One night, for a few terrifying seconds, he'd come within inches of backhanding her.

"Some tree-huggin' son of a bitch went and cut our fence, Row," he finally said. All five strands of barbed wire. He searched for shoe prints and then tire impressions on the road, but the escaping cattle had trampled them. *Must round up the strays.* No sight of them on the rolling slopes all around. "I'll walk from here to the pit," he added.

"You still gonna cut the alfalfa?"

"If there's time." Cinch rose. "Go back and phone Olin. Have him pick up Augie. I'll need their help."

"You want me to get the sheriff's office?"

"Later."

Rowena slid across the front seat and took the wheel. She drove the dark green GMC down to a wide spot, then made a U-turn and started back toward the house, shifting clumsily right in front of Cinch. He tried not to show his displeasure. She was hard on the worn clutch. She had no feel for machinery.

He checked his father's watch. The old man was gone, but he'd chained Cinch to time before going. It'd be a good two hours before Olin Peters, Rowena's brother, and Augie Dietz, Cinch's part-time hired hand, would arrive. Time enough to drive the tractor up to the barn and hitch on the mower.

He'd had Rowena leave him off here because the road made a big switchback just below and he could save time—*time again*—by walking straight down the slope.

But he was too beat to move right away. He'd spent

all of yesterday stringing new fence with Dietz. At supper, his arms had been so sore from driving in metal posts it'd hurt to bring food and drink to his mouth. He watched the dust from the pickup sift up against the sun, golden. Rowena drove under the telephone line that, in the past year, had begun to sag, thanks to a wobbly pole. One more thing to fix.

Then he passed through the breach in his fence and started down the slope.

It was more frightening than he'd ever admit to Rowena: that the Hollands had enemies who came in the night to try to force them off the land. The first of his family had arrived in Cayuse Valley when it was just another nameless basin beyond the southern Rockies, driving their herd of longhorns all the way from Texas. That had been two years after the Civil War. They'd spent the first winter in a cave on Cayuse Mountain. Fought the Shoshone by themselves because no cavalry was close by.

But they'd hung on. Five generations.

He plunged on down the steep slope, digging in his heels to keep from sliding. He could see the gravel pit, an ash-colored scar in the sage.

His great-grandfather had opened it in the 1890s, and the family had made free use of the gravel ever since— until three years ago, when the BLM informed him by certified letter that from now on he'd have to file a mining claim. Somebody from the Wilderness Conservancy Alliance had asked to see the claims by which local ranchers were taking ''common varieties minerals'' from public lands. Nobody had ever filed. It would've seemed like petitioning to use air. But Cinch had then filled out the forms, and the WCA accomplished exactly what it'd set out to do: forced the ranchers to spend the one thing they could least afford: *time*.

Cinch slid the last few yards down into the pit, the soles of his boots rasping over the gravel.

He looked his tractor over, then dug the key out of his pocket. He'd purchased a locking cap for the gas tank, so the engine couldn't be gummed up with sugar, which had been done to Tom Wheatley last fall. The sons of bitches knew that livestock operators had their equipment spread all over kingdom come.

Nursing the choke, Cinch fired up the engine. It ran all right, and he sat back, relieved.

He'd wanted to get the tractor yesterday, but Augie Dietz had been in a rare mood to work, and the two of them had gotten to stringing the new fence as soon as breakfast was done.

Cinch raised the bucket and started up the road, the engine puttering.

The iron seat was far from comfortable, but he sat back and tried to relax. This might be the only idle time he'd have until God knew when. He, Olin, and Augie and the others were going up onto the mountain tonight. They'd all go, even if Cinch couldn't find his strays before nightfall. He'd made up his mind about that.

The tractor's engine suddenly died.

Quickly, Cinch braked, swearing, then immediately restarted it. But as soon as he let out the clutch the engine seized and stopped again.

He sat quietly for a minute, gazing up at the clump of cottonwoods that hid the ranch house from view, the green square on the mountainside that was his alfalfa field. It was waiting to be cut so he might have some cash to pay a few of his bills and limp on for another month or two.

He got off the seat and checked for the gear oil plug.

It was gone.

He turned and traced the ribbon of glistening oil that went all the way back to the gravel pit.

Dee Laguerre turned off Highway 95 onto Cayuse Mountain Road, the main artery into the wilderness study area. She had no intention of going all the way up onto the mountain before nightfall. To her right was Ranch Road. Along it were the alfalfa fields and head-quarters of most of the valley's cattle operations. She could almost feel the eyes of the ranchers following her. On her left sprawled Alkali Dry Lake, achingly white under the morning sun. On its ancient shoreline stood a shanty that looked neatly whitewashed until the rain rinsed off the salt dust. Augie Dietz's hovel. Dead ahead loomed Cayuse Mountain itself, the only scar of human activity on its slopes the Holland Ranch.

But reaching the foothills, she turned again, this time north onto a trace that had once been used to service a telegraph line, abandoned now. Tall sagebrush screaked along the sides of the Bronco as she roller-coastered over a series of gullies and ridges.

Gambel's quail skittered in front of her, tilting forward like little bowling pins about to topple.

Last winter, seven years of drought had finally given way to normal snowfall, and now there was a population explosion of small animals. Most of the moisture in this, the West's *cold desert*, fell as snow, even though staggering amounts of rain could come from a summer cloudburst, sweeping cars off Highway 95 as if they were toys.

Still, Dee preferred rain over snow.

Her father had lost three toes to frostbite his first winter in a small tent on the open range. And her parents had died in the snow.

The dust made her sneeze, suddenly. It wafted in like smoke through the door seams. She flipped on the air conditioner, the fan creating just enough cabin pressure to stave off the worst of it. But her sunglasses were a mess again.

She cleaned them once more, thinking.

The choice to go up on the mountain tonight was entirely hers. For all she knew, the locals were planning a stag party. It'd happened before. They'd carted along a generator to run a projector for porno flicks, alfresco.

But she was sure that wasn't the case this time.

No, it was something illegal, something falling under Dee's jurisdiction. Otherwise, Jewell would've kept her mouth shut.

Deer poaching and even cattle rustling came to mind, but while the locals might bag a few bucks on the sly they'd never steal livestock. Invariably, that was done by outsiders, rustling syndicates that used bobtail trucks, slaughterhouses on wheels.

Jewell had been warning her, maybe even intimating that the sniper who'd fired the shot at Dee last May under the cover of darkness would be among them tonight.

Dee slowed.

A white pickup truck was shining on the flats below. On its driver's-side door was the same inverted blue-and-green triangle that marked her own vehicle.

All at once, she wanted to turn around. The déjà vu of past shouting matches came over her like a wet blanket.

She knew that if she were male she wouldn't think twice about asking for a backup tonight. But it seemed that every request for help, no matter how reasonable, was used against her by the man who'd parked that white truck out in the sage. Proof that a ''split-tail'' couldn't hold down a remote beat by herself.

Still, she wouldn't grovel. And she'd go up alone if she had to, for she knew deep down that the local ranchers were putting together another wild horse kill. Massed rifles and Jim Beam whiskey—great sport. Mustangs, protected by federal law, competed with livestock for scarce forage and even scarcer water.

She could see two male figures sifting through the brushy growth on the plain below the truck.

She stopped and rested her chin atop the wheel, running through the alternatives before she drove the last few hundred yards down. Ask the sheriff for a deputy to go with her. But that was the same as phoning one of the ranchers and saying that she was on to their plan for tonight. Most of the deputies came from ranching families. Rabe Pleasant was on days off in Las Vegas. The middle-aged wildlife biologist was the one BLM male employee in the Cayuse Resource Area she could rely on to help her without counting it a moral victory. But Rabe wasn't due to report back for another two days, and she could only hope that he'd return early to the Pyrennes Hotel, where he rented the room directly across the hall from her.

That left only Jack Reckling, the range con, to ask.

Sighing, she depressed the gas pedal and drove on toward the white truck.

Sometimes she tried to see things as Reckling did. He'd joined the bureau in a time when female employees were clerical support. His own wife had never worked outside the home, just baked pies and knotted macramé plant holders in their bungalow on the federal housing compound a mile south of town. So, in the eighties along came a crop of young women who didn't want to type and answer the phone. They wanted to be in the field. When the old guard in the Department of the Interior tried to stonewall this, lawsuits followed. Then came the consent decrees, agreements between the government and women's groups to keep the issue out of the courts. *Presto*—fifty-five-year-old Jack Reckling had a convenient excuse, other than his own alcoholism, for why he'd never been promoted: affirmative action for split-tails.

Dee gritted her teeth as she watched him work, a lank figure waist-high in the sage. Catching the engine noise, he glanced up and stared at the approaching Bronco. Then, without a wave, he went back to making checkmarks on his clipboard.

"Fuck you too, Jack," she muttered.

One such consent decree had obligated the Nevada office to fill a number of its ranger vacancies with females. Not that she'd needed it, she believed. She'd wound up first in her class at the federal law enforcement academy in Georgia. A class that had been ninety-five percent dribblers and squirters.

She pulled alongside the white truck and cut her engine.

Reckling was still ignoring her. She could just see the other man's head, jet-black hair glistening in the strong sunlight. He was the botanist from the Reno office, Milton Kwak. She knew that, as far as Reckling was concerned, she was personally responsible for Kwak's being down here, draining Jack's budget on "some political bullshit."

She stepped outside and loudly shut the door. Folding her arms over her badge, she leaned against the Bronco. The wind had risen strongly out of the southwest, tropically moist. She could smell the promise of rain on it.

Reckling gave her his back. A streak of sweat had already worked through his calico shirt.

She turned away, tempted to leave. Reckling could go to hell.

The two rangers in Cayuse before her had been split-tails. Both of them—thanks to endless griping from Reckling, hostility from the livestock operators, and numbing loneliness off duty—had quit. The state ranger coordinator hadn't believed his luck when Dee walked into his Reno office—a divorced split-tail with no espousal career to worry about, a native Nevadan, *and* a Basque to boot. A people with a legendary capacity to endure the solitude and privation of life on the open range.

She rested her elbows on the roof to gaze eastward. Instantly, she jerked them away. Hot.

Cayuse Mountain rose above her, immense. If pulled flat like a wrinkled carpet, it would be larger than New York's Long Island. And that gave her another problem in going up alone tonight. The road went in on this, the west, side and came out thirty miles to the east inside the nuclear testing site, which the locals easily ran by turning off their headlights and keeping to the branch roads.

If things went reasonably well with Jack, she'd ask him to bring his truck tonight. Two vehicles that way.

Meanwhile, the range con went on pretending that she wasn't standing fifty yards away.

She reached inside the cab for the public address microphone. "Jack," she boomed over the external speaker, "this is the skinny Basque bitch. . . . " She knew that he called her this behind her back. Reckling gave no reaction, but Kwak stuck his head up out of the brush and laughed. "Hi, Milt. Jack, can we talk? I can throw a bullhorn out to you."

At last, Reckling lowered his clipboard to his side. But he wasn't quite ready to stroll up the gentle slope. He fished in his shirt pocket for a pack of Lucky Strike regulars, lit one, and let out a long stream of smoke before starting her way.

Reckling stopped ten feet shy of her, said nothing.

"Morning, Jack," she said. "How's the work going?"

He had a gaunt, humorless face, and eyebrows bleached white by years in the desert sun. He took a deep pull off his Lucky, then hooked his thumbs behind his silver belt buckle, a mannerism he'd probably picked up from his cowboy buddies. "Well, Laguerre," he drawled, "we been out here since seven, and the China-man still can't say if it's *Eriogonum ampullaceum* or *Eriogonum davidsonii* or some goddamn mix of the two nobody's heard of yet." Reckling took pride in the fact that he didn't sound or act like a man with a sheepskin, even though he'd gotten a bachelor's in Wyoming. Not exactly Ivy League, but still his put-on accent made her wonder why he felt it necessary to sound like Slim Pickens.

"Korean-American," Dee corrected.

"How's that?"

"Milt is Korean-American, not Chinese."

"Whatever you say, Laguerre," Reckling said, scratching his leathery cheek with the same two fingers that clenched his cigarette. "For a little gal, you're sure keepin' me busy."

"Oh?"

"First a whole new range inventory, which I still ain't half done with, and now this—tryin' to figure out if we got us a patch of threatened and endangered *Eriogonum ampullaceum* or just its plain-Jane cousin, *Eriogonum davidsonii*."

"I didn't bring the eriogonum to the bureau's attention, Jack," she said evenly.

"No, but your friends with the WCA sure as shit did."

"Friends aside, I had nothing to do with it. And I'm tired of you insinuating I did."

But he was on a roll now. "Sent an amateur botanist out here all the way from 'Frisco. Had her tramp her cute little fanny all over this country for three months with one express purpose—find every picayune endangered plant species she could so Congress would turn the whole shebang into designated wilderness. No more grazin', all for some little plant even John Muir woulda tromped on without a second look."

"This range could use some rest, Jack," she said, realizing that she shouldn't have as soon as it flew out of her mouth. She'd come to get backup for tonight, not wade into the grazing controversy that had divided the BLM itself.

"What the hell d'you know, Laguerre?"

"Not much, Jack," she said, feeling her blood rise. "I've just got a worthless master's in resource management."

"Master's," he grunted, as if the word were an obscenity. Then he walked off a short way and looked out across the valley toward the approaching storm. "*Cowburnt*. There's another one."

"What about it?"

"That's what you and your renegades called my range in your report to the director. Catchy word. You whizkid rebels make it up?"

"No," she said. "Edward Abbey did." The late environmentalist was one of the first to sound the alarm that cattle were turning the Southwest into a cat box. And the rebels Reckling was referring to were her fellow dissidents of Federal Employees for Environmental Responsibility, mostly BLM and U.S. Forest Service midlevel careerists who'd had enough of business as usual, of the government's invariably siding with the livestock and mining interests. She was president of the Nevada chapter, which would probably block her own chances for promotion. Not that she wanted to trade the field for a desk.

"Fuckin' Abbey . . . it figures." Reckling dropped the cigarette butt to the sandy ground, snuffed it out under the toe of his rawhide chukka boot. "An American Gobi. You put that down too, right? My range is being severely overgrazed and trampled into an American Gobi?"

"We did."

"This honestly look like the Gobi Desert to you, Laguerre?"

"Not quite yet. But close. Give the graziers a few more years."

"Christ, woman—your own daddy was a grazier." Reckling tried to smile, but the expression turned into a scowl. "Hell, I remember you ridin' in his ol' Studebaker truck when he came to get his permit renewed . . . you no bigger than that blue-eyed sheepdog of yours." Dee kept silent. With another man there might have been some genuine fondness attached to the memory. But not with Jack Reckling. "Now, I know he and your mama are gone . . . what—nine, ten years now?"

She nodded. Nine years, six months. A solo car rollover on the drive back from Gold Mountain in a snowstorm.

"But let's pretend he wasn't. And what's more, let's pretend you're in my shoes. What would you say to him? No more sheep permits, Papa Laguerre, 'cause this country is all used up? It's *sheepburnt*." Then Reckling offered a travesty of a warm smile. "Now be truthful—would you have the heart to tell him that?"

She'd had enough. "You found the heart to cut his allotment in half, just to brown-nose your cattle friends and lease them the acreage. That's what got him off the range, Jack, not the environmental movement!"

He sighted down his forefinger at her. "Now hold it right there, sister!"

"I've been holding it a long time, Jack, and it's starting to stink." She took a step forward and shoved his finger aside. "I never claimed to know what's best for this range. *That's* why I pushed for an inventory. Let the specialists come in and look it over. The flora and fauna, the whole ecosystem. Then we'll really know what the carrying capacity for livestock ought to be. Scientifically. Not somebody's guesstimate. I don't know what the hell you're so pissed off about. If you're right, the inventory'll prove it!''

"It's a waste of taxpayers' money!"

"No, Jack," she said. "The waste comes from renting grazing allotments to your cronies for pennies an acre!''

Then both of them realized that Milt Kwak was standing on the other side of the vehicles, looking embarrassed, twirling a sprig of sage in his fingers. She would've expected him to be examining some eriogonum. But it was just common tall sage. Ubiquitous *Artemisia tridentata*, the plant that had won the West because of grazing.

"What?" Reckling snapped at him.

"Came in for a drink," Kwak said, keeping his eyes on the ground. "Then I'm gonna start widening the search." He walked to the back of the truck. Before reaching for the water cooler, he carefully slipped the sprig of artemisia into a Baggie he was stashing in his front pants pocket.

"Well, Laguerre," Reckling said, throwing up his hands, "we get to widen the goddamn search area now." Then he chuckled bitterly. "Shit. You and your rebs start the wilderness ball rollin', and I'm the one who gets the death threats."

"What're you talking about, Jack?"

Reckling shook another Lucky out of the pack, then struck a kitchen match on his thumbnail. "Just what I said—I been gettin' calls."

"At home, you mean?"

"Yeah."

All at once, Dee recalled the throaty bang of the high-powered rifle going off in the alfalfa field and the rustle of the bullet going past her head. "Has Topsy taken any of these calls?" she asked.

"Just me. He knows when I'm home."

"Recognize the voice?"

"Nope."

"Same caller all the time?"

Reckling yawned.

"Why didn't you report this, Jack?"

But Reckling just walked back out into the brush.

Kwak was lifting the cooler over his head and letting the water trickle down into his mouth.

"Bet you've been having a ball," Dee said to him.

Kwak wiped his lips on his sleeve. "Well, I can't say that I've been made to feel like family."

"Consider yourself lucky. You should see how he treats his wife. Anything she does to him short of decapitation I'm going to call a suicide." Dee paused. "Does it look like ampullaceum to you?" The endangered variety.

The botanist hesitated, but then said quietly, "I think so. But if you don't mind, I'm gonna mail my findings to Jack."

"Don't let him get to you, Milt."

"He won't," Kwak said cheerfully. "I'm giving notice in a couple weeks."

"I'm sorry to hear that."

Kwak said, "Thanks, but enough's enough." Then he joined Jack back out in the scrub.

Frowning, she got inside the Bronco and immediately set the air conditioner on full blast. Muggy. She wasn't used to it. Five or six percent humidity was the norm in the high desert. Last summer in Georgia had nearly killed her.

She popped a eucalyptus lozenge. The shouting had rekindled her chronic dust cough.

Turning the Bronco around, she noticed a glint on the slope just above. She stopped and broke out her binoculars. Nothing, just bitterbrush thickets. And it'd been close enough to the old telegraph line to make her think that sunlight was reflecting off a broken glass insulator.

She continued on toward Cayuse Mountain Road.

Alone tonight in the wilderness study area. That's what this spat with Reckling meant. But now she didn't care if every drunk rancher within a hundred miles was up there with a rifle and a festering grudge toward the BLM. She wasn't about to ask Reckling for help ever again. "And good going, Jack," she said to herself. "It'll be months before we get a replacement botanist."

Her radio squawked to life. The scanner picked up the transmissions of every federal, state, and local agency within range. This time it was the sheriff's office dispatcher sending the resident deputy in the valley up to the Holland Ranch for a monkeywrenching.

She parked near the intersection and slowly cooled down as she waited for the cruiser to appear. She told herself that, no matter what, she had to work with Reckling. And in fairness, she reminded herself that he'd held the line here against grazing abuses for a quarter of a century. Much of that time he'd been alone. The problem was that it hadn't been an especially firm line.

The black-and-white Dodge came past, spraying gravel against the side of the Bronco. She fell in behind the deputy.

CHAPTER**THREE**

Monkeywrenching had been Edward Abbey's battle cry to end grazing on public lands. By that, he'd meant for environmentalists—not the armchair kind, but bona fide rural guerrillas who'd make no compromises in the defense of Mother Earth—to throw a monkey wrench into the gears of the federally subsidized livestock industry. Make it ungodly expensive for ranchers to maintain their operations. Cut fences so they'd have to spend time chasing their stock. Bury salt and mineral blocks. Flip over water troughs. Drop chunks of iron down well casings. Spike the roads used for the fall roundup. Sabotage machinery. Shoot cows. Toss wrench after wrench into the guts of the works, stand back, and watch the industry grind itself to pieces.

That was the game plan, and young men and women from the world over, undaunted by the risks of arrest or ranchers' gunfire, were enacting it all over sagebrush country.

Dee knew that grazing on government allotments had to go. It was just too hard on the land for the small return it gave the American public: only two percent of the total production of U.S. beef. But monkeywrenching wasn't the way to end it. Not against a rugged, well-armed people who held private property to be the most sacred of their rights. Sabotage would bring a backlash, one far more violent than an ecology prophet like Abbey could ever have envisioned. After all, he'd never been a cop. Angry people hadn't been his specialty. He'd been a visionary, and visionaries can seldom imagine an indignation stronger than their own.

Dee now sped around the big curve on the dirt lane to the Holland Ranch.

It gave her an odd thrill, a delicious sense of danger to have come this far and still be heading up the hill. She'd never been to the house, although as a teenager she'd ridden on muleback to the bluff above the curve. From there, she'd seen the homestead through the winter-bare cottonwoods and, happily, Cinch Holland, too. He'd been in a rawhide coat with a fleece collar, pitching alfalfa off the back of a haywagon into the snow for the cattle, which came running from the edges of the pasture, their breaths steaming.

Thin dust began enclosing the Bronco.

She slowed as once again she drove up on the rear bumper of the resident deputy's sedan. The Dodge was fishtailing slightly on the rough road, which was badly in need of grading.

The deputy waved, his plump hand sparkling from two or three Indian-style rings.

Dee waved back for a third time.

His name was Paul, but everybody called him Pancake. His tan uniform looked like a Coleman tent with buttons, but nobody complained to the sheriff. The locals seemed to prefer their cops fleshy. She'd heard that at one time the department had required an annual physical checkup, but then two deputies had suffered heart attacks—one fatal—during the treadmill test. So that ended that foolishness. The rest of rural Nevada law enforcement was on the way to modernization. But not Pinyon County S.O. The sheriff refused to cooperate with state peace officer standards and training. In his view, Carson City was a "foreign power."

Pancake led the way through an open gate and parked in the dooryard of the house. He got out and his side of the chassis sprang up six inches.

"Mornin', Dee," he said. Then, chortling, he pointed at her nightstick, which she'd slid into her Sam Browne ring. "You altogether sure you'll be needin' that baton?"

"Like a seat belt, Pancake. You never know when."

"You ain't changed one bit, Dee-Dee," Pancake then said. She wasn't quite sure how to take it. They'd known each since high school. For one thing, nobody called her Dee-Dee anymore.

They went up the front steps together, and Pancake knocked on the screen door.

Waiting for someone to answer, Dee turned and looked the place over. It was more run-down than she'd imagined. The saddlehouse and other outbuildings hadn't been painted in at least a generation. The original log cabin had tumbled in on itself, and just outside the garden fence lay a junkyard: a wooden freight wagon, a Model-A pickup, and cast-off pieces of farm machinery, all half cloaked by a rank growth of sedges and prickly poppy.

But the Hollands still had something infinitely precious in this country. Water. It leaked from a mossy gash in the hillside, formed a willow-shaded creek that fed into a pond near the house. It was a rare riparian grassland surrounded by miles of dry scrubland, the portion of the homestead Cinch hadn't put in alfalfa. A pair of dragonflies were whirling in courtship a few feet above a bed of blue flag iris.

"Yes?"

Dee started slightly at the sound of Rowena Holland's voice. She hadn't heard it in ten years.

Cinch's wife must have seen only Dee at first, for as she neared the screen door she said less sharply, "Oh, hi there, Pancake. Thanks for comin'."

"Glad to, Row."

Dee worked not to appear too pleased. Rowena looked like a frump. Thirty pounds overweight. Two chins, and one more on the way. But she had those same vapidly pretty blue eyes that had been alternately glued to the King James Bible and Cinch Holland on that long bus ride.

"Hello, Rowena."

She took so long to answer that Dee began to wonder if the woman had recognized her. But then Rowena said expressionlessly, "Dominica. Somebody told me you was back."

Cinch, Dee hoped. "Yeah, going on a year now. Surprised we haven't bumped into each other."

"I don't get down the hill much."

"How old's your little boy?" Dee asked, although she already knew the answer. Almost to the month.

"Cody's ten."

And then the two of them ran out of things to say to each other. Rowena tried to smile. Dee tried harder. Thankfully, Pancake broke the silence. "Cinch inside, Row?"

"No, I'm sorry—he's in the barn with my brother and Augie. They're gettin' set to ride after the strays. You wanna go on through the house? It's quicker."

"Naw," Pancake said, "no use trackin' up the carpets."

"Nice seeing you, Rowena," Dee said.

Rowena just nodded, then stepped back out of sight.

Pancake and Dee had to skirt the truck garden fence to reach the barn. Along the way was the woodpile, and an ax was frozen in a round of locust wood, probably where it'd been left the very first morning spring came to the high range. It told her something about Cinch's life, that ax. He was racing from one chore to another, and never coming close to catching up.

They were going through the corral gate when Dee felt eyes on the back of her neck.

She stopped dead and turned, letting Pancake go inside the barn by himself. Her gaze was drawn to a second-story window, where a figure sat motionlessly. For a split second, Dee thought that it was a mannequin, the little boy's idea of a joke. Then she realized that it was Mother Holland, who'd been cut down by a stroke six years before. Jewell had told her that the matriarch was a living ghost, unspeaking, unseeing, unfeeling, dependent on her daughter-in-law for "spoonin' the food in and diaperin' it out." The rusted mesh of the screen

made her features seem surreal, as if her somber face
had been painted there by Andrew Wyeth. But Dee
could almost feel the same old hatred spilling from those
dull eyes, hatred for the "foreign bitch" who'd seduced
her son. The seduction—in the Hollands' GMC on a
knoll south of town—had been spontaneous and mutual,
and Dee couldn't recall who had led and who had followed. In that, it'd been uncommonly innocent, her first
time.

She could hear Cinch's voice coming from inside the
barn. It was older, but still soft and unassuming. He was
telling Pancake how the monkeywrenchers had cut his
fence and frozen up the differential gear on his tractor.
"They loosened the plug just enough so the vibration
from startin' the motor would shake it off. . . ."

Dee didn't hurry through the big doors.

Over the past year they'd waved while passing each
other on the highway. That had been it. Cattlemen didn't
frequent Gabrielle's bar in the Pyrennes. And Dee was
far from welcome in the cowboy tavern across the street,
the Snake Pit. She'd seen Cinch driving a new one-ton
diesel truck until recently. Jewell said that it'd been re-
possessed.

Dee stepped inside the barn.

Sunlight was slanting down through the holes left by
missing roof shingles. Cinch stopped talking and looked
at her. His bay gelding was saddled, and he was holding
it by the bridle. For an instant she thought that he was
displeased she was there, but then he slowly smiled and
said, "My God."

"Cinch." She could tell that she'd caught him completely off-guard by the way his eyes darted around her
face. He wasn't as lean as she remembered, but still
sinewy with a flat belly. His long sleeves were rolled
midway up his biceps, as far as they'd go without cutting
off circulation. The color had risen in his tanned cheeks,
so she rescued him by asking, "Where was the tractor?"

"Down at my gravel pit."

Not his. The public's. The pit lay on federal land. But
she let it slide. "When'd you leave it?"

"Evenin' 'fore last. Like I told Pancake—I was fillin' a rut in my road with gravel."

She took the hint and shut up while the deputy went on with the questioning. Cinch smiled quietly at her once more before shifting his attention to Pancake, although now and again his eyes would suddenly pull at hers.

She became aware of the other two men, besides the deputy, in the barn. Olin Peters, Rowena's brother, was a bruin of a man, balding, with a serious paunch. He was doing his best to ignore Dee. The shot fired at Dee had come from his alfalfa field, although a neighboring rancher swore up and down that Peters had been with him in town at the time. The other man, Augie Dietz, kept looking at her with a twisted grin from atop a drum of diesel fuel. No doubt he'd perfected his jailhouse stare during the seven years he'd spent up at Carson City for a homicide committed during an armed robbery. Killed a liquor store owner after he'd shot Augie in the face, leaving a deep scar under his right eye. Dietz was a wiry little misfit who made ends meet by prospecting, trapping, and hiring out part-time to local ranchers. He wasn't accepted, exactly, but he'd found a niche for himself in rural Nevada's Old West tolerance for the outlaw.

"You wait and see," Olin Peters was saying, finally glancing at Dee, "some blood's gonna be spilt 'fore this is over."

"Whose, Olin?" she asked.

"Depends."

"On what?"

"How far folks get pushed."

"Do you feel you're being pushed too far?"

Peters turned sideways and smiled at Dietz, who shrugged, still grinning, and said, "Everybody's got a button what can be punched up, Miss Dee."

"And what's yours, Augie?"

Briefly, his face went to stone. "You don't wanna know." But then he laughed under his breath.

"Well," Cinch, clearly uncomfortable, told Pancake, "we gotta be goin'." And then he said to Olin and Augie, "I wanna be back here by four, no matter what."

Dee found that odd. Under these circumstances, the typical cattleman would stay out as long as it took to find his strays. She had to ask. "Why's that, Cinch?"

He looked questioningly at her a moment, then walked his mount toward the doors. "Got things to do here," he said over his shoulder, sounding irked all at once. "Like that goddamn float valve for the corral trough, Augie. . . . " The device automatically filled the basin as soon as the water level dropped. "You seen to it yet?"

"Not yet, Cinch. It's on my list."

"Well, get it done—or you're on *my* list."

Dee was last out behind the horses, the taste of ammonia on her tongue from the swirling dust. Olin was sauntering stiff-legged in front of her. He'd suffered some kind of war injury, but she couldn't remember which war.

Rowena was waiting at the corral fence, their towheaded son beside her, using the fence as a jungle gym. The boy looked more like Cinch than her.

The three men looped their reins over the hitch rail, and Augie asked Cinch, "You wanna pack along the Colt?"

"May as well take it for snakes, Aug."

Dietz went through the gate and strolled over to Cinch's old pickup, opened the driver's-side door. It was the same pickup in which Dee had lost her virginity. Starry December night. Cold. Steamed windows. She was distracted by Rowena asking, "You want some iced tea, Dominica?"

"No thanks, Rowena," Dee said. "I've got to be going myself." Pancake had determined absolutely nothing of value about the monkeywrenching, but Dee knew that her own questions weren't welcome.

"I'll walk you down to your car," Cinch said to her.

She avoided Rowena's eyes. At that moment Dietz strolled past, a nickel-plated revolver dangling muzzledown from his fist.

"That yours, Augie?" Dee asked.

"Why no, Miss Dee," he answered in that oily, cell

block solicitude of his, "wouldn't think of it. . . ." Neither would the law; he was an ex-felon. "This here is Cinch's service weapon."

Cinch took the wheelgun from Augie, stowed it in a saddlebag. Like most of the able-bodied men in the sparsely populated county, Cinch was a reserve deputy sheriff, the ongoing legacy of the frontier posse. That was another worry for Dee in enforcing environmental law: Some of the worst violators were part-time cops with the right to conceal handguns on themselves and under the front seats of their trucks.

Dee glanced up at the window. The sphinx was still there, as unmoving as a corpse.

"Well, take care, everybody," Dee said, trying to wring a smile out of Cody with a wink. He didn't respond. "And nice seeing you again, Rowena."

She set off alone for the Bronco, giving Cinch an out if he thought better of being alone with her.

But he didn't.

She heard his boots scuffle the ground as he caught up. At arm's length, his eyes looked red-veined and exhausted, but he smiled again. "Dee Laguerre," he simply said, as if in wonder.

"You've got a nice boy, Cinch," she said.

He just nodded. She'd never heard him brag. Nor did he try to justify anything he ever did. She'd once thought this behavior silly, almost vain, but then she'd married Tyler Ravenshaw, who'd spend ten minutes justifying why he'd chosen paper instead of plastic bags at the grocery store. Maybe Cinch just realized that human perfection is unattainable.

Dee felt awkward knowing, without turning, that Rowena was still standing at the corral fence. "How's the ranch?" Dee asked.

He slowly let out a breath. "All right, I guess." But then he added, "Goin' to a yearlin' operation."

"Are you sure?"

"Yeah."

It was more dire for the Hollands than it sounded. Like his father before him, Cinch had always operated on a "cow-calf" basis. He bred calves from his own stock, grazed them from late June to October on the public range he leased from the BLM, then sold all but the mother herd before the first snow flew. Now, trying to save a sinking ship, he would put all his cattle, including the precious mother herd, on the auction block in November. That way he could sell his alfalfa crop for cash instead of using it for feed. A 130-year-old breeding program wiped out just to keep his nose above water another season.

"I'm sorry," she said. She genuinely was. Cinch Holland was the least reactionary of the local ranchers. "Jack Reckling tells me you're going to the Savory Method."

"Yeah, I took the leap."

"That's good."

He gently took her by the elbow, and they both stopped. He pointed to the sloping lands below them. Three or four miles off were the flats on which Reckling and Milt Kwak were still hunting for the elusive *Eriogonum ampullaceum*. But nearer, she could see several new fence lines radiating out from the Holland homestead like the spokes of a giant wheel. "Two more legs of fivestrand," he said, "and I got it done."

The Savory Method, named after the African-born cattleman who'd developed it, called for intense grazing in a limited enclosure for a short period of time. It was softer on the range than the old way, even beneficial to native plants by letting the hooves of the cattle turn under the wild seed. But it had a big price tag. "What's fence costing you?"

"Fifteen hundred a mile in materials alone. Ten miles."

"And whatever you're paying Dietz, it's probably too much."

Cinch nodded. "You got that straight. Olin and me waited two hours for him to show this mornin'. Told us he's got business concerns of his own to look after. Can't find decent ranch labor no more, unless it's Mexican. And then you got Immigration breathin' down your neck.''

Dee got inside the Bronco, and Cinch leaned on his arms against the door, his calloused fingers gripping the few inches of window glass she'd left rolled up. ''Sorry I ain't been 'round to see you.''

''I don't want you to,'' she quickly said. ''Unless it's like this, today.''

She could tell that she'd stung him by the way he stood up and gazed off. His eyes were on the cloudbank, which was building ever taller and darker in the southwest. ''Sure can use the rain,'' he said, then started back for the corral.

CHAPTER**FOUR**

Dee parked in the old handball court behind the Pyrennes Hotel. Even as late as her own childhood, there would've been at least two herders playing on a summer afternoon like this, the ball echoing off the concrete walls of the enclosure. The sheep bosses would periodically drag them in off the range to Gabrielle's place, mostly so they wouldn't become *soraturik*, "sheeped" or loneliness-crazed, and start shunning human company. With most Bascos, the adaptation to solitude worked all too well. So there was Gabrielle to shock them out of it, a garrulous and carping hunchback who kept after them until they started talking again. When a young shepherd proposed to her, it was the sign that he was ready for the range again, and his boss picked him up in a rattly stake truck, usually with a sheepdog perched on the roof, snarling at the cowpunchers filing into the Snake Pit, across the street.

Going in through the back door, Dee hurried down a dim corridor lined with scarred wooden doors. There was just time for a quick lunch, but she had to be concealed somewhere along the western approach to Cayuse Mountain long before four o'clock, the hour Cinch had let slip that he meant to return to his ranch.

The lobby was filled with Japanese tourists and diesel fumes from their bus, which was idling outside the propped-open main entrance. The Pyrennes had no air-conditioning.

"Merde," Dee said. There went lunch.

But Gabrielle, who was herding the Japanese through the dining room door as if running sheep through a dip-bath, pointed toward the kitchen. She'd set a table for Dee in there.

Dee mouthed the word *Merci,* and drummed up the stairs toward her room to wash. She paused briefly at the heavy oak banister along the mezzanine and looked down on the milling Japanese. It was like an electrical storm, the flash cubes going off. Was their world so uniform and sterile that a run-down turn-of-the-century hotel with skid row ambience could fascinate them? Turning, she almost bumped into a middle-aged couple. They both gave a cursory bow, and the husband asked in decent English if he could take Dee's picture.

She started to roll her eyes, but then said, "Sure."

"Is it possible you aim six-shooter at camera?"

"Nope."

"Sorry?"

"No. Against the rules."

His expression stayed the same, and his flash went off, blinding her for a few seconds.

"You sheriff?" he asked.

"Infidelity police."

He grunted in bewilderment.

"I'm part of a special force of women that patrols hotels making sure husbands remain true to their wedding vows."

It took a moment, but he finally got it.

His wife asked him something, no doubt for a translation of what Dee had said—but he refused to tell her.

Dee moved on down the second-story hallway and pounded on Rabe Pleasant's door, bawling, "Everybody out! I want to see your marriage licenses!" She couldn't resist glancing back at the couple. The husband's jaw had dropped.

Dee hoped that Rabe would stick his head out into the hall, his red toupee slightly askew, and ask, "I beg your pardon, sweetness?"

But he was apparently still in Las Vegas.

She made up her mind to stop hoping for help tonight. There was probably enough time to phone the Reno office and arrange for a ranger from another resource area to speed here. But for what? Some vague tip that the buckaroos might do something on the mountain after dark? She'd have to reveal her informant, and Jack Reckling would just love to learn that it was the madam of the local cathouse.

Throwing open her door, she saw that the green light on her answering machine was blinking, but ignored it for the moment.

At the sink, she palmed some water onto her face, then studied her dripping reflection in the mirror. A good Basque face, as Gabrielle often said. Crow's-feet just beginning to show at the corners of her eyes, thanks to the merciless Nevada sun, but still a young face. Frank brown eyes. But something in them at the moment disturbed her.

Fear.

Still, she needed that. It'd keep her sharp tonight, distrustful enough to look out for herself first.

The message was from Tyler Ravenshaw, her ex-husband. The call had probably come in shortly after she'd left this morning for Jewell's. Now and again, it was his habit to drink until dawn and then call her in a fit of boozy self-pity. His sober self was never maudlin. "Something occurred to me tonight, Dee," his recorded voice was saying, tinged with a slur. She could hear a foghorn in the background. "I probably would do anything to get you back. I would—" She erased the message and reset the machine. *Probably.* Good old T.R.

Downstairs again, she squeezed through the Japanese and into the kitchen. Hector, the Mexican cook, noted her entry with his timeworn greeting, proudly telling her that he had *mucho carne* for her anytime she wanted it.

"Fuck off, Hector," Dee said, sliding into a chair at a small table that reeked of freshly diced onion. "All you male bastards promise that, then deliver Vienna sausage."

She folded her hands together, then rested her chin

atop them. Cinch Holland had looked good this morning.
Too good for him to be knocking on her door some
evening after she'd had a few after-dinner drinks.
Something had gone faster inside her, seeing him again.
But however good he'd looked, tonight he was going up
the mountain. She was almost sure of it. As sure as she
was that she could arrest him, if it got down to that. All
by herself. The whole group of them. Spurs and beer
bellies.

She suddenly got up and went to the wall phone.
She'd no sooner dialed than Gabrielle swept in and began setting a place for her.

"Who you ringin' this tine, Dominica?" the old
woman asked in her heavy Basque accent.

"Local," Dee reassured her.

"Snake Pit," a voice drawled over the line. The on-
duty bartender.

"Charlie?"

"Speakin'."

"This is Dee Laguerre."

A long silence, then: "Uh-huh."

"Jack Reckling there?"

"Ain't seen him."

"Damn," Dee said, then paused exactly as long as
Charlie had.

"Why?"

"Well, I'm driving in to Gold Mountain this afternoon. May not be back till morning, and I just wanted
Jack to know. If you see him, will you tell him?"

"Okay." *Click.*

Smiling wickedly, Dee returned to her chair. Charlie
would also let every rancher within a hundred miles
know. She had no intention of going to the county seat
this evening, but the Bascos had learned long ago in
their war with the cattlemen that if you don't have numbers you resort to guile.

Gabrielle set an enormous bowl of *iapikua*, Basque
stew, in front of Dee and told her to eat it all, that Dee's
hips were womanly enough but she needed more filling
out in the chest to get a man.

"I had a man," Dee said, realizing for the first time that she was hungry.

"You din't have a man," Gabrielle said. "Not for lon', at least. Know why? 'Cause you went lookin' outside." Dee had shown the old woman her wedding photos, and Gabrielle had immediately dismissed T.R. as being too pale and soft-looking. A true man worked with his hands out in the sunlight, not preparing briefs on a word processor. "Eat pleny now."

Dee shrugged but did as she was told. She wasn't having what the Japanese and Germans would dine on today. French tourists avoided the Pyrennes like the plague; they knew that mammoth quantities of chicken, ribs, and spaghetti didn't constitute authentic Basque cooking. But Gabrielle kept a separate menu for landsmen. And screw the French: They'd guillotined her grandfather for sedition. "Good *iapikua*," Dee said.

Gabrielle's wizened face grew even tighter. "Of course. How can you act surprise?"

Smiling, Dee asked, "Rabe phone when he's coming back?"

"No. He fall asleep on the road and is dead out in the sage." The eternal optimism of a long-oppressed minority.

The spoon stopped before it reached Dee's mouth, and a clove of garlic plopped back into the bowl. "Sage," she half whispered.

"What you say?"

Dee shot up for the phone again. Dialing long-distance, she had to briefly pause while spinning the rotor to assure Gabrielle that the call would be on her government credit card. Compulsive Old World frugality. Once arrived in Nevada, Dee's father had mailed his passport back to the homeland so his look-alike brother could use it.

"Battle Mountain Research Station," somebody male finally answered, sounding annoyed at having been interrupted.

"Shannon Touhey, please."

"Hang on . . ."

Milton Kwak, the botanist, had mystified her when he revealed that he was collecting samples of common sage. That wasn't what he'd been brought down from Reno to do. He was to differentiate between two related plant species, and then, if he found the endangered kind, determine the extent of its range. Did the Nevada director have some agenda for Cayuse Mountain he was keeping to himself? It'd happened before in other states, the brass undercutting the field staff and opening up whole new areas for agriculture and commerce.

"Touhey," Shannon finally answered. Dee could almost visualize the research geneticist impatiently twirling the phone cord around a finger. She headed the upstate facility for range studies and ran marathons on the weekends to relax. Dee had met her at an ecosystems seminar in Reno where everybody called her "Fooey Touhey" for her weak expletives until, with the help of some vodka brought by the Russian delegation, she was encouraged to utter her first *fuck*.

"Dee Laguerre, Shannon."

"Hi."

"Quick question." Dee knew that Shannon tolerated no other kind. "Why would a field botanist be collecting sage leaders like a tea picker?" Leaders were the outermost growth on a plant.

"Shit," Shannon said, "I don't know." Obviously, the seminar had served her well. "What're you talking—black sage, silver, big . . . what?"

"Big sage."

"Okay, it's a good indicator of water and soil conditions at a given site. The root system on an average *Artemisia tridentata* covers an underground area the size of a three-bedroom house."

"That much?" Dee asked.

"Yep. How tall's the sage there?"

"Oh, maybe five feet."

"Then it's arable land," Shannon said. "That's the rule of thumb. Any place with artemisia taller than three feet can be planted with crops. Is that the plan?"

"I don't think so. At least I hope not."

"Are you guys going to rehabilitate the area with native species?"

"Nope," Dee said, alarm bells going off inside her head. "It's just a sensitive plant study area. Potential wilderness overlaps."

"Then you got me. Anything else?"

"That's it. Thanks."

"Anytime." Shannon promptly signed off.

Twilight came early because of a towering wall of clouds in the west. The front was coming slowly, which only told Dee that it meant to stick around for a while. She knew that the rain wouldn't keep the ranchers home tonight. It'd make them even bolder to realize that their tracks would be washed away. She glanced up through the windshield at Cayuse Mountain. Its summit was still bathed in late sunshine, the sedimentary rock there a vivid chartreuse-yellow in contrast to twilit slopes below the eight-thousand-foot level. The storm's shadow on the peak was constantly changing shape in keeping with the restless billowing of the line of thunderheads drifting over the valley behind her.

Dee was using a jeep trail that wound northeast through the foothills. She recalled that it suddenly ended near an overlook of the junction of Holland Ranch Lane and Cayuse Mountain Road, the one she was sure the ranchers would use at dusk, if not sooner. She crept along at only a few miles an hour, raising as little dust as she had to. Still, it curled in through the door seams. If a bullet didn't get her, she figured silicosis would. Alkali dust looked like broken glass under a microscope.

Jack Reckling's voice, trying to raise her, came over the BLM frequency. She started to reach for the mike, but then stopped.

Let him think she'd gone to Gold Mountain.

Coming to the foot of a sandy ridge, she saw that she could drive no farther. She turned the Bronco around in the arroyo there and parked it high on the opposite slope, well above any sudden water that might surge down the ravine later even if it wasn't raining at this spot.

Reckling tried again, then quit.

She sat a moment in the still vehicle, listening to the catalytic converter tick as it began to cool. The wind was picking up, making the brush tremble. She uncased her binoculars, hung them by the warm plastic strap around her neck. The sultry heat made her yawn. If she could get Milton Kwak aside from Jack Reckling, she'd ask him what the hell he was doing with the sage. Reckling probably knew, but he'd deny any knowledge until the day some big agricultural outfit, with friends in the Department of the Interior, bladed off the native species for alfalfa and sank a well. Land swap. The government wrote off one area to enhance another. Is that what was secretly planned for Cayuse Mountain?

Dee removed her gold badge and nameplate, then tossed them into the glove box. Too shiny. "Well, Dominica," she said to herself, sighing, "let's go fuck with the cowboys."

She trudged up the slope, fine sand flowing around her ankle-high boots like water. But still it felt good to walk.

Flakes of black obsidian were littered all over the ridge, evidence that the Shoshone and the nameless tribes before them had used the same overlook. She could imagine them: stocky, nut-brown men squatting here five thousand years ago, waiting for the approaching storm to move the deer or mountain sheep down off the pinyon-furred slopes, wiling away the afternoon by chipping projectile points for their throwing spears. She wondered if they'd found life any less complicated than she did.

Probably not.

Kneeling behind a low copse of desert peach, she swept her field glasses up to her eyes. Nothing on the road. Too soon, as expected. But just to make sure, she traced the road's switchbacks all the way up to the first bench, a broad flat on the mountainside. Nothing but rock and thick trees.

She sat. A gust made her shut her eyes for several seconds while the sand bit into her face.

* * *

Cinch's GMC pickup inched down Holland Ranch Lane. Dee checked her wristwatch—ten minutes after five o'clock—then peered through her binoculars. Six men altogether, three sitting in the cab and three sprawled in the bed. Still too far to tell who they were, although she had no doubt that Cinch was behind the wheel. No weapons were visible, but one of the men in the back was pillowing his head on a big canvas bag.

"Turn right, Cinch," she softly begged. Toward Highway 95 and Holland Station. Away from the cleft in the mountain known as Jubal Canyon through which the road climbed eastward. "Drive down to the Snake Pit. Get knee-crawling drunk and forget for a few hours that you're going broke."

But the pickup went left into the canyon and started up the long grade onto the mountain.

"*Merde,*" Dee said. Another hard gust made her spin away. She protected the lenses of the binoculars with her palms until the wind ebbed, then glassed the road again. Through the rear window of the GMC's cab she could see Cinch at the wheel. Beside him was Olin Peters, and slouching with his tattoed arm hooked out the passenger-door window was Augie Dietz. He had a beer bottle going and was laughing. In the bed were three other local ranchers. The Wheatley twins, Bill and Tom, known poachers, and Wade Russell, who'd raped a girl in high school and gotten away with it.

"Fine company, Cinch," Dee grumbled.

She waited for the pickup to reach the first switchback at the head of the canyon, then she rose and ran down the slope to the Bronco.

The wind was steady and hard now. No use worrying about the tires kicking up dust; it was rising everywhere, skirling along the ground in visible eddies. She backtracked in the Bronco to a stock trail, a virtual boulevard trampled through the rabbitbrush, and followed it down to Cayuse Mountain Road.

She wanted to stop the pickup, knowing that the

ranchers, Cinch especially, would call off the slaughter if she confronted them.

But she wouldn't do that.

It was time to set limits with these people. If they went down for killing mustangs that might be the end of it for a long while. But if she let them off with what amounted to a warning, they'd be back on the mountain tomorrow night.

Still, she wasn't sure how she'd feel—arresting Cinch.

Pulling over to the side of the road, she waited for the GMC to reach the bench. If she moved anytime before that, one of the men might spot her. Checking her watch again, worrying that the pickup would get too far ahead, she dipped into the glove compartment for a handful of shotgun shells and stuffed them down the right front pocket of her trousers.

Cinch would never put up a fight. But she wasn't about to trust her luck with the others, Olin and Augie especially. Dietz was known to have killed. And last May the bullet had come at her out of Peters's property.

She realized that Cinch would see arrest as a personal vendetta. The very idea that he'd think that infuriated her, but she knew he would. A year older than him, Dee had gone on to college in Reno with every expectation that he'd follow. But meanwhile, back in the valley, Cinch had eased his loneliness by knocking up Rowena Peters. Dee's mother had to tell her that he was married—he'd simply stopped writing. She hadn't stood face-to-face with him again until this morning, and then her anger had failed her. His sad, weary face had defused it.

"Well, there is a God," Dee said, driving on again, "and at least I'm not stuck being Mother Holland's nurse."

She glanced up the willow-choked side road that led to Lower Cayuse Spring—and saw a shirtless young man turn on his heel and vanish into the lacy growth.

"Oh yeah?" She braked and put the Bronco in reverse.

Thin tire impressions lay on the side road, unbroken by hoof marks. A vehicle had only recently gone up that way.

Wood smoke. She could smell it wafting through the air-conditioning vents. A fire in this kind of wind—idiocy.

She took out the shotgun, jacked a round into the chamber, and laid the piece on the floorboards under her legs. Then she started up toward the spring.

The willows soon engulfed her, the foliage pressing against the glass. Dead twigs clawed at the Bronco's finish, setting her teeth on edge. She reached the young man's footprints. And they were just that. He was barefoot, something she hadn't noticed in the split second before he'd disappeared.

She shifted into Park, then punched in the radio frequency for Clark County Metro. Plenty of authoritative cop chatter was coming in clearly from Las Vegas, so she put it on the external speaker to create the illusion in this idiot's mind that there were more like her within calling distance.

She got out and quietly locked up, leaving the shotgun. Too cumbersome in the growth.

She followed the footprints down the faint suggestion of a trail game used to approach the water. She halted and listened.

Voices, low and urgent, were coming from the direction of the spring.

She broke from the willows onto a sunbrown meadow, and there they were near a rusted Volkswagen van, two men and a woman, all in their early thirties, kicking dirt onto a small cooking fire. Dee saw the barechested man who'd given her the slip among them, but she reminded herself that one more member of the party might still be out in the willows. Behind her somewhere.

The woman was striking-looking, with sharp features and red hair shorn down to a half inch of fuzz.

Noticing Dee, the threesome finally stopped trying to bury the last wisp of smoke. The woman clasped her hands behind her. The shirtless man tucked his in his armpits.

"Hello," Dee said. Calm. Nonconfrontational. "Would you all please keep your hands down at your sides?"

They complied, murmured their own hellos. She thought she detected a few foreign accents. She glanced at the rear plate on the van: California, with registration tags that expired three months ago. And the plate holder advertised an auto dealership in seaside Santa Cruz, explaining the rust corrosion. There was a state university there, but they were a bit too old and jaded-looking for even the graduate program.

Dee quickly made up her mind. Cinch could go on for the moment. She'd gamble that she could find the GMC later on the mountain. Just looking at the threesome, she knew that she had the monkeywrenchers.

The tallest of them asked with a slight German accent, "Is there some problem?"

"Yeah," Dee said, strolling up to within a few yards of them. "You've got an open fire going on tinder-dry range in the middle of a windstorm."

"It will rain soon," the German said as if she were slow for not realizing this. His blond hair swept back into a long ponytail. Handsome in an obnoxious Teutonic way.

"Might," Dee said, smiling. "Might rain buckets here. And then again it could fall all around, leaving this meadow as dry as bone. What're you doing here?"

The German smiled back at her. "Must I give you a reason?"

"Either that or your campfire permit."

"We don't have one."

"No wonder," Dee said. "We're not issuing them due to the fire danger." She felt that, unlike the Japanese tourists, they knew exactly what her duties were.

"It was a very small fire."

"They all are at first." Then Dee rested her left hand on her nightstick. "What are you doing here?"

He grinned as if he couldn't believe this. "Camping.

Out enjoying the freedom of the Wild West.''

The shirtless man added "For sure." American.

"We came to photograph the mustangs," the woman said, less sure of herself than the others, not realizing that she was giving the standard alibi for illegal activity in this particular resource area. Like the man with the ponytail, she too was probably German.

"I doubt you'll see any cayuses this way," Dee said. "You're camping right on top of one of the few places they can find water. Who built the fire?"

"I did," the German male said.

"Alone?"

"Yes. It's my night to cook dinner."

"How egalitarian." But she slipped her leather-jacketed citation booklet from her back trouser pocket.

"What is that?" he asked, instantly suspicious.

"I'm going to cite you for having an open fire."

"I see no reason for that."

Dee said, "I see plenty of reasons." Not the least of which was identifying the threesome. Later something might develop linking them to the monkeywrenching on the Holland Ranch. And if Cinch had been hit, other ranchers would soon discover their own damages.

"There is no reason for that," the German said more adamantly.

And then he started to step toward her.

Before he'd taken his third stride, her nightstick was out. Gripping the short side handle, she laid the length of the hard vinyl baton along her left forearm and used it to shove him against the side of the van.

He tried to move, but she froze him in place by pressing the stick against his throat. Not enough to choke him, but enough to make his eyes bulge a little.

Her right hand was on the backstrap of her revolver as she barked, "Everybody stay put. Understood?"

Heads bobbed.

"I meant nothing," the German said. "I was just going to entreat you to be reasonable."

"I know that. Otherwise you'd be out cold on the ground right now. What's your name?"

"Eric," he said sullenly. "Eric Brenner."

"All right, Eric," Dee said, backing out of the reach of his arms. "I'm writing you a citation. If I have any reason to believe that you don't intend to appear at the given time and place, I'm taking you forthwith to the federal magistrate. If I have any reason to believe that you intend to resist or try to intimidate me, I'm taking you to the hospital in Tonopah, *then* to the magistrate. Now . . . do we understand how things are here in the Wild West?"

Brenner nodded.

Ordinarily, he would've been handcuffed by now. She had touched him, and you arrested whatever you laid your hands on. Cardinal rule. But she figured she could still catch Cinch's pickup if she got the cite written in the next few minutes.

"I want to see identification for everybody," she ordered.

"It's in the van, lady," the American said. He probably hadn't called a woman "lady" in years.

One by one, Dee had them go in through the sliding door and rummage through their dirty belongings for driver's licenses and passports. She stood back, hand on her Smith and Wesson, watching each and every move. She couldn't search the interior herself at this point. There wasn't probable cause, and the case would be thrown out even if she discovered something. But if—in plain view—she saw bolt or wire cutters, or sacks of sugar that could be used to ruin gas tanks, they were all under arrest.

But the threesome revealed nothing suspicious to her inside the Volkswagen.

Eric Brenner and Karena Heinold, his shorn ewe, were from Cologne. That rang a bell. Tyler had met in San Francisco with Greens from that city. Cleaning up the Rhine River. Part of his around-the-clock push in the last year of their marriage to make the Wilderness Conservancy Alliance a worldwide environmental organization—with him at the helm, of course. Blaine Chapman, the American and the registered owner of the van, was from Half Moon Bay, a small town on the coast between Santa Cruz and San Francisco. Tyler and she had frequented a seafood place there.

"Do you belong to the Green Party?" Dee asked Brenner and Heinold.

Brenner just gave her a messianic stare, not unlike Augie Dietz's jailhouse variety.

"I asked you a question," Dee said, writing, trying to keep the cite from flapping in the wind. It was warm and humid, just the way it felt before a rain squall. Then she gave them her own look.

Karena said, "We used to be."

"Greens too tame for you?"

"Tame . . . ?"

Brenner gave her the equivalent in German, and before he could warn her off with a glare, she said, "Yes."

"And what group do you belong to?" Brenner demanded.

"The Wolf Pack."

His forehead wrinkled.

"Alumni Association, University of Nevada." Then she gave him the ticket and wished them all an enjoyable visit.

the exit from Half Moon Bay, a ranch home to the dual and then back and forth between Yuba and San Francisco.

CHAPTER**FIVE**

As usual, Augie Dietz was going on about his great plans, how he was working on having a ranch of his own, how a stepbrother had screwed him out of the spread that had been rightfully his. Half listening, Cinch watched his temperature gauge needle creep upward. The Wheatleys and even Olin had newer trucks, but all were either white or fire engine red, not the deep emerald green that had caught the eye of Cinch's father so long ago on a used car lot in Reno. The same green as the pinyon trees that grew above the ranch. A funny-looking pine, the pinyon—shaped more like an apple tree than a conifer. Sweet, plump nuts his mother used to buy from an old Indian woman each fall.

"Hell, Olin," Augie suddenly complained, "Cinch ain't even hearin' me out on this."

"What's that, Aug?" Olin asked, winking at Cinch.

"Christ awmighty—does *anybody* listen to me?"

Olin laughed and swiped Augie's beer for a quick sip. "Cinch don't listen to nobody. He's too busy stewin'."

I'd stew a lot less, too, if I had a disability check coming in from the government each month, Cinch thought. But then he quickly decided that that wasn't fair. Olin's legs were still messed up from the collapse of that Marine barracks in Beirut, so the money was his by rights.

"But I heard you, Aug," Olin went on. "Somethin' about usin' the land up to its potential."

"Exactly." Augie hocked some phlegm, then spat between his knees onto the tattered rubber floormat.

"Don't do that," Cinch said, disgusted. Prison manners.

"Beer gives me phlegm," Augie said. "Don't you have no whiskey, Cinch? Olie?"

"This ain't a party." Cinch checked the needle again. He figured he could reach the bench before the radiator needed a rest.

Augie flipped his windbreaker window around for some breeze. "Times are changin'. You can't think no more in terms of just one use of this country, like ranchin'. Now me, I got jewed outta my spread early on, so I had to broaden my outlook. Hell, there's more mineralization in this county than any other in the whole of Nevada."

"Minerali*what*?" Olin asked, winking over at Cinch again.

"Gold, silver, lead, copper, tungsten—shit, we even got coal in spots."

"So you think Cinch and me oughta become coal miners, Aug?"

"I think you oughta do what needs doin' to survive."

"I'm not gonna dig in the ground for my bread," Cinch said quietly, firmly. "I like it out in the sunshine. And I don't like what minin' does to the land. I seen that big pit up north in Esmeralda County, and I don't want that here." Cinch braked, then backed into a cove in the trees where he felt the pickup couldn't be seen from below. Briefly, the GMC was veiled in its own dust. He got out and raised the hood, flinching from the heat that flowed up around his face.

"What's wrong?" Wade Russell asked sleepily from the back. He'd admitted spending last night at Jewell's. Cinch had no idea how he got away with being such a heller. Wade was married, and Dixie Russell had a temper. If the truth were known, her real estate business was keeping Wade afloat.

"We're either boilin' or close to it," Cinch said.

"It's them lard-asses in the bed," Olin said.

Cinch had Augie give him his binoculars from under the seat. "I'm gonna have a look down the road."

"Good idea," Tom Wheatley said, although he didn't volunteer to go along. Instead, he popped another Coors. His twin brother immediately did the same. Tweedledum and Tweedledee.

Cinch headed downslope.

He liked the sound of the wind in the pine needles, the creak of the rocking boughs. He especially liked the sense that rain was on the way. It did something magical to this country, summer rain. Somehow made it seem less stark and forsaken. But he hoped it'd hold off for a few hours more. The horses wouldn't come to the spring if they could water at the short-lived puddles a thunderstorm left everywhere. They knew that springs were natural killings grounds.

He found a clearing and gazed westward. He'd forgotten the term for it, but he could see dark skirts of rain that were almost reaching the ground, in this case the pearl-white playa of Alkali Dry Lake.

Hope.

Maybe that was the term for things that almost came through—but never did.

Lifting his glasses to his eyes, he began searching the entire length of Cayuse Mountain Road from where it started at Highway 95, past the turnoff to his own place, and then up Jubal Canyon to the switchbacks they'd just climbed. He was focusing on Lower Cayuse Spring when rustling through the pinyon branches turned him around.

It was Augie and Olin come to join him, each of them nursing a beer.

"Anythin'?" Augie asked.

Cinch focused on the spring below again. "Yeah, some kinda panel truck or van in the meadow."

"How many people?"

"Too far to see."

Augie took off his sweat-stained hat and slapped Olin's arm with it. "I told you I smelt smoke down there in the canyon," he said, delighted with himself.

Olin nodded. "Yeah, maybe we shoulda had a look in the willows. Could be our tree-huggers."

"One thing at a time," Cinch said. "Might wind up good for us they're down there, whoever they are. Horses will use the upper spring for sure, now." *Unless it rains soon.* But he left that unsaid. There was enough bad luck in the world without tempting more of it.

Dee opened the rear window of the Bronco and reached inside the cargo net for the camera case. From the direction of the van she could hear Eric Brenner giving somebody the devil in German—Karena, no doubt, for having admitted that they were greener-than-thou. As if Dee would ever believe that they were doing a spread on wild horses for *National Geographic.*

Walking forward through the tunnel of willows, she found some tire impressions from the Volkswagen she hadn't driven over in the Bronco. They were in mud from one of numerous seeps fed by the main spring. Sharp, as if they'd been chiseled there. She set the detachable flash on the ground next to the track and snapped the shutter button. Insurance for prosecution, should Brenner and his friends decide to stick around and try to end grazing in Nevada on their own.

In the Bronco again, she was backing out of the thicket when she suddenly stopped. The twilight was deeping, but it was by no means nightfall. She checked her watch. Another hour to that.

Cinch wasn't a fool. He'd keep an eye to the rear. He might even set a guard on the road, maybe along one of the hairpin switchbacks.

She reached around for her spotting scope, ten times as powerful as her binoculars, then got out and carried it through the willows to their edge. There she lay down and scanned the road from the head of the canyon to the benchland.

Nothing.

A big raindrop plopped into the thirsty dust beside her elbow. It shriveled and vanished almost instantly. She expected more to come. But a minute passed and the storm held off, except for the wind, which was now whipping the slender branches nearly to the ground.

She swung the scope along the lip of the bench, carefully checking all the openings in the trees. She went past one such clearing, then rushed back to it, adjusted the focus, and waited impatiently for the dust to ease up for a moment.

When it did, she saw three figures standing on the overlook. Two of them were holding beer cans. Augie Dietz and Olin Peters. The third man was glassing the canyon below, seemingly looking directly at Dee herself. Cinch Holland.

"*Merde,*" she said.

Now she knew she'd have to wait until nightfall.

Cinch drove up the darkening road without using his headlights. It grew rougher the higher up the mountain it wound, taxing his concentration, and at one point he told Augie to shut up long enough to help him look for fallen rocks.

Dietz obeyed for a minute, but then laughed bitterly. "You think I'm shit, don't you, Cinch Holland?"

"Oh, come on now, Aug," Olin said, lighting a Marlboro.

Cinch made up his mind not to get entangled. Augie Dietz *was* shit, but that was beside any point that meant anything to him at the moment.

"Well," Augie went on, "can't say I'm hurt. Damn near all my life folks been talkin' to me like I'm a cow chip. Started when I was small like Cody, and they'll be talkin' that way over my casket. They'll always find a way to cut me down to size. I can sit a horse as good as anybody, but they'll say I'm no buckaroo. Just a laborer. A drifter. I walk 'most everywheres to help me cogitate on things, but they'll say I'm too lazy to buy a car—"

One of the men in the back pounded on the roof of the cab, and Cinch immediately braked. "What?" he asked out his open window, heart racing.

"You oughta see all the lightnin' to the west," Bill
Wheatley said.

"Christ, man—don't do that," Cinch said, acceler-
ating again, hoping that no one below had seen his
brakelamps wink on.

"Relax," Augie said, "and you might have some fun.
Life's a hopeless bag of shit, but that don't mean you
can't enjoy yourself."

"Killin' horses fun to you?" Cinch asked.

Augie just grinned in the greenish cast of the dashboard lights. Cinch needed them to keep an eye on the
temperature gauge. Dietz's old gunshot wound to the
face looked so deep Cinch wondered how he'd ever survived it.

"We wouldn't even have to be doin' this," Olin said,
"if the gov'mint hunters hadn't kilt all the lions back in
the fifties. Cats would trim this herd in no time."

Too edgy for arguing, Cinch didn't point out that the
livestock operators, his father included, had insisted on
those hunts. An occasional calf or sheep was being
dragged off in the night, but nobody had foreseen that
shooting and poisoning all the mountain lions would
have consequences on a mustang herd that had been the
same size for more than a century. Some said that the
local cayuses were from Spanish conquistador stock, but
that was romantic hogwash. The Hollands had found no
wild horses on their arrival in the valley. Jubal Holland,
the family pioneer, wrote in his diary that a year after
the Civil War some California wranglers were herding
several hundred mounts toward horse-starved Texas
when a score of head escaped in a dust storm. The stal-
lions of that original group then began enticing away the
Hollands' own horses. So, tonight, Cinch would be snuff-
ing out a bloodline that, in part, went all the way back
to the horses his ancestors had ridden.

He thought of asking Olin for a cigarette, but finally
didn't. He'd quit last year. Just too damned expensive.

Olin cackled, but didn't explain why right off. More
and more he was sounding like an old woman when he
did that.

"What's ticklin' you?" Cinch asked irritably.

"Just thinkin' of the look on that sissy-la-la biologist's face when he takes a look at the horse census after we're done. He's gonna think the cats are back."

Cinch wasn't as amused as Olin, but he knew that that was the point of tonight's hunt. After decades, the BLM was putting together a new range inventory. Reevaluating how much use the land would bear. Mustangs were voracious grazers whose impact on the carrying capacity of the range would be figured in Rabe Pleasant's wildlife tally. Fewer cayuses meant the BLM would have one less argument for cutting back on the cattle it meant to allow on public lands from now on.

"But it is a shame to shoot horses," Olin went on expansively. "It's them BLM-ers we oughta gun down." Then something chilling came into his voice. "Lure 'em out into the sticks and do 'em righteous. One shot to drop 'em and one to the head to finish 'em. Every last goddamn specialist and bureaucrat."

"Don't talk that way," Cinch said, slowing for a rocky stretch.

Olin was jostled against Cinch's shoulder by the lurching chassis. "Why? It's just us jawin'."

Cinch kept silent.

Augie leaned forward so he could look directly at Cinch. "You sayin' you don't trust me?"

"No."

"Well, coulda fooled me, Cinch."

The humidity was rising fast. Cinch had to wipe the steam off the inside of his half of the windshield with his bandanna. He trusted nobody when it came to breaking the law. Other than drunk driving now and again, he'd had only one other experience akin to what he'd do tonight. He and some high school buddies had trashed a rack of mailboxes with baseball bats. He hadn't gotten home before one of the boys had sung to the deputy, who phoned Cinch's dad. The old man met him on the front porch with a roundhouse blow to the chin.

So much for trust among lawbreakers.

But that had been simple hell-raising. This was dif-

ferent. He had to do this. If the BLM cut back his Animal Unit Months, the bureaucratic measure of what a
cow and calf or five sheep would eat off the range each
month, he was finished. He could never raise enough
alfalfa to feed his herd, and buying hay was out of the
question.

Olin had been quiet for several minutes when he
asked, hushed, ''You figure we oughta try to hide the
carcasses when we're done? Cover 'em over with brush
or somethin'?''

Cinch thought about it for a moment. ''No. You can't
see the upper spring from the road. And the turkey vul-
tures will stop circlin' and start feedin' off them by
noon.'' Dee Laguerre was in Gold Mountain until tomorrow, according to Charlie at the Snake Pit, and the
chance of her coming up the mountain in the next several days was small. The coyotes would soon dismember
the carcasses and scatter the bones.

''Somewheres along here, Aug?'' Cinch asked in an
earnest tone, trying to make amends. It wasn't good to
go into something like this with bad feelings.

''Sure,'' Dietz said. ''This is close enough.''

Cinch slowed and turned on his headlamps just long
enough to find a place in the pinyons where he could
hide the truck. Then he parked behind a tree with
branches all the way to the ground and went on to Augie, ''You go on down there alone and have a look. Hell,
you could sneak up on yourself, Aug.''

There was just enough daylight left to see that Augie
was grinning again. ''You got that right, Cinch. And I'm
so goddamn slick I can get away with the same trick
twice.''

Dietz got out but didn't close his door. He whispered
what was up to the men in the back, then disappeared
into the pinyons.

Cinch leaned his head against the rear window and
shut his eyes. He saw Dee's face, and it gave him a
smoldering ache. She had seen right off that he still
wanted her—and had shot down that fancy fast enough.
He hadn't even realized that he was thinking about

knocking on her door one night until she'd warned him not to. It had been good with Dee, and he'd no sooner rolled off Rowena that one time than he'd known that he'd made the worst mistake of his life. He could probably blame teenage horns and potent malt liquor, but he didn't. He blamed himself. And he'd be rich today if he had a dollar for every hour he'd thought about Dee Laguerre these past years.

"Dietz *is* a sneaky little shit," Olin said. "Part Cherokee, he told me."

Cinch snorted under his breath. "Cherokee were farmers, Olie. They couldn't sneak up on a plow. And if everybody who says he's part Cherokee really was, that'd make them the horniest tribe that ever was."

"Maybe it was Comanche he said."

"Maybe it was Chinese," Cinch said, opening his eyes and yawning. "He's as dinky as a Chinaman." The windshield was speckled. As quietly as Augie before him, Cinch stepped out. The wind had eased, and a fine mist was falling. He turned his face up into it and opened his mouth. Cool, sweet-tasting.

"Can we break out our slickers?" Tom Wheatley asked in his normal drunken voice, which seemed like a shout.

Cinch shushed him, then whispered, "Too noisy. We should be back to the truck before it really starts comin' down. Then you can put on your gear." A fib. The heavens could break open at any second. But he hadn't come this far just to listen helplessly to the mustangs running away.

Off to the west, he could see the lightning through the approaching rain, which was blearing it into burstlike glows. Still, he could barely hear the thunder.

"Where the fuck is he?" Olin hissed from inside the cab.

Cinch was impatient, too. The light was going fast. "Might as well get set, boys." Wade Russell opened the canvas bag and began handing out the carbines, highway flares, and big dry-cell flashlights.

"Give me my revolver, Olin," Cinch said. He

strapped on the holster belt before accepting his Winchester from Wade.

Olin got out and took a carbine.

"Where's my Weatherby magnum?" Cinch asked. He'd loaned the rifle to Olin for deer season last fall and this afternoon had made a point of asking his brother-in-law to bring it along tonight. He wanted at least one heavy rifle for this business, even though it might be hard to sight through the scope.

"Oh," Olin said evasively, "I ain't cleaned the damn thing yet."

"After all these months, for chrissake?"

Then Augie was standing on the other side of the truck. "We got 'em, Cinch," he said happily. "They're down there. Even that big ol' white stud."

The rain started with a single drop, seemingly as big as a grape, that popped against the roof. Two more quickly followed, and then a sudden roar enveloped the Bronco as the squall line caught up with Dee. The surface of the hood became a chaos of big drops breaking apart into smaller ones.

She flicked on the wipers but left the headlamps off.

Within a minute, the road was glistening from runoff, which made it easier to follow in the twilight but harder to get the traction she needed to climb the last few hundred yards up onto the bench. She stopped, got out, and ran to the right front fender, stooping to turn the hub so she could go on in four-wheel drive.

The raindrops were so stinging she half believed that they were hail.

Lightning flashed almost directly overhead.

"One-Mississippi," she counted as she hurried around the grill to the other hub, "two-Mississippi—" Then came a crack and a deep-throated roar. Two miles away. "Close enough for government work." The cloudburst was so drenching she got back in the vehicle through the passenger door and crawled across to the driver's seat.

She used the lining of her jacket to dry her face.

It defied logic—how a land so parched could get so instantly wet. She was soaked to the skin, miserable, but still she cracked her window so she could smell the pine and sage, both scents enlivened by the deluge bruising the needles and leaves.

Driving on, she figured that Cinch had about five miles on her. But he had quite a load of men, and with a bit of luck she could catch him. Or, with bad luck, one of the ranchers would catch her with a bullet out of the darkness. Last May, as she'd set out on a night patrol, she'd never expected to be the near victim of a sniping. She'd seen a flashlight blink on and off three times from the old canal that ran along the edge of Olin Peters's alfalfa field. Stepping out of the Bronco to see who was signaling her, she heard the distant blast and then, almost simultaneously, the whir of the heavy-caliber bullet a few feet over her head. No one had been near the canal by the time she'd gotten there, and a sense of having been violated gave way to anger when Pancake asked her if it might have been a backfire she'd heard.

Suddenly, her side of the Bronco began a sickening downward tilt. "No!" She resisted sharply jinking the wheel, instead gradually steering back toward the middle of the road.

She braked and looked behind.

Her water-filled track almost went off the edge of a tumbling precipice. She realized where she was, the cliff just below the bench, and her stomach fluttered.

But she jammed the gear lever into Low and drove on.

It was the only water trap in the county, a closed, steep-walled canyon with a spring at its bottom. This disadvantage of Upper Cayuse Spring hadn't been lost on the canny mustangs, who'd found an almost invisible trail up the north face, giving them another route to escape danger should the lower canyon be blocked by a predator.

Cinch knelt at the outlet to this trail on the rimrock. He took two flares from the waistband of his Levi's and laid them on the ground beside him. He couldn't see the main herd from this spot, but he could hear them below, sheltering against the overhanging wall. Hooves clopped skittishly, a colt snorted. They, no doubt, as he, could hear the rain coming, a dull roar building out of the west.

Augie had gone down a hundred yards to seal the narrows, where the canyon was no wider than twenty feet. A smaller band of five or six yearling studs was waiting just above that spot for the old white stallion Augie had seen to clear out from the spring with his mares and colts. Only then could these outcast bachelors drink. All in all, twenty-five or more wild horses. A lot to find in one place. But water in August was a magnet.

It was Cinch's job to block the top of the trail. Olin, the Wheatley twins, and Russell were strung out across the edge of the rimrock, lying on their bellies, carbines cradled in their arms and flashlights within quick reach.

The old white stud could thank the ranchers for the unusually large size of his harem. They'd been picking off the monarch stallion of this and that band for years, whenever they figured they could drop one and get away with it.

At last, Augie's voice echoed up the canyon. "Fire in the hole, boys!" A red, throbbing blaze erupted on the sandy floor of the narrows. It grew brighter as Dietz pitched more and more flares over the cliff.

The bachelors trotted up the canyon into view, but then stopped and froze, ears uplifted, their fear of the flares now matched by their fear of the old white stud. All were either blacks or browns, not the Appaloosas, palominos, and creamellos people preferred to adopt. But they had nice manes and tails, well combed by the trees and brush they ran through.

Cinch uncapped a flare, waited.

He could hear the horses of the main herd scuffling back and forth below, the white stud not sure what to do yet.

Rain began to fall as if a heavy curtain were sweeping up the mountainside.

"Christ," Cinch said under his breath.

But he was glad it hadn't started ten minutes ago, before they were all in place. The horses might have left the spring then, and he didn't want to come out again on this chore anytime soon. Once a summer was all he had the stomach for. The BLM had an adoption program, which the tree-huggers and animal rights activists thought was the solution to a problem that had tripled in size since the wild horses had fallen under the protection of federal law in 1970. But the truth was that most mustangs were unfit to be pets. They were just too wild or broken down, and a good number of the adoptees wound up back in the government corrals within a few weeks, from then on caught in a bureaucratic limbo that ruled out either death or release.

Cinch figured a bullet was kinder than that.

He pulled his hat brim low over his eyes. Water was pouring off the crease as if from a spout. He knew the others were cussing him for not allowing them to wear their slickers.

Finally, he could hear hooves thudding up the trail toward him.

He lit a flare and hurled it down the trail. He waved a second one over his head like a big sparkler. The flashlights came on along the rimrock, the beams slanting down through the rain on the bright, glassy eyes in the bottom of the canyon. The bachelor studs. One screamed and went down, his forelegs folding under him.

"Jesus Christ," Cinch growled, then tossed down the second flare a few yards in front of him. He never wanted to do this again. Period.

But he picked up his Winchester and levered a cartridge into the chamber. Hearing no more hoofbeats on the trail, he supposed that the white stud had wheeled to take his chances in the canyon bottom. The flashlights were turning it into a mosaic of light and shadow, through which the mares and colts were running helterskelter. Blood bays and sorrels and grays. Neighing and snorting and even some defiant stamping from the yearling studs.

This is shit, Cinch thought, unable to bring himself to shoot.

But then he could hear something charging him from just beyond the glow of the flares. The old white stud. He reared about ten feet from Cinch, flailing his hooves. Scars from a half dozen fights could be seen on his hoary legs and chest. He had a heavy jaw and furious eyes.

Cinch fired.

By the time the thin smoke cleared off, he saw nothing where the stallion had been—except red pencils of rain streaking down through the light of the flares. Then he heard a crash against loose rock as the stud hit bottom.

Wade Russell, who was farthest up the canyon, shouted something.

Tom Wheatley asked Wade to repeat himself, and everybody quit shooting.

"Hold it, boys," Russell bawled, "Augie's comin' up the narrows!"

Nobody had said anything about working the canyon floor, but Dietz was sprinting toward the spring, firing from the hip at any horse that tried to gallop past him. He dropped three in this way, then reloaded and smirked up at the men. "You see that, fellas?"

"Get outta there," Cinch angrily ordered.

But Augie charged what must have been the few remaining survivors, huddled against the base of the overhanging wall.

A mare tried to bolt, but Dietz broke her back with another shot from the hip, and she toppled, screaming.

"Damn you," Cinch cried, "heart or lungs!"

Augie cupped his hand behind his ear. "What?"

"Finish her!"

Augie shrugged, then did so.

Cinch grabbed his flashlight and started down the slippery trail. The others on the rimrock rose to their feet, their soaked clothes squishing as they moved, and followed him down.

Augie was breathing heavily, his eyes shining in his wet face. "We did it fine this time—didn't we, Cinch?"

"It's a goddamn mess." Cinch looked roundabout. "Half of 'em are just wounded. Dammit. Damn it to hell."

"Hard to shoot straight in this kind of light," Bill Wheatley said, trying to hold down a grin. "Man, we never got this many in one whack before."

Cinch decided that he was too disgusted to say anything more. He just leaned his carbine against a boulder and unholstered his revolver. Then he went from horse to horse, shooting those that needed it in the brain. He came back from the last one, a white-legged colt that lifted its head to look at him, with hands trembling so bad he had to hide them from the others behind his body.

"Let's clean up our shells and the flares," he said in a low rasp. "Rain'll take care of our tracks."

At first, Dee thought that it was an old pinyon snag fallen across the road. Stopping, she threw her plastic poncho over her head and snapped up the sides before getting out to have a look. She held her fingers over the lens to her flashlight, cracking them just slightly to let the barest amount of light leak onto the sodden ground before her.

"Oh, for *merde*sake."

It wasn't a log. It was eighteen inches of mud and fist-size rocks oozing down out of a draw and spreading across the road.

But she immediately went back to the Bronco for her trenching tool.

Mustangs watered at early morning and evening, so her best guess had always been that Cinch and his cronies were headed for Upper Cayuse Spring. She thought she was less than a mile from it, but there was no telling for sure in the darkness. Of course, she wouldn't put it past some ranchers to leave a salt block 'most anywhere on the mountain, then return a few nights later to gun down the horses. Locals did the same thing to poach deer.

Tramping up to the slide again, she widened her stance and began shoveling. But for every shovelful of mud she tossed over the bank that much more ooze slid into the hole. And there was no use in trying to drive across the flow. Four-wheel drive had its limits.

She stood straight, surveyed the road. At least the slide was on a curve. Cinch wouldn't see it until he'd rounded most of the bend. If he came out this way—and not through the nuclear testing site on the east side of the mountain. Yet, this was the only bet she had left.

Her boots slapping over the mud, she rushed back to the Bronco and parked it in the trees, but so that her headlights could shine directly at the GMC pickup. If and when it came to a halt on the far side of the flow.

"If," she said out loud, exasperated.

Her case was getting weaker by the minute. Now, she'd given up any hope of catching the men in the act of killing the horses and was simply hoping to identify them as being in the general area at the approximate time. It'd help if she heard the shooting, saw the muzzle flashes over by Upper Cayuse Spring. That way she could reasonably search the pickup for weapons, although the ranchers' defense attorney would still give her a hard time on that one: *How did you know, Ranger Laguerre, that at that time you rummaged through Mr. Holland's vehicle a number of wild horses had been killed? And is it possible that these horses were killed after you conducted this unreasonable search?*

Dee rolled her window down six inches—to listen for distant gunfire. But the rainfall was still drumming loudly on the roof.

Sighing, she put up the hood on her poncho, grabbed the shotgun and flashlight, and got out one more time.

The raindrops struck her poncho with a sound like popcorn popping. She guessed that two inches had already fallen, and there was no sign that it was letting up. Earlier, she'd heard on the AM radio that the National Weather Service had issued a flash flood warning for the desert south of Tonopah.

She hiked up the steep slope through the heavily dripping pinyons, zigzagging toward a small pinnacle. The lightning had shown the outcrop to her. From there, she felt she could see the canyon that enclosed the upper spring. She might even hear gunshots if she got far enough away from the Bronco, which sounded like a tin drum in the torrent.

Water was on the move everywhere, chuckling streamlets in every draw.

She wondered what Tyler would think if he could see her right now—camouflaged poncho, gripping a shotgun. She smiled to herself. He'd once called her an amazon, but that had been after a backpacking trip in which she'd wound up carrying both packs down out of the Oregon Cascades. He loved the outdoors, but from a comfortable distance. On Sierra Club calendars. In John Muir's writings. More recently, he'd called her "the willowly Basque beauty who never took my name—fuck you from the bottom of my heart." That had been the last endearment he'd left on her answering machine, other than this morning's plea for reconciliation, which would be forgotten as soon as he sobered up.

But, in all fairness, Tyler Ravenshaw was good at forming lasting coalitions out of seemingly implacable foes. His biggest talent was persuasion, which had played no small part in her leaving Reno and going to San Francisco with the boyishly handsome environmental attorney, sharing with him an apartment that overlooked the yacht harbor and Mount Tamalpais across the bay. That much was fine. T.R. was intelligent, engaging, boundlessly enthusiastic, and hellbent on changing how people used the land.

Her mistake had been marrying him.

Boundless can also mean "consuming." He lectured, traveled to ecological hot spots, lobbied Sacramento and Washington, and stayed up late at night writing briefs. While he forged a number of small grass-roots organizations into the powerful Wilderness Conservancy Alliance, Dee took a part-time job downtown with the Southwest regional office of the U.S. Forest Service, writing environmental documents, mostly. This amused Tyler, but horrified his haute ecology friends. Their place in the ecosystem had been secured by inheritances or marrying well, so they were free to host cocktail parties feting flint-eyed radicals of Eric Brenner's ilk, fundraising to cover the legal fees incurred by ecoterrorists who'd been caught blowing up power transmission lines and such.

Two years of that was enough.

Dee faxed Tyler a note of explanation from Donner Lake on the way to Reno through a late spring Sierra blizzard. "If you look carefully around the place, you might notice that I'm gone." That was followed by the lyrics of the chorus from "Home on the Range." "Love, D.L." Naturally, there was a postscript. One seemed fitting after three years of sharing the same bed. She finally explained why she'd never used the name Ravenshaw. "In the Basque homeland, children more often take the name of the mother than the father. So, the children of the House of Laguerre must be Laguerres, no matter who the sire. Or the hubby. Sorry."

Reaching the pinnacle at last, she inched around its slippery base to the leeward side, then wrapped the poncho tighter around herself and gazed eastward, waiting for muzzle flashes.

Lightning struck the peak above her, illuminating the pinyons. Their needles turned an electric white for a split second.

CHAPTER**SIX**

Jack Reckling raced his BLM truck along the old telegraph line, splashing through the puddles that dotted the track. The cloud cover had broken this morning, but he could feel more rain on the way. The air was satiny and warm. Thunderheads were already building in the southwest.

He reached down between his legs for his beer and took a swig.

Kwak's government jeep was parked out on the flats, but the botanist was nowhere to be seen. "Nice try, you son of a bitch," Reckling said, getting mad all over again. "Think you can pull ol' Jack on like a rubber boot, don't you?" He parked next to the jeep and laid on his horn for a full minute before scanning the brush with his binoculars.

"Shit . . ." Kwak was halfway to the dry lake, nearly a mile away.

Waving, Kwak started up the long slope.

"Mornin' to you too, Zip." Reckling finished the last swallow in the can, then exchanged it under the seat for a fresh one.

It was Saturday, his day off. He'd had a few screwdrivers with the boys while cooking eggs for the cattlemen's association pancake breakfast. Good cause—to benefit the volunteer fire department, although a lot of folks hadn't shown up because of the threat of weather. Stepping across the highway to the post office, he'd

71

found a receipt in his box from Howbert's Assay Laboratory in Gold Mountain. Two hundred bucks had been paid out by the bureau's clerk before Reckling even saw the bill, which had been signed by Milton Kwak.

He polished off the second can, stashed it out of sight, then stepped out of the truck. It'd been cool at first light, following the all-night downpour, but now the air was quickly heating up again.

"Hurry up, will you!" he shouted down to Kwak, who continued toward him at the same unflappable lope.

Reckling's eye was drawn to a speck of white and brown turning off Cayuse Mountain Road onto the old telegraph line track. He grabbed his binoculars off the dashboard and confirmed what he'd thought—it was Dee Laguerre's Bronco, mud-splattered.

"What now?"

Had she gone up the mountain this morning after returning from Gold Mountain?

Reckling was never sure what she was doing. Or who she was really working for. She had no loyalty to the bureau, he knew that much. Bascos had no loyalties to anybody but their own kind. They were like Orientals in that way. And if he were a gambling man, he'd bet his last dollar that her campaign to end grazing in the resource area was on the orders of old Julian Arrache, her distant kinsman and the head of the last big Basque clan in the valley. Most of the present-day livestock allotments were for cattle, not sheep, thanks to the preference the Taylor Grazing Act had given in the thirties to those first on the land, those who owned and paid taxes on their hay ranches—the cattlemen, in short. The kind of seminomadic sheep operation run by Laguerre's father had slowly died out. Dominique Laguerre hadn't even owned the old silver-painted travel trailer he'd lived in with his rawboned wife and skinny daughter on the outskirts of town; he rented it from an Indian. Most of the Basques had moved on, opened restaurants all over the West, gone into gaming and even politics. There was no denying that Basques did well. They were like Jews in that way. Success was their religion.

Kwak strode up to Reckling just as Laguerre pulled in alongside the other two vehicles.

"As soon as she clears off," Reckling said to the botanist, "you and me're gonna waltz."

Kwak dropped his gaze. Guilty as sin.

Laguerre got out of the Bronco. Her uniform looked damp and her bobbed hair was a mess.

"I thought you went to Gold Mountain," Reckling said.

"I heard that rumor, too." She paused, and Reckling realized that she was worked up about something. Her face was slightly convulsed. "They took out the whole mustang band, Jack."

"What band?"

"Cayuse Mountain."

It sank in, and he swore. Now the horse lover groups would descend on the valley, blame him for not protecting them. Well, that was Laguerre's job, not his. And she'd failed, something that offset his worry a little. "How many?"

"I counted thirty-three carcasses at the upper spring."

"Shit awmighty." That was the entire band, all right. "You see anybody there?"

"No. They must've gone out the east side."

"Any idea who they were?"

She looked at him full-on, and he remembered old Dominique glaring at him the same way. Eyes burning with contempt. "You tell me, Jack. I don't have a stool with my name on it down at the Snake Pit."

Reckling took a step backward. Had she smelled it on his breath? He was on his day off, but he'd used his government truck, figuring that his face-off with Kwak would be official business. He tried to think of something to snap back at her, but his mind was spinning. There'd been some noticeable absences at this morning's breakfast. The Wheatleys. And Olin Peters, who'd been scheduled to help Reckling fry up the eggs. "You positive they went out through the nuke site?"

"Positive. A slide kept me from driving into the spring last night. I had to hike in this morning."

Then she'd been tipped off. He just knew it. Nodding, he decided on another tack. "You all right?" he asked gently.

"Okay."

"Honey, you look pretty shook to me."

Her face went perfectly still. "Don't try to make a case out of it, Jack. You weren't there. You didn't see what those bastards left behind. I did, but I'm still in control. You understand?"

"I'm not makin' a case, Dee. I'm just sayin' you're just human like the rest of us."

"That's right," she said. "No more, no less."

Easy does it, Reckling reminded himself. He'd never met a full-blooded Basco who wasn't three quarts of suspicion and one quart cunning. But he was beginning to feel slightly more hopeful than he had when she'd first told him. The report of a mustang slaughter would hit the papers, and some horse-loving gadflies would come down from Reno and run their own investigation. He could weather that. But a prosecution was an entirely different thing. The relationship he'd built up with the ranchers all these years—and he had no doubt that the local ranchers were involved—would go belly-up if the BLM put together a solid case and took it to federal court. Reckling felt the sweat break out on his skin. He intently eyed Laguerre a moment, before asking in a voice as smooth and calm as he could make it, "You find any physical evidence up there?"

But damned if she didn't sniff out what was making him sweat. "It'll all be in my report, Jack."

"And when do I get a look at that?"

She turned, without saying, and headed back toward the Bronco.

"I'm talkin' to you, sister!"

"And every livestock operator in Pinyon County. So you'll get the report when they do, Jack."

"You can go straight to hell, Laguerre!" Reckling cried. There was a pause in which he inwardly told himself to shut up, but it came too late and too weakly. The voice of caution passed like a puff of breeze. He looked at Kwak, who was smiling sardonically at him. "Both of you can go to fuckin' hell!"

Laguerre then stopped and faced him again.

"Time when this whole area was mine alone to look after," Reckling went on, "and now I can't even find out what gives with my own outfit!"

"*Outfit*'s a livestock operator's term, Jack," Laguerre said evenly.

Reckling wanted to hit her so badly he forced himself to focus on Kwak. "You tell me, boy," he said, whipping the folded paper from his shirt pocket, "what the fuck does a vegetation assay have to do with a range inventory?"

Kwak kept his eyes on the ground.

"Tell me, dammit!"

"Nothing, Jack," the botanist finally admitted, looking hangdog. "It's for my doctoral thesis in plant-soil symbiosis. I'll reimburse you out of my own pocket. I meant to in the first place. Just forgot."

"How's that help my budget? That money has to go back into the general fund. I won't ever see it, Zipper!"

Laguerre said something to him, but his blood was pumping so hotly in his ears he had to ask, "What's that?"

"I said watch the racist bullshit, Jack. You're on duty."

Reckling laughed triumphantly. "Wrong. I came out here on my day off to square this with Zipper—so it's First Amendment time!"

"That's debatable."

"Put a lid on it, Laguerre!"

"That's my advice to you, Jack."

"No, it's time I finally spoke up! What the hell is happenin' to this outfit!" Reckling took off his Stetson and flung it to the ground. "Token cunt. Token slant. We even got us a token queer. Christ, we'd have a token whale if we could squeeze one into a uniform!"

"Jack, you're drunk—"

"*I'm* the goddamn minority around here! *I'm* the threatened and endangered species!"

Laguerre strode over to her Bronco. Reckling thought she was going to drive off, but instead she reached through her open window for the microphone. She tried to raise the BLM dispatcher at the office in Gold Mountain.

Instantly, Reckling's rage shriveled, his blood began to cool, and he realized that he'd gone too far. He avoided Kwak's bewildered stare. Years of rage suffered in silence. He wanted to explain that, how he and Topsy had looked forward to moving to Reno on the wings of a promotion to the state office—and how a woman with half his years in the BLM and only a tenth of his range experience had gotten the job, thanks to a consent decree. He just wanted to make himself clear.

He expected Laguerre to have the dispatcher log her grievance. But she didn't. She simply signed off duty and came back to Reckling.

"What'd you do that for?" he asked, puzzled.

"So this token cunt could exercise her own First Amendment rights and say something sexist to you."

"Sexist?" he echoed, completely deflated now.

"Yeah, but it just hit me that you're a dickless bastard, Jack Reckling—so how can I be sexist by calling you a worthless alcoholic prick!"

Dee trooped into the lobby of the Pyrennes just as a large group of German tourists filed out the front door into their bus. Great. She was in no mood to put up with their complaints about only God knew what. Someday, one of them would finally realize that the Japanese paid half of what they did for the family-style meal. But Japanese ate half of what the Germans did. She'd thought one of them was a very good pianist until the Greyhound pulled out for Las Vegas and the delicate Chopin étude continued from the aged upright in the alcove bar.

She dropped her crime scene equipment bag to the threadbare Belgian carpet and looked in on the player.

He smiled up from the keyboard at her, perhaps the most gorgeous young man she'd ever seen. Luxuriant black hair and unblemished olive skin.

"Beautiful," Dee said, wearily easing onto a bar stool.

He accepted the compliment with a dreamy-eyed nod.

Then, from the lobby, came Rabe Pleasant's Mississippi accent, arguing with Gabrielle that he knew damned well she was hiding a bottle of French champagne and he wanted it. Price was no object. The old woman contended that Rabe had raided her only magnum the last time he'd returned from Las Vegas with a guest.

Dee softly laughed, then asked the young man, "Have you ever been hooted?"

His fingers froze in mid-measure and he asked innocently, *"Hooted?"* Either a Spanish or a Portuguese accent. "No, miss, I don't think so. Maybe . . ." A silly laugh followed that made everything perfectly clear. "You're Dominica, are you not?"

"Yeah." Sitting in the confined space, she realized that her uniform smelled like used gym socks.

"I've heard very much about you, Miss Dominica."

"All of it in warning," Rabe said, sweeping in and sliding behind the bar to examine the bottles, "that you're a cold-blooded vamp." He pointed at the young man, who went on coaxing some exquisite Chopin out of the brittle felts and strings, and said sotto voce to Dee, "Dibs on that, sweetness—do we have an understanding?"

"Of course," Dee said, "I've always been a realist."

"The best policy, especially the way you look today. My God, woman, have you been out mud-wrestling again?"

"How kind."

Rabe settled on a bottle of absinthe. "Got caught in the rain this morning?"

"Last night, all night."

The wildlife biologist paused in the middle of taking three small glasses off the dusty shelf. "Something up?"

Dee hesitated. She didn't want to ruin the last few hours of Rabe's holiday. And the chances of prosecuting Cinch and the others were now practically nil unless she got some unlikely forensic support from the state office. A veterinarian would have to be contracted for the necropsies, which would cost the bureau a small fortune. So it wasn't worth upsetting Rabe about the mustang slaughter. He was inordinately fond of animals. He'd once confessed that they'd been his only comfort as a child on the Delta. "It can wait."

"You sure?" Rabe asked, making sure in the mirror behind the bar that his five-thousand-dollar toupee was on squarely. "Talk to me, sweetness."

She sighed. "Reckling's being an asshole."

"Oh, shock."

"Like I said, let's forget it for now. How're you doing?"

"Wonderful." His freckled face beamed, flushed giddily. "Mad in love."

"I gathered that much. We haven't been introduced."

"Sorry. Ramaloche . . . ?"

The young man swiveled around on the piano stool. A smile that could disarm the Balkans. "Yes, Rabe?"

"I'd like you to meet my only friend in this inhospitable wilderness . . . Dee Laguerre."

Ramaloche offered his hand. The palm was heavily calloused, which was explained when Rabe added, "Ramaloche is the marimba player with *Oba, Oba.*" A Brazilian extravaganza currently running in Las Vegas.

"A pleasure, Miss Dominica." But then the young man's brow furled as Rabe came around the bar with the glasses. "Rabe, what is a hooting?"

The biologist frowned at Dee.

"Now, don't get on me, dammit," she said, taking a tiny sip of the mind-bending green liqueur. Almost instantaneously, it could transform impulses into actions, an effect Rabe was no doubt counting on. "Remember that great universal truth we stumbled upon the other night, Mr. Pleasant?"

"No. We were shit-faced."

"All lasting relationships begin with absolute trust."

Rabe looked doubtful, then took a breath and said to Ramaloche, "I go out at night and broadcast a recording of the mating call of a particular species of owl. Hoping a live one will answer. It's the easiest way I have to find a bird of the same feather, so to speak.''

"I see.'' Then Ramaloche turned to Dee and grinned. "Yes, I have been hooted.''

She burst into laughter.

"You have a wantonly vicious sense of humor, woman,'' Rabe said, trying not to laugh himself.

But suddenly, for no particular reason, Dee saw something strikingly unfunny in her mind's eye. Dead horses. Clouds of meat bees drawn to them. She quickly knocked back the rest of the absinthe and got to her feet.

"Bath,'' she announced.

"Please do,'' Rabe said.

She went out, picked up her bag, and hurried up the stairs, the liqueur making her reach for the banister once. She felt much better now that Rabe was back. Not so alone. Rangering for the BLM was police work with none of the camaraderie of the precinct house, no getting together over a couple of beers to "debrief'' and talk away the tension, the occasional horrors.

In the morning she'd lay everything on Rabe Pleasant about the slaughter, hoping that he'd see some way to proceed she herself hadn't.

Rabe and she were the only government employees who didn't live in the compound south of town. He, of course, had taken a room at the Pyrennes because he could never traipse past Jack and Topsy Reckling's bungalow with the latest bird he'd bagged on a hooting trip. But for Dee, living in this old hotel had been coming home to the smells and accents of her childhood. She'd desperately wanted to feel at home after San Francisco. Those years on the bay had left her feeling *leku barik*, the old expression that so typified the Basque experience—"without a place.'' Now she was home, all right. Back in the middle of the range war she'd found so intolerably stupid as a college student, so much so she'd vowed never to return to Cayuse Valley.

She immediately went to her desk with the equipment bag. Aching for the soothing warmth of some hot water, she nevertheless took out her fingerprinting kit and a small plastic bottle that held the casing from a spent cartridge. It was the remnant of a .30-.30 round, probably fired from a Winchester saddlegun, the traditional weapon of ranchers.

She had found the casing just above the narrows in Upper Cayuse Spring canyon, the only shred of physical evidence a two-hour search of the area had netted. Other than the gunshot wounds to the horses, which she'd photographed. To extract the bullets without damaging them would call for an expertise she didn't have, and budget cuts had limited investigative support to the most serious crimes. Shooting wild horses was still only a misdemeanor. Political pressure from the mustang lobby might help jar loose some funds for her. Maybe.

Holding the brass hull on the eraser end of a pencil, she gently brushed it with a fine, black volcanic powder that would cling to any oils left by human touch.

She did it twice, but no latent fingerprints materialized.

"Merde," she said, tossing down the brush.

The rain and scouring sand had left her with absolutely nothing to place any of the ranchers in the canyon—other than the bullets. Even if she could recover them, she knew that there was little hope that they were in any shape for laboratory comparison to bullets from a weapon fired by one of the ranchers. Collisions with bone and skull had most likely transformed them into shapeless nuggets of lead.

"Shit."

She stripped and jammed her filthy uniform into her already full wicker hamper, then threw a terry cloth robe around herself and trekked down the hallway to the common bathroom.

There, she made the mistake of stepping up to the mirror while she ran the taps. Her face was streaked with slurry from the dust and rain. "My God." If Ramaloche had felt any faint stirring for the opposite sex, this ghoulish mug had quashed it forever. She giggled helplessly.

Slipping into the warm water, she closed her eyes. It

had been the epitome of luxury to generations of shepherds, this old claw-footed, cast-iron tub. The pleasure
of it made her want to sing. "... seldom is heard, a
discouraging word ... and the skies are not ... are
not ..." Her eyes snapped open, fixed on the pebbled
glass of the high window. The sky was darkening with
clouds again. But, inwardly, she was seeing the signature
page of the Western Nevada Comprehensive Wild Horse
Plan. Cordell Holland had signed it. The document had
been completed while she was at the academy in Georgia, but Cinch, Olin Peters, the Wheatleys and Wade
Russell had all solemnly agreed with their John Henrys
that the way to manage the size of the herd was through
the pet adoption program. Not bullets.

She sat up, bent forward from the waist, and dunked
her head. She came up, sputtering, cursing Cinch Holland for being a two-faced son of a bitch.

She finally understood what last night meant.

It was more than a horse hunt to the ranchers. With
it, they were serving notice that they had no further intention of honoring any agreements and rules. They were
in full revolt against the government of the United
States. The Sabebrush Rebellion had returned to Cayuse
Valley, and Cinch Holland was its ringleader.

"Well then, Holland," she said, rising from the tub
and reaching for her towel, "I may not be able to nail
your ass in court on this one, but I sure as hell can serve
my own notice."

CHAPTER**SEVEN**

Dee sped through an open gate and down into a grassy hollow. There was an old shack at its bottom, half hidden in a clump of stunted aspens. Beside it was Cinch's GMC pickup, the hood propped open with a forked stick as if to cool the engine. The pasture, dusty and wind-blasted for months, had already drunk up most of the night's rainfall. But one large puddle remained, gleaming like polished steel under the cloudy sky. Dee splashed headlong through it, almost catching Cinch with the spray. He was standing in the middle of the corral to one side of the shack, wearing a yellow slicker. His calves scampered around him like chickens. A big syringe was poised in his gloved hands.

She stopped and got out, slamming the Bronco's door behind her.

Cinch watched her coming at him, his jaw muscles working under two days of reddish-blond growth. He lowered the syringe.

She vaulted over the top rail and landed in the mud in front of him. His gaze was steady, expressionless, and he was breathing through slightly parted lips.

She slapped him, hard.

He did nothing, said nothing—until she reared back her hand to strike him again. He caught it in mid-flight. "You can arrest me, Dee, but I'm not gonna let you hit me."

Then, stepping past her, he climbed over the fence

and went inside the shack, leaving the door open.

She leaned on her arms against the corral fence. A few drops streaked past her eyes, and then, instantly, a downpour was rattling in the leaves of the aspens. From an adjoining pen, a cow and her leppie, a stunted calf, stared saucer-eyed through the rails at her.

"You signed the wild horse plan, Cinch Holland!" she shouted at the shack, spinning around. "You gave your word, dammit!"

Silence came from the darkened doorway.

She hadn't meant to slap him, that had never been her intention on the drive up. But the look in his eye had made her. He wasn't gloating over last night, which she'd expected, hoped for even. His look said that he was beaten and waiting for somebody to take him down the hill to jail. That's what had infuriated her more than anything else. Holland was folding without a fight.

Her face felt hot. She turned it up into the rain for a few seconds, then went over the fence again and put down the pickup's hood before the engine got wet. Her hair and shirt were getting soaked. She plodded up to the shack. It had been built in the 1880s to shelter cowboys working more than a day's ride from the ranch headquarters, and its tin roof was sagging from last winter's crushing weight of snow.

Cinch was sitting on the cot in the dim, single room, braiding a horsehair rope. He didn't glance up at her.

"I'm just trying to understand," she said. "I figured you were different."

"From who?"

"The others you went with."

His busy fingers went still. "Nobody's different. Not when it's all said and done." Then he went on braiding. "How'd you know where to find me? Rowena tell you?"

"No." Dee took a chair at the dust-covered table. It was shoved up against the wall beneath the only window. She watched the glass being etched by rain as she said, "You always come up here to wait out bad news."

"I tell you that back when?" He looked her way for the first time.

She nodded. "I'd guess you came up here when Rowena told you she'd missed her monthly."

He said nothing for a long moment, then: "I did. Spent five days in this ol' line shack before Olin found me. He was home from the service. In his gyrene uniform with medals all over his chest. It was like God and country tellin' me to do right by Rowena Peters."

"Did you do right, Cinch?"

"No," he said, dropping his gaze again—and then his voice to a whisper as if the knotholes in the pine walls were ears. "I din't love her, so it was wrong all around."

"Where'd you get married?" she asked after a bit.

"Vegas." He snapped the new section of rope between his fists to tighten the braid. "I remember standin' at the hotel window that night, lookin' down on the Strip and wonderin' what the hell I'd gone and done. I remember wonderin' what you were doin' that minute up in Reno." He paused. "So what's the bad news this afternoon, Dee?"

"You tell me." She could see the veins in his hands stand out as he flexed the rope tighter.

"I'm in no mood for games," he said. "Do what you come for. If it's cuffs, it's cuffs. You know I'd never lay a finger on you."

That only made her feel worse about having slapped him. "Talk to me, Cordell."

"Only Mama calls me that. I mean, used to. When she was herself. Seems like somebody else's name, it's been so long."

"Why'd you break your word?" she asked.

"Sounds like attorney time, Dee."

"Maybe not."

"What d'you mean?"

"I won't use this talk against you. But I may use something else. That's just fair warning."

"Then what's the point in me talkin'?"

"Like I said—I want to understand."

Cinch laid the unfinished rope aside, then stretched his back and said, yawning, "I woulda never signed that damn wild horse plan had I known a new range inventory was in the works. Fact is, Jack Reckling promised all us operators there wouldn't be one. Situation was stabilized."

"That wasn't his to promise."

"Well, he did—that's all I'm sayin'."

"I believe you," Dee said. Reckling couldn't quite get it into his head that he was one cog in a resource management team—and that his word wasn't law on this range, as it'd once been when he was the only BLM employee in Pinyon County. "I've seen Jack pull that crap before."

Cinch said, "He ain't half as popular as he thinks he is. The operators just pump him with booze for information. That's the only reason they put up with his bullshit, lettin' him think he's a buckaroo or somethin'. He's just another goddamn bureaucrat. I don't care how long he's been here."

Hail began beating against the tin roof. Dee turned and looked through the open door: ice pellets were dancing in the grass, dimpling the big puddle. "What are the ranchers feeling right now, Cinch?"

He laughed knowingly. "You don't wanna hear."

"Yes, I do."

He started to pick up the rope again, but then clasped his hands together in his lap. "It was you what lured us cattlemen out here in the first place."

"Me?"

"Sure . . . the gov'mint."

So he thought she was government more than herself. Flattering. But she asked, "You mean through the Homestead Act?"

"That's right. 'Come out west, and we'll give you one hundred and sixty acres.' Hell, we both know that's nothin' out here. You can barely graze enough cattle on that to feed your family, let alone earn some cash. But come, you said. Feed the army. Feed the railroad men, you told us. Help us turn little towns into great big cities

like 'Frisco and L.A.'' A cold breeze blew inside and
fanned Cinch's hair. The hail had gone to rain again, but
a sudden chill was left behind. He got up and shut the
door. "Well, we done it for you. And to prove it, we
got us a family plot filled with Hollands who died before
their time. Shoshone raids. Blizzards. Range wars with
the sheepmen. . . ." He was careful not to look at her as
he said this. "Cholera. Plain old exhaustion. But we
done it. Fed half a nation. And now, instead of sayin'
thanks, you made it all happen out here—what d'you
do, Uncle Sam?'' He laughed again. "You say our
time's up. We're bad for the land. Walk away from
everythin' you own, cowboy, everythin' you know—do
it for the good of the world.''

"Nobody's driving you out, Cinch," Dee said.

"You hit the nail on the head, lady. That's the bitch.
It ain't a person. I could fight a person, knock him on
his ass. It's rules and regs. Filin' an environmental as-
sessment before I step out my front door with a tool in
my hand. Twelve-hour workdays, and then tryin' to stay
awake in your 'bury the hatchet' meetin's with a bunch
of snot-nosed tree-huggers who're so far up the food
chain they've forgotten they got teeth, cud, and assholes
like the rest of us.'' His eyes were now damp with anger.
"Somebody's gonna get kilt if this goes on, Dee.
There's gonna be one helluva backlash to all this. Times
are hard, and if somebody takes your livin' he might as
well take your life. These people 'round here, they din't
lay down for the Shoshone, and no tree-hugger from
'Frisco is half as tough as a Shoshone brave.''

"Could you kill another human being, Cinch?" she
asked quietly.

To his credit, he thought about it. "On the wrong day,
I suppose. It makes me afraid, Dee—how I wake up
feelin' these days. I was never angry like this before.
Oh, I got pissed off from time to time, broke some of
Row's china, or somebody's nose if he got in my face
down at the Snake Pit. But it was never all the time, like
now. It just never gets out of my system, no matter what
I do.'' Rubbing his eyes with his fingers, he yawned

once again. "Nothin' like bein' on the edge, Dee." He laughed as if embarrassed now, but then said in a faltering voice, "I look over and see nothin' down there for me. But I can't even jump. Promised Mama before her stroke I'd carry on for Daddy's sake. For Grandpa's too. I'd keep the place off the auction block for all them that went before. If she was in her right mind, I could maybe explain how hopeless it's all turned . . . how . . ."

Then he buried his face in his hands and choked off a sob before it could fully break from his mouth. He was motionless, silent, mortified.

After a moment of not knowing what to do or say, Dee went to him, eased down beside him on the cot and tried to lightly touch his shoulder. But he sprang up as if her fingers had burned him, half sobbing and half laughing, and went to the door. He leaned against the rough-hewn jamb and said, gazing wetly out over the pasture, "Sorry—you just caught me on a low day."

"Maybe I'm glad I did," she said.

He nodded—appreciatively, she thought. "Don't care much for rain," he went on. "I always look forward to it, but then remember I don't like the way it takes away the light. We got good, strong light in this country. But rain's good for the grass. Recharges my springs—"

He sharply pivoted at her fingers on his back, not having heard her cross the floorboards because of the rain on the roof. The words came hard, and she realized that suddenly her speech was thick. "I've got to go, Cinch."

"Sure," he said, drying his eyes on the back of his right hand. But then, as he began to move, he took hold of her by the crook of the arm and whispered, "Don't, Dee."

"Got to."

"May not come for us again."

Thank God, she thought, *I won't be able to walk out on this twice*. But she said breathily, "I know."

His grasp slid down her arm. He brought her wrist up

to his lips and kissed it just below her palm. "Don't . . . *please.*"

"Got to."

Then, gently, he pulled her back into the room. "I never stopped lovin' you, Dee Laguerre."

"Yes, you did," she said, but then helped him undo the snaps on his slicker. It fell crinkling to the floor, and he began helping her with her uniform shirt buttons.

Jack Reckling went straight home from the plant study site, although in driving past the Snake Pit he was tempted to duck inside and tell the boys what had happened between Laguerre and himself. He knew that all of the cattlemen disliked her—distrusted her, even, for her blood ties to the Arraches. They'd see in a minute how she'd do anything to get back at Reckling for having reduced her daddy's grazing allotments. Ancient history, but a Basco had a memory like an elephant. The boys' sympathetic words would go down like smooth whiskey, but Reckling sensed through a dull headache that the fewer who knew what he'd said to Kwak and Laguerre the better.

By the time he'd soaked his head under the shower he fully realized what was bound to follow.

Laguerre would argue that he had been on duty—he'd been in a government truck and had confronted Kwak over a BLM matter. With that established, she'd press for disciplinary action. Failing to convince their superiors of that, she still might force the issue just enough to land Reckling in an alcohol-abuse program. Not exactly discipline, but enough to castrate him in terms of having any authority over range matters.

Topsy stuck her head inside the steamy bathroom. "You ready for dinner, Jack?"

"Later."

"What's that mean, honey?"

"I'm goin' back out for an hour. Maybe a little more."

The door shut, swirling the steam back over the top of the shower curtain. He shut off the taps and stared down at his chest hair. Completely gray now. Too late to become a private range consultant at this point. Besides, he had no savings to see Topsy and him through the year or two it might take to get established. Too late to do anything except stick it out with the BLM. Eat shit and stick it out. Just after college, he'd been offered a job by the Rhodesian government to run its range program. He wondered how things would be different for him had he taken it. "Hell," he muttered to himself, "I'd still be dead. The nigger rebels woulda shot and roasted me."

He dried off, brushed his teeth, and gargled, then put on his uniform. He seldom wore one. Alienated the locals.

"Later, Topsy," he said on his way out the door. Getting into his truck, he made up his mind not to rehearse the speech he would give to Kwak. The whole idea of apologizing was still so galling it only fired up his anger again, so he tried to think about nothing as he passed a long string of motorhomes on Highway 95. Each of them had at least one dirt bike mounted to the rear bumper. That's what Laguerre should concentrate on: dirt bikes tearing up the range. Took decades for nature to repair that kind of mindless damage.

Turning off Cayuse Mountain Road onto the old telegraph line track, he had to flick on the wipers. A misty rain was falling, turning the dried bugs on the windshield to gelatin.

Kwak was working along the very base of the mountain.

Reckling tapped on his horn twice to announce himself, then got out of the truck. Realizing that the rain was coming down harder, he reached behind the bench seat for two olive-drab ponchos, one for himself and one for Kwak. He donned his and hiked up through the brush to the botanist, who didn't immediately look at him.

"Figured you might find this handy, Milt," Reckling said, offering him the poncho.

Kwak hesitated, then accepted it. Just in time, too. The rain began pelting them.

"How much more you got to go?" Reckling asked.

"Just this last transect," Kwak said, gesturing to indicate the dimensions of the strip he was going over.

"This won't be easy no matter what, so I'm just gonna come out with it, Milt," Reckling said, falling in alongside him. "I'm sorry. For flyin' off the handle like I did this mornin'."

Kwak just kept shuffling along, head inclined, inspecting every square inch of ground for eriogonum.

"I was wrong," Reckling said, feeling the shame spread over his rain-streaked face.

Kwak put up the hood to his poncho and asked, "About what?"

A black-tailed jackrabbit gave up its shelter in a sage hummock and darted away. "Well, for one thing—your vegetation assay."

"I said I'd pay for it, Jack."

"Hold on—I don't know if I want you to now."

"Why not?"

"Well, it could be of use to the range inventory. I mean, what's one more piddly-ass bill?"

Kwak halted and turned toward him, his almond-shaped eyes as blank as agates. "I'm going to pay for it, Jack."

Reckling felt as if he were slowly sinking into the earth. Kwak was going to team up with Laguerre against him. There'd be a hearing in Reno, and he could already hear his own voice going as dry as dust under questioning. "Milt . . ." He didn't want to sound desperate, but he was out of ploys and his neck was on the chopping block as it'd never been before. "What the fuck do I have to do to prove I'm sorry?"

Kwak snapped off an artemisia seed head and began mashing it with his fingers. "You're not sorry, Jack—you're scared."

"Okay," Reckling said, "you're right about that. The last part, I mean." He almost choked on the words, but made himself go on. If he quit and walked back to his truck now, it was the same as walking out on twenty-eight years. "I'm plenty scared, Kwak. You're young and you're a minority. I'm gettin' old and I'm too white to get hirin' preference anywheres. It's your world now. Yours and Laguerre's. I accept that. All I want is the cheese that's due me and a little hole to crawl in.''

Despite the downpour, Kwak lowered his hood. He was smiling ironically. ''When I hired on, the state director said, 'Welcome to the family. The bureau is a family.' ''

''Used to be that way, Milt.''

''When it was all white, Jack?'' The botanist laughed, then put the seed head in his front pants pocket and took off his rain-speckled glasses. Carefully, he wiped them with his handkerchief. ''Well, I've already got a family, Jack. I don't need another. My old man and Mom worked eighteen hours a day unloading produce at Central Market in L.A. till they could afford a small grocery of their own. They gave up their house and slept in the back of the store to put me through Stanford and my sister through Berkeley.''

''Well, I never said you weren't an industrious people.''

Kwak laughed again. ''Not the point, Jack.''

''All right . . . what is?''

''That's the kind of family that deserves my loyalty. Not a bunch of assholes who call me 'slant' behind my back.''

''Blood's thicker than water. I can understand that.''

''Yeah.'' Kwak put his glasses back on, his eyes now shrewd behind the lenses. ''Let's deal.''

''Okay, that's what I'm here for.'' Reckling, feeling hope again, had to fight down a smile. Kwak was caving in.

''I need to run several more geochemical assays through your budget.''

''How many?''

''Six.''

''Jesus.'' Reckling almost whistled. Twelve hundred dollars. He wanted to wince, but he managed to nod. He'd find a way to cover them. Postpone a riparian rehabilitation project slated for this fall. Kwak was the key. With the botanist on the sidelines, Reckling figured he could hold Laguerre to a draw in a hearing by testifying that she still resented Jack's having cut back her father's grazing permits. "And you don't say nothin' about this mornin', Milt?"

"That's right."

"What about the words that passed between Laguerre and me?"

"I must've been out of earshot."

Reckling extended his hand. "You won't regret it, Milt."

"I know." Kwak was just reaching out to accept the shake when his back seemed to buckle. He collapsed against Reckling, bowling him over flat against the ground. Astonished, Jack was wondering if the botanist had fainted or was even attacking him—when he heard the thunderous echo roll over them. A big-caliber rifle.

Kwak was lying heavily atop him, his chin hanging loosely over Reckling's left shoulder.

"Milt . . . ?"

Raising his head a few inches, Reckling could see a bloody, finger-size hole in the back of Kwak's poncho.

"Christ!"

He lifted Kwak's torso slightly off his own chest and watched in horror as gouts of blood and tissue poured from the big exit wound in the botanist's side. Was he himself hit? No, he didn't think so. Miraculously, the bullet had been deflected while passing through Kwak's body.

Revulsion made him want to roll the corpse off him, but then wet sand spurted up from the ground within two feet of his face.

The same rumbly echo quickly followed.

Reckling couldn't tell where the shots were coming from, although common sense told him the slope above. He held fast to the body, positioning the slack head to protect his own.

"Oh, Jesus Christ," he moaned, shuddering as he felt Kwak's blood trickle down into one of the side slits of his own poncho. The flow was warm, and he could see steam rising off it through the rain.

He took deep breaths, trying not to get sick.

Then it came to him. He should have played dead from the beginning. He had to run now. Bullet after bullet would come at him, and the first one had sliced through Kwak's body as if it were butter. But his truck and Kwak's jeep were parked on the most exposed part of the flats. No use trying for one of them.

At last, he threw off the corpse and staggered to his feet. He meant to run immediately, but his legs were like wood and his lungs felt scorched. He stole an upward glance but saw nothing but rain and mist scudding over the western slope of the mountain.

Hobbling, trying to fall into a gait, he started downslope. It was hailing, and the next bullet made an evil clicking sound as it zipped through the sheets of falling ice. Three or less feet above Reckling's head.

On he ran, trying to keep low as he leaped over hummocks and threaded through the brush.

Ahead, no more than a hundred yards, was an arroyo. Six feet deep, the gully meandered all the way down to Highway 95. It was a virtual tunnel to safety. First, Reckling had only to cross a small playa, which was ankle-deep with muddy water. The slimy bottom sucked off a boot, but he kept hobbling toward the arroyo.

CHAPTER**EIGHT**

Cinch Holland sat on his disabled tractor. Far to the west he could see a narrow opening in the storm, a red seam in the clouds. The air was unusually cool, but he could hear winged insects whirring about. A bat was after them, testing the calm between downpours. The last deluge had left the willows around the pond heavy with rain, the branches drooping almost to the muddy ground.

From the house came Rowena's voice calling Cody to his bath and then supper. The boy was up on the slope with his octagon-barreled .22 rifle, hunting jacks—just as Cinch himself had a lifetime ago. Strange to think that there could be fun in this place. But the Holland Ranch of his father's day had had its joys: hayrides on fall evenings and roping contests on Sunday afternoons. And there'd always been the bunkhouse and its resident cowpunchers, men with luminous eyes and faces like dried apples. Where had they all gone? These days, no operator could afford more than a little part-time help, and a whole breed of cowmen had gone extinct. *Poof.* Now and again, one had come along who liked to make up poems. As far as Cinch could tell, not a word was ever written down. He often wished that he could recall some of those verses. When he went up to the line shack, it was with a faint hope he'd hear some of those poems whispering around the walls.

The outdoor bell to the telephone chimed twice before Rowena answered.

Cody came trooping across the dooryard, his rifle draped across his bony shoulders. Cinch thought to shout for him to make sure that the chamber and magazine were empty before he went inside. But he couldn't find his tongue.

He didn't feel up to correcting anybody.

The screen door slammed, and Cody was gone from sight. It creaked open and shut again a few seconds later. Cinch knew without looking that Rowena was coming down to him. He thought about standing up, but then realized that he might not know what to do with his hands.

She stopped ten feet from the tractor and looked at him—through his skin to his yellowish marrow, it seemed. The skin Dee had touched with her lips and somehow made transparent.

When she said nothing after a long moment, Cinch mumbled, "Good sleepin' weather." Immediately, he realized that it was the damndest thing to say, given the afternoon. The nightfall was almost complete, but he feared that she'd see the color rise in his face. "Goin' back up to the shack tomorrow mornin'," he quickly said, "finish shootin' the dope to those calves. All we needed right now—screwworm."

"Cinch . . . ?"

He gripped the clammy steering wheel. "Yeah?"

"That was Julian Arrache on the phone."

He blinked at her a moment. "You sure?"

"It sounded like him all right."

"Say what he wanted?" Cinch asked.

"You to come up to the hacienda this evenin'."

"Anythin' more?"

"No, that was it."

Cinch let go of the steering wheel, wiped his palms on his Levi's. His revolver was still under the front seat of the pickup. At least he'd have that with him, although he had little doubt Julian's sons would frisk him before he'd be allowed to see the old man. "What'd you tell him?"

''Nothin','' she said, then paused. ''You're not thinkin' of goin' . . . are you?''

He stood. The red slit in the clouds was gone. ''The Arraches've had a hundred chances to gun me down out on the range, like they did Uncle Howard.''

''Cinch—''

''Rowena, I can't see 'em crappin' in their own nest now.''

''You don't know that for sure.''

But he had already set off for his truck. ''Phone Olin and Wade if I don't get word back to you by nine.''

Dee sat in the darkness of her room, her heels resting on the windowsill. For the last ten minutes, there had been a spectacular display of lightning in the southwest. Big, white-hot branches of the stuff struck the hills there several times a minute. Some of it streaked parallel to the horizon, as if slithering along in search of a victim. One bolt seemed to rocket up from the ground before dissipating in the sky.

Somebody rapped on her door.

''Who is it?''

''Colin Powell's worst nightmare.''

''Come,'' she said, then took a sip from the glass she was nesting between her legs.

Rabe Pleasant was wearing a cinnamon-colored kimono and matching carpet slippers. The wildlife biologist left the door open, and the neon from the hallway fixture spilled in. ''Can I turn on a lamp without spoiling the mood?'' he asked.

''Nope. And I doubt you could turn on anything in this room.''

''Don't underestimate me.'' Rabe made straightway for the half dozen bottles she kept on top of her bureau. ''What're you drinking?''

''Sun and shade,'' she said.

He made a face. ''Why would anybody in his right mind want to toss clear anisette and dark amber cognac into the same glass?''

''No Basco's in his right mind.''

"Tell me about it," Rabe said, turning a bottle label into the light from the hallway. "Both you and Gabrielle tried to hit on poor Ramaloche. Sweet Jesus, don't you have anything tasty to drink?"

"Try a *sol y sombra*," Dee said. "You're ambiguous enough to enjoy it."

"You win. I'm too bushed to go down to the bar." He mixed up the concoction, then swallowed tentatively. "Well . . . ?"

"It tastes like a fucking contradiction."

"That's the point, Rabe—it's a liquid metaphor for life."

He sprawled on his belly atop her bedspread. "I can think of something else that fits that definition."

"Shut up." She heard thunder for the first time; the squall line was creeping toward Cayuse Valley. "So what d'you want to talk about tonight?"

"The contradiction of love."

"No," she said, "not tonight."

"Oh . . . ?" Rabe rolled onto his side and propped a hand behind his head. "Do I hear what I think I'm hearing?"

"Yes, but it was a mistake that won't be repeated."

"That's two of us, I suppose," he said desolately, his voice almost cracking.

She wanted to smile, but knew that there was meanness in the urge. Had she honestly done better than Rabe in this department? "Ramaloche's gone, then."

"Don't make it sound so goddamn final."

"Sorry."

Rabe took a healthier quaff of *sol y sombra*. "Not bad, really. I can see how it might grow on you. Parasitically, but still it could grow on you. It tastes like Yogi Berra talks. And yes—dear Ramaloche borrowed three hundred rupees to keep from being thrown out of his apartment and got on the Gray Dog back to Vegas. Said he'd call as soon as he arrived. Anytime now."

Twisting around in her overstuffed chair, Dee saw across the hall that Rabe had left his door open as well— to listen for his phone.

"Rabe," Dee said thoughtfully, "something serious . . ."

"You want me to change first?"

"No, just listen. And tell me what you think."

He sat up, his shiny face reflecting the spurts of ever-closer lightning. "Fire away."

"There's an old Basque saying—too much use of the dogs makes a band nervous. Hard to control. Dogged sheep can go crazy, even refuse to eat."

"So?"

"Is that what we're doing to Cayuse—?"

Rabe interrupted, "Who's us?"

"Jack, you, me. All the specialists we call in. Are we dogging these people to the point that they're going crazy?"

"Maybe."

"Then should we lighten up on them?"

"How?"

"Look the other way now and again. Let a thing or two slide."

Rabe swirled the last inch of drink in the bottom of his glass. "Depends. If you're talking about this mindless horse massacre, I say no—"

His phone rang, and he bolted for his room, the hem of his kimono snapping against his shins. He shut her door on the way out, leaving her in darkness again.

The storm cell was now poised over the southwestern rim of the valley, a basaltic bluff called Shepherder's Mountain.

Minutes later, her own phone rang. "Laguerre."

"You alone, Baa?"

"It doesn't mean I'm a failure, Jewell."

"No, it don't. You're a failure because you came back to this shithole when you had a fancy lawyer in 'Frisco willin' to keep you in furs and sweets as long as you kept his hormones jolly."

"You make it sound like it was prostitution," Dee said.

"It was. So what? There's two legalized kinds, mine and marriage. My deadbeat husbands made streetwalkin' look good. You, Dee Laguerre, had yourself a prince.''

"Ask Princess Diana what that can be like. Also, be honest, you were looking for bouncers, not husbands."

"True." Abruptly, Jewell Farley dropped her voice, and Dee could visualize the madam checking over her shoulder for eavesdroppers. "I got a tidbit you might find interestin' . . ."

"Okay."

"Cinch Holland is headed up to the Arraches' place. He's probably there by now. Julian invited him."

"Your informant's drunk, honey."

"Yes, but a drunk man can speak a sober mind."

Dee mulled it over a minute, then asked, "Did Cinch go alone?"

"That's what I heard."

It convinced Dee more than anything. An inebriate would have had Cinch and a dozen of his rancher buddies going up to the Arraches' to settle an old score. This version was more credible, but no less disturbing. Other than in court, the Hollands and the Arraches had never come together without gunplay erupting. "Thanks, Jewell. I'm on my way."

"Bye."

Dee flipped through her hamper for her least dirty uniform shirt and quickly dressed. Yet, by the time she'd strapped on her Sam Browne belt she realized that her showing up at the hacienda might not prevent her distant cousins on her mother's side, the Arraches, from doing whatever they had in mind. She was blood, and they might count on her to at least keep quiet, if not take their side. Regardless of ties, her BLM uniform might only inflame the situation. And nothing Jewell had said told her that the federal government had jurisdiction in the matter.

She phoned Jewell back. "Listen—have one of your new girls contact the sheriff's office. Anonymously. Report a disturbance, whatever, up at the Arraches'."

"Should she mention Cinch bein' there?"

"Absolutely, otherwise Pancake might not bother to respond."

Hanging up, Dee heard the door creak open.

Rabe stepped inside. He was in uniform as well. "Oh, good, I take it you've already heard."

"Yeah, but I think we should let the sheriff's office get there first. We might check in on the hacienda later."

"Then you know where Jack is?" Rabe asked, sounding surprised.

"*Jack?*"

"Topsy just called. I thought she got hold of you, too."

"No, what's with Reckling?"

"He's a couple hours late coming in from the field. She's worried—called the Snake Pit, but nobody's seen him this evening. Nothing on the office log. Any ideas where he went?"

Dee thought for only an instant before saying, "One."

Driving, Cinch thrust his free hand out the open window of the truck into a light, ticklish rain. The series of cloudbursts over the past twenty-four hours had so darkened the highway its asphalt seemed to swallow the light from his headlamps. But the smell of sage was nice. He turned his windbreaker window inward so that the bittersweet perfume flowed over him. Really wasn't sage, at least the garden kind. Artemesia was related to the sunflower. He remembered that from somewhere.

His mind felt curiously sharp, his senses keener than they'd been in years. He was so beaten down from trying to get around things, it was suddenly exhilarating to go at something head-on. Yet, his grandfather would have a fit if he were alive to realize that Cinch was about to call on the Arraches. The old man would flatly forbid it. "There's a helluva lot more Arraches than Hollands," he'd say. "They know that. They got fingers and toes. So they're countin' on us to come back at them. My Howard would understand. We'll play tit for tat the day we get the upper hand, and not before."

Cinch had been born a quarter century after his father's older brother, Howard, was gunned down on the range. But he'd been out to the spot and stood on the small, rocky knoll where Julian Arrache's own brother crouched and fired two rounds of double-ought buck from a shotgun. The first blast brought down Howard's horse. The second wounded Howard in the legs. He then bled to death in a light, dreamy snowfall.

Both killer and victim had been eighteen years old. Boys. Yet they'd always seemed like men in Cinch's imagination.

Julian's brother fled back to Spain or France, or wherever in those heartless mountains the Arraches called home, and the Hollands buried Howard in the family plot alongside all the other casualties of putting beef on America's tables.

Only a year before he died had Cinch's father told Cinch that Howard had pistol-whipped an Arrache while busting up a sheep camp they'd pitched on the Hollands' allotment. And in truth, it'd been the Arraches' range until the federal Grazing Service—the outfit that eventually became the BLM—handed it over to the Hollands and other cattlemen. Those who'd been first on the land. First to grab the grass. The Basques were latecomers. "A people so surly and piss-poor backward," Cinch's grandfather had said, "we paid 'em no mind till it was too late, and they'd taken root."

The old man lived long enough to see that Bascos were anything but backward. Most of the Arraches went to Reno and Las Vegas and climbed the money ladder from restauranting to gaming. Only Julian and his sons had stayed on in Cayuse Valley, running a few sheep but mostly providing a getaway for the rest of the clan— and anybody else who could pay. Years ago, the FBI had gone up to the hacienda with a warrant to search for a Basque terrorist wanted by the Spanish authorities. Julian was too cagey for the feds, and they came away empty-handed. But the incident gave the rest of the valley an idea how Julian managed to make a living with virtually no range to call his own.

Highway 95 curved around a hill, and Cinch could see the floodlights of the hacienda up on Sheepherder's Mountain, the blazing lights of a suspicious people. A clan waiting all these years to get bushwhacked. Maybe that's what this invitation was about. Julian was getting tired of waiting for the other shoe to drop, and he wanted to cut a deal with the last adult male Holland. Or failing that, he planned to kill him.

If that happened, Cinch didn't want Cody to try to avenge him. For the first time, he realized that he wanted his son to move on and find another life. It gave him an unexpected pleasure as he braked for Arrache Road—to imagine Cody going to college, or even riding rodeo for a living if that's what he wanted. A life far removed from crushing labor. From killing horses in the idiotic hope that it'd keep you afloat another couple of months.

He turned off the highway and started up the dirt road, one he had never been on before, not even in the most reckless days of his youth. He reached under the seat and was reassured to feel his holster belt, a few of the round-nosed cartridges.

Lightning lit up the sky directly behind, and then the rain came down.

Dee Laguerre put the wipers on their fastest setting, but still the windshield was a wavery blur. The flats beneath the mountain had finally absorbed all the water they could, and the old telegraph line track looked like a canal. A loud splashing sound was reverberating through the Bronco from the wheel wells, making Rabe Pleasant raise his voice to be heard. "Uh, sweetness, I think you're going off the side."

He was right. Thorny brush could be heard scraping the right front fender.

Dee stopped, closed her eyes to rest them. No decent sleep in two days now.

"Jack could've had engine trouble," Rabe said, trying to sound hopeful.

"Maybe." But she didn't say what she was thinking. Jack's truck would be found parked next to Milt Kwak's jeep, and it was unlikely that both vehicles had broken down.

Rabe went on, "Or a flash flood cut them off. Happened to me once up on Silver Peak."

"Must've been scary."

"Utterly terrifying. All I had were C rations and country and western on the radio."

Dee opened her eyes and inched forward again. The Bronco wallowed through a foot-deep brown creek in the bottom of a usually dry ravine and then churned up the muddy, rutted slope beyond. "But we've made it this far, Rabe, and both those guys have four-wheel drive, too."

"Well," Rabe said, "I'm sure there's an explanation."

"There's always an explanation."

"I mean a happy one." Yet, his left hand was tight around the barrel of the shotgun.

She crowned the next rise and parked, then flicked on her spotlight. The rain looked like Christmas tree tinsel as it passed through the beam. She probed the plant study site. The brush was jeweled, glistening.

"There, Rabe," she finally said, letting go of the handle that swiveled the spot. The truck and the jeep—side by side, just as she'd expected. There was no sign of either man in or around either of the vehicles.

Rabe reached for the PA microphone and called out for Jack.

"Don't," Dee said, taking the mike from him and clipping it back on the radio stack.

"What's wrong?" Rabe was looking at her as he never had before, his eyes large. "What is it?"

She killed all the lights and then the engine. "I don't know," she said. "I just think we ought to go down there on foot as quietly as we can."

"In this?" he said, falling silent for a moment so she could hear the rain pounding on the roof of the Bronco. "We'll have to do breaststroke."

She reached for the flashlight she kept in the glove box, her poncho making a crinkling sound as she leaned across Rabe. Just as Cinch's slicker had as she'd rolled it off his shoulders onto the floor.

"You want me to carry the shotgun?" Rabe asked.

She didn't really have an obvious reason to break it out. But she wondered what had made Rabe ask. Was it the same thing that was gnawing at her?

"No," she finally said, "but grab that big flashlight in the bag just behind you."

Rabe didn't budge. She couldn't see his eyes in the dark but sensed that they were fixed steadily on her. "Dee," he asked, his voice strangely hesitant, "how'd you know Jack came back out here?"

"I just did."

"He could've gone a thousand places, including Tonopah for a snort, but you drove straight out here."

Wearing the poncho had made her sweaty, yet her hands and feet were cold. Only her belly felt warm, but it was fluttery. "After what happened this morning," she then said, "I knew Reckling would go home and sober up enough to know he'd screwed the pooch by calling Milt a token slant and me a token cunt. I'm proud of what he called me, but Kwak might not be so broadminded. I figured Jack would come back out and try to suck up to Milt. Jack never goes on patrol after five. He might catch some of his Snake Pit pals doing something they shouldn't. Satisfied?"

Rabe slowly let out a breath. "Where's that flashlight?"

"The bag, behind you." She made sure her revolver was snugly holstered. "By the way, Jack called you a token queer."

"What a filthy lie."

"Oh?"

"Lots of queers work for Uncle Sam. A matter of fact, how come Sam isn't married?"

"Come on." Yet, with one hand on the door latch, Dee paused. She didn't want to hike down to the vehicles, but the notion of driving down onto the flats with lights blazing made her feel even more vulnerable. Then, impulsively, she unlocked the shotgun and took it with her.

"Oh, Jesus," Rabe said, getting out a second after her.

She stood beside the Bronco, the rain beating against her face. She looked for movements out in the sage, tried to hear something, anything, over the roar of tons of water rustling in the scrub.

Rabe came around to her. "I don't like this, do you?"

"No," she admitted, then started walking.

Each time lightning struck somewhere near, she quickly pivoted, trying to glimpse either Reckling or Kwak on the flats before the flash dimmed again. Far below to the west, headlamps crawled along U.S. 95 and Jewell's landing strip beacon blinked.

Rabe asked low, "Could they've walked cross-country down to the highway for some reason?"

Dee had been thinking the same thing. But why hadn't they driven out the way she and Rabe had just approached the plant study site? Unless a flash flood, some hours ago, had blocked the road and then receded. "I don't know, Rabe. Nothing adds up, and that's what I don't like more than anything."

Five minutes later, they came to the vehicles. Her right hand on her revolver grip, she lit up the interior of Reckling's truck. Nothing. Kwak's jeep was empty, too, except for the usual jumble of gear that came with being on detail in the field. She opened Reckling's cab door, and a gust stinking of stale beer hit her. The keys were still in the ignition. She reached for the radio microphone, raised the Gold Mountain dispatcher, and asked, "How do you read me?"

"Clear as a bell, Dee."

One more thing that made no sense. Whatever had gone wrong, Reckling could have radioed in.

"Here's a possibility," Rabe said. "One of them got hurt, broke a leg, something like that—and they holed up together to wait out the downpour. What d'you think?"

Squatting, Dee shined her light along the ground. A line of elongated dimples in the sand led upslope. "You're the tracker, Rabe—are those footprints?"

He knelt beside her, not minding that the knees to his trousers were instantly soaked. ''What's left of them.'' But he rose and began following the tracks. Dee fell in behind him, keeping the muzzle of the shotgun barrel pointed downward. She illuminated the brush for a second or two whenever a shape seemed even vaguely human to her.

All at once, Rabe went to his knees again and began sweeping his flashlight beam along the edge of some tall sage. *''Dee,''* he said urgently.

Eyes, metallically orange, glinted from the maze of leafy branches. Two pair. No, three. Dee peered down her shotgun barrel at them, then lowered the weapon. ''What the hell are coyotes doing out on a night like this?''

''Scavenging,'' Rabe said, sounding sickened. ''They'd only get wet for some damned easy pickings.'' He got up and hurried on, scattering the small pack before him.

She fell in behind him.

''Oh, Christ.'' And then Rabe was running, his light dancing wildly around the ground. Dee caught up and soon saw what Rabe had seen.

She grabbed the tail of his poncho and yanked him to a halt. ''Easy,'' she said, surprised by how shuddery and high her voice sounded. She handed Rabe the shotgun. ''You stay out here. Beyond my light.''

He accepted the gun without a word, but then seemed to throw off his shock. His retired army colonel father had forced him to hunt bobwhite quail in Mississippi, so he smoothly jacked a round into the chamber. ''Which way do I watch?'' he asked.

''Every way.'' Then Dee approached Milton Kwak. He was lying on his right side, that arm pinned beneath him and the left outstretched as if beckoning her to come all the way forward. One eye was closed, but the other, destroyed, bugled milkily from the socket. She knelt over him, made a fist to stop her fingers from trembling, and forced herself to touch him. He had no carotid pulse. And no flesh color flowed back under his thumbnail after she pressed it. She'd known at once that he was gone, but she also realized that if she did everything as she'd been taught she might not get sick, or be overwhelmed by the thought that this had been someone she'd known and liked.

This was her first homicide.

"Is he . . . ?" Rabe called to her, hushed.

"Yes," she said.

"Shit."

She looked for tracks around the body, but there were none that she could recognize as human—only little water-filled divots from the coyotes, who'd shredded Milt's poncho with their claws and teeth to get at his wounds. She knew that there were wounds from the bloodstains. They were pinkish from having been diluted by the rain. Straddling the corpse, she ran her beam along the length of his body. She stopped in the middle of his back and inspected a blood-rimmed hole in the poncho. With two fingertips, she pressed a few inches directly above it. The spine. The bullet had broken his back, and death had no doubt been instantaneous.

This gave little sense to the second wound she discovered.

Kwak had been shot in the back of the skull as well. The scalp around the entry hole showed tattooing, stippling from tiny hemorrhages caused by the discharge of burned powder. Milt had taken this second bullet from only inches away.

A coup de grace.

Dee closed her eyes again, but only for a few seconds before she began examining the body again. "Exit wounds," she said to herself, running down a mental checklist.

"What's that?" Rabe asked.

The shot to the head had almost exited through an eye. A handgun bullet, most likely, for a rifle round at this range would have kept on traveling. Gingerly, she rolled Kwak onto his back. He was almost in complete rigor mortis, which made her feel a little easier in one way: the killer was most likely long gone. Stiffening this thorough came only after several hours.

Looking at the massive exit wound in Kwak's side brought the taste of bile to her mouth.

She spun away, took several deep breaths.

"You all right, sweetness?" Rabe asked.

She inhaled deeply one last time, then rasped, "Yeah. I guess." The high-powered rifle bullet had blown out a section of Milt's side the size of a cantaloupe. She got up, her legs numb beneath her, and searched for this bloody clump of tissue and bone. Not finding it, she went back to Rabe with the strange sensation that she was walking a few inches above the soggy ground.

"Jack was near him when he died," she said, switching off her light, thankful for the darkness.

"How d'you know that?" Rabe whispered.

"I think he got splattered. I can't find a big piece of . . . you know."

Rabe could be heard breathing shallowly through his mouth.

"He's still out here," she said. A trickle of rain went down her nape, and she shivered.

"Let's wait for help, Dee."

"He might be wounded, Rabe. Badly. I'm not going to wait."

"What'd he call me again? A cunt or a queer?"

"You're the queer. I'm the cunt."

"Okay, as long as Jack wasn't just singling me out. Take this." Rabe handed her back the shotgun. Turning on his light, he began circling the corpse on a radius of about twenty feet. He stopped once and stared off toward the vehicles. "You'd think he would've made a beeline back for one of the radios."

"Not if he was using his head," Dee said. "Nothing to hide behind that way."

"All right."

A few minutes later, Rabe found foot impressions heading downslope. They angled away from the vehicles but on a line that would eventually end at Highway 95. They were faint, and Rabe lost them several times. The final time was at the edge of a pool that had formed in a shallow alkali sink. "If it's Jack, he went swimming from here on," Rabe said, then looked sharply at Dee. "God, you don't think he's under that water, d'you?"

She knew that there was only one way to find out. Wading out, she took the live shell out of the chamber, then used the stock of the shotgun as a probe. The deepest part of the sink was up to her knees.

"Got something, Rabe," she said near the pool's far shore.

"Oh, Jesus."

She groped in the khaki-colored waters for a moment, then brought up a chukka boot. Rawhide. One of Jack's.

Rabe, standing where the tracks entered the pool, was using his thumb to sight along a line that passed through where Dee had recovered the boot. Suddenly, he was running around the sink.

"What . . . ?" Dee asked.

But Rabe had halted in silence before what Dee had taken for a boulder. She slogged out of the pool and joined him.

Reckling had almost made the cover of a ravine that was now half filled with muddy water. Wordlessly, she entrusted Rabe with the shotgun to keep guard while she went up to examine the body.

Within minutes, she believed that she knew how Jack Reckling had died.

She stepped over to Rabe, who gave her a quick embrace. It was just the right thing to do, although she was left with the urge to cry. The rain had stopped, and a few stars were showing between the thick swatches of clouds. She cleared her throat and said, "Rifle bullet dropped him. Hit him in the thigh. Lots of bleeding. And blood on his hands from putting pressure on the wound. So he wasn't dead at that point."

"Then what got him?" Rabe asked.

"Two bullets to the face."

CHAPTER**NINE**

The hacienda wasn't what Cinch had expected. With all the power and wealth the Arraches supposedly had, he'd thought that the place would be fancier. The walls of the house were white stucco, which was cracked around the red-trimmed windows from earthquakes set off by testing on the nuclear reservation. The terra-cotta roof tiles down near the eaves had been chipped by winter's ice buildup and left unrepaired. Slowly, he drove over the unpaved courtyard, through puddles that were reflecting the glare of the floodlights. It was like a prison compound in that way: a harsh light on a tall pole in each corner. There were no lawns or ornamental bushes anywhere, but that was just sheepmen. Wherever they went with their hooved locusts, desolation followed, so maybe they acquired a taste for barrenness. A cattle family, at least, always had a lilac bush or a cottonwood.

He stopped, turned off the engine.

Nobody was in sight.

None of the curtains in the house windows parted or jiggled. Small windows, almost like gun ports.

If the Arraches meant to take him down in cold blood, he figured it would come now, before any words were exchanged. He cranked down his side window to listen. The rain had quit, and everything was silent. Twisting around, he carefully looked over the big aluminum sheep trailer parked across the yard. No movement was visible through the round ventilation holes in its side.

Then Cinch held his breath for a moment. He could hear a car racing up the road behind him.

Suddenly, headlights on high beam swept over the roof, and he started to grab under the seat for his revolver, sure that the Arraches were going to block the courtyard gate and hem him in.

But it was a sheriff's car that came splashing through the puddles, the rear amber light blinking.

Pancake bailed out as quickly as he could dislodge his belly from behind the steering wheel, and huffed up to Cinch's window. "You already been?" the deputy asked breathlessly.

"Been where?"

"Inside, dammit."

"Yep."

"Everything okay then?"

"Nope."

"What d'you mean?"

"I shot 'em all in the head, Pancake." The deputy's jaw dropped before Cinch smiled.

"Not funny, Holland."

"Who told you I was comin'?"

"Half the valley, includin' the Arraches."

Cinch asked in surprise, "*Julian* wanted you here?"

"I guess. Dispatch says it was his daughter-in-law askin' me to keep the peace. Stay put."

Pancake started for the house, the clump of keys on his belt jingling, but Julian Arrache's sons were already filing out the front door into a cloud of moths hugging the porch light. Bittor was first, tall, vaguely sneering as always. The oldest and the most brutal. Years ago, he'd stabbed a Shoshone with his sheep knife in a brawl outside a Gold Mountain tavern and served a year in county jail for it. Cinch had heard that Bittor had once had designs on Dee. Pello followed, a deceptively soft-looking man, for flab was frosting on a stoutly muscular body, and he'd once beaten Wade Russell within an inch of his life. Mikel, or Nino as he was called, was last, poker-faced. The youngest son. He and Cinch had gone through twelve grades of school together without having traded a single word. If one of them was picked to lead the Pledge of Allegiance, the other clammed up.

Warily, Pancake approached them. "Evenin', boys." Silence.

"Try sign language on 'em, Pancake," Cinch sang out from the truck. "They're only two generations outta the caves."

Pancake flashed his palm for Cinch to shut up, then lit a cigarette to look nonchalant. He launched into some rigamarole about his just being there to keep a lid on things. He wanted nobody to be packing a gun on his person, and to prove this he asked Cinch if he had any weapons.

"Just my service revolver."

Frowning, Pancake returned to Cinch's truck and said, "I'll hold it till you go."

"Ain't you forgettin' somethin'?"

"What?"

"For chrissake, Pancake—I'm a reserve deputy."

"You ain't here on sheriff's business, Cinch, so I'll take your piece. Let's not argue in front of these people."

"Fuck these people."

"Cinch, *please* . . ."

Sighing, Cinch reached under the seat. As soon as he brought up the gun belt he knew something was wrong. Too light.

"Where is it?" Pancake asked, eyes on the empty holster.

Cinch got out with his flashlight and stooped, shining the light under the seat. "Hell if I know." Cody sprang to mind, but his son had been warned, and Cinch couldn't imagine his risking the licking he'd get for even touching the revolver without permission. "Just frisk me, goddammit," he said, standing. Then he raised his voice. "And frisk those dagos, too. They carry knives you could gut a buffalo with."

"You're not layin' a hand on us," Bittor said with menace.

But then an old man's voice drifted from inside the

house. "Do as the deputy says." Some quieter words followed, but Cinch couldn't make them out. Maybe they were Basque.

His cigarette tucked in the corner of his mouth, Pancake patted around Cinch's waist, squeezed the pockets to his Levi's jacket. "Clean," he said, then went up onto the porch and gave the three Arraches the same cursory search.

At that moment, Julian strolled out, straight-backed even though he had to be in his seventies. He had silver hair and a prominent nose. Pancake said, almost sounding apologetic, that he couldn't find Cinch's revolver, then started to frisk the old man's light woolen sweater and baggy trousers.

"Never mind that, Pancake," Cinch said, strolling up to the front door. "Julian knows that I can take a bullet and still find some way to gouge out his eyes."

The old man gave a hoarse chuckle. "Please come inside, Cordell," he said, the hard, insistent voice of a sheep boss. He turned to his sons as Cinch walked slowly past them. "Stay out here and keep the deputy from gettin' lonely."

None of them gave any reaction Cinch could see.

Julian led the way inside. The house smelled different to Cinch than any he'd ever entered. Foreign. They went through the first door into a den. Again, nothing special, although the furniture was upholstered with sheepskin. "Sit down, Cordell."

As he did, a woman, thirtyish, swept in carrying two tiny glasses on a tray. She was pretty in the way Dee was, full-lipped with frank brown eyes. Cinch couldn't recall having ever seen her before.

Julian said. "My new daughter-in-law, Errukine. Mikel's wife. This is Cordell Holland."

Cinch stood again. "Pleasure, ma'am," he mumbled.

"Are you Dutch?" she asked with a thick accent. Not shy at all.

That caught Cinch off guard for a split second. "Uh— no, ma'am. My granddaddy told me we was English 'fore we turned American. Someplace over there called Essex.''

Smiling, she set the tray on a cigarette-scarred coffee table and withdrew. They had a way of making you give them all your attention, Basque women.

Cinch sat again, and Julian handed him a glass across the table. "*Ossagaria*. Your health," he said, jerking back his head and downing the clear liquor in a single gulp.

Cinch drank his. He thought for a moment that he'd been given white gas, but then the burning in his throat eased and a queer mellowness took hold of his belly.

Julian sat back and gazed at him, full-on. "His name was Bittor. I named my oldest boy after him."

"Who you talkin' about?"

"My brother, who killed your uncle."

It was Cinch's turn to lock eyes.

"He's dead," Julian went on, not intimidated in the least. "Shot dead by the Spanish army a couple years after he got back to the homeland." A bitter smile followed. "He always was hot-blooded, Bittor."

"I don't know about that," Cinch said.

"Oh . . . ?"

"Takes a cold-blooded son of a bitch to bushwhack a man. What Howard did, breakin' up your camp, whippin' one of your kin, was done in hot blood. So there was a difference, Julian." Cinch then thought he could feel a rise of Basco temper coming.

But the seconds ticked away without an outburst, and the old man just went on showing his false teeth in a smile. "Julen."

"What?"

"It's really Julen, not Julian."

"Well, that's news to me. I always heard it as Julian."

"My mistake for not correctin' everybody early on. For signin' papers that way just to fit in and get along. You know, years and years ago, *Euskal Telebista*—TV in our homeland—come over to do a show on the Basque shepherd in Nevada. That damn crew wore out two sets of tires and found only us, the Arraches, still on the range. From that day on, I made up my mind I was Julen, like my mama and papa named me. We been swallowed up by your way of life. We'll be forgot unless we remind ourselves every day what we are. So I stopped callin' my Bittor Victor, like we all did sometimes outta laziness. And Pello stopped bein' Peter. Mikel, Michael.'' The old man's expression had darkened, but now he suddenly grinned. ''Still, you call me Julian—if your tongue's more comfortable that way. And it's sad what happened between our families back then. I din't ask you here to stir up the past, Cordell. I want to bury it—before they bury me. That's what I want to leave for my sons and their children. Your son, too.'' Then he added pointedly, ''Cody. An end to this *bullshita* for little Cody's sake.''

Cinch set down his glass, his mind racing. Dee had once told him that a clan could hold a grudge for centuries, so he didn't trust a word Julian was saying. He didn't even believe that Howard's murderer was dead. It was all just sugarcoating to cover the taste of poison. And Julian's knowing Cody's name somehow smacked of a threat. ''What's the payoff, Arrache?''

''We can all relax. Sleep good at night.''

Cinch shook his head. ''I know you people better'n that. You don't give a damn about relaxation. What's the practical thing you want out of a truce?''

Julian laughed. In grudging admiration, Cinch thought. ''All right, Cordell, I'll level—the new range inventory.''

''So?''

''I wanna nip it in the bud. If the BLM cuts back the allotments, you know as well as me what'll happen. The sheep operators have always sucked hind tit, so we'll be left out in the cold before anybody.'' Then his eyes blazed for an instant. ''Thanks to your goddamn Taylor Act.'' But he quickly paused and visibly calmed down. ''That's the old way talkin'. Gotta put it behind us. We're all livestock operators, all in the same leaky boat, and the wilderness boys want us all off the land.''

''You're right on that score.''

Julian nodded. "Good, Cordell. I'm glad we agree on somethin'. That's a start. You want another drink?"

"Nope. I'm still healin' from the first one."

Julian chuckled.

But Cinch cut it short with: "What're you pro-posin'?"

"An operators' coalition," the old man said. "Now, me and my sons sure as hell can't join your cattlemen's association, can we?"

Cinch softly harrumphed.

"But, Cordell, we can throw in lots with some new kinda outfit to stop the BLM and the wilderness boys dead in their tracks."

"Wait," Cinch said. "Before we talk about throwin' in lots, why don't you square away your own kin?"

"Who?"

Cinch hesitated, but then said, "Dee Laguerre."

"What about Dominica?"

Cinch realized that he didn't want to go down this road, but there was no changing the subject now. As he spoke, he saw her face beneath his, her head rocking from side to side. "She was the one to get the damn ball rollin'. Without her gettin' the wilderness crowd on board, there'd be no inventory."

Julian's lips thinned across his artificially perfect teeth. "You don't know much about Basque women, do you?"

Cinch wanted to say, *More'n what you think, old man.* But he didn't.

"Dominica has her own mind," the old man contin-ued, "and even I don't understand it. Errukine I under-stand. She's got her own thoughts, but she's from the old country—so I can see what she's gettin' at most of the time. Dominica and me don't see eye-to-eye on any-thin'. Like those mustangs what got kilt up on the moun-tain this week. I think that was a good thing. Good for the range. Good for the operators. How about you—what you think?"

Cinch kept silent.

"You figure Dominica's been up there to investigate yet?"

"No idea," Cinch lied.

"Well, it's not like they're antelope or deer or somethin' like that, Cordell. Right? Man brought the horse here, and it's his right to take it off the land. This is the kind of thing we should come together on, all the graziers. Sheepmen and cattlemen alike."

Cinch realized that the old man had raised his voice slightly in the last minute. Furtively, he glanced around the room. Two cords were plugged into an electrical outlet and wound behind the couch on which Julian sat. One led to the lamp on the end table. The other had no purpose he could see.

"I'm for doin' everythin' we can to keep as much stock on the range as it'll carry," Cinch said. The old man's eyes brightened at this. "But killin' horses is against the law, and I'm not for it."

Julian nodded, trying to hide his obvious disappointment.

Both men started a little as the front door boomed against an inner wall and footfalls, those of several men, approached down the hall. Bittor came into the den first, followed closely by Pancake and then the two other Arrache brothers. "Listen to this, Papa," he said with a trace of a smile as he stood aside for the deputy.

"You're never gonna believe what Dee Laguerre just found," Pancake began.

Dee watched their progress through her binoculars.

Sheriff Neeley, who was also the county coroner, was riding up to the plant study site in the ambulance, followed by an open jeep crammed with deputies and reserves. Dee could see them stop as soon as they turned off Cayuse Mountain Road and chain up the wheels of the ambulance before churning along the old telegraph line toward her.

Rabe Pleasant was sitting in the shotgun seat of her Bronco, head slumped. The storm-chilled air felt curiously like refrigeration, but she still preferred being outside. The last of the thunderheads were bunched blackly along the eastern horizon, and the sky overhead and to the west was flecked with stars.

Quietly, Rabe got out and strolled to her side. "Topsy's got to know soon. Otherwise somebody might phone her to ask how she's holding up. That's no way to find out."

Dee nodded.

Rabe gestured toward the two BLM vehicles still parked out on the flats, chrome glinting in the starshine. "Maybe I could take Jack's truck back to the compound."

"Can't, Rabe. I'm going to leave everything just as it is till I can get some investigative support down from Reno. We've got to go over those vehicles for prints." Dee paused. "Why don't you hitch a ride back to the hotel in the ambulance, then take your own truck out to the compound?"

"All right."

Dee swatted at a mosquito that had been bumping against the back of her neck. "Unless you want me to handle it later."

"No, sweetness—the sooner the better, like I said."

Details. She felt woolly-headed and queasy, but there were so many details to handle. Reaching the Bronco after leaving Jack Reckling's body, she'd radioed the dispatcher to advise Reno of the homicides, hoping that the lateness of the hour, midnight then, meant that no police band snoops were listening in. The on-call agent at the state office had yet to get back to her. His name was Gundry. He'd recently transferred in from Alaska, and she didn't know him.

So far, she controlled the situation. But she realized that that would soon be under attack.

The ambulance and the sheriff's department jeep labored up the last slope to her Bronco. She could see Cinch Holland in the back of the lurching jeep, grasping the roll bar. To avoid him, she stepped around to the passenger side of the ambulance just as the sheriff stepped out. "Hello there, Missy," Neeley said.

"Hello, Garvis."

"Everything's okay now," he went on in his annoying nasal twang, "so you just sit back."

"It's been okay for hours. And I don't feel like sitting back."

The sheriff looked carefully at her. "Where's the two victims?" Garvis Neeley was a short man with a crew cut. He'd been a truck driver before running for sheriff. "You hear me, Missy?"

Dee said, "I'll lead you down as soon as I hear from our agent in Reno."

The sheriff laughed in dismay. "The hell you say, Missy. These homicides occurred in my county. Lead the way, *now*."

In one regard, he was on solid ground. There was no U.S. code for homicide. But federal law superseded all other, so Dee said, "The way I see it, Sheriff, two government employees have been assaulted. That *is* a federal crime. Now, I'll be glad to share the investigation, as we usually do in these cases—just as soon as I clear it with the state office. We've got a new agent up there, so I don't have any idea what he's going to say. He might say fuck the sheriff of Pinyon County and tell him to quit calling you Missy. You're a federal officer, not a tour guide at Opryland U.S.A."

The little man pulled himself taller. "I'm goin' down to the crime scenes, *Missy*, and get my ID man busy."

"Well, your ID man's going to spill a lot of fingerprint powder if you try to drive over the top of my Bronco."

Pivoting on his heels, the sheriff looked for another way around. There was none.

The dispatcher's voice blared from Dee's exterior speaker, trying to raise her. She went back to her microphone, Rabe close behind.

"You *are* a cunt," he whispered.

"It's getting easier all the time."

She answered the dispatcher, who wanted to know if Dee had access to a telephone. This request came from Agent Gundry in Reno. "Uh . . . yeah, hang on. I think the ambulance on the scene has a cellular.'' Her own request for one had been denied. Budget constraints.

Two minutes later, she was talking to a gruff, sleepy voice. ''Dutch Gundry, Laguerre—what happened down there?''

Stepping away from the ambulance and a smoldering Sheriff Neeley, she told the agent in as few words as possible.

He made a surflike sound into his mouthpiece, then asked, ''Any suspects?''

She hesitated, glancing at Cinch, who was leaning against the side of the jeep, watching her. ''I don't know.''

''Reach, Laguerre. You gotta start somewhere.''

''I just don't know.''

''How long you been in service?''

''A year,'' Dee said.

''Less academy time?''

''Including.''

''Shit,'' Gundry said. ''Well, do the best you can. That pretty empty country down there, population-wise?''

''It doesn't get much emptier in the Great Basin.''

''Start developin' some leads for me. Go back through any warnin' tags or citations you might have. You got any from the last few days?''

''Yes. Some possible monkeywrenchers camped a few miles from the crime scene . . .''

''Anythin' of note in between them and the scene? Houses? Other campers? Anythin' at all?''

''No,'' she admitted.

There was a rustle of sheets on the other end of the line, and Gundry suddenly sounded wide awake. ''Christ, Laguerre—those're your suspects.''

''I'm not so sure, Gundry,'' she said. ''And I want the jurisdictional thing cleared up with the local sheriff before he gets out of hand. He wants to take over the ID work, and these rural departments aren't known for their technical prowess.''

Gundry asked, ''Is he available?''

"Standing about twenty feet away."

"What's his handle?"

"Garvis Neeley."

"Put him on. I'll be down there by—say—shit, what time is it?"

Dee glanced at her luminous dial. "Almost one."

"I'll be down there by eight. Just hold the fort till then."

She went to the sheriff and handed him the cellular phone. "Agent Gundry for you." Then, yawning, she walked a short way out into the brush. Her hands were cold, so she slid them into her jacket pockets. The view was crystalline, the lights of Holland Station seemed a mile away instead of the ten that they actually were. Roisterous stars.

She suddenly frowned; Neeley was already calling the agent "Dutch," and they were jawing about moose hunting in the Yukon. So far, she wasn't overly impressed with Gundry.

Someone came up on her from behind.

She spun around and faced Cinch Holland, who backed off and said, "Sorry, Dee—didn't mean to startle you." His features were lost in shadow, his blond hair like frost in the glow of all the headlights. For the first time in memory, he seemed vaguely inhuman to her. A cowman. An enemy. "You okay?" he asked, something eerie about his gentleness.

The mustangs on the mountain and Jack and Milt had all taken shots to the head. Revolver shots, most likely. She fought a rising disgust and somehow managed to say, "Yeah, I'm fine."

"Well, Missy," the sheriff announced, grinning as he tossed the phone to the ambulance driver, "we got us a shared jurisdiction here."

"Let me talk to Gundry," she said, stepping around Cinch.

"Dutch already hung up. Why didn't you tell me about them terrorists camped at Lower Cayuse Spring? Hell, Missy—that's our first priority, taking them bastards down. The ID work can wait. Dutch agrees entirely. You got a damn fine man for a boss there.''

"He's not my boss."

"Well, he oughta be," Neeley said sourly.

She accelerated up Cayuse Mountain Road with Pancake beside her in the Bronco. The Wheatley twins were so obviously drunk even the sheriff had seen the wisdom in leaving them on the flats with Rabe to keep the coyotes off the bodies. A sergeant from the jail in Gold Mountain was at the wheel of the jeep, leading the way toward the spring, careening muddily around the curves. Cinch and Wade Russell were standing up in the back, hatless, each hanging onto the roll bar with one hand and a carbine with the other.

Cinch half turned and gazed into her headlights, his eyes narrowed by the wind. He'd turned up the collar to his Levi's jacket.

Damn him for leaving her in an investigative limbo. It might be as long as two days before the autopsies were done, although she believed that the examiner would establish the times of death as soon as possible. She wouldn't really know how to feel toward Cinch until she saw those findings. Damn him. And here she was speeding toward one group of suspects with at least two other suspects—Cinch and Russell—backing her. If Eric Brenner and his friends could be called suspects. She'd seen no long rifle when they'd sifted their belongings for identification, and that's what a reasonable search would hinge on.

"Who the hell would go'n kill ol' Jack Reckling?" Pancake asked philosophically for the second time since entering Jubal Canyon. "Don't that just take it? Somebody up'n shootin' poor ol' Jack?"

"And Milt. The son of a bitch killed Milt Kwak, too."

"Well . . ." Pancake let his voice trail off.

As in the frontier days, Orientals didn't figure in vital statistics. Most of the mining camps had unrecorded Chinese populations equal in number to the whites.

"We're coming to the last turn," she said, letting up on the gas pedal.

The sheriff had promised her that they'd all stop here, well below the spring, and send two men ahead on foot to reconnoiter. Brenner and his friends might not be camped in the same place, let alone even in the county. But rather than showing brake lights, the sergeant began to pull away from the Bronco.

"What gives?" Dee asked with rising anger.

"What's what?"

"Neeley said he'd stop first."

"Well," Pancake said, lighting a smoke, "he's always eager to get it on. He's an eager beaver, ol' Garvis."

"He's a lying sack of shit."

"Oh, come on now, Dee-Dee. You don't mean that."

Dee plucked the cigarette from between his lips and chucked it out her open window. "Quit calling me Dee-Dee."

At least the sergeant shut off his headlamps as he neared the willows surrounding the spring. Dee quickly did the same, although a few frightening seconds passed in blackness until her eyes adjusted to the starlight.

"Here we go," Pancake said, laughing witlessly.

Dee could just make out Cinch and Wade crouching as the jeep bounded through the growth along the narrow trace. Then wet branches were whipping the sides of the Bronco, flailing at her face through the window.

She could smell wood smoke, which told her that Brenner's party was still here.

The jeep's spotlight came on, shifted back and forth through the thin mist given off by the spring—then zeroed in on the rusted Volkswagen van. It was just where she'd left it yesterday afternoon, although now a backpacking tent was pitched beside it.

She reached for the switch to her own spot, but then realized that she'd only backlight the sheriff and his men, who were already bailing out of the jeep. Through them, in the mist, she could see two figures standing near the van, half dressed, gaping at the carbines and revolvers trained on them. One of them was definitely female.

Pancake lumbered out of the Bronco and slammed the passenger door so hard Dee thought the glass would fall out of the window.

Two figures, she reminded herself. Not three.

She reached for her nightstick, which had fallen onto the floor during the jolting ride up the canyon.

The sheriff was hollering for Brenner's party to kiss the ground, but at the same time Pancake ordered them to clasp their hands behind their necks and interlace their fingers. The result was that neither Blaine Chapman nor Karena Heinold did a thing. Too stunned to move, they just stood and stared. Wade Russell worked behind them, squarely into the line of fire should things turn violent, and began booting the backs of knees to force them down into the sodden meadow grass.

Drawing her handgun, Dee about-faced and began jogging back along the willow-choked lane. She halted out on Cayuse Mountain Road, held her breath and listened. The jeep's spot was spilling dim gray light all over the canyon.

The creek, ordinarily dry, was running noisily, but over it she suddenly heard a clatter of rocks.

She ran in that direction for a minute, then slowed and began picking her way through the rabbitbrush down to the water course. The bank was steep-walled, crumbling in places from the muddy flow. She could hear small boulders being knocked against one another beneath the swift waters, but that wasn't the sharp, dry sound she'd caught from the road. The sound of feet or hooves disturbing rocks.

She wanted to use her flashlight to search for tracks, but didn't.

Slowly, avoiding the brush to keep it from whisking against her trouser legs, she inched upstream. Her revolver was clasped in front of her. Deer. It could have just been a muley who'd been browsing near the spring when Neeley and his men charged in like the cavalry.

The sheriff could still be heard bellowing, "Do what I say, you hippie motherfuckers!"

Then Dee felt a hand wrap around her ankle.

She started to kick it off, but too late—she was tumbling through the air. Reeling, she tossed her revolver up onto the bank in the split second before the cold water had her. She burst up from a depth of only a foot and a half, but the current was so fast and powerful she couldn't swing her legs around and brace herself.

The taste of mud filled her mouth. She gagged.

A blow from behind rocked her chin against her breastbone, and then hands were closing around her throat. Large male hands. She and the man were being swept along, but he refused to let go.

She tried to pry his fingers off, only to find them too strong. Driving an elbow toward his nose did even less: He simply turned his face and took the blow harmlessly on the side of his head.

Over her shoulder, she could see a large rock splitting the stream into two channels. She could still feel her nightstick in its belt ring. Using it as an anchor, she scuttled around so that he was leading the way. She was getting light-headed.

His back struck the rock with a thud, and his hands flew away from her.

Sucking in a big, wheezy breath, she struggled to her feet and managed to stand. He rose as well, staggered briefly, then waded ponderously toward her.

"Keep coming, Brenner," she said, "and I'll give you a broken bone for every step you take."

He kept coming, his hands fisted, his breaths escaping in sharp bursts. "No, you won't," he said.

She struck his knee, hoping to collapse him. But she had so little balance, leaning against the heavy waters, the blow was too light to do anything but slow him for a moment.

"You've ruined it all!" he cried, almost howling. "You've ruined it for everybody!"

He was reaching for her throat again when Dee saw a boot swing off the bank at eye level and slam into

Brenner's jaw. There was a crack, and he went down.

Hurriedly, Dee grabbed the scruff of his hair to keep him from floating away.

Cinch leaped down beside her, falling to his buttocks but springing right back up. "Shit, that's cold," he said. "I'll take him."

She leaned against the bank, shivering in the darkness.

"He went down awful damn hard, Cinch," she said between gulping breaths. "I've never had anybody go like that." Hard enough to have just committed two homicides, she realized. For almost anything else, Eric Brenner would have taken his chances with the courts.

"Yeah, well—no wonder." Cinch muscled Brenner up so that his chest rested on top of the bank, then he turned toward Dee. "They din't want us to search that Volkswagen in the worst way. Know why? They had a case of forty percent dynamite hidden under one of the seats. And a timin' device, we think."

"Did Chapman give consent to the search?"

"No. Why?"

Because there was nothing to link the threesome to the homicides other than the fact that they were outsiders in the same general area as the victims. It probably made sense to Neeley, but this argument would never fly in court. She wanted to groan. Improper searches were why most cases were thrown out. She'd had that fact drummed into her at the academy, with push-ups used to punish any lapses of memory. Lacking a warrant as they had, she would have preferred getting permission from the van's owner. A long shot, but maybe Chapman would've caved in with the right persuasion. A rural sheriff berating him was not that kind of persuasion. "You find any weapons?"

Cinch paused, then swung Brenner's legs up onto the bank. "No . . . no guns."

Soft. The search was terminally soft. The discovery of a rifle or a handgun, instruments of the crime, might've justified it—with some creative embellishment of probable cause in the report. But not dynamite, no matter how illegal it might prove for Brenner and his friends to possess it.

The German had run and then resisted arrest, but that was now meaningless in judicial terms.

Cinch climbed up beside Brenner, made sure he was breathing, then lowered a hand to Dee. "We'll have to drag him like a dead buck," he said, pulling her up.

"First I've got to find my revolver," she said, gritting her teeth to keep them from chattering.

Cinch chuckled. "How the hell did you lose it?"

CHAPTER **TEN**

Dee awoke to what she believed to be a murderous hangover. The buzzing she'd thought to be inside her skull turned out to be from the digital alarm clock on her bureau. Eleven o'clock. She'd forgotten to pull down the shade, and strong daylight filled the room. She threw off her perspiration-soaked sheet and padded across the linoleum to kill the incessant sound. Her back ached. As did her arms and knees. And her throat was sore; not as if a cold were coming on, but rather as if she'd been strangled.

That brought it all back to her.

"Uh...," she moaned, instantly feeling the same numbing sadness she'd felt upon turning in, completely sober, at eight o'clock this morning. So she'd had three hours of restless sleep, of bumbling through endless, nonsensical investigative chores that made her half believe she was still on duty, of being unable to turn her sight away from blood, from gaping wounds and Milton Kwak's ruined eye. She'd met Dutch Gundry, hadn't she? A thickset boor. Or had she only dreamed that, too?

"Piaf," she resolved, shuffling over to her stereo.

It was a good morning for the Little Sparrow. That brave voice, defiant even in the face of senseless death. Romantic in the depths of loss and pain.

Fighting dizziness as she leaned over the turntable, Dee found her favorite band and brought down the worn needle. *"Non, Je Ne Regrette Rien."* "No Regrets." Yet, she'd felt regret at first light this morning as she sat in the Recklings' bungalow with Topsy, able only to mutter banalities. She'd regretted that Topsy and she had never become even casual friends, for it'd been obvious from the woman's desperate clinging that she had none.

Dee was brushing her teeth when a knock came at the door.

Thinking that it was Rabe making sure she was up for the evidence search Gundry had organized for noon, she answered in the T-shirt and panties she'd worn to bed, clenching the toothbrush between her back molars.

It was Tyler Ravenshaw, her ex-husband.

Swiftly, she shut the door.

Laughing, Tyler opened it again, stuck his head inside, his cologne overcoming the taste of Crest. "Brunch in fifteen minutes downstairs. I invited your cohort— Rabe, isn't it? He said thanks but no thanks. Matter of principle. Says he belongs to some group called Gays Against Brunch." Tyler paused to closely examine her face. "My God, Dee, you've been fighting, haven't you?"

Then his head was gone from the doorway.

A count of three later, she peeked out into the hall.

He'd known that she'd do this, for he laughed over his shoulder at her, then went jauntily down the stairs. Definitely Tyler. Same crisp white shirt. Same breezy charm, although for the first time it struck her as being ridiculously transparent.

She rushed to the mirror over the sink. Not only was her hair matted from sleep, most of her left cheek was a deep purple. The worst bruises always seemed to come from the blows she didn't feel at the time.

She spat out a mouthful of toothpaste, then pushed up her nose with a finger to complete the ghoul mask.

Ten minutes later, she hurried downstairs in her last fresh uniform. A worried-looking Gabrielle directed her away from the usual midday throng of tourists and toward the kitchen door. "I had to rent him a room," she explained defensively. "It's the law."

Being under the same roof with Tyler again was not good news, but Dee said, "I know."

"But don't you go alon' with this one, Dominica. He's a snake."

"Tell me about it."

She pushed through the door alone and saw that the small table had been covered with a linen cloth. Tyler, smiling over fingers he'd steepled beneath his chin, was sitting at one place, and a single red rose was waiting for her at the other.

"What're you doing here, T.R.?" she asked, ignoring the rose. Roses were to her what reparations were to war-torn countries.

Undaunted, Tyler went on smiling. "Good to see you, too, Dee. I've asked my friend Hector here to make us a shrimp-and-avocado quesadilla. Just like they did at that Mexican place across the bay at Tiburon. What was its name—?"

"Just coffee," Dee said to the cook. "I've got to be out in the field in twenty minutes." Then she couldn't resist adding, "How come you're not telling me about your big *carne* this morning, Hector?"

The man grinned pathetically, almost fearfully.

"Inside joke?" Tyler asked, his eyes revealing a flicker of self-doubt for the first time. Jealousy had always been the Achilles' heel in his calm reserve. Spasms of extreme possessiveness followed by weeks of neglect.

"Yes," Dee said. "Inside joke."

"Listen, if you don't have time right now for a chat, how about dinner?"

"I can't make any promises today, T.R. Two of our people have been—"

"I know," he said quietly. At that moment, Hector brought coffees to the table. "Thanks, *amigo*. Just what I need, Dee. Drove all night, most of it on a mountain road behind the same asinine, gas-guzzling Winnebago." He waited until the cook had withdrawn, then asked, "Did you get my message?"

"Half of it. Something's wrong with my machine."

Tyler frowned. "Which half?"

"Something about doing anything to get me back. Or get back at me. That's where it got garbled."

"I'm serious, Dee," he said with an intent stare that didn't suit him. No doubt he thought he was being sincere.

"You came all the way to Cayuse Valley for this?"

"No," he said. "Seems you've gone and arrested the brother of a friend."

"Brenner?" she asked, her eyes widening.

"Uh, not quite. Chapman."

It hit Dee almost immediately. "Elsbeth Chapman."

Tyler avoided her eyes. "Some coincidence, what?"

A mild one, but still it was discomfiting. The Chapmans and the Ravenshaws were both old San Francisco money. Their fortunes had come out of Comstock mining companies whose milling practices had left the soil of much of modern-day western Nevada laced with mercury, lead, and cyanide. Dee didn't know Elsbeth Chapman well, but their few brushes had left her thankful about that.

"I want you to remember something, Dominica," Tyler went on. "I left that message before this homicide thing ever popped up."

"Who's representing Hansel and Gretel?"

Tyler smiled after a moment. "Mr. Brenner and Ms. Heinold have asked me to represent them as well at their initial appearance."

"Will you?"

"Yes."

"You're not a criminal attorney."

"No, but give me some credit—I might be able to hold off the lynching until a competent one can get here for the arraignment."

Dee sighed. "I wasn't putting you down, T.R. I'm just surprised that you're so directly involved." Tyler had lawyer friends all over the West. He easily could've arranged for one to drive here this morning from Reno or Las Vegas. Yet, he himself had come four hundred miles from San Francisco on a moment's notice. "Is the alliance going to foot the bill for their defense?"

He leaned back. "I'm really not at liberty to say."

"Then Elsbeth must be some friend."

He gave her another brittle stare. "She's proving to be."

"Good, T.R. That makes me feel better about your coming here."

"Oh?"

"I'd hate to think that the WCA intends to get involved this way."

"And what way is that, my dear?"

"Bankrolling the defense of people possibly involved in the murder of two federal employees," Dee said. "No matter what FEER thinks of your other efforts, the membership isn't likely to take support for Brenner and company kindly."

"*Possibly* involved?"

"Don't fish, T.R. You'll get a copy of my report as soon as I'm finished with it. Which, come to think of it, means dinner's out of the question. And you'll get a letter from FEER's steering committee as soon as we meet later this month."

"To scold us?"

"We'll see."

"That would be running with low beams." Tyler lumped all worldviews into two categories: high beams, which described his outlook and that of his organization; and low beams, which described the rest. He smiled wryly at her. "Federal Employees for Environmental Responsibility—something of an oxymoron, wouldn't you say?"

"Right up there with 'gentleman' and 'honest difference of opinion.' "

Tyler chortled. "My God, I've missed you." He checked her reaction, then consoled himself with a sip of coffee. "Mr. Brenner claims that you broke his jaw."

"All in the report."

"You're ferocious, Dee."

"So's Mr. Brenner."

"Only when provoked," Tyler said. "You have to understand something about him. His grandfather was a

Nuremberg defendant. Spent the remainder of his life at Spandau. Made quite an impression on young Eric. Needless to say, he was left with a healthy contempt for authority. All authority.''

''Then you should be careful taking on allies like him.'' Dee gulped down the last of her coffee and rose. ''One of these days you might convince the American people that you should run the show. Then you'd be the authority figure.''

She could tell that Rabe Pleasant was no more eager to return to the plant study site than she was. He sat glassy-eyed in the shotgun seat, running the skinned knuckles of his right hand back and forth across one of the air-conditioning vents. ''What happened to your hand?'' she asked.

''Fell down lifting one of the body bags onto the ambulance gurney.''

She didn't want all this to evolve into something grimly sacrosanct. She had to prick this black balloon now. ''Whose?''

''Whose what?''

''Body bag.''

''Does it matter?''

''Which one?''

''Jack's.''

''Good for you.''

Rabe giggled helplessly, freeing up something inside—as she'd hoped. ''Oh, you rotten cunt,'' he said.

''And so Jack Reckling's words live on in the hearts and minds of his friends.'' She turned off Highway 95 and up Cayuse Mountain Road for what seemed the thousandth time that week. Already, despite the rains, a light dust was being stirred by the tires. Out of habit, she reached for a lozenge. ''What'd you think of my ex?'' she asked, sucking.

''Been meaning to discuss him with you.''

''Okay.''

''Is it entirely over between you two?'' Rabe asked.

"Entirely," Dee said. "Even the Pope would sign the annulment, if I bothered to go after one."

"Then you wouldn't mind if I . . . ?"

"Oh, you rotten queer."

Over twenty vehicles were now parked at the site, including Jack's and Milt's, which were cordoned off with yellow streamers and stakes. Yet, the federal and local agencies were segregated, Dutch Gundry's sedan and the FBI technician's Dodge van parked on one side of the impromptu lot and the sheriff's cruisers and his reserve deputies' private pickup trucks grouped on the other.

Dee parked in the middle.

She and Rabe got out. It was August-hot again. The air was stifling, but only a few cumulus were to be seen, and they were too far to the south to throw any shade on the flats.

Dee looked for Gundry.

The agent was yucking it up with the sheriff. She had no desire to barge in on their love feast, so she leaned against a front fender of the mud-caked Bronco. Rabe sat inside again, leaving the door open.

The small, scattered throng seemed curiously like mourners waiting in a mortuary parking lot for the casket to be borne out to the hearse. Men smoked and talked in low voices, although now and again a burst of laughter broke the quiet before trailing off into sudden self-consciousness. The deputies and ranchers seemed respectful enough, but Dee sensed an "I told you so" in how they glanced at her.

Cinch was sitting on his heels by himself, a gold star clipped to the pocket of his cambric shirt. He looked at Dee briefly, his eyes never really centering on her, then gazed off toward Alkali Dry Lake.

At last, Gundry came over to her, his high forehead pearled with sweat. He was a large man, and she could tell that he enjoyed being large. The shape of his mouth was slightly lopsided, which made his grin seem all the more disingenuous. "Lookee at that shiner," he boomed. "Does it hurt?"

"Not much."

"Great. Well, did ol' Garvis finally get you squared away last night?"

She couldn't believe her ears. "What?"

"Did the sheriff show you how to get an investigation rollin'? That's what I asked him on the phone to do. Nursemaid you along."

"Then I want to thank you, Agent Gundry."

"Call me Dutch." He took a pinch of tobacco from a tin of Red Man and tucked it between his gum and cheek. Then, quickly catching her tone, he said evenly, "And I was just lookin' out for you, Laguerre, bein' a rookie and all."

"You sure did." She struggled not to raise her voice. "You hamstrung me to jolly a pompous jackass whose sole law enforcement training consists of a week of traffic school. And that was just to work off the speeding tickets he got as a truck driver."

Gundry stopped chewing. "He told me he's got years in the field."

"Three of them, in which time he hasn't learned search and seizure from Shinola. He did manage to get me involved in a felony takedown based only on the fact that the suspects weren't locals."

Gundry spat down between his shoes. "Case of dynamite says otherwise. You'll learn we got us some pretty broadminded magistrates."

Dee fell silent. There was no easy answer to search-and-seizure issues; the courts were reinterpreting them all the time. But she knew damned well that last night's fishing expedition had not been a clean, logical search arising out of the urgent need to locate the murder weapons—and the case against Brenner and his friends would ultimately suffer because of it. Dutch Gundry was telling her nothing that convinced her otherwise. He wasn't even trying.

The agent suddenly laughed and chucked her on the arm. "Laguerre, I'm gonna chalk up this little fit to fatigue."

"Chalk it up to be being pissed off. I'll sleep eight

hours tonight and still be pissed off tomorrow.''

He looked at her a moment longer, then turned and shouted for everybody to gather around him. He gave instructions for the search, twice repeated a warning that anything found, no matter how seemingly insignificant, was not to be touched until the technician had a look at it. As an afterthought, he cautioned everyone not to trample the eriogonum. ''What's it look like, Pleasant?''

Rabe told them. A few of the ranchers twitted.

Then Gundry formed the group into a long line, which began sweeping up toward the spot where Rabe and Dee had found Milt Kwak's body. They moved at a snail's pace, eyeing every square inch of ground, bending back the sage to examine the clumps.

Dee walked with Rabe on one side of her and the technician, a soft-spoken Puerto Rican named Melendez, on the other. She tried to keep her mind on the search, but kept wondering why Gundry felt so pleased about the discovery of the case of dynamite. Eric Brenner had been running headlong from something. The reason he'd brought the explosives to Pinyon County, most likely, which the bureau might never learn. But even as she'd tussled with him in the flood-swollen creek, she hadn't sensed that he was fleeing from the homicides. They had occurred several hours before, and only a fool or a psychopath would go on camping within a few miles of his victims' corpses.

Melendez started as a jackrabbit streaked off from the far side of a bush he was probing with his camera tripod. ''Jeez,'' the technician said, madly backstepping, ''did I disturb his hole or something?''

''The black-tailed hare doesn't dig burrows,'' Rabe said. ''Lives completely out in the open.''

''Then how does he keep cool on a day like this?''

Rabe poised his hands atop his head like big ears. ''They act like radiators, cooling the animal's blood.''

''Amazing.''

''Yes,'' Rabe said earnestly, ''it really is. Thanks for reminding me.''

Dee saw that the line was herding more and more

jacks before it. Shoshone clans had done much the same thing in the old days, driving jackrabbits and cottontails into nets woven from plant fibers. The bounding targets proved too much of a temptation to somebody. Dee heard four shots cranked off in quick succession.

The entire line shuffled to a halt.

"Goddamit," Gundry roared, "are you a complete fuckin' moron!"

Tom Wheatley had no better answer than to lower the .45 automatic he'd just fired, apparently without hitting a single hare.

Gundry rushed over to Melendez and growled, "Take that idiot's pistol and hold it . . ." He then raised his voice so all could hear. ". . . in case we got to run a useless comparison test on bullets some moron just jacked off all over my crime scene!" He walked past Dee on his way back to the center of the line.

"Well, Dutch," she drawled, pausing to spit between her boots, "these boys finally squarin' you away?"

CHAPTER**ELEVEN**

By four o'clock that afternoon, Dee was thinking of Gabrielle's cubbyhole of a bar in ways she never had before. She realized how perennially cool it was, how sheltered from harsh light. She wanted a vodka drink with a sprig of mint in a tall, sweating glass. But she was still plodding along with the rest of the search line, the rays of the sun flat in her face, the sand baking her feet right through the soles of her boots.

The searchers had trekked up the slope, well beyond where Kwak had lain, and found nothing, not even Tom Wheatley's slugs. Gundry had then led them back down to the vehicles, watered them, then started the second tedious sweep down to where a wounded Jack Reckling had rolled onto his back only to take two bullets in the face.

Rabe took off his wide-brimmed straw hat and began fanning himself. In the hard sunlight, his toupee was a more lurid red than his natural hair. "Had a nice chat with Agent Gundry over a cup of water," he said quietly enough so that only Dee could hear.

"I saw him take you aside."

"He's been told, sweetness."

"About what?"

"Bad blood between Jack and you."

Dee turned over a pebble with the toe of her boot. For a second, it'd looked like a bullet. "What'd you tell him?"

"Everybody working in the resource area put a contract out on Reckling, and I fulfilled it." Rabe shrugged at Dee's smile. "I needed the cash."

Suddenly, the sheriff whooped from the right side of the line. "We got us a gun, Dutch!"

A tired cheer rose from the searchers, who immediately stopped. Rabe flopped down in the sand, and Melendez jogged over toward the find, grasping his tripod in one hand and the strap to his bulging gear bag with the other.

Dee followed the technician at a distance.

In the last ten minutes, the line had come to the gully Reckling had almost reached. It was no longer flowing with muddy water. The searchers had then crossed it and shuffled out onto an expanse of rabbitbrush, already blossoming golden. The first hint of autumn Dee had noticed. Halting, she now gazed back up at the red-flagged stake Gundry had driven into the ground beside Jack's body. She strolled on, then stopped again at a spot in between this marker and the cluster of tan-shirted deputies who, like curious boys, were watching Melendez photograph the weapon. She traced this imaginary line on down the slope toward Alkali Dry Lake, shimmering two miles distant through waves of heat; then to Olin Peters's spread, no more than four miles away; and finally, to the hay ranches, marked by a succession of double-wide mobile homes, belonging to Wade Russell and the Wheatley twins.

The killer might well have walked. Last night, she'd seen no tire tracks coming out of the study site.

Within minutes, Melendez was hurrying past Dee on his way back to his van, carrying the revolver in a cardboard box. A string had been drawn through the trigger guard, suspending the piece and keeping it from touching the sides of the box. A .38 special or .357 magnum-caliber Colt. It was nickel-plated, which wasn't unusual for this part of the country. The salt dust soon abraded blued finishes on weapons.

She went back to Rabe, feeling little gratification that

she'd probably been right about the head shots being from a handgun.

The sheriff was bawling for somebody to bring down the metal detector in the trunk of one of the cruisers. Gundry had paced off a grid around the point where the wheelgun had been found and wanted it electronically searched.

Rabe had found some shade under a desert peach shrub, and she eased down beside him.

"No dignity in this," he said, rubbing some Chapstick over his lips.

"I suppose not," she said.

"We've all got to go, sweetness, but I hope to God I'm never murdered." Rabe wiped his glistening lips with a finger, then the finger on one of his socks. "Had a friend in West Hollywood who went like this. Just out walking his dog, and some gang-bangers shot him to death. He had a toy poodle. I sometimes wonder if he'd still be alive had he owned a bulldog."

Dee watched Gundry go back up to the van to see how Melendez was doing.

"What'd you tell Topsy?" Rabe asked.

"Nothing. At least nothing that meant anything. Just held her hand."

"Me, too. Except she held mine like she thought I was HIV positive."

Dee flopped back and laid her dark brown campaign hat over her eyes. *"Merde . . . merde . . ."* She must have dozed off with surprising suddenness, for next thing she knew Rabe was shaking her.

She sat upright. "What?"

"Gundry's screaming for you."

Light-headed, sun-blinded, she strode toward the agent, careful not to show any haste. Gundry could scream all he wanted. Sand tickled down her nape from her hair. She stopped a moment to brush it clean with a hand.

Gundry watched her approach as if he were looking right through her.

"What's up?" she asked, resting a boot on the bumper of his sedan.

He looked away from her, gripping a cellular phone. His eyes seemed to be counting the deputies, who'd come back to the parking area to mill around a big ice chest. The search was finished; beers were being passed out. Gundry spoke at last. "Just got the registration return on that Colt's serial number from Carson City . . ." And then, in the split second before he went on, Dee realized that she knew precisely what he was going to ask. "Which one of these yahoos is Reserve Deputy Cordell Holland?"

Her head was swimming; she felt like a stone bouncing down the plunging wall of a gorge.

"Laguerre?"

"What's the—"

"Just answer me."

She pointed at Cinch. Thankfully, he wasn't looking her way.

"Is he popular 'round here?" Gundry asked.

"More than that. Respected. But he's been under a lot of pressure lately. His operation's going bankrupt. But these people would do anything for him."

"Swell." The agent clasped his free hand to the back of his neck. The skin looked hot. "We got ourselves a situation that can turn to crap real fast. Can you rule him out as a suspect?"

"Anything back on the postmortems?" she asked.

"What're you gettin' at?"

"Estimated times of death. I need to know."

Gundry checked his watch, the crystal glinting as he turned his wrist. "Pathologist from Reno probably hasn't even cracked the bodies yet."

"I thought the times were established as soon as possible. Temperature probe in the liver."

The agent squinted at her. "Why do they matter so much to you?"

Shaking her head, she stared off. She saw the inside of the line shack roof, heard the rain beating on its tin.

"Laguerre, can you rule Holland out?"

She started to brace her hands against the hood of Gundry's car, but the metal was too hot. "How's Melendez rate his chances of finding latents on the weapon?"

"Lousy to none. The revolver was half buried in sand and rained on for hours. But the worst came today with this hot sun. Probably melted the fingerprint grease." Gundry patted his thick neck with his handkerchief. "You playin' cat-and-mouse with me, Laguerre?"

"No. It's just more complicated than it seems."

"Then let's simplify," Gundry said. "You ever seen Holland with a nickel-plated Colt thirty-eight special?"

"Yes."

"How recent?"

Dee tried not to hesitate, but each word seemed like a betrayal. "Two days ago. Up at his ranch."

"You friends with Holland?"

"Used to be. Cinch and I went to school together. His wife, Rowena, too." Then she realized that this would never do. Jack and Milt were *dead*, and whatever conditional promises she'd made to Cinch didn't stack up against two men from her own agency murdered. "I suspect he was involved—along with some others who're out here today wearing badges—in the slaughter of a band of mustangs earlier this week."

"So? Ranchers dust wild horses every chance they get. We both know that. I'm here for the homicides, Laguerre. Fuck the cayuses."

"Some of them were finished off with shots to the head."

Gundry looked like he'd been slapped. "Christ, lady," he fumed, "why didn't you tell me this last night?"

"Never got the chance." He'd been too busy bonding with ol' Garv.

She thought Gundry was going to blow up, but after a moment he just put away his handkerchief and said, "Okay, I didn't understand how mixed-up things are down here. But two feds are coolin' on stainless steel tables, and I'm not just walkin' away from the man who most likely pulled the trigger on them. Go get Pleasant. I want him and Melendez to watch our backs while we put the cuffs on Holland.''

''Don't do it like that, Dutch. . . .''

Gundry's eyebrows arched, but then he surprised her. ''I'm listenin'.''

''Cuffing Holland would be an insult. Even if he stands for it, his friends won't. It's more than us against them. It's big government against little government. You were in Alaska; you know how deep this runs. We could spark something out here today that might not end for years.''

''You mean we just scoot on out of here empty-handed?''

''No,'' Dee said. ''We drive out of here with Cinch's word. If he gives it, he'll keep it. He surrenders to the federal magistrate in Gold Mountain tomorrow, say eleven o'clock. We go with our own prosecution on assault because I doubt the county D.A. would file even manslaughter on Cinch Holland.''

''Damn, I'd like to test his hands for gunshot residue before that.''

Dee didn't know what to say to that. They were back to square one.

But then Gundry said, ''Forget it. Been twenty-four hours, at least. GSR material seldom sticks to skin for more than six hours. Does Holland wash before he eats and after he pisses?''

Dee smiled wanly. ''Probably.''

Gundry sighed again. ''Okay, Laguerre—when in Rome . . .'' Then, sounding amicable enough, he called for the sheriff and Holland.

Cinch looked bewildered for a moment, but then his face grew taut. He set his beer can on the tailgate of a sheriff's pickup and came over. Sheriff Neeley was behind him, beaming as if he expected to trade more moose hunting yarns with Gundry. ''What's next on the agenda, Dutch?''

Dee said coolly, ''Agent Gundry just got a return on

the Colt from Carson.'' She looked straight at Cinch. ''It's registered to you.''

Then she fell silent to let it sink in.

Cinch stared at her, his head tilted back slightly. After a few seconds it was clear that he had nothing to say. But the sheriff snorted, ''That's impossible, Missy.''

''No, it ain't, Garvis,'' Gundry said somberly. ''I checked the numbers myself. Twice.''

''Well, shit,'' Neeley went on, ''even if it's registered to him, don't mean a thing.'' A sudden inspiration lit up his face. ''Hell, Cinch, din't you report it stolen recently? I swear I saw a report like that cross my desk.''

Cinch, still looking at Dee, said, ''No, Sheriff. It musta been some other gun you're thinkin' of.''

''You have an attorney, Cinch?'' she asked.

''Kinda.''

That probably meant he owed his lawyer too much to take on something this involved. Dee asked, ''One can be appointed for you.''

''No,'' he said, quieter. ''I'll find somebody, Dee. Where and when?''

''The federal offices trailer in Gold Mountain. Eleven tomorrow morning.'' She reminded herself not to mention ''surrendering'' himself. There was a gentler way to tell him that he wouldn't be at immediate liberty to leave. ''Does that give you enough time to handle any pressing chores around the place?''

He nodded, catching her drift—for his eyes glazed over. She guessed that he was thinking of what he might say to his son.

Then she added, ''Hopefully, the autopsy reports will be available pretty soon. They'll tell us a lot. Times of death, especially.''

''Reports never tell it all,'' he said. ''Nothin' tells the whole story.''

Gundry asked the sheriff, ''This way of doin' it okay with you, Garv?''

''It's monkeyshit.'' But Neeley didn't argue. Instead, he turned to Cinch and said, ''I'll be there with you in the mornin'. I'll ask the county supervisors along, if you want.''

"No," Cinch said, "let's not make this a circus."

At twilight, Olin Peters rode his little motorbike down Ranch Road toward the salt-encrusted shores of Alkali Dry Lake. His alfalfa fields stretched out on both sides of him into the gathering darkness. Ordinarily, he came out twice each evening, once after supper to set up his wheel lines for the night's irrigating, and once at eleven o'clock to make sure that the sprinkler heads hadn't plugged. His well was gradually going bad, pumping sand.

He'd skipped supper tonight, thanks to an acid gut.

He left his fields behind and followed the road out into the scrub. The land was quickly giving off the day's heat. A pair of mourning doves fluttered up a rut and streaked out into the low sage, their wings whistling even above the sound of the engine. The playa gleamed directly ahead of him, blue-white like exposed bone, and beside it stood Augie Dietz's shanty. Hell of a place to live, but Augie claimed that he liked the almost constant wind, the grit sizzling against the pitted glass of his windows. Cinch said that he was bound to get lung disease, breathing all that junk off the lake bed.

Cinch.

Olin inwardly saw his brother-in-law going from horse to horse like a zombie. Heads jerking as the revolver slugs crashed through the skulls. He could hear the mares screaming in the high-pitched whine of the motorbike's engine.

Augie's windows showed light. "Good," Olin said, slowing.

But what was this?

A bronze-colored Land Rover was parked in front of the shack. As Olin shut down the bike, Dietz came out on his porch and stood with his thumbs hooked in the corners of his pant pockets, shaking his head as if he didn't want any more company than what he obviously had. "What you need?" he demanded.

"We gotta talk, Aug."

"Later."

"Somethin's happened. Somethin' you gotta hear 'bout."

Augie frowned, swore, but then flapped his arms in resignation and said, "Come on in, dammit."

Seated calmly in the midst of the usual clutter and filth was a man in his early thirties. He had nice hair. He'd tied the arms of a windbreaker around his shoulders, the way Hollywood stars did in the movies after playing tennis.

"Olin Peters," Augie said, "this here's Guillaume."

"Hello, Mr. Peters." Foreign accent.

Olin knew that he could never pronounce the name, so he just said, "How do," as he sat at the table.

"Guillaume's all the way from Paris, France," Augie went on expansively. "He makes pictures."

"Movin' pictures?" Olin asked the man.

"Yes. Documentaries."

"He wants to do one about Nevada wild horses." Pulling up a chair for himself, Augie winked slyly at Olin. "And if anybody can find mustangs, it's ol' August Earl Dietz."

Olin's mouth went dry just at the mention of horses. He forgot the Frenchman for the moment. "I came by this mornin' and knocked most of five minutes. Where you been?"

"Reno. Day 'fore last, I took the bus up to meet with Guillaume here. Told him we got more mustangs here in Cayuse than the rest of the state altogether. So he's down for a look-see."

"That's right," the Frenchman said. "And it all seems quite promising. But now I must be going." He rose. "Mr. Peters, a pleasure."

Staying seated, Olin nodded through his gnawing distraction. While Augie walked the Frenchman out, Olin glanced around for a bottle. There was a pint of Jim Beam on the sinkboard. No piped water, but Augie had himself a sink. He lived like a pig.

"Help yourself," Augie said sarcastically, coming

back inside in time to catch Olin taking a greedy pull off the bottle.

"Sorry, Aug, but I needed a jolt bad."

"Why?"

"The feds arrested Cinch."

Augie sank into a chair. His eyes got small, almost as if he were backing away from Olin on tracks. "For the horse killin'?"

Then it struck Olin. Augie didn't know. He'd been gone. "Christ, no—somebody shot Jack Reckling and that Chinaman. Deader'n dead."

Augie sat quietly for several seconds. Then, shocking Olin, he smacked the table with a fist and gave a shrill, giddy laugh. "That takes the prize, don't it? Cinch won't even slaughter that miserable leppie calf he's keepin' at the line shack pen, but now he's in jail for doin' two men!"

"Well," Olin said, "he ain't locked up yet."

Augie's look turned serious again. "Why not?"

"I don't know. Some kind of deal. He's supposed to turn himself in tomorrow."

"Well, that's the gov'mint's mistake. We can drive Cinch down to ol' Mexico tonight."

Olin reached for the bottle again. "I don't know, Aug."

"What don't you know?"

"He won't go for that. Cinch ain't that way." Olin could hear the wind picking up, moaning between the weather-shrunken boards of the shack. "It's us I'm worried 'bout," he finally admitted, then took a swig to wash the taste these words left in his mouth. Us. Not Cinch. "See, they found his gun where the bodies was. And word has it Laguerre went over the dead horses. She knows a lot of 'em took head shots."

Dietz shrugged as if confused.

"Aug, Jack and the Chinaman was shot in the head, too. So don't you see what we gotta do?"

"Nothin'. We already doin' exactly what we oughta."

"No, mister—we got to go to the BLM and admit we helped Cinch shoot the mustangs."

Augie screwed up his face, then started to laugh again.

But Olin cut him off with: ''Otherwise, they'll think we was in on the man killin's, too. I can't have that happen.''

Augie asked, ''Why not?''

Olin lowered his gaze to the bottle in his hands. ''See, somethin' happened in the service over there in Lebanon. On sentry duty. I shot an Arab.''

''Just up'n wasted him?''

''No,'' Olin said sharply, ''I only meant to scare him. It was just a potshot. But I guess instinct and trainin' took over.'' He paused, reliving the moment. ''It was all political, Aug, even the captain said so—but I wound up in a red-line brig. I never been to prison like you, but that's as close as I ever wanna get. . . . '' On the verge of choking up, he took another quick swallow. ''The Judge Advocate Gen'ral told my daddy 'bout the court-martial and all. But Rowena still don't know. Cinch neither. And I never want 'em to. So don't you see?''

''I think I do,'' Augie said, his tone suddenly chilly.

''Sure you do. I shot one man the gov'mint knows about, so they'll just assume I did more of the same here. I know how the gov'mint figures, Aug.''

Dietz smirked. ''It was horseshit, wasn't it?''

''What?''

''That Marine barracks fallin' on top of you, ruinin' your legs.''

Olin wanted to slide down through the wide cracks in the floor, but he finally nodded. ''The nigger guards beat me bad in that brig, Aug. Went over my knees terrible with their sticks. So bad they got disciplined for it, and the corps shushed me up with a disability pension.'' Then he felt the fear jangling him again. ''They'll take us away, Aug. The feds. They'll jail us for what Cinch done.''

''Neither.''

''How can you be so sure?'' Olin asked.

Dietz reached into the left front pocket of his jeans for a tiny black automatic pistol that was no larger than his palm. He slammed it on the tabletop. "This says they don't take us." Then he took a silver handcuff key from one of his rear pockets. "And this says they don't jail us. They never search you for tiny shit till they strip you in the bookin' tank."

"Jesus, Aug," Olin said, turning his face, "I don't even want to see that shit on you."

"Why not?"

"You an ex-con, man!"

" 'Xactly!" Dietz exclaimed. "It ain't you they'll come lookin' for if Cinch talks. It's me. Shit flies to an ol' con like metal filin's to a magnet. But it goes back farther'n that. I was five, and it flew to me on my step-daddy's fists. That son of a bitch hit me like I was a man, not a kid." He paused. "You listen—I was at Harrah's Club in Reno the whole time, winin' and dinin' the Frenchie, but damned if they won't find some way to pin this thing on me. There's injustice in this world you ain't never dreamed of, Olin Peters." Deitz drank, his Adam's apple bobbing. "Other night goin' up the mountain to the high spring . . . ?" He left his words dangling in the dusty-smelling air.

"Yeah?"

"I recall you sayin' it was the BLM-ers we oughta gun down instead of the cayuses. 'One shot to drop 'em, and one to the head to finish 'em.' I got a memory for words. That's what some counselor up at the State House told me. And I ain't no pathological liar. You put me on the lie box and you'll get a true readin'."

Olin could feel his guts going cold. "Don't you never repeat that, Dietz," he said, his voice shaking, "or I swear I'll . . ."

Augie sneered. "You'll what? Shoot me like you done Jack and the Chinaman? Maybe instinct and trainin' took over one more time . . . right?"

Olin was too flustered to speak. He was consciously holding down his hands, for almost of their own will they wanted to fly up and close around Dietz's throat.

"I don't care who done it," Augie said serenely, slipping the pack of Marlboros from Olin's shirt pocket. "I

don't care why he done it.'' He shook out a cigarette.
''We say nothin' to nobody about that night on the
mountain. All of us, we stand by Cinch. Sad commen-
tary on these times, ain't it? A shit-for-brains jailbird
remindin' a respected rancher about loyalty to his own
brother-in-law? But in case loyalty means nothin' to
you—lemme say this. I kilt a fella on a robbery. Did
seven long years for it. I'll do seven more for killin'
you, Olie, if'n you drop the dime on Cinch, tryin' to
save your own skin. I want you to cogitate long and
hard on that.'' Then he smiled, and asked, ''Got a light?
I'm short on kitchen matches.''

Dee sat alone at the bar in the Pyrennes, her second
vodka collins of the evening locked between her fingers.
She was wearing a pair of khaki shorts and one of Tyler
Ravenshaw's old white dress shirts, left untucked. A few
years ago, while they were still married, the collar had
gotten frayed, and she'd rescued it from the rag box,
meaning to paint the apartment in it. But then she'd settled on a fresh life, not just a fresh coat of paint, and
the shirt traveled home to Nevada with her.
     Suddenly, as if she'd unintentionally conjured a ghost,
Tyler slid onto the stool beside her.
     ''The shirt was part of the settlement, T.R.,'' she said.
     ''What?'' he asked, glancing around for the bartender,
who didn't exist. Except for Gabrielle, who mixed drinks
only for the German tourists. ''What settlement? Ours?''
     ''Nothing,'' Dee murmured.
     ''Where's the barkeep?'' he asked.
     ''Dead.''
     ''Within the last couple minutes?''
     ''No,'' she said, ''years ago. He hanged himself in
your room.''
     ''Over love?''
     ''Prostate cancer.''
     ''Then how does one get a drink?''
     ''Honor system. Unless you're kraut. Then the honor
system doesn't apply. Gabrielle tried it once, and they
went Nazi on her.''

"Very well." Tyler stepped around to the other side of the bar and began examining the wine bottles. "Old Basque saying . . . wine has four feet and no eyes. How's that for a memory?"

"Très bien."

He quickly gave up on the assortment of screw-capped bottles and settled on some cognac with a label too dusty to make out. Sitting again, he winked suggestively at her. "Hi. What's your sign?"

"Caution—Bitch Crossing."

He rolled his eyes. "Last time I come here on ladies' night."

"Speaking of krauts, have Brenner and company bailed yet?"

"Nope, and they refused an offer of help in that regard. They seem to have taken a kind of monastic liking to Pinyon County Jail."

"Aid and comfort from the WCA?"

"Don't fish, Dee," he said, throwing her own words back at her. But then he volunteered, "I suspect Mr. Brenner sees political opportunities arising out of his legal problems. I also believe he wants to make some kind of statement to the media, but that's rather difficult right now. What with his jaws wired shut." He took a sip of cognac, winced. "Lovely—Chateau Texaco. I understand that you've made an arrest, or are in the process of making an arrest . . . however the local custom goes."

"Yes. Cordell Holland, a local rancher. We found his revolver at the scene today."

She could tell by the sudden stillness in his face that Tyler recalled the name. She'd told him about her high school relationship with Cinch. A mistake. Until that moment, she'd had no idea how jealous Tyler could be. But now he apparently decided to steer clear of the personal. "Does this arrest mean that the government will finally come to its senses and drop its sundry and unspecified charges against my clients?"

"Still the little matter of a case of dynamite and a possible timing device," she bluffed.

Tyler raised his eyebrows. *"Possible?"*

"It's a timing device, T.R. We're just waiting for the lab to confirm the obvious." She swung her legs around toward him, then leaned his way, slightly. "Actually, I'm glad I ran into you this evening."

"Really?"

She took four folded copies of a government bulletin from her back pocket and handed them to him.

"What's this?" he asked.

"Read it."

"Too dark."

"It's a security circular from the nuclear testing site just over the mountain here. The Department of Energy sends one out to all neighboring law enforcement just prior to an underground test. The next is scheduled for noon, two days from now. I made separate copies, one for each of your clients."

Tyler asked, "How does this involve them?"

"Cayuse Mountain Road is the largely unguarded backdoor into the site. That's where they were arrested. I don't know precisely how this involves them, but I'm willing to discuss it with any or all of them. One of them will eventually crack and talk. Tell them for me that it's always better to be first than last. And tell them that the San Francisco office of the FBI and Interpol are already prying into their heroic lives."

In silence, Tyler tucked the fliers in his shirt pocket.

Dee glanced at her watch. "Gotta go, T.R."

"Go where?"

"Out with the girls . . ." She leaned over the bar and grabbed a fifth of sloe gin, then left a twenty-dollar bill under the salt shaker. "Girl, actually . . . woman . . . oh, hell, she's a whore, but don't let her catch you saying that."

Tyler swiveled around on his stool. "May we talk later?"

"Nope."

"Why not?"

"I'll be deaf mute drunk."

He rose and caught her by the elbow. His voice was

almost a growl. "How far do I have to go to get your attention?"

"You had it once, Tyler. Big-time. Then you pissed it away."

He set his mouth hard, but then released her.

Outside, as expected, Jewell Farley was waiting in the minivan she'd bought for the coach to tool her Little League team around the state. Her cigarette coal winked redly through the darkness as she took a deep puff.

"Always on time," Dee said in admiration, hopping in and rolling down the side window. Tyler had never been on time. Quite proudly, he'd claimed that important men weren't punctual. The quality would trivialize them.

"Honey, I'm trained. A good cathouse runs on the clock—" Then Jewell noticed the bruise. "*Goddamn*, did he hit you?"

"Who?"

"Your ex-hubby."

"What?"

"He's here, ain't he? Damn that son of a bitch!" Jewell threw the shift lever into Park and started to bail out.

"Where you going?"

"Kick his ass!"

Laughing, Dee grabbed her. "Honey, I got this taking down a prisoner."

Jewell continued to boil for a few seconds more, then said, "But Ravenshaw is here, correct?"

"Correct."

"Any chance I get to meet him?"

"Nope."

Jewell's face looked crestfallen in the dash lights. "You ashamed of me, Dee Laguerre? Has it finally come to that?"

"No, I'm ashamed of myself. For having fallen for somebody like him back then. If I introduce my best friend, he'll take it as a sign I'm still interested."

Jewell roused up after a long, wounded silence. "Honest?"

"Honest."

She slipped the bottle from Dee's hands. "Oh, Jesus-Mary—sloe gin."

"What's wrong with that?"

"Baa, I can't drink sloe gin without pukin'."

"We drank it the last time we did this."

"That was in high school, and we both wound up pukin'." Jewell made a U-turn that ended across the highway in front of the Snake Pit. "Hang on," she said, then got out and went inside.

Through the open door, Dee could hear a shout of surprise fly up from the patrons, and somebody said, "Why, Jewell Farley, I swear I ain't seen you out in ten years."

"Well, Charlie, I don't get out much because you get it in all the time." Then she said over the raucous laughter, "Package me up two pints of Bushmill's Irish."

Waiting, Dee wondered if she'd made a mistake in telling Tyler about the nuke test. She had only intuition and common sense to tell her that this is why Brenner had come to Pinyon County. Yet, if that could be confirmed, a problem then arose with the monkeywrenching at the Holland Ranch. Why risk arrest for petty malicious mischief when your aim was to stand the entire military-industrial complex on its ear?

Jewell emerged from the bar clutching the bottles in a brown paper bag. The two missing fingertips were especially noticeable because of the plum-colored polish on the surviving nails. "Shit, I'm glad I didn't send you in."

"Why?" Dee asked.

"Nobody's 'xactly pleased over this thing with Cinch."

"Me neither," Dee said.

Jewell drove them a mile south of town, then turned off Highway 95, the minivan's headlights sweeping over the rain-washed sage. The dirt lane wound up to the summit of a small reddish knoll. The plug to a volcanic cone that had eroded away. But Dee hadn't known that the first time she'd come up here with Jewell. It was simply a high place from which they could watch the lights of town or the stars. And with Cinch, it had been their only bedroom.

Jewell parked and took two low-to-the ground beach chairs from the back of the van. "I know Cinch Holland longer than you, and I'll swear on my poor busted maidenhead that he's never kilt a soul in his life."

"Watch for snakes," Dee warned.

"Fuck the snakes." Jewell plopped down in a chair, the pints of Irish clinking together as she held them to her bosom. "We're talkin' about Cinch."

"I don't want to talk about him tonight." Dee sat.

"Yes, you do. That's just why you dragged me out here. We talked about Cinch Holland way back then, and damned if we won't again tonight."

Dee tried her sloe gin, then spat it out. "Oh, God, you're right. This is urine."

"Save it for snakebite." Jewell handed her one of her bottles. She never let Dee drink after her, and from this she realized that Jewell still serviced customers on occasion. "Now, Miss Laguerre—d'you honestly believe in your heart of hearts that Cinch did Jack and that other fella?"

"No," Dee admitted, "but I can't rely on how I feel about this thing." The whiskey was like velvet. "Back at that academy in Georgia, they really fill your head. Most of it goes in one ear and out the other. But one thing stuck. It came from an old cop, and he told us, 'Most of the time when you take down somebody for something really vile, just remember—you're catching a good man on the worst day of his life.' " She craned her neck, looking for the Big Dipper. "But this may be beside the point."

"Why?"

"I was with Cinch that afternoon."

Jewell scooted her chair closer. "When you say 'with,' do you really mean with?"

"Yes."

"What was he like?"

"Sexually?"

"Hell, no. Don't bore me. His spirits that day."

"Low," Dee said. "It was scary how low he was."

"Jesus, Baa—low is one thing and murderin' is another." Jewell drank noisily. "Were ol' Jack's danglies mut'lated?"

"Of course not."

"Then you can take Topsy Reckling off the list."

Dee giggled. At last, she was beginning to feel better. The rain had left the starriest sky she'd seen in months.

"But what about the other boys you told me about on the phone?" Jewell said. Her speech was already slightly slurred. She always got drunk fast and hard. Dee realized that she'd have to drive back.

"What other boys?"

"Went up the mountain with Cinch that night to kill the horses."

"I've been thinking about them," Dee said. Before Dutch Gundry had headed back to his motel in Gold Mountain, Dee had fully briefed him about the slaughter. Everything she knew, except that which hinged on what Cinch had confessed to her.

"Well, let's go over 'em," Jewell said, the slosh of her bottle telling Dee that it was already half empty. "There's the Wheatleys. But if one of the twins kilt your people it was most likely a huntin' accident. They're that retarded."

Dee sensed that Jewell might be trying to overcome pangs of conscience about professional privilege and tell her something important. "And Wade Russell?"

"He's a maybe. Mean enough. He'd be mean to my girls if he weren't scared shitless of me. But I'm not sure 'bout him."

"Olin?"

Jewell chuckled knowingly. "Peters has his secrets, but it's not for me to tell 'em." Yet, then she went on, "Paper said a high-powered rifle was used on your people."

"That's right. Every rancher I know has one, along with a Winchester carbine."

" 'Cept Cinch."

"How's that?"

"It's become somethin' of a joke," Jewell said. "He loant his Weatherby to Olin last huntin' season, who then lost it."

"Lost?"

"That's what Peters claims. But now he just can't work up the nerve to tell Cinch. They got a pool down at the Snake Pit. Winner had to come up with the best excuse. Cinch won it in a cattlemen's association raffle."

Dee watched a falling star plunge into the lighter band of darkness along the horizon. She wished that this could all be over. "Then that leaves Augie Dietz," she said, "who served time for homicide."

"I know the type as well as the man. Augie wouldn't shit in his own nest. Oh, he might drop the hammer on somebody in Vegas or Reno. But not here. Not where he's known." Jewell loudly yawned, then said, " 'Member how we used to get that station from Calgary up here?"

"Uh-huh."

"Ian and Sylvia. I loved those two. 'Four Strong Winds.' " Jewell started to hum the melody, but then stopped and asked, "Whatever happened to 'em?"

"They split up. Divorced."

"Figures." Jewell got up in the darkness, hiked her long skirt a few inches off the stony ground. "Well, I'm gonna find us that station anyways." Humming again, she started for the van but then tripped over her chair and fell to a clatter of aluminum and a tinkle of broken glass.

Dee shot up. "Jewell, you all right?"

"Dandy," she answered after a moment, " 'cept I just broke my goddamn arm."

CHAPTER **TWELVE**

At five minutes to eleven o'clock, Cinch Holland, alone, stepped out of the hot sunlight into the air-conditioned chill of the federal offices. They were in a triple-wide mobilehome across the street from the Pinyon County Jail in Gold Mountain, a turn-of-the-century mining boomtown now reduced to three hundred working poor. The county seat had always seemed run-down to him, but this morning it looked desolate. He ran his eyes over the shacks and trailers tucked among sulfurous yellow heaps of old tailings, the ore digested and excreted by the stamp mills that had once run night and day.

A federal marshal was waiting for him in the small lobby. A broad-shouldered black man in a charcoal gray suit. "Cordell Holland?" he asked.

"Yeah."

He gave Cinch a quick frisking, then said, "Down the hall. Second door on the left. Lead the way."

The sheriff hadn't shown. And Cinch's attorney had never returned his calls. He really couldn't blame the man. His fee for the gravel pit fight was still outstanding, and representing a rancher going under was like doctoring a penniless cancer patient. Yet, despite his aloneness, Cinch felt a strange sense of release as he walked down the corridor. Last night, he'd slept well enough, even though it'd taken a couple of hours to drift off. And this dawn, for the first time in years, he'd sat on the front porch and lingered over a third cup of coffee—instead of plunging right into a day full of chores. The hardest part in all this had been explaining to Cody, but that was behind him, too. All pain and weight were behind him.

The second door on the left opened onto an office. Nothing like a courtroom. And sitting behind the desk was an elderly man in a Western-cut shirt and a string tie.

"Hello," Cinch said, "I'm Holland."

"Have a seat," the old fellow said, then went on chatting with a bored-looking man in shirtsleeves on the sofa. A Jew, Cinch believed. "So I marked that spot on Charleston Peak where I saw my four-pointer drop. . . . " He formed two liver-spotted fists, placed one in front of the other. "Did it by linin' up two junipers on where I saw the dust rise. Then I went back to camp for help 'cause it was gettin' dark, and I didn't want the coyotes to have the best damn buck I ever shot in my life. . . . "

Cinch took one of two hard-backed chairs, figuring that they'd been set apart for himself and the public defender, who had yet to show.

The marshal sat beside the man on the sofa.

"We formed a line and started workin' up the slope. . . . "

Cinch folded his hands together in his lap. He felt small.

The door opened, and a plain-faced woman hurried in with a dictating machine under her arm. She was followed by a dumpy young man. A pimple on his chin had been freshly squeezed. He apologized all over himself to the old fellow, a federal magistrate up from Las Vegas, then introduced himself to the man on the sofa, who turned out to be the U.S. attorney. The young man then stepped up to Cinch and, shaking hands, repeated his name. But it was Polish-sounding and wouldn't stick in Cinch's brain. All he knew was that this chubby boy was his court-appointed counsel.

And then Cinch found himself in the middle of it, straining to make sense of the murmurings of the three men.

The U.S. attorney said something about having only "preliminary information" for a complaint due to time constraints. He handed one copy to the judge and one to Cinch's lawyer, who accepted it with a trembly hand. The old man glanced up and told Cinch that he had the right to a hearing—was this it?—and to legal counsel, noted as present. He also had the right to remain silent.

"I'd like to take you up on that, Your Honor," Cinch said, "for the time bein'."

But nobody seemed to have heard him.

Without apparent interest, the U.S. attorney peered through the window at the gallowslike headframe over an abandoned mine shaft while the judge went on reading the preliminary information he'd been given. "How long have you lived in Pinyon County, Mr. Holland?" he asked after a minute.

"All my life. My family settled this area even before it was a county. Jubal Holland was the first sheriff."

That also went in one ear and out the other.

Cinch felt that no matter what he said, even if he went to his knees and confessed the killings, it'd go unnoticed like a shout under a bridge with a train roaring over. Everything was on track, and nobody wanted to risk derailment over anything an ignorant rancher said.

"I'll allow freedom on bail," the magistrate said. "Let's say two-fifty, given the seriousness."

Both lawyers launched respectfully into him over that, the government man pressing for no release and the public defender for a bail reduction.

Cinch ran the figures behind his shut eyes.

Then it came to him.

The old man was talking about $250,000, certainly not $250. The surety bond on that amount would cost him $25,000, which was out of the question. He wasn't going home this afternoon or even anytime soon. But somehow he'd known that as he set out from the ranch this morning, the road to Gold Mountain glinting like an iron bar through the sage.

Then it was apparently over. The bail amount stood. A minute later, Cinch was out in the scorching light again, flanked by his lawyer and the marshal as they crossed the street to the jail. The asphalt patches felt mushy beneath the soles of his boots. He glanced behind, hoping to see the back side of Cayuse Mountain before he had to go inside again. But the roofline of old man Howbert's assay lab blocked the view.

"Sorry, Cinch," the sheriff said, meeting him in the jail lobby, "the feds wouldn't let me come. Claimed I had no business at your first appearance."

"It's okay, Garv," Cinch said. "Wasn't all that much to it."

The marshal said that he'd stand by for the booking process, then could be reached at his motel.

"Cordell Holland," the sheriff said, raising his voice, "you cartin' any guns, knives, or bombs on your person?"

"No," Cinch said quietly.

Looking at the marshal, the sheriff said, "Then consider yourself booked, Cinch."

A man, roughly Cinch's age, came smoothly over to him and, before the marshal could intervene, offered his hand. "Cinch, is it?" he asked, smiling.

"Yeah."

"I think introductions are finally in order. . . . " He wore a blue blazer and white shirt but no tie. His face was handsome, but Cinch found it unpleasant for some reason. Maybe the eyes were too bright. "I'm Tyler Ravenshaw."

"I know you?"

"Perhaps. You certainly know my ex-wife, Dee."

Still ignoring Ravenshaw's outstretched hand, Cinch said, "Yeah, I guess I do."

Ravenshaw chuckled and lowered his hand, his face slightly reddened, and asked Sheriff Neeley, "Is there some legitimate reason I can't see my client, Mr. Brenner, right away?"

"He's eatin' lunch."

Ravenshaw consulted his watch, a Rolex. "It's ten after one."

"Takes a while to suck your lunch through a straw."

"Why can't I talk while he sucks?"

"Jail rules."

Ravenshaw shrugged. "So it goes in Mayberry."

"Then, Ravenshaw," Cinch said, "you're gonna have to tell us poor ignorant peckerwoods how things're done up on top of the food chain."

"I just might."

"Please do."

"Well, for one thing, we go through life with our high beams on. Less damage that way."

"What's that suppose to mean?"

"Ask Dee," Ravenshaw concluded. "You still see her from time to time, don't you?"

Turning, Cinch went through the prisoner intake door, followed by his attorney and the sheriff, who asked, "You wanna eat or talk to your lawyer first, Cinch?"

"Talk to this fella, Garvis. I got no appetite, so don't let Margie think it's her cookin'."

The sheriff deposited them in the interviewing cubicle, and the young attorney began emptying the contents of his briefcase onto the tabletop.

"All this shit for just one case?"

"And more coming," the young man said, then opened an official-looking envelope. "Autopsy reports." He leafed through the pages, his hands still unsteady. "First things first. Let's see here . . . approximate time of death on Reckling and . . ." He clumsily switched papers in his hands. "And on Kwak . . . ah, the same . . . between two and four o'clock that date." He looked up at Cinch with an uneasy smile. "Quickest way out of this mess—can anybody vouch for your whereabouts during those hours?"

Dee parked above Upper Cayuse Spring. She, Gundry, and Melendez got out, locked their doors. The agent stretched so tall that the cords in his neck showed, then he spat tobacco juice onto a Mormon tea bush. The sight almost made Dee retch. Her hangover was precariously balanced between nausea and dizziness. They'd had to wait an hour on the road below while a Caterpillar from the BLM fire station bladed through the dried mudslide, which had set up like concrete.

"You married, Dutch?" she asked, trying to overcome her irritation with him, with the blinding midday sun, the heavy air.

"All my life."

"What's your wife think of you chewing?"

"Hell, Nadene chews, too."

"No way."

"Honest. Most those Alaskan gals do. Helps 'em stand up to the winters."

Gundry chuckled, but then his expression slowly turned stony. So far he hadn't zeroed in on her past relationship with Cinch Holland, although she guessed that he'd inquired around enough to know about it. His not asking made her believe that Gundry was patiently tinkering with a snare—and she might wind up the trapped prey unless she was wary. For this reason, she wouldn't bring up the postmortem reports to him again, knowing that she'd already shown too keen an interest in the times of death. She was almost going out of her mind, waiting for this, the information the pathologist had no doubt determined before anything else.

What if, unexpectedly, Reckling and Kwak had died at an hour that only heaped more doubt on Cinch's innocence?

Melendez had told her that no prints on Cinch's Colt revolver had survived exposure to the elements. In the cylinder, he had simply found three unfired cartridges and three spent casings. The bullets were silver-tipped, not with the actual metal but with an alloy of that color.

Lowering the back window, she looked out into the pinyon forest. The stillness there felt like expectation, the lull before the first winter storm.

Melendez reached over the tailgate to retrieve the two equipment bags he'd brought. "Let me take one of those for you, Luis," she offered, although the last thing in the world she felt like doing was hiking in loaded down with forty pounds of crime scene gear.

"Thanks." Melendez was yawning, probably not realizing that it was in hunger for oxygen. "Man, have I got a headache."

Me, too, she thought. But hers came from a mixture of Bushmill's Irish and sloe gin. "The altitude, Luis," she explained. "It does that if you're not used to it. Let me get you some aspirin out of the first aid kit."

"Ready?" Gundry asked, frowning at Dee.

Two minutes later, they were threading through the trees in single file, Dee bringing up the rear. A pinyon jay was flitting from branch to branch, inspecting the cones. They'd just taken form: tiny, prickly fists the color of pea soup.

"Where were you last night, Laguerre?" Gundry asked over his shoulder.

"Why?"

"I phoned around eleven-thirty."

And left no message, which told her that he'd hoped to catch her half asleep, her defenses down. She shifted the bag to her other hand. "Had to take a friend to the hospital in Tonopah."

"Anything serious?"

"Fractured arm," Dee said, catching a sickly sweet smell as they came closer to the canyon.

"How'd he do that?"

"She. Girlfriend. Moving a chair."

"Furniture'll do it," Gundry said with conviction. "That's what almost ruined my back. A goddamn antique oak buffet Nadene bought at an estate sale in Anchorage."

They emerged from the trees, and the stench became overpowering. "Nature calls," Dee said just before copious saliva welled in her mouth.

"*Now?*" Gundry asked.

"Go on. I'll catch up in a minute."

Gundry chortled under his breath to Melendez. "That's one thing a consent decree can't give 'em—field gear for pissin'."

Dee ducked behind a rock, waiting with all her resolve for the sound of footfalls to fade. Urination wasn't her problem at the moment. Making up her mind to get it over with in private, she thrust her middle finger down her throat.

"You all right?" Gundry asked as soon as she rejoined them.

"Fine."

"Well, you look poorly," the agent prodded.

Melendez, to his credit, kept walking, blank-faced.

Dee said, "Rattler almost nailed me."

"You're kiddin'," Gundry said, eyes getting big.

"Thank God I'm not a man, otherwise it would've gotten me right on the tip of my field gear."

Melendez laughed, and a smirking Gundry led them out onto the rimrock. "You got a mouth, Laguerre," he said. "I'll give you that much."

They stopped and gazed down on the bloated carnage.

"*Ay,*" Melendez said, pinching shut his nostrils with his fingers.

"Well," Gundry said, "let's get it done."

They crept down a barely visible horse trail to the canyon floor. The coyotes and other scavengers had been busy over the past several days, stripping and dismembering the carcasses, scattering the gnawed bones everywhere. Dee dropped Melendez's bag and sat on a flat-topped boulder while the two men took it all in at ground level.

"They even shot up the colts," Gundry said, mopping his face with his handerchief. "That's cold. Real cold."

She had told him this, but he'd had to see it for himself to understand how far this kill had gone. "I don't think anything got away."

Gundry came over and stood near her, his stunned eyes still roving over the slaughtered band. "Bastards who'd do this would do anythin'," he said.

"Got that right," Melendez echoed.

She was no longer so sure, understanding now how close Cinch and perhaps some of the others were to bankruptcy, how fearful they all were of the new range inventory. But she'd felt much the same as the two men on the morning she'd hiked up here from the mudslide and first seen it.

"You know," Gundry went on, "we gotta stop thinkin' in terms of one suspect. This was a team effort, and could be the homicides were, too."

Dee had considered the possibility, but something about it didn't sit right with her. Homicide was nearly always a private affair in this part of the country. Even the range wars had been fought one man against another. One Arrache had killed one Holland. But who could really say at this point? Maybe it had been a conspiracy, and Cinch had been forced to go along.

Gundry said, "Tell me more about the yahoos who came this way in Holland's truck."

She didn't feel like going through the list again. Instead, she pointed out that she had no physical evidence to place any of them here at the blind spring that night. She'd seen them going up Jubal Canyon, but the government might as well try to hold someone for a bank robbery in Manhattan on the basis of having seen him enter the Lincoln Tunnel. Nor had she spotted any weapons in the GMC.

"Yeah," Gundry argued, "but you found that thirty-thirty casing. I'm already workin' on locatin' the saddlegun that fired it. The magistrate'll give us a warrant on that in a minute."

"It might've been fired by a deer hunter last fall."

"Maybe."

Dee went on, "Reckling and Kwak were brought down by a big-caliber rifle, I'm sure of it. Not a carbine. You saw the wounds."

"We'll see, Laguerre. All in due course." Then Gundry shouted Melendez over. "I want bullet extractions from any cranium that shows an entry wound."

The technician puffed up his cheeks, then blew out a gust of air. "That'll take a lot of time, Dutch."

"We got nothin' but. Besides, Laguerre'll help you."

"You bet," she said, jumping off the boulder and grabbing the bag again. She wanted to get busy.

Melendez asked, "What about shots to the bodies? You want them, too?"

"Second priority," Gundry decided. "Later. If we decide on full necropsies."

Side-by-side, Dee and Melendez trekked downcanyon to the farthest dead horse. He set up his camera, shooed the blowflies off the hide with a squirt of insect repellent, laid a numbered card against the ear, then snapped two photographs. The smell proved too much even for him, for he broke out two dust-type masks and handed her one. "You want to learn a thing or two?" he asked, his voice muffled.

"Sure."

"The secret to extracting a bullet," he continued, "is never pry it out. That'll ruin any value the projectile might have for microscope comparison."

"Won't these bullets be messed up? Horse skull is really thick bone."

"Sometimes you get lucky and can make a comparison off a mangled bullet, but yes—I've got an inkling Dutch is going to be disappointed this time." His eyes suddenly smiled at her. "Stink still getting to you?"

She had to nod.

"Me, too," he admitted. "You like cigars?"

"Nope."

"All the better, then." Melendez took two enormous ones from a bag. "The cheapest and smudgiest you can buy in all the Caribbean. I gave Dutch one and told him it was a Havana."

Dee could see the agent wandering among the carcasses, shaking his head.

Lowering the mask around his throat, Melendez lit a cigar, sucked it to life, then passed it to her. "Gundry loved it. Wants to know where he can get more. Any burro pen in Puerto Rico, but he doesn't have to find that out."

She shed her own mask and took a tentative puff. It burned her throat, but within a few seconds she could smell nothing but the smoke. "Thanks, Luis."

"*De nada.*" He got his own cigar going, then took out a battery-driven saw. "Okay, we cut away the bone or desiccated tissue and the bullet in one piece. . . . "

*   *   *

Dee rested in a bitterbrush thicket on the slope over-looking the plant study site. The sun was half gone be-hind the crest of the mountains in the west, and she'd expected to be back at her room in the Pyrennes at this hour, nursing her hangover. But on the drive down from the blind spring, Dutch Gundry had made up his mind to use the last bit of daylight. He and Melendez would search the lower spring, where Brenner and his friends had camped, for additional physical evidence. Dee would take the Bronco farther down Jubal Canyon, then hike across the front slope of Cayuse Mountain to the general area where the killer had peered through his scope at Reckling and Kwak.

Gundry had walked this slope himself, but admitted that it was easy to miss something.

Dee had the feeling that his real purpose for splitting up the threesome was to discuss something in private with Melendez. The technician had recovered five mu-tilated silver-tipped bullets from the heads of that many horses. He'd said that they might well be .38 special caliber, although there was no telling for sure at this point. Had this finding somehow weakened Gundry's case against Cinch?

Dee started moving through the thickets again.

It was almost eight-thirty. Soon she'd turn back for the Bronco to pick up the men before nightfall.

She halted.

Three long shadows had caught her eye. They stretched up the brushy mountainside from three rock piles. The cairns were man-sized. They formed a right-angled triangle. One stood about five hundred feet below her; the two others lay about a quarter mile apart on a line roughly level with her. For all she knew, there could be more of them behind the first ridge to the north.

Then she realized. They were stone boys.

The crude monuments had been erected by immigrant Basque shepherds in the old days. They'd built them out of loneliness. It consoled them to glance up from their flocks at what had once been a barren ridge and see even a hint of something human. Another side of this aching loneliness made them carve the flesh-white bark of aspens with female depictions that bordered on the pornographic.

The stone boys were historical relics. Must tell the district archaeologist about them: The vote would be close, and this was one more argument for Congress to designate the mountain a wilderness area. A thousand years from now, these might be the only works left by an Old World mountain people who'd come to the Great Basin, herded sheep for a time, then vanished.

The sun went, leaving great streamerlike rays to fan over the valley. She turned back for the Bronco.

This land never failed to surprise her. It grudgingly doled out its secrets a thimbleful at a time. She'd glanced up at this hillside untold times, yet only now had the light been precisely right to show her the cairns in the thickets.

Gundry and Melendez were waiting out in the road for her. She could tell just looking at them that they'd found something.

They bounced inside, smelling of perspiration and sage, and Gundry slammed his door.

"Bingo," the agent said, grinning.

Melendez half leaned over the front seat, offering her a glimpse inside the small cardboard box he was gently holding. It held an automatic pistol, almost elegant-looking.

"What kind is it?"

Melendez said, "A Walther nine-millimeter."

"Sounds German," Dee said.

"It is." Then Gundry impatiently ordered, "Get us back to the van right away." They'd parked it at the intersection of Cayuse Mountain Road and Highway 95. "This piece was tossed under a bush, and Luis thinks he'll be able to lift latents off it."

"Almost sure of it," Melendez added.

Dee turned around and accelerated. "Where'd you find it?"

"Between the road and that dry crick."

Where she had pursued Brenner. "Luis, can a nine-millimeter bullet be confused with a thirty-eight special?"

"We found just one round in the magazine, none in the chamber," Gundry butted in before the technician could answer, obviously taken with his own train of thought. "That magazine holds seven or eight shots. Somebody's been doin' a little plinkin', wouldn't you say?"

"Yes, Dee," Melendez finally had the chance to say, "they can be confused. Particularly since this bullet is a hundred and fifteen grains of alloy. Heavier than most nine-mil slugs."

"Is it silver-tipped?" she asked.

Melendez said nothing, but Gundry finally muttered, "Yes."

Dee realized that the twilight was gone. She turned on her headlamps, then clicked them up to high beams.

CHAPTER **THIRTEEN**

Dee felt a corner of her bed sink. She hesitated, trying to decide how awake she was, not sure if the sinking sensation was part of a dream. A tractor-trailer loudly rumbled below her window on its way south, jake brake hissing. That was enough to convince her to slide her right hand under her pillow, although her eyes remained tightly shut. Then, opening them, she sprang up and went to her knees, gripping her revolver in both hands before her.

"Dee!" Tyler Ravenshaw cried, falling off the mattress as he scrambled backward on his hands and heels.

She lowered the handgun between her thighs. "Oh, shit."

He cowered on the floor a moment longer, then recovered his dignity with a feeble smile and stood up. Slowly. "How long've you been keeping a gun under your pillow?" he asked.

"Just started," she said. "How'd you get in?"

"The door was unlocked."

"Damn." She'd forgotten. She ordinarily didn't lock it. This was Holland Station, after all.

"Revealing, Dee."

"What?"

"You invite danger. But only on your own terms."

The daylight pouring in through the window made her cover her eyes with part of the rumpled sheet. She'd been having a nightmare when Tyler awakened her.

Three autopsy tables in a shadowy room. Jack Reckling lay nude on the first. Milt Kwak tallow-yellow on the next. And finally herself. As she watched, Reckling was cut and sawn open. Then Kwak. And finally it was her turn, although she was alive, or at least conscious of the pathologist's every move. She just couldn't tell him that she wasn't completely dead. "Who invited you in here, T.R.?"

"Nobody."

"Then get out."

"Rabe just told me you were still in bed," Tyler said, sitting again on the foot of the bed, "and I thought maybe you were sick. You never sleep in. Bascos are always up before the ram mounts his first ewe of the day—remember telling me that one?"

"No. There's no such Basque saying."

"You sure?"

"Positive. What time's it?"

"Almost noon. What *are* you doing, woman?"

Dee lowered the sheet from her face. What *was* she doing? Then she recalled. "They made me take a day off."

"Oh?" His antennae up.

"I've been burning up the overtime budget, and there's no money left in it. Nobody to take my place either, should I want compensatory time off."

"Things sound pretty rough with the bureau."

"Don't gloat, T.R." She put her revolver in the nightstand drawer. "There will always be a U.S. federal government. Even if Sony and Mitsubishi have to bankroll it."

"The Japanese are finished. One more glittering bubble gone bust thanks to predatory economics."

"Still driving a Toyota Landcruiser, T.R.?"

Tyler chuckled. "Maybe I can interest you in some haute Basque cuisine here at Chez Pyren—"

All at once, the walls of the room were rocking and her bed was swaying in counterpoint. Her answering machine clicked on, and she could hear herself saying that she couldn't come to the phone right now.

"Earthquake," Tyler said, trying to sound calm, although his voice had spiked half an octave higher. "Stand in the doorway, Dominica."

As she huddled between his heaving chest and the doorjamb, she realized what it was in the same instant the rocking ended. It was twelve o'clock. "Man-made, T.R.," she said.

"How?"

"The underground nuclear test I told you about."

"All that from one bomb?" he asked incredulously. "My God, we've got to stop that insanity."

"Talk to Brenner. I believe he has an idea or two on that score." She saw Rabe across the hallway in his own doorway, simpering at Tyler and her. Ravenshaw was dressed, but she was in her usual nightclothes, her most frayed T-shirt and panties.

"Oh, that explains it," Rabe said.

"Shut up, Rabe," Dee snapped. "You too, Ravenshaw." He was laughing. She was getting ready to close her door on both men when she turned and asked Pleasant, "You heard if there's a return from the postmortems yet?"

He held up his palms apologetically.

But Tyler said, "I got my copies yesterday afternoon, Federal Express from the U.S. Attorney's office in Vegas."

"You *what*?"

"Darling, it's called right of discovery. I'm sorry if it offends you, but the prosecution ordinarily gives the accused a peek at the deck they've stacked against him." Tyler paused. "What's wrong?"

She turned and drifted back inside.

"Talk to me, Dee."

Wearily, she sank into her overstuffed chair. If Tyler had gotten a copy in the afternoon, Dutch Gundry had gotten his even before he, she, and Melendez had gone up to the blind spring. The devious son of a bitch.

Tyler asked, "You want to take a look at my copies, Dee?"

"Yes," she said, pounding the arms of the chair with her fists. "Hell yes."

A minute later, he returned from his room with the autopsy reports. She riffled noisily through the sheaf and quickly found the times of death. She checked them again, then lowered her head and pensively rolled the inside of her cheek between her teeth.

"That engrossing? Maybe I won't wait for the movie," Tyler said, sitting on the bed, crossing one leg over the other. "Good news?"

"Could be."

"Care to share it with me?"

"Nope."

"What about discovery?"

"Doesn't apply at the moment." She plunged on through the lengthy reports. In the writing at least, the pathologist had paid scant attention to the three bullets he'd extracted, two from Jack's brain and one from Milt's eye. But he'd noted their poor condition, which may have explained Gundry's interest in conducting a wider evidence search yesterday evening and then his glee at finding the Walther pistol. There was now a good possibility he couldn't prove that Cinch's Colt had fired the fatal bullets, even though the government had some circumstantial support in the fact that three spent casings had been found in the cylinder.

Gundry had purposely kept her in the dark yesterday. That had to mean that he was still working Cinch as a suspect—and didn't trust her to help him without prejudice. As soon as she got some coffee in her, she was going to phone the agent. It was time to lock horns—or find herself with no meaningful role in the investigation.

"Dee," Tyler asked, "rumor has it you people found a forty-five automatic near Brenner's campsite."

She thought a moment, then said, "No, it was a German automatic. Nine-millimeter."

"All right. Thanks. Anything else?"

"Yes, the FBI technician called me late last night. He has a positive match. The latent fingerprints on the weapon and Brenner's jail print card."

Tyler nodded. "I'm a lesser light on the defense team at this point, but thank you. A big gun got in yesterday evening from Berkeley to take it from here."

"Who's that?"

"Syd Konigsberg."

She grunted. The last great hippie lawyer. An incorrigible obstructionist with gray, shoulder-length hair and a social conscience he wore on his sleeve. He'd recently done the impossible, gotten an acquittal for an environmentalist who'd grabbed a peavy, a pole with an iron spike, from a logger in a scuffle and bashed in his skull with it. This in timber county in northern California.

Tyler was staring at her—sadly, she realized.

"Have you been fired, T.R.?"

"Oh, not really. Let's just say Brenner and Konigsberg are more in tune with each other. And this is Syd's specialty. I shag sandwiches and send faxes."

"T.R.," she said, "if you've got no real business here, do me a favor—go home."

He turned intensely quiet all of a sudden, and he took his time before answering. "I've got all kinds of business here."

"Such as?"

"First off, foremost . . . you."

"That's flattering, T.R., but—"

"No, it isn't. It's obsessive." He glanced at the window screen, against which a yellowjacket was buzzing in frustration. His speech became slightly halting, and the moisture rose in his eyes. "I've been seeing a . . . a therapist."

It was all Dee could to keep from asking, *You?*

"He suggested," Tyler went on, "that now was the time I should see you again."

"Why now?" she asked. Nearly a whisper.

"I'm getting married."

She expected him to smile, but he didn't. "No jokes, T.R."

"No joke. Matter of fact, it's finally come over me how serious a decision this is."

"Who?"

"Elsbeth Chapman."

The news made her feel curiously hollow, maybe the echo of rejection in it, but she could hear herself saying, "Felicitations."

"Not a done deal yet, Dee. As I said, I had to see you first."

"For my blessing?"

He shook his head. For once, he was at a loss for words.

"Good, that'd be a little too quaint, T.R."

"Dominica," he asked carefully, deliberately, "is there any possibility, however remote, that you and I might someday—?"

"No, T.R. Close the deal with Elsbeth."

He stared at her a few seconds longer, then smacked his palms together once, sharply. "Well, I suppose that's the bitter pill I needed. Just what the doctor ordered." He stood, buried his hands in his pockets, and sighed. "Won't bring it up again. Promise. But there's other business keeping me here. After all these years, the grazing pot is ready to boil over, and Pinyon County is where it's going to happen. I'm sure of that."

"Why?"

"Because Brenner wants it," he said. "And I have the feeling Eric has a gift for making things happen."

"Like what?"

"You'll see." Tyler started to go out, his face grim, but then he turned at the door. "Was I cruel, Dee?"

"Sometimes. But you were always interesting, T.R. You never bored me."

He nodded distantly. "It's funny. Being obsessively in love with your ex-wife is a disease. Being the same with your wife is the height of well-being. All in timing, I suppose."

Cinch Holland strolled across the street from jail to the dirt parking lot where he'd left his pickup the day before. A broiling sun had driven everybody indoors, and even the shadows looked hot, like patches of fresh tar. The main street of Gold Mountain was deserted, except for a white cat that shifted its weight from one side to the other as if the pavement burned its paws.

Taking the worn truck key from the coin pocket of his Levi's, Cinch glanced around one last time for a man in a suit or a nice car. He figured that the man from the state cattlemen's association had come in a suit and a nice car. But there was no one to be seen.

He fired up the GMC's engine, gunned it briefly, then set out for home.

Shortly after lunch, the jail sergeant had burst into the interviewing room, which had been given over to Cinch so he could study the paperwork on his case, and clapped him on the shoulder. "You're outta here, buddy," he said, grinning from ear to ear. "The association just posted for you." Within minutes, he was outside on the street, looking for his benefactor. Maybe the lawyer, for he supposed the fellow was the association's attorney, expected Cinch to join him in the bar at the Gold Mountain Hotel. But he didn't feel like a drink. He wanted to go home. He felt grimy and used up, the same way he'd felt after Rowena and he had had that big fight the first year they were married and he'd limped home from Las Vegas after two days of drinking and hell-raising.

He turned left at the only stoplight in town, a flashing red light suspended on cables, and drove west.

In one sense, it hadn't been a bad twenty-four hours in the Pinyon County Jail. He'd never been put behind bars, other than for a brief charade staged in a cell when the federal marshal came over just before lights out to make sure Cinch hadn't escaped. The sheriff had let him spend the night on the leather sofa in his office, watching the *Tonight Show* on a television set the sergeant had brought him from the property room. But as first light showed through the venetian blinds, it hit him hard: He couldn't go outside. And as kind as the deputies were, they still wouldn't let him leave. They were his jailers and only coincidentally his friends.

The road straightened out atop the mesa north of Cayuse Mountain, and Cinch leaned his head out the side window into the searing wind. The sky, cloudless, seemed bigger than yesterday's.

He brought his face back inside.

He felt no worse than he had a minute before, but suddenly he was crying. Sobbing. It lasted for miles, all the winding way up to Cayuse Summit—then stopped, leaving him to feel as dry and pithy as an old elderberry stalk.

He noticed dust rising from a side road in a ravine, but thought nothing more of it until he glanced in his rearview mirror and saw that a line of cars and pickup trucks had fallen in behind him. Horns began honking. In the lead was Wade Russell driving his El Dorado convertible with his wife, Dixie, standing on the backseat and waving a Confederate battle flag.

Cinch waved back, but he couldn't bring himself to smile. He didn't want this. Not today. Not ever. He realized that the horns were for him to pull over, but he didn't want to talk. He wanted to go home, see his mother, then ride among his cattle before it got dark and he faced one more sleepless night. Maybe he'd sleep if he could do ordinary things, sink into routine again.

Wade pulled up alongside Cinch, seemingly oblivious to the fact they were on a blind curve.

"Snake Pit, boy!" he hollered.

"Tired," Cinch shouted back.

"Bullshit."

"Dixie Mae—get down, for chrissake, 'fore you fall on your ass!"

"I'm built for fallin', Cookie Face!" She slapped her fanny with both hands. "Pinyon County just seceded from the U.S. of A.—and you're our new president, Cinch Holland!"

He forced a grin, although he had no intention of going to the Snake Pit. He needed home. But five minutes later, when he signaled a turn off Highway 95 onto Cayuse Mountain Road, Wade Russell roared alongside again, laying down a pall of white exhaust smoke, and kept him from turning for the ranch.

"All right . . . the goddamn Snake Pit," Cinch said,

giving up, offering Wade an exaggerated nod. "Before you go'n kill some poor innocent bastard, Russell." And he didn't want this many excited people to follow him up to the ranch. The ruckus would be bad for Mother Holland.

The cortege—Cinch had counted sixteen vehicles—sped into town, horns blaring again, and parked helter-skelter around the Snake Pit.

Before the dust had settled, Japanese tourists came pouring from the Pyrennes, some with napkins still tucked into their collars, and began photographing what they probably took to be some local festival. What they were seeing was an outbreak of the Sagebrush Rebellion, and it made Cinch want to hide when he realized that he was the cause of it. The attention made him feel like a fake. Big yellow ribbons were tied around the awning posts of the saloon, and somebody had written NO BUREAUCRATS in shaving cream on the front window.

A tall, elderly man in a seersucker suit came down the steps and strode over to the GMC. He was shaking Cinch's hand even before he could shut off the engine. "Cordell, I'm Jim Bailey from the association," he said. "We met once in Elko, didn't we?"

"Yes, sir. I believe we did. You gave a talk on how to whip the tree-huggers in court."

"Sorry I ran out on you in Gold Mountain, but your neighbors didn't want me to spoil the party."

Cinch looked past the lawyer and saw Rowena and Cody standing together in the open door. His heart sank. She was putting on a smile, but the boy looked darkly thoughtful. "I appreciate all this, Mr. Bailey—but I don't feel like no party today. I just want to gather up my family and go on home."

"I understand, son." Bailey patted Cinch's arm in a grandfatherly way. "But these folks *are* the association, and you've gotta thank them by sharing a drink or two. They need you as much as you need them." His patting hand suddenly gripped as he said, "Too bad you can't find somebody friendly to ranching to help you with an alibi."

"Yeah, but workin' out of a line shack can be lonely."

"I understand." Bailey backed off.

Cinch sat behind the wheel a moment longer, then got out and started accepting handshakes. Tom Wheatley tried to press a beer on him, but he said he wanted to say hello to Rowena first. He stiffly went up the steps and stopped in front of his wife and son. "Row," he said, not knowing how to go on.

She gave him a quick peck on the cheek. "You din't shave, Cinch."

"No, I guess not. Forgot my razor. Suppose I coulda asked for one, but I din't." Cinch knelt. Cody shrank from him. The movement was almost imperceptible, but Cinch wanted to break something—it hurt so bad. But he made himself say a few words. "Tomorrow we'll go ridin', you and me. How's that?"

Cody didn't answer. His nervous eyes were on the throng, which then forced Cinch and Rowena inside with a flurry of backslaps and kisses and talk that was much too loud.

"Who's with Mama?" he asked Rowena as they were pressed up against the bar.

"Ginny."

Olin's wife. Their sister-in-law. Cinch didn't think that Mother Holland was comfortable with Ginny, but he decided to let it slide. They'd be home soon enough. "We lost Cody."

"I'll latch on to him," Rowena said, squeezing between Pancake and Bill Wheatley, who pretended to try to pinch her ass.

Dixie Russell wrapped her bony arms around Cinch's neck and gave him a sloppy kiss that tasted of gin. "Would you smile, Cookie Face?"

"Cookie Face ain't gonna smile till we get him shit-faced," Wade said, popping a Coors for Cinch, dousing him with the fine spray.

"Where's Olin?" Cinch asked Wade.

"Ain't seen him in a couple days." Then he added

in a low voice, "Watch him. He's drinkin' again. Feelin' the heat. Keep an eye on him."

"I ain't watchin' nobody, Wade," Cinch said, holding the man's gaze for a moment. Then he stood on his boot toes, searching for Bailey. He'd realized that he needed to set up a time to talk to him. Not today. Maybe not even tomorrow. But soon.

Augie Dietz had a sallow-faced outsider by the arm, leading him through the crush of bodies. "Cordell Holland," he said, as if overnight the name meant something special, "this here fella is from *Time* magazine. He wants to talk to you."

Cinch hiked his shoulders. " 'Bout what?"

"You. The Sagebrush Rebellion."

"I don't know anythin' 'bout that."

"Do you feel that the BLM is strangling the Western livestock operator?"

Cinch turned and rested his elbows on the red Naugahyde bar bumper. He took a sip of beer, then said, "There's others know more about this'n me."

"Yes, but they're not accused of murdering two BLM men."

Cinch started to spin around, but then, straining inwardly, he forced himself to remain hunched over the bar. "Get this guy outta here."

The Wheatley twins grabbed the reporter and dragged him off; he knew enough to go limp and say nothing more. They accidentally knocked Dixie Russell over on the way to the door. Cinch helped her up. "Honey, you okay?" he asked, checking to make sure that her glass hadn't shattered in her hand as she tumbled.

"Don't tell Rowena I fell down."

"You din't. You got trampled."

"Thank God," she said, then began snapping her orange-nailed fingers at Charlie for another drink.

Augie was still at Cinch's side. He looked angry now. "You are dumber than dumb, Cordell Holland. You are the most ignorant son of a bitch I ever come across."

Cinch laughed helplessly. He began to take a swallow of beer, but then laughed again. "You know, Aug, damn if that ain't refreshin' to hear. I left Gold Mountain a fool and arrived home a genius—and I'm not sure I like the reason why everybody suddenly can't say enough good 'bout me. I thank you for your honesty. It's a ray of sunshine on a dark day.''

"I'm serious, Cinch. I was tryin' to negotiate somethin' for you with that fella from *Time*, but you're too backward to see that there's money in your story."

"Have him drop by the county jail. There's some Huns and a tree-hugger there I hear are just dyin' to sell their story."

Augie was right in his face. "Will you just cogitate, for once? All of them Hollywood television producers go through the papers and magazines for their movie ideas."

"I'm not a movie idea, Aug."

"No, you're a backward fuck with manure under his fingernails. Know what your problem is? You ain't got a dream, and a man without a dream has no imagination."

Rowena returned with Cody. "I got a booth for us."

"Good," Cinch said. "Gangway, fellas, please."

They had a minute or two of privacy after they first sat down. Charlie brought Rowena and Cody sodas and another Coors for Cinch. He could tell that she wanted to ask how he was doing, but he had nothing to say, other than to mumble once, maybe twice, that he was beat. God, how he was beat. A county supervisor came over and excitedly told him that the board was going to draft an ordinance calling for the arrest of any federal bureaucrat who interfered with a reasonable business pursuit through the enforcement of any environmental law. Before Cinch could say how he felt about this, the man rushed back to the bar.

Rowena took Cinch's hand under the table.

"I never knew attention could wear like this," he said.

She held on tighter to him.

"Daddy," Cody piped up for the first time, "you feel the quake this mornin'?"

"Yes, son, I—"

"Holland," a heavyset man said, "I just wanna thank you for single-handedly stoppin' that wilderness junk."

Cinch could recall the face but not the name. A cattle-man from neighboring Nye County. There was a fine tracery of red all over his nose and fat cheeks, booze-ravaged capillaries. "I din't stop nothin'," Cinch said, watching Cody, who suddenly quit chewing on the straw he'd plucked from his soda bottle.

The man dropped his voice to a conspiratorial hush. "The hell you din't, friend. You kill a couple BLM-ers, like you done—and believe me, they'll get the message in Washington."

Cinch saw Cody's eyes flare and bore into his.

Then it was over before he could think. He'd raised up a few inches off the seat and slammed his fist into the rosy face. The man bowled over and fell out of sight. A woman screamed. Rowena, he realized a moment later.

Cody had ducked under the table. Cinch found him there, curled up like a fetus.

It was like old home week in the bar of the Pyrennes. Dee had just descended the stairs into the lobby, hoping to grab a late lunch in the kitchen, when Tyler called her over for a drink. She was in uniform, expecting Dutch Gundry to pick her up in twenty minutes, and so she took Ravenshaw's offer as something of a taunt, particularly after the uncomfortable moments they'd shared upstairs earlier. "Sure, T.R.," she said, stepping up to the bar. "It's every man's secret desire . . . a drunk woman with a loaded gun." Then, through the dimness, she saw the company he was keeping, most of the ex-ecutive committee of the Wilderness Conservancy Alli-ance.

Belatedly, Elsbeth Chapman laughed at Dee's quip, although her eyes remained aloof from the laugh. "It's wonderful to see that you haven't changed one iota, Dominica."

"Here for the Labor Day rodeo, Ellie?" Dee asked.

"Rodeo?" She blinked up at Tyler.

"She's joking. Her frontier wit." Then he added, "We're here for the duration, hell or high water."

Dee detected some dissension in the way the others glanced at him.

"At least through my brother's trial," Elsbeth qualified. Then she wrinkled her nose at Dee. "Blaine's an awful black sheep, but he really is authentic."

"An authentic what?"

Elsbeth laughed again. "Goes without saying, Dominica."

"I'm sure it does." *Authenticity*. The new indefinable measure of personal worth in the circle. If you had to ask, you didn't have it. Dee nodded to Jerry MacMillan, mentioned that she'd seen his new photographic essay on Tibet in a Reno bookstore.

"And didn't buy it, love?" the sun-bronzed photographer asked, rising off his stool to kiss her on both cheeks.

"At sixty bucks? Uncle Sam's not my sugar daddy."

"At least you didn't call it a coffee table book."

She nodded to the others, seven altogether including Tyler, and not one of them a person of color. She had been their first ethnic, and after all these years she could still perfectly recall the ringing silence that had followed her admission that she'd grown up in a thirty-foot-long travel trailer. She'd been naive enough to think that they'd be amused.

Elsbeth's stare was flickering between Dee's uniform and the bruise, which had begun to yellow. "It all really becomes her—doesn't it, Jerry?"

"Or is she becoming it?" Tyler said with no levity in his voice, his eyes cold.

"Excuse me," Dee said, then crossed the lobby toward the front door. Through the window, she had just glimpsed Cinch Holland rushing from the Snake Pit. She'd learned from Rabe that the cattlemen's association had covered his bond.

She no sooner reached the boardwalk than Rowena and Cody emerged from the tavern and stood along the street. They were apparently waiting for Cinch to bring the pickup around from the parking lot. Rowena looked preoccupied, and she failed to notice Dee sink into one of two weathered captain's chairs Gabrielle left outside for the town's duffers.

Tyler eased into the other chair. "Hope you didn't mind my little witticism. It was a bit more tense than I thought I'd be."

"What witticism?"

He decided to let it go. Instead, he raised his white wine and a twist toward the Snake Pit. "The natives are restless."

"And then some."

"Well, that's their mistake."

"Whatever you have in mind, T.R.—these people aren't going to take it lying down."

"I never expected them to."

"Then what *do* you expect from them?"

"Change," Tyler said. "For that a crisis is required, and I have to thank you, Dee. Whatever your reasons, you've given us the head-on collision with grazing we've needed all these years."

Cinch sped from the parking lot, his tires scattering gravel that pinged off the other vehicles. He braked sharply in front of the Snake Pit, then leaned across the seat and flung open the side door for Rowena and Cody.

"Be careful, T.R.," Dee said. "You may not be the one to walk away from the wreckage."

She tried to catch the look on Cinch's face, but the late afternoon sun was glinting on the windshield. As soon as his family was in the cab, he accelerated north—toward home, she imagined. He'd go up to the line shack, if he could, and the image of him there, on the cot, gave her a moment of bittersweet longing. Dutch Gundry's government sedan passed him coming the other way.

Rising, Dee intertwined her fingers and stretched her arms out. Then she chuckled. A bit cattily, she realized.

"What?" Tyler asked.

"*Not* Ellie, T.R.," she said, still chuckling.

He reddened. Spectacularly.

"And I didn't mind the jokes about my uniform. It made me really understand for the first time that I'm home. Oh, I know it's brutal here and the locals don't know an ecosystem from an eclair. But it's where I belong. Do thank Ellie for me, won't you? She removed all doubt for me."

"About what?" Tyler asked.

Gundry stopped in front of the hotel but kept the engine idling. Dee went over to him, and he snapped, "Hop in. Hurry. Let's go."

That took her aback. She had demanded the showdown.

Taking her time, she got in, adjusted the air-conditioning vent so it wasn't blowing on her sweat-damp skin. "You're a sneaky prick, Gundry," she said for openers.

He gawked a moment at her, then said, "Tell me somethin' I don't know."

"Damn you," she went on, straining to hold down her temper, "you withheld the autopsy reports from me."

"What're you doin' in uniform?" Gundry backed up, then drove north. "I gave you the day off."

"My supervisor suggested I take the day off. As of now, I'm back on duty. This is business, and I mean to get to the bottom of it."

"Stow it, Laguerre," he said, swinging his sun visor around to the side. "It slipped my mind, okay? Happens now and again. I'll have copies for you first thing in the mornin'." He passed the old GMC pickup, but Dee forced herself not to stare. Cinch probably felt as if the entire world were staring at him. "Got me a call at the motel in Gold Mountain. Voice said that if we want to hang Holland—that's him right here, isn't it?"

"Yes."

"Well, he ain't free for long. If we want to hang Holland we oughta lean on his brother-in-law, Olin Peters. We're headed in the right direction?"

"Yeah, turn off on Ranch Road. Half mile more."

True to form, the conspiracy—whatever it involved—was breaking up. Fear worked on men like frost broke apart granite. "The caller identify himself?" she asked.

"No, but he had an accent."

"Southwestern, you mean?"

"Naw, foreign."

Dee fell silent for several seconds. "Was it like this?" She recited "Mary Had a Little Lamb" as her father would have.

"That's it. What is it?"

"Basque," she said. "Did it sound like a two-pack-a-day voice?"

"Yeah. Know who he is?"

"Julian Arrache, I'd bet. You should take whatever he says about Cinch with a grain of salt. The Arraches and the Hollands have been feuding since the turn of the century."

Gundry slowed for the turnoff. "Anythin' else I should know about these players?"

"Cinch was my high school steady. Julian is a second cousin on my mother's side." As they sped past Wade Russell's ranch, Dee blurted, "Who're we working here—Cinch or Brenner? Square with me, will you?"

"Both, for the time bein'." Gundry reached into his shirt pocket for his tobacco tin. "We got us two weapons that fired silver-tip bullets. I've sent all the slugs, or what's left of 'em, plus the unfired rounds back to Technical Services at FBI headquarters. Alloy comparisons. Let those boys eliminate either Brenner or Holland. Till then, we get us a jump on both suspects. Fair enough?" He eased up on the gas. "What's this?"

A motorbike lay on its side just off the road, a deep, comma-shaped gouge in the dirt marking where the rider had lost control. On the far side of the fence, Olin Peters was sitting like a stone Buddha out in the alfalfa, watching his sprinklers irrigate another part of the field. The breeze-driven mist was banded by a vivid rainbow that seemed to transfix him. He didn't budge as Gundry and Dee came up on him from behind, their shins thrashing through the lush green crop.

"Olin?" Dee asked gently. There was a nasty abrasion on his forehead and nose, and his skinned knuckles were covered with dried blood. She could smell the liquor. "Are you all right?"

He twisted around, unsteadily, and squinted against the sunlight. "Lost it," he croaked.

"You need medical attention, hoss?" Gundry asked.

Olin faced the rainbow again. "I did say some things, but it was all bullshit. It was the beer talkin'."

Gundry knelt beside him. "What things?"

"Shit," Olin said, grinning wetly, bitterly, "you know."

"No, I don't."

"You got to understand Cinch. Dee here does. It's a matter of understandin'."

She was surprised that, in his state, he'd recognized her.

"You gotta understand," Olin went on in drunken adamancy. "He's scairt. He can't do nothin' else than this. . . ." He limply waved at the alfalfa, his cattle dotting the public range beyond. "Me, I can. I was a professional soldier. I can go back to it if I gotta. I can kill for a livin', and everybody knows it."

"Did you kill those horses up at the spring?"

Olin peered off a second longer, then dropped his face into his hands and wept.

"That's all right, hoss," Gundry said.

"That's all I done, I swear. Shot up some goddamn cayuses."

Gundry winked over Olin's bowed head at Dee. "Who went with you that night, Olin? Cinch, of course."

The rancher nodded, snuffling.

"Who else?"

He took in a gasping breath, then sighed miserably. "Shit. It comes to this. My hand on the table." Once more, he sighed. "The Wheatleys. Wade Russell. Me."

"That it, hoss?"

"I can't think of nobody else."

Dee asked, "What about Dietz?"

In a blink Olin stopped crying. "No, I don't think he went along." He wiped his nose with his fingers, opening the abrasion again. "Hell, I don't remember. Augie coulda been, but I just don't remember. Cinch could tell you. I was blind drunk the whole time. We all was."

"What'd Cinch think of Jack Reckling?" Gundry asked.

Olin took a moment. "Hated him, I guess."

"Either you hate somebody or you don't. Which was it?"

"Well, I'm just goin' by what Cinch said."

"Which was?"

Bowing his head again, the rancher closed his eyes. "He told me he was scairt he might snap. He'd taken all he could from the BLM, and one day he might up'n shoot Reckling."

"Why Reckling and not other folks with the bureau?"

"He's the one what broke Cinch, pressurin' him to go with the Savory Method and all. Chokin' him to death with all that red tape."

Dee asked, "Anybody else hear him say this?"

Olin opened a single, sullen eye on her. "You callin' me a liar, Dee Laguerre?"

Gundry frowned at her. "Nobody's calling you a liar, Olie. Where was Cinch the day of the homicides, say from two to five or so?"

Dee came within a breath of speaking up. It was time to stop this insanity. Truth or not, Olin's testimony would help convict Cinch unless she spoke up. But once again, since seeing Tyler's copies of the autopsy reports at noon, she realized that the decision to reveal Cinch's whereabouts that rainy afternoon wasn't hers alone. The consequences went beyond herself.

"Workin' somewhere on his place, I guess." And then Olin turned testy. "Hell, he's my brother-in-law. Not my kid. We got back from shootin' the horses in the wee hours, and I didn't see him for quite a while after. I ain't responsible for him. He married my sister, that's all."

"Olin," Dee asked, ignoring the look Gundry shot at

her, ''where were Tom and Bill Wheatley that afternoon?''

''Not a clue.''

''Wade Russell?''

The rancher just shook his head, which made it ache, for he groaned.

''Augie Dietz?''

''That I do know. He was up in Reno, playin' Hollywood.''

''Doin' what?'' Gundry asked, taking over again.

''He met some Frenchie director, and they talked 'bout makin' a movie on the mustangs down here.''

Dee butted in, ''How d'you know that's true?''

''Met the Frenchie myself at Augie's dump. He told me so.'' Olin tried to stand, but his ankle folded under him. ''You gonna haul me off to jail now?''

''No,'' the agent said. ''I'm gonna get a doc to look you over, then I'll bring you straight home to Mama. You're helpin' me get the picture around here, Olie,'' he said to Peters, although he was watching Dee, ''and Dutch Gundry always returns a favor.''

''Dutch,'' Peters murmured thickly, a drop of blood hanging off the tip of his nose. ''That mean you're a Dutchman?''

''No, Irish and German. I got the nickname because I always split the tab. I always play fair, Olie.''

CHAPTER**FOURTEEN**

After breakfast, Cinch set out to teach Cody how to ride fence, how to look for weak places where the barbed wire was sagging, where erosion had left the poles wobbly and ready to collapse. But as they rode side by side, Cody on an aged pinto pony and Cinch on his favorite gelding, he saw no point in passing along the skills his own father had taught him. May as well teach Cody to trap beaver or repair wagon wheels.

Giving up on the lesson, he tried to take comfort from the land itself. But it seemed as if he could only see it as the environmentalists wanted him to, the withering of the vegetation and the gullying. He kept an eye out for Indian rice grass, the rich provender of this range that had made his ancestors decide on Cayuse Valley. But for the first time ever at the close of summer he couldn't find a single patch.

Cody had asked nothing about the things that had happened over the past days, and Cinch—after a few halting attempts—just couldn't find a way to explain them. It seemed the weakest thing a man could do: to try to defend himself with words. A man was the summation of the things he'd done and, maybe more important, the things he'd chosen not to do. If he'd lived decently, the tone of his life was self-evident. And if he hadn't, all the explaining in the world wouldn't matter.

Last night in bed, he'd asked himself why he believed this, wondering if it was one more useless piece of bag-

gage from the dead past that was weighing him down in
the present. In Pinyon County Jail, the public defender
had casually asked him for an alibi, never realizing that
he was asking Cinch to justify himself, his entire life.
Jim Bailey had asked the same thing outside the Snake
Pit, but at least he'd known enough to be embarrassed.
Even now, that old weight was keeping the alibi down
deep in his throat, a weight that had grown ten times
heavier by the simple act of Rowena's taking his hand
under the table at the tavern yesterday. In that instant,
the unexpected intimacy of his wife's touch raising the
hair on the back of his neck, he'd seen that in all the
universe he had but one place to be, his home. If he left
his ranch, he would step off into black space, forever.
Prison was something that could be outlasted. But the
destruction of his home could not.

He realized that he'd said nothing to Cody in some
minutes. Time to make conversation.

"Question for you," he said.

The boy sat up in the saddle. "All right, Daddy."

"What's the best wild grass we got for feed?"

"Indian rice grass," Cody said, barely giving Cinch
time to get the question out.

Cinch nodded. His father's nod had been praise
enough. Too much praise weakened a man. The range
praised no one, and it ate up the weak. "Let's see who
spots some rice grass first."

The boy put the old pony into an achy-looking canter,
but Cinch called for him to halt. "Where you goin'?"

Cody peered back over his shoulder, holding the reins
high. "To look."

"What chance do I got if you break trail?"

"Well, I—"

"Forget it." Cinch smiled. "Go on."

"I won't, Daddy, if you want."

"No, go on and tell me what's comin'."

Cody had no sooner ridden ahead than Cinch saw dust
rising from the big curve. Not wanting the boy to meet
the vehicle first, Cinch started to dig in his spurs—but
then saw that it was the BLM Bronco.

"Knew this was comin'," he said to himself, drawing rein, then running his fingers through the gelding's tangled mane. He recalled the lovely, pinyon-branch-combed manes of the cayuses he'd shot.

Dee Laguerre braked to smile and say something to Cody, who remained wary throughout the brief exchange. Then she drove up toward Cinch, and Cody turned back, protectively, as if he didn't want his father to be alone with the law.

"No," Cinch said sharply, "go on like I said, boy. I'm serious 'bout findin' that rice grass. I'll catch up in a few minutes."

Reluctantly, Cody wheeled his pony.

Dee yanked her shift lever into Park and stared up at Cinch.

He found it hard to meet her eyes. They were hurting. She said nothing at first, just looked at him, waiting.

"Jim Bailey, my lawyer, said if anybody from the gov'mint tries to talk to me, I'm suppose to say that I've invoked my rights."

"I'm not here for the government, Cinch."

"Seems I fell for that once before."

"You didn't fall for anything. I promised I wouldn't use anything you said against you. I never promised I'd let you and the others skate."

After a moment, he said, "That's true. That's just what you said."

Dee switched off her key. The engine noise died, replaced by that of the dry breeze sighing in the brush. "I have to tell them, Cordell."

Tight-lipped, he watched Cody and the pony getting smaller along the fence line.

"You hear me, Cinch . . . ?"

"Ain't it peculiar, though?" he said, his voice thin and airy.

"What?"

"You think of your kid gettin' bigger, then gettin' so big he moves out one day. But that ain't the way it happens at all. Too much work or worry makes kids smaller in your life. One day, they get so small they just disappear. And you're alone." He flicked his chin up toward the ranch house, but he was thinking of the cemetery plot behind it. "That was the real beauty of this place. In its time. Its day. Nobody disappeared to the family. Even when they died. Nobody got small in your life."

Dee's face softened. But only briefly. "I have to tell them where you and I were that afternoon."

"No, you don't. As of yesterday, my lawyer says you don't have much of a case against me."

"That's the point, Cinch."

"What is?"

"That was yesterday. Each day Gundry is putting a stronger case together. It's like building a barn. One board at a time. The FBI is doing some tests back east that can put you right back in the hot seat." She paused, making him glance at her. "Olin's talking against you. About the horse slaughter and more. I know it's pure crap from a scared man trying to save his own skin, but Cordell Holland's brother-in-law would make a hell of a witness for the government."

His gelding began prancing, and Cinch gently patted his neck to calm him. Now this. Betrayal by one of the few people he had counted on.

"Don't tell Rowena," he said, trying not to sound like he was begging. But he knew that he was. "Just do me a favor, Dee, and don't tell her. I realize it'll be a shock no matter what, but she's not up to one more jolt right now. She thinks the world of her brother."

Dee said, "I don't believe this." But then her look got determined. "I'm going to volunteer to go on the polygraph. It's the only way I have to end all doubt for good."

He considered that, briefly. "You have to say how long you was with me . . . and everythin'?"

"Yes. I have to tell the whole truth, otherwise there's no point. One lie, even a fudge about something that's not even material, would invalidate the test."

He started to nod, but then he saw red and heard himself barking at her, "You do that, Dominica—and you'll kill Rowena. She looks strong, but she ain't, really. You'll save my worthless ass and kill my boy's mama!"

Tears showed in her eyes. "Damn you, Cinch Holland."

"I'm sorry," he quickly said, seeing how badly he'd stung her. "Shit, I shoulda invoked the minute you rolled down your window. I just got nothin' to tell you."

"If I keep quiet," she said, angrily wiping her eyes with the heels of her hands, "you'll be sent to prison. Be executed, even. What will that do for your boy's mama?"

He saw that Cody had gone as far down the road as he could comfortably go. The boy was coming back, holding something in his free hand. "You should think of yourself," he said.

"Why?"

"I wouldn't be surprised they can fire you for bein' with me like that."

"They don't have the balls."

Cinch chuckled, despite himself.

"Besides," Dee continued, "I accidentally logged myself off duty before I drove up to the line shack. Using the Bronco to visit you might become an issue, but not much of one. My Fiat is still in the shop, and how else can I get around?" She had to blow her nose into a wad of Kleenex, which made her even madder. "If you're worried about shaming me—don't. I've been ashamed before and lived through it." Then she held out her left hand to him. "Give me the word, Cinch, and I'll stop this right now."

Cody had come galloping up, and Cinch backed his gelding away from the Bronco. Dee withdrew her hand.

"You find any?" he asked the boy.

Cody held up a clump of spiky, almost menacing-looking seed heads in his fist.

"No, son," Cinch said, "that's cheatgrass. It's no good for feed. No good for nothin'."

"Then I didn't see no rice grass, Daddy."

"I don't think there's any left. I was hopin' new eyes

might find some. But it's all gone, just like Jack Reckling said.''

Then he touched his fingers to the brim of his hat at Dee and started for home with Cody.

The polygraph examiner disconnected Dee from his machine. He reminded her of one of the placcid, eversmiling monks who'd run a religious retreat in Arizona she'd gone on as a girl.

''Am I absolved?'' she asked, standing.

''I'm only a GS-eleven,'' he said, indicating his government service pay grade. ''You've got to be at least a GS-thirteen to grant absolution. But I can give you this.'' He took a lime-green lollipop from the pencil drawer of his desk and presented her with it.

''And what's this mean?''

The FBI examiner shrugged. ''Well, I could've given you a red one.''

''Any other flavors?''

''Yes. Lemon . . . for those poor lost souls who don't know what the truth is. Good afternoon, Ms. Laguerre.''

She paused at the door. ''How long have you been doing this?''

''Nineteen years.''

''Do you honestly believe that there's such a thing as truth?''

''Oh yes,'' he said, still smiling. ''It's my bread and butter. I've got to believe.''

Rabe Pleasant was waiting for her out in the corridor.

She'd deposited him in the coffee room, but he explained as they started for the elevator, ''Some agents came in, and they nearly killed me with their boring talk. Football. Betting spreads. How can the FBI be so boring?''

It felt good to hear him prattle. The examination had left her feeling violated, weakened. ''What surprises you about that? It's just another federal bureaucracy, like ours.''

''But I was sure that Hoover, being of the persuasion,

had left his stamp on it. You know, provided some atmospherics.''

''*J. Edgar Hoover* was gay?''

''As a fritter. Oh, God, didn't you know that? I'm sorry to be the first to tell you.''

They stepped into the elevator. She'd worked hard to tell the absolute truth. Maybe it was the laboring that had left the aftertaste of deceit in her mouth. Whatever, she never wanted to go through this again. It was confession without spiritual release. A car wash for moral stains.

''You okay, sweetness?'' Rabe asked.

''Oh, kind of blue.'' She tried to smile.

Tenderly, he kissed her on the cheek just as the doors opened on the lobby of the federal building. A pair of agents stood there, smirking.

''My reputation is saved,'' Rabe whispered.

Outside, she threaded her arm through his. ''You hungry?'' she asked.

''Eternally. How about you?''

''Not yet,'' she had to admit. ''A drink would be nice. It might give me an appetite.''

''Isn't that the truth? Drinking and driving are only mildly dangerous compared to drinking and eating. I've wiped out entire buffets thanks to alcohol. A week of six-hundred-calorie days, then two highballs and I'm burying my face in a guacamole bowl.''

They stopped in the middle of the Virginia Street bridge over the Truckee. The river was low, just a languid trickle through the cobbled bed of melon-size stones.

''You okay?'' Rabe asked again.

Her eyes began to burn, and a few seconds passed before she trusted herself to say, ''I feel dirty, Rabe.''

''I know, but you're not. Absurdly honest, yes. But dirty . . . no. You have a *thing* for this guy. That's chemistry, not dirt.''

She gave him a peck on the cheek, but his words hadn't put a dent in her mood. On the drive up in the Bronco, all at breakneck speeds with the rear amber light going to ward off the highway patrol, she'd felt nothing but certainty that she was doing the right thing. The feeling had seen her through the one-hour meeting with her supervisor and Dutch Gundry's boss at the BLM state office. But it had collapsed as soon as she went on the polygraph. Then, for the first time, she couldn't shake off what Cinch had said this would do to Rowena—and she began questioning her own motivation for being so forthcoming.

Rabe's voice suddenly brightened. "Oh, we're in a movie."

She glanced around for cameras, crews. "Where?"

"That scene in *The Misfits*, sweetness—you know, where Marilyn Monroe and Thelma Ritter stand right on this spot after leaving the courthouse there. And old, homely Thelma tells young, gorgeous Marilyn that if she throws in her wedding ring she'll never get divorced again."

Dee leaned over the parapet and dropped her lime sucker into the silver ribbon of water below. She smiled, watching it float out of sight under the bridge. "You know, it does make you feel better." But then she saw that Rabe looked positively doleful. "What's wrong?"

"I've just had the most horrible epiphany," he said. "I'm Thelma Ritter, aren't I?"

"We both can use a drink. Come on."

Arm in arm, they strolled northeast a few blocks to Louis' Basque Corner, where they drank a rich red wine and shared dinner with four generations of the same family at one of the common tables. The warm press of bodies began to make her feel better. Safe. A *buro zuri*, an old whitehead, sat across from her, the great-grandfather of the clan, his granddaughter explained. His warm but rheumy eyes shone from beneath his rakishly skewed beret.

"You have a good Basque face," he told Dee. Shades of Gabrielle.

"You do too, *Abuelo*." Grandfather.

He laughed, opening a mouth full of gold. "Yes, but

I am not beautiful. I am still stron', but not beautiful. Not in a lon' tine, anyways.''

"He's hitting on you," Rabe quietly said, neatly tearing his bread into bite-size pieces.

"So what? It's working.''

"You're a lewd people.''

"Lusty, not lewd. They'll have to use a sheep knife to get the lid closed on this guy's coffin.''

"Then you must tell me what's in this food," Rabe said. When she didn't respond, he added, "That was a joke, my dear.''

"I'm sorry," she said, staring at the portrait of the old woman on the wall. Iron-willed. Face of stone, eyes of flint. "I was just thinking . . .''

"What?" Rabe asked.

"*Abuelo*," she said, "please tell me about stone boys.''

The old man winked at her. "What's to know?''

"Did you ever build one?''

"Many tines. To make a friend when no friends 'round. One to watch over me. To listen to my songs.''

"Did you ever build three of them in a triangle?''

The old eyes twitched in confusion. "No, never.'' Then he took a big bite of tripe.

Rowena hung up the wall phone and came back to the kitchen table. She walked stiff-backed, as she did when she had some duty to perform in church, and then failed to take her chair.

Cinch stopped chewing and asked, "Who was that?''

Rowena reached out and overturned the table. Dishes broke and bean soup slopped against the pantry door.

Cinch reared back, toppling his chair behind him, while Cody remained frozen, his fork upright in his fist.

"What the—?''

"Congratulations, Cinch Holland—charges been dismissed against you," she said, her words slow with fury. "Your lawyer'll be callin' any minute with the official news.''

Cinch stood motionless, half crouched, his hands feeling the empty space between his wife, his son, and himself. All at once, the light seemed dazzling, and he wanted to smash the circle of bulbs in the wagon wheel chandelier, but it'd only frighten Cody more than he already was. The fixture was swinging, and he realized that he must've brushed it when he jumped up. "Who was that?" he asked, avoiding her eyes.

"What the hell does that matter!"

Unsettling to hear her cuss. Cinch steadied the chandelier.

"Why don't you tell Cody what you was doin' when those BLM men got kilt?"

That lit his own temper. "Stop it, Row—don't drag him into the middle of this."

"He was *born* in the middle of it."

For a moment, he thought that she'd started crying. But a glance showed that she wasn't. Still, he'd never seen her face so devastated.

"Is it true, Cinch . . . where you were?" Her voice broke.

He sank to his knees, outstretched his hands, and cradled Cody's face in them. "It ain't you. It's me. All foolish me, pretty boy." He'd last called Cody that when he was a toddler.

"Tell us!" Rowena shouted.

He rose again. "Yes, I imagine it's true. If you're talkin' about Dee."

"Get out."

"And go where?"

"Life up at the line shack seems to treat you damn good."

And then he was blindly furious. He folded his arms over his chest so he could grip his biceps. He realized that unless he clutched himself like this he might smack her and not even know it until he saw her mouth or her nose bloodied. "What the shit 'bout Olin?" he seethed. "The son of a bitch told the gov'mint I was good for it. He told that agent I had it in for Reckling!"

"This is 'tween us, and you know it."

Her sudden calm infuriated him, but he had to admit

that she was right. "Yes, that's true. Everythin's true. Every goddamn word." And like that, his anger was gone, replaced by a heaviness so great he feared he couldn't move his legs to get himself out of Rowena's sight. "What 'bout Mama?"

"I'll do as I always done. Changin' her diaper and spoonin' baby food into her mouth."

Cinch nodded. "Lemme say good-bye."

Rowena had no argument to that, so he went upstairs.

The old woman was staring into her reflection on the inside of the window glass, so he put down the shade. Then he lifted her out of the rocking chair and into the bed. For that brief moment, she rested the side of her face against his neck, and he thought that there was a spark of feeling in how she did it. Her eyelids had slid shut, but she was breathing as she did when awake.

Sitting on the floor, he took one of her hands in both his and pressed it to his lips. "I'll be bunkin' at the line shack for a spell, Mama." He paused, doggedly hopeful that she might say something back. " 'Member that time couple months ago when you just up and smiled at Row? 'Member? See what if'n you can't do that again, Mama." Then she began quietly snoring, and he was talking to himself, without a doubt. "When you're last of a line, the end don't come quick enough, does it? You'll forgive me, won't you, Mama, if I find an end?"

CHAPTER**FIFTEEN**

Dee flipped down the visor against the rising sun. She started the Bronco's engine, gunned it a few times to blow out the night's chill, then tuned in the Tonopah FM station to catch the state and local news. She expected to be the featured item this morning and only hoped that the reporting wouldn't tend toward the lurid. *BLM siren leads Pinyon County buckaroo astray.* The announcer was going through the livestock prices, so she put the volume on a murmur.

Last night, upon returning from Reno, she'd made up her mind to keep busy during what she knew would be the worst day of the coming ordeal. Thankfully, she had something to do: go back out and take a closer look at the three stone boys on the mountainside above the plant study site.

A city was cluttered with the unusual, most of it meaningless. But out in the desert the unusual most often had significance, human or otherwise. Rocks strung out in a line across a playa might prove to be the boundary of a makeshift landing strip for drug smugglers. A rock in the center of a shallow crater was most likely a meteorite. A solitary quartz crystal on an overlook, an Indian hunting talisman. The stone boys had a meaning, one out of the ordinary. Perhaps related to the homicides. Perhaps not.

Suddenly the passenger door flew open, and instinctively Dee's right hand went to her holster.

"Someplace private, Dominica Laguerre," Rowena Holland said, getting in, "and no, I ain't gonna shoot you, much as I'd like."

"Where?"

"You pick it."

Dee backed away from the Pyrennes and started south on the highway.

Rowena rode in silence, the dawn rays highlighting the fuzz along her jawline. Her eyes were inflamed by either sleeplessness or crying.

"Put on your seat belt," Dee said.

"Go to hell."

She figured that the knoll was as good a place as any, and she drove up the dirt road to the top, parked, but left the engine running.

"Why not?" Rowena said, growing even more provoked as she looked over the site. "It's fittin'. Here's where I lost my girlhood."

Dee rolled her eyes, inwardly cussing Cinch Holland.

Rowena went on, "I see they din't fire you."

"No, I got the word last night. They're going to make me work three days without pay."

"That's all?"

"What'd you want them to do? Burn me at the stake?"

"Don't make jokes on me, Dee Laguerre."

"I wasn't, Row."

Neither of them said anything for a minute or two. The radio noise was annoying Dee, but she realized that if she turned it off the snappish quiet would be even more uncomfortable.

"Was it vengeance?" Rowena demanded. Dee correctly decided that she didn't want the question answered. "If it was, well, I deserve it. What I done with Cinch back then on this hill tore your heart bad. Tell me it was vengeance workin' itself out, so we can call it even and I go on with Cinch, maybe."

Dee vacillated, but finally said, "It wasn't, Row."

Rowena's voice crumpled as she asked, "Then why'd you love up my husband, woman?"

Dee just stared out across the sage at Holland Station. It looked like a ghost town on the golden, brushy land.

"Give me a reason," Rowena said. "That's all I'm askin'."

"All right. You and everybody else know I've always had a weakness for Cinch. But that wasn't it. Not really. It wasn't a happy afternoon up there, Rowena. I don't want you to imagine that it was fun."

"But there was still sex . . . right?"

Dee sighed, then nodded. Luckily, her temper was still under wraps, for she'd almost added, *Damned good sex.* But then Rowena's pain-twisted look cooled her down even more. "I guess it was the only way I had to bring him back from the brink, Row. You should've seen his face. It wasn't right what happened between us, but I think I'd do it again under the same circumstances."

"Shit," Rowena said, probably for the first time in her life. "Afraid you'd say somethin' like that. Me, I got nothin' left to bring him back, and we both know it. This whole valley knows it." Then she started to cry.

Dee wanted to comfort her with a touch, but knew that that wasn't possible.

"Well," Rowena went on, hiding her eyes behind a hand, "you saw that look in his face just one afternoon. I seen it mornin' and night for years now. And you put it there, lady, you and the whole heartless Bureau of Land Mismanagement. You got no idea how you've tortured that man."

Dee shifted into Reverse. "Let me take you back. You drive down in the pickup?"

"No, my sister-in-law, Ginny, brought me."

Dee quickly braked. The radio announcer was talking about a development in the murder of two BLM employees in Pinyon County. She wanted to switch it off, but Rowena had obviously heard, too. ". . . German national Eric Brenner has startled federal and local authorities with the contents of a handwritten statement he entrusted yesterday to a Las Vegas reporter. . . ."

Augie Dietz hiked north across the dry lake bed, his

boots crunching over the salt crystals. The distant ridges wavered through the midday heat. He carried a shovel over his shoulder and a canteen on a web belt. Over the slosh of water and his own footfalls, he heard an approaching whine. Looking skyward, he saw nothing but the contrails of San Francisco–bound jets, flying far too high to be heard.

He turned.

Racing at him from the direction of the shanty was Olin Peters on his motorbike. He was rippling through the mirage, leaving a rut in the salt pan as deep as a bowling alley gutter.

"What the bejesus happened to you?" Augie asked as the rancher rode up and stopped. He had scabs on his face and hands.

"Fell off this piece of Jap junk," Olin said, planting the heels of his boots in the dried mud. He spat off to one side of the handlebars, then said, "You heard?"

"Heard what?"

"On the radio." Olin had yet to meet Augie's gaze, and he didn't care much for that. "The German, the one they got in jail for the dynamite, he says he whacked Reckling and the Chinaman."

Augie sniffed for booze. The smell was on Olin, but it was stale. He looked reasonably sober. "Why would he go'n do that?"

"Claims it was self-defense."

That was even more unbelievable. Reckling and the Chinaman had carried no guns, ever. "You're making no sense at all, man."

"I know, but that's what they said on the radio. No sense to you and me, but I guess it does to the Hun. Brenner's his name. Brenner says the gov'mint is killin' off the land bit by bit, which'll make life impossible for most folks. So he had no choice but to stop the gov'mint before there's no more land to save."

Augie shook his head, trying to clear it. "That ain't no kind of self-defense."

"I know, but Brenner thinks so."

Augie took a thoughtful swig from his canteen. "He

say if the others with him was in on it? The girl and the American?''

"No, just him. He pulled the trigger. The sheriff already found the pistol.''

"Then where's the rifle he used?''

Olin shrugged. "Give me a sip, Aug.''

"No," Augie said, putting his canteen back on his belt. "I could be out all day on foot, walkin'. Can't afford no scooter like you. You're just minutes from your kitchen tap. This water could be the difference 'tween life and death for me.''

Olin didn't protest. He just licked his lips. "What d'you think the German's up to?''

Dietz swung the shovel off his shoulder and pounded the lake bed with it, once, hard.

"Aug . . . ?''

Then, leaning on the handle, he gave Peters a long stare.

Olin wiped his skinned nose with his fingers and said, "Listen, Aug—there's talk goin' 'round you oughta pay no attention to.''

"Like what?''

"Oh, that Cinch and me's had a fallin'-out.''

"Have you?''

"No way. Blood's thicker'n water.''

"You and Cinch ain't blood.''

Olin chuckled weakly. "Well, close. Now, I got to admit I din't like him not goin' along with the rest of us. Havin' you wrap our Winchesters in plastic and buryin' 'em till this all blows over. But that's just Cinch. He won't never bend." Olin paused. "It confounds me, though—what's this Brenner kid up to?''

Dietz tapped his temple with a finger. "Cogitate, man.''

"I been tryin'," Olin said.

Dietz could see it as plain as day: It wasn't the German who was pulling the strings in this; it was the government investigators, pumping out a smoke screen so they could make their next move in secret. He'd bet his life on it.

But all he said to Peters was: "Shouldn't even let the sons of bitches in the country."

"Calculated martyrdom," Rabe Pleasant said, topping a Saltine cracker with a hunk of salami. "Here. *Bon appetit.*"

Dee took her right hand off the wheel to accept the only lunch she and the biologist would have today. The two of them had been forced out of the Pyrennes by reporters from as far away as Denver who refused to be convinced that neither of them was authorized to speak for the federal government on Brenner's unexpected confession. "Is it true that Eric and Karena were members of the Baader-Meinhof terrorist gang before turning to radical environmentalism?" Faced with that question, Rabe had grabbed Dee and begged her to take him along back out to the plant study site, where she still meant to examine the stone boys.

Now, driving up Cayuse Mountain Road, she munched on the salami and cracker, mulling Rabe's supposition over. "Meaning," she said, "that Brenner came here with the intention of murdering two of our people, then sacrificing himself for the sake of a showcase trial?"

"Something like that."

"Too direct," she said after a pause.

"Why?"

"Brenner packed along the makings of a bomb. Terrorism at arm's length, that's what he wanted. A bomber chooses that means because he wants time to get away."

"Okay then," Rabe went on, using his Buck knife to slice off some salami for himself, "accidental martyrdom. Things got screwed up, out of control. Brenner and his friends got arrested because of something they didn't do, but he—the most hard-core of the three—decided to seize the opportunity, figuring the docket is a bully pulpit to rail against grazing and environmental abuse."

"Yes." That struck her as being closer to the truth. And it was in line with how Tyler had behaved this morning: taken aback, apologetic even, because of the bizarre tack the defense had taken. It was clear to her that T.R. had expected something else from Eric Brenner, not a confused appeal to the spirit of the Nuremberg trials, in that a moral man must resist—forcibly, if necessary—the evil state. It was just the kind of argument Syd Konigsberg loved. But it was too much for poor Tyler, who had told her that the WCA had never and would never sanction the murder of federal employees, even to save Mother Earth, and he wanted that conveyed to FEER, Dee's own organization. T.R.'s whole manner had convinced her of one thing. He now genuinely believed that Brenner had murdered Reckling and Kwak.

He wasn't alone in that belief.

Dutch Gundry had phoned her from Gold Mountain and, pretending that there were no hard feelings, said, "Looks like we got a wrap on this one. You're clear to go back to your routine patrol duties. . . . " He then added that he was going to pursue the mustang slaughter case on his own and try to close it before returning to Reno. He was in the process of getting search warrants to obtain the .30-.30 carbines of the ranchers involved. "I'll use Olin Peters's statements to lean on the others, startin' with August Dietz. Peters seemed a bit too eager to keep him off the list of who went up to the spring that night. I prefer handlin' this by my lonesome, Laguerre. That way when if the locals get bent out of shape a little, you don't wind up the bad guy. Okay with you?" The question was hollow. She knew that she had no voice in the matter. She was being disciplined. Her stock with the state office was almost worthless at present. It was a bad time to press the ranchers, right after Cinch— one of their own—had been falsely accused, but she simply signed off with: "Whatever, Dutch."

Slowing, she came to the jumping-off place for the stone boys. "I got kidnapped this morning," she said, parking on the edge of a wide spot.

"Really?" Rabe asked, sitting up.

"Kind of. Rowena Holland."

"Oh, this *is* juicy. Was she armed?"

"Only with righteous indignation."

"Did it come to blows?"

"No, tears."

Rabe's smile vanished. "Whose?"

Dee reached for her radio microphone. "I'll be away from my cruiser on the west slope of Cayuse Mountain for an hour or so," she advised the dispatcher in Gold Mountain. "Pleasant is with me."

"Aren't we being punctilious," Rabe said, getting out.

"That's what happens when you get your teat caught in the wringer."

They approached the bitterbrush thickets from a lower route than Dee had used at dusk two days before, and the trick of light was confirmed: The rock piles were virtually invisible within the growth and would remain so until sundown, when their long shadows crept up the slope. In this, the builder had taken care, making the stone boys as unobtrusive as possible yet never trying to deny that they were part of the landscape.

She let Rabe go up alone to the first of them. Standing back, she felt oddly exposed. She scanned the brush for the glint off a telescopic scope, fragments of human shadows. That rainy evening, Reckling and Kwak had been as alone as she and Rabe now were. She could usually sense lightning before it struck close by. If she now felt a similar tingling, she wouldn't hesitate to tell Rabe to drop, then hug the ground herself. She wondered if Reckling or Kwak had had any inkling.

Hands on his hips, Rabe strolled around the pile twice, then stooped and examined the spaces between the rocks. "No signs of nesting of any kind," he said.

"Did you expect some?"

"Sure. One critter or another is bound to look upon this as a virtual fortress." Rabe stood again and inspected the topmost rock. "Not much guano. How old should one of these things be?"

"I don't know. Fifty years, at least."

Rabe shook his head. "Sorry."

"What d'you mean?"

"Several generations of some raptor—red-tailed

hawk, for instance—would've shit these upper rocks white by now. This is a superior hunting vantage, and they're rare below the pinyon-juniper forest.''

''Then it's no relic?''

''I doubt it's been here more than a few months.''

She started for the next one, which was directly below, at a near run.

''Wait, dammit,'' Rabe said, following.

The second stone boy was equally clean of nests and bird droppings.

Dee, ignoring Rabe's pleas for her to slow down, moved diagonally up the slope to the final pile. From the high ridge there, she could see mile after mile of tubular white posts set in two rows five hundred yards apart, stretching northward along the base of Cayuse Mountain into what was roadless terrain. The triangle was actually a rectangle, for the last corner of the first claim was hidden below the ridge line and marked by a PCV post.

As Rabe huffed up, she turned and began tearing the stone boy apart with her hands.

''Hold it, woman,'' Rabe said. ''I'm not a thousand percent sure it isn't a relic.''

''I am,'' she said, and to prove it she produced a rusted Prince Albert tobacco can from a niche deep within the pile.

''Ah,'' Rabe said, recognizing its purpose at once.

Dee pried the lid open with her fingernails and took out the notice of location. Often the writing on the form faded to illegibility within a few years, but this ink was fresh. ''Ever hear of Sidewinder Mining Company?'' she asked.

Rabe shook his head.

''Well,'' Dee said, gazing off at the white corner posts marking the multiple claims as required by law, ''it looks like Sidewinder has staked out the entire north end of the valley.''

''After what?''

''Doesn't say. Left blank.''

''Why build three sham relics?''

Pivoting, Dee saw that this, the first claim in a long line of them, could be seen from the jeep trail along the old telegraph line below, particularly if marked by the glaring white posts most miners used. "Sidewinder Mining is trying to keep it quiet. I never got word of this operation, did you?" she asked, not adding that the BLM geologist in Gold Mountain, who processed the permits, seldom informed her of new applications.

"Crazy." Rabe's hands went back to his hips as he surveyed the extent of the potential mining operation. "Crazy to claim half the county. This side of the mountain has never supported a single mine for more than a few months. Even that lead outfit went belly-up. Just crazy."

"Maybe not." She started down the slope toward an outcropping, skidding on the soles of her boots.

Along the way, she paused at a small pit. Six feet deep with sand heaped all around it.

"Lady, I happen to have bum knees," Rabe complained, catching up.

"High school football?"

"Sure." He, too, then noticed the hole. "You think he shot Jack and Milt from here?"

She checked the line of fire, then moved on again. "No, that outcrop's in the way."

She threw out her palms and stopped her descent by bracing against the reddish knob of rock.

Rabe came down the last steep incline on the seat of his trousers, then sat still a moment, choking in his own dust. "What're you taking specimens for?" he finally asked.

"An assay," she said, pocketing the small pieces of stone.

CHAPTER**SIXTEEN**

She had peeked in the same window as a child. Her father came to Gold Mountain from time to time, usually to handle some immigration paperwork for a sheepherder he'd hired for the summer. While he took care of his business in the courthouse, she would drift across the street to steal a look inside this shop. Basques didn't take to mining—it was too sunless a trade—so the dim interior of the assay lab was strangely forbidding to her. It was a sorcerer's workshop, every nook and shelf crammed with elixirs and powders, dusty fragments of earth and stoneware crucible cups. Through the glass, she'd listened to the soft evil roar of the propane-fed oven.

It was now cold.

The sign said CLOSED. But, seeing light spilling under a black curtain at the back of the shop, she knocked.

It was a quarter past nine, dark now, and two hours since she'd forgone supper and left Rabe off at the Pyrennes.

The curtain rings clicked along a metal bar, and a hunched male figure could be seen moving slowly toward the front door. He stopped in the shadows and said, "Closed. Tomorrow."

"Tonight," she said, raising her voice. *"Please."*

With difficulty, he unlatched the mortise lock and cracked the door. His fingers were knobbly, as her father's had been in his last years. Arthritis. "Come back in the mornin'."

"I can't, Mr. Howbert. This is an emergency."

She could tell by the slow lowering of his head that he was taking in the uniform. "Gov'mint business?"

She hadn't wanted to say this. "Yes. A quick assay. The sooner the better." She raised the brown paper bag in which she'd put the specimens from the outcropping. "I can wait."

The assayer fell silent, except for a slight bronchial wheeze. She thought he was on the verge of locking up again when he said, "It'll cost you extra."

"That's fine."

He took the bag from her and shut the door.

Dee thought of grabbing a bite to eat, but then again realized the lateness of the hour. She went across the street to the courthouse and called the county recorder from the pay telephone out front, fudging that the bureau needed some information out of the mining book, immediately.

The woman sighed thunderously in the receiver, but told her to wait on the steps.

Leaning against the rail, she gazed down the street toward the jail. A reporter, microphone in hand, awash in lights, was using the building's facade as a backdrop. "Milk it for all it's worth, Eric." She was more sure than ever that Brenner and his friends would walk on the explosives charge, thanks to the weak probable cause that sent the sheriff off looking for firearms and winding up with dynamite. It still didn't gel for her, Brenner's having shot Jack and Milt. As for his murder confession, it was simply meant to shock, she was convinced of that, and he could back away from it anytime he wanted by screaming duress and coercion. The sheriff's office had broken his jaw, hadn't it? She doubted that the government would prosecute him for lying to it. Everybody lied to the government. It was the American way.

Forty minutes later, a Chevy Malibu with badly oxidized paint pulled up under the only streetlamp in town. A blue-haired woman in her sixties got out.

"Hello, Ms. Dolan," Dee said, hoping she might be recognized.

But the county recorder scarcely looked at her as she took an ancient skeleton key from her purse. "I do indeed hope this is important," she said, opening the door with Dee's help. The ground beneath the century-old building was riddled with mining tunnels, and the staff had been fighting a losing battle against sagging floors and sticky doors as long as Dee could remember.

The recorder flipped on a globe fixture in the high ceiling, then stepped around the counter, her low heels echoing. She assumed her may-I-help-you stance. "Now, who is the claimant?"

"Sidewinder Mining."

"Repulsive name," she said, taking a huge book with worn corners off the oak table behind her. "Did you know my Eddie passed on this winter?"

Dee said that she hadn't heard, but commiserated. She realized then that she'd been recognized—but not fondly. To these people her father had been a little foreigner, stinking of sheep.

The woman cracked open the book, moistened her fingertips, and began leisurely turning pages. "Sidewinder Mining . . . oh, my goodness, look at all the notices."

"How many?" Dee asked, trying not to sound as antsy as she felt.

"Thirty-five . . . no, thirty-six standard claims."

"Who's their agent?"

"That isn't put down. There's no space in the book for it."

"*Merde.*"

The woman said in a brittle voice, "I beg your pardon?"

"I really need to know that information, Ms. Dolan. That's what I came all the way here for."

"Sometimes I pencil it in over the mailing address. If he's a local."

"Did you?" Dee asked hopefully.

"A moment, *s'il vous plaît.*" The woman lifted a snide eyebrow at Dee, then perused the watermarked page. "Yes, I did indeed. August Earl Dietz, president."

Dee gripped the edge of the counter. "Any other officers or agents listed?"

"None. Just Mr. Dietz."

Two minutes later, she was knocking on the assayer's door again. Howbert was busy with mortar and pestle, but he frowned and let her in. "I barely got goin'."

Dee nodded, trying to contain her impatience.

"But I do know this ore, young lady. It's Carlin Trend stuff. I knew that as soon as I took it from the bag."

"What d'you mean?"

He went back to his worktable and picked up one of the specimens she'd collected. "Carlin Trend is a big geologic zone that runs up and down the state. Looks like any other stretch of desert, but it's peppered with microscopic particles of gold."

"Rich ore, then?" she asked.

"Just the opposite. Piddlin'. At best, a third of an ounce of gold per ton."

"Then where's the value?"

"In volume." Howbert clipped a magnifying monocle onto the frame of his glasses and examined the reddish stone. "Thanks to cyanide heap leachin', it's profitable. The operator piles up damn near a mountain of low-grade ore like this, then lets cyanide solution trickle down through it. He retrieves the gold from a pond below the heap."

"What's that do to the land?"

"Heap leachin' turns a lot of acreage inside out. It's got a big appetite for ground." Then he astonished her. "Your jasperoid here probably come from the west slope of Cayuse Mountain."

"How'd you know that?"

"I seen this stuff twice in the last month," Howbert said, licking the stone before inspecting it again. "First sample came from Aug Dietz, and then the same exact jasperoid from a Korean fella."

Dee took a breath. Everything was coming too fast. "You mean Milton Kwak?"

"No, not Milt. A relative of his, I figure."

"Wait," Dee said. "How d'you know Milt?"

"He ran several sagebrush assays for Carlin gold through me."

The assays that had been charged to Jack Reckling's budget, pissing him off. "I thought those were for a soil survey."

The old man winked. "Well, I suppose you could put it that way. But it's all geochemical exploration in my book. You know anythin' about the root system of *Artemesia tridentata*?"

"Only that it's extensive."

"And deep. Those roots suck up elements from as far down as twenty-five feet. I ash the sagebrush, then—"

"Hold on," Dee interrupted. She needed to understand this from the beginning. "How does the process start?"

"You go out and collect the samples on a grid basis, snip off the branch leaders or seed heads . . ." Kwak's furtive tea-picking at the site, she realized. "You then wash it real good," Howbert went on. "I take over from there and burn it down to fine ash, then chemically analyze what's left for a suite of elements. Sometimes I find gold itself. Other times arsenic and antimony—which're dispersed 'round gold deposits more'n gold itself, if that makes any sense to you."

"What about the samples from Dietz and Kwak?"

"Lousy with arsenic and antimony," Howbert said, grinning with professional satisfaction. "I never seen anythin' like it. In the last month, Aug's been diggin' down six foot or so for straight soil samples. . . ." The pit she'd found between the stone boys. "This was so I could test for mercury and thallium. Two more surefire indicators of gold, but they don't get concentrated so good in plants, so you gotta take to the spade."

"And the results?" Dee asked.

"Lousy with both 'em."

"Then you're telling me Cayuse Valley is a prime candidate for cyanide heap leaching."

"Prime."

Dee wanted to laugh, it was so ironic. The ranchers, BLM, and environmentalists had been arguing about the extent of grazing in Cayuse Valley while at least two separate parties, Dietz and Kwak, had been quietly initiating an operation that might end with hundreds of square miles of range being displaced by huge shovels and rinsed with cyanide, one of the most toxic compounds known to man. "Milt and his relative . . ."

"Yes?" Howbert asked, already back to work, grinding with his pestle.

"Did they come in together?"

"No."

"Did Milt say a relative would be dropping by with a mineral sample?"

"No."

"Then how'd you know they were related?"

"Well," the old man said, smiling, "I didn't for sure. But first one Kwak comes in for me to ash some sagebrush for him, and then a week later another Kwak comes in with a Carlin sample. Now, I don't wanna draw no conclusions, but it seems to me a federal botanist could do a mess of geochemical exploration on gov'mint time, then alert some kin of his to follow up on any hot spots he found."

"Did you tell Dietz about this?"

"Well . . ." The assayer glanced away. "Ol' Aug's a local, ain't he?"

At eleven o'clock, just before Olin Peters set out to make his final check on the irrigation, Wade Russell phoned. Olin, not wanting Ginny to hear, took the call in the kitchen. He'd known that Russell would be getting hold of him one way or another, and it had weighed on his mind all day.

"You lyin' piece of shit," Wade said right off.

"What?"

"That fed, Gundry, saw me this afternoon. He says you told him we kilt the mustangs."

Olin had been drinking beer most of the evening, but now reached up into the cabinet over the refrigerator and took down a bottle of bourbon. No time to think. Wade had to have heard it wrong. Gundry had said nothing about using Olin's words to confront the others. Dutch would never do that.

"You still there?" Wade demanded.

"I'm here."

"Gundry knew it all. He named every last one of us."

Olin asked hesitantly, "Augie, too?"

"Shit, yes!"

The walls of the kitchen seemed to close in on Olin. He saw no way out, just shrinking walls. "I had to, Wade."

"You *what*?"

"To save Cinch. They was gonna use the horse kill against Holland to get him on the murders, too."

"You expect me to buy that?"

"No, I probably don't." Olin took a swig from the bottle. "That's 'cause you don't understand the law. Reasonable cause. Usin' one thing to go'n explain another. That's how the law works."

"You blew the whistle on us. That's all I understand. The fed leaned on Augie this evenin', and he din't crack. Neither'd I. Just you, Olin." Then he said in a quiet but enraged voice before hanging up, "And I'm not about to let it slide."

For several minutes, Olin stood at the sinkboard in the darkened kitchen, drinking, gazing out the window. A low mist lay on his alfalfa fields from the chilly night air resting against the sun-baked earth.

Ginny asked sleepily from the living room, "What was that all about?"

Thankfully, he recalled that he had to check on the irrigation. "Nothin'," he said, taking one last gulp. He realized that he'd polished off a quarter of the bottle. "Wade and Dixie just askin' how Cinch 'n Rowena's doin'."

"You tell 'em everythin'?"

"No," Olin said. "Don't worry."

"Good, none of their business. God knows Dixie and him have their own problems."

The warmth in his belly made Olin feel better, but he still went to the bedroom and grabbed his .45 automatic.

Wade Russell had a surprise coming if he thought Olin Peters was going to be caught flat-footed.

Then he limped out the back door into a moist gray hush, silent but for the crickets.

He started up the bike, revved the motor a few turns of his wrist, then accelerated down his driveway and out to Ranch Road. He began to get mad. Wade had had no call to talk to him that way. Who was he to talk? Just a drunk and a whorehouse regular.

By the time he turned left toward his northernmost fields, he was as mad as he could be. At Dutch Gundry as well as Wade. He opened the throttle all the way. The mist stung his face. The agent had pulled him on, said that the important thing was the homicides. From that Olin had trusted nothing would really happen about the horse slaughter. Gundry had even acted as if he approved of shooting the damned pests.

The mist became thicker as he neared the slough, an old canal filled with two feet of scummy water after the recent rains. The road narrowed here to cross the ditch on a culvert bridge. Olin saw no headlights coming at him and kept up his speed. He glanced at the stars, fuzzy because of the dampness in the air.

He looked forward again, and suddenly he was squeezing the lever for the feeble brake with all his might. The bike barely slowed, not that he noticed anyway. Ahead, he could see cows and calves. His own cattle were filing out onto the road just beyond the bridge. Trotting with their tails hoisted as if something had just spooked them.

His pasture fence had been breached, he realized with a feeling that seemed to disconnect him from the moment, a sense that none of this was really happening.

The bike fishtailed wildly under him and the tires made a crunching noise as they skidded along. But the dull, glinting eyes of his livestock just got closer and closer.

He made up his mind to veer off into the softer ground of the field and lay the bike down there on its side.

He dipped the handlebars to the right. His leg burned

as it was pinched between the bike and the road. Then he was airborne. He thought he would come down right away, but he didn't. He tumbled through the darkness forever, his arms outstretched.

Then, abruptly, he was cold, and a bubbly sound filled his ears.

His head was under the water. Gagging, he tried to raise his mouth above the surface, but even the slightest attempt at movement set off stunning pain all over his body. He strained to hold his breath, but the pain wouldn't let him. Water filled his nose and poured down his throat.

Somehow, he managed to roll onto his back and suck in some air. Heaven. At this instant, he was sure that he would live. But then, as he began slowly to sink, he shifted around to brace his arms against the silty bottom—and found them useless.

Broken, he figured. His legs as well.

He whipped his torso back and forth, testing for a motion that would keep him afloat.

Almost directly overhead, standing on the bridge among the milling cattle, was the silhouette of a man. He was grasping something in one hand. A leafy branch. He waved, then began to carefully sweep the ground with it.

Olin started to cry out to him for help, but the effort only made him retch. The water lapped over his face. He tilted back his head to hold his mouth above the surface, yet the cold water kept flowing over his bottom teeth and down his throat.

Twice, Dee drove completely around the Jackpot Motel to make sure Dutch Gundry's sedan was gone. Only then did she go inside the office. A tiny bell attached to the door jingled. The room was paneled with knotty pine and smelled of fried onions and cigarette smoke. Along the front windows were two tired-looking poker machines.

She glanced at the wall clock. Eleven-fifteen. Gundry could return to the motel at any moment.

The night manager finally came through the door from the attached living room. Gray-blond hair sweeping back from a long face. "Room?" he asked hopefully. The construction of Highway 95 thirty miles to the west had left Gold Mountain off the beaten track, and its tailings piles and ramshackle architecture didn't exactly make it a destination resort.

"No room. May I have a look at your register?"

He hesitated, then grinned off into whirling space. Horse teeth. "Oh . . . you must be workin' with Dutch on the murders."

She kept a blank expression. "Yes."

"I can tell you nobody involved stayed here. I'd turn 'em away right now."

A sign on the cash register reserved the right to refuse service. Especially homicide suspects, she gathered. "Dutch just asked me to make doubly sure."

"Well, okie-doke." He slid the register across the counter to her, then grinned again.

Within a minute, she found a late June entry for a Kwak Jae Kyn of Seoul. Under "representing," he had written "self." "You still have the paperwork on this guest?" she asked.

He looked at the name and date. "Sure do."

Milton Kwak's apparent relative had paid with a corporate Visa card in the name of Morning Calm Mining Company. Korea, the land of morning calm. She'd seen it on a Korean Air commercial.

On a sudden inspiration, she asked, "Have any other mining reps stayed with you over the past several months?"

"Lots." Then the night manager added in a burst of local boosterism, "Gold Mountain's comin' back." Gold Mountain had been coming back every year since 1906, when the big mines had closed for good.

"Any of them go out to Cayuse Valley?"

"Uh . . ." His eyes dimmed as he concentrated. Like lights on an overloaded circuit. "Yes, the Frog."

"French Basque, you mean?"

"No, Canuck." The manager produced another account. It was only a week old. Guillaume Lenoir of Quebec. Thunder Bay Mining Company. "He borrowed the phone, tried to get somebody's number over there in Cayuse."

"August Dietz?"

"That sounds like it. One of the months. July Dietz, maybe?"

The bell on the door tinkled, and Dee turned her head, then slowly straightened and faced Dutch Gundry.

He smiled, but his eyes bored through her. "What's up? Office tryin' to locate me?"

"No, Dutch," the manager blurted, "she checkin' my register for the murderers, like you said."

Gundry's smile went out. He was still holding his car keys. He began jiggling them in his fist. "You were cleared to go back on routine patrol. Period. That was the agreement."

"Listen, I've learned something—"

"No, you haven't learned a goddamn thing. Patrol. No investigatin'. Just patrol."

"I have yet to hear that from my supervisor."

"My word not good enough?"

Dee knew better than to answer.

"Phone," Gundry ordered the manager, who quickly complied. The agent took a small red book from his jacket pocket. Three minutes later, he was explaining the situation to her supervisor at home in Reno. Not the way she herself would have explained it. "Glad to," he said, then dropped the receiver into Dee's hands as if it were a hot potato.

"Laguerre?"

"Yes, sir."

"Finish your disciplinary days off at home," the groggy voice said at the other end of the line. "Do not report to work during that time. Do not drive your government vehicle. Do nothing except catch up on your soaps. Understood?"

CHAPTER**SEVENTEEN**

"Listen . . . Olin Peters was just found dead."

It took Dee a split second to realize that the voice was Jewell's and that she herself had somehow managed to answer the phone. Rising on her elbows, the handset tucked against her neck, she glanced at her digital clock. It was almost four. Her window was still dark, and through the screen flowed the smell of ground fog. "How?"

"He din't come in from his late irrigatin', and Ginny got worried."

"No—how'd he die?"

"Accident. Got his fat ass throwed off that scooter of his. Fell in the old canal and drowned."

Dee sat up. All at once, she was wide awake and her heart was racing. "Like hell."

"Well, that's what Pancake said."

"Screw him."

"Baa, Pancake could cash in his retirement, hock his gold star—and still not get a hand-job off me." Jewell had never liked Olin either. She then groaned as if going through a catlike stretch. "Well, just thought I'd let you know."

Dee's first impulse was to alert the sheriff's office, but then she calmed down enough to realize that no one would listen to her. Even Gundry hadn't listened to her. "Phone Cinch."

"Me?"

223

"All right, have your handyman call for you. Rowena's bound to hang up on any female voice at this point."

"I can't phone Cinch. Nobody can."

"Why not?" Dee asked, swinging her legs over the side of the bed. "Something wrong you're not telling me?"

"Rowena kicked him out of the house. He's bunkin' in his line shack."

Dee winced in the darkness, but then said, "Got to run," and hung up.

Before dressing, she crossed the hall and was about to pound on Rabe's door when she recalled that he'd left yesterday evening for Las Vegas. Ramaloche, at long last, had phoned. Rabe had slid an ebullient note under Dee's door that she'd found upon returning from Gold Mountain after midnight.

She floated back inside her room and went to the window.

Leaning against the sill, she gazed down on the Bronco. Not her Bronco, the federal government's. A half-moon was inching over Cayuse Mountain. Its glow was making the emergency light bar look almost as if it were on. Her fingers tugged idly at her lower lip.

"Well," she finally said, "I was looking for a job when I found this one."

She passed a tractor-trailer rig at eighty miles an hour, then swerved back into her lane to avoid a Maserati coming south almost as fast as she was going north. A low fog wreathed the alfalfa fields along Ranch Road, but the rest of the valley was clear. The salt crystals coating Alkali Dry Lake were glittering like frost. She could pick out the speck on the ancient shoreline that was Augie Dietz's shanty.

The urge was strong to confront him right away. But she couldn't. Not yet.

Pancake, no doubt, had destroyed any physical evidence along the canal that might have established Olin Peters's death as foul play, and Dutch Gundry, eager to get home to Reno, was content to close his investigation with Eric Brenner's confession.

She needed time to take Dietz down, and she knew that she could find the patience for this within herself— as soon as she saw with her own eyes that Cinch was safe.

Just north of the dry lake, she turned off the highway onto a narrow road. It cut east across some flats Cinch had planted some years ago with crested wheatgrass, then wound up several switchbacks onto the mountain. As a child, she'd come this way many times. Yet, her father had always taken the branch that led away from the Hollands' line shack and dead-ended in a high meadow ringed by aspen.

Here, on the Arraches' last local allotment, the valley's Basque families had once picnicked in late spring, to eat and drink and ward off the coming isolation of the summer range. She could recall creeping past a Holland Ranch stock truck pulled over in one of the turnouts, the leather-faced cattlemen squeezed together in the cab, looking at her father with eyes made small by what they felt for him. Sometimes a towheaded boy was riding in the back of the truck, seemingly on the brink of smiling at her before the dust had him.

Making a sharp left, she started up the spur that led to the line shack.

Little frenzies of nerves came and went. She could be fired for this, she kept realizing. Her Fiat wasn't even running, so how could she hunt for another job? At least she'd put the assay on her personal charge card.

Mist was rising from the hollow. Tendrils of the stuff, turned silvery by her headlights, sifted up the road toward her. She could barely see the GMC pickup, which Cinch had parked near the outer gate. Probably to keep the tires from tearing up the rain-softened pasture. A Winchester was visible through the rear window in the rack. For a moment, she was gratified. He hadn't scuttled his carbine, the one he'd no doubt used on the horse kill.

She drove nearly all the way down to the shack. She wanted her own long gun to be close at hand. Her radio, too, although using it would be the same as writing her own pink slip.

She hoped that her lights sweeping over the shack's window would bring Cinch to the door.

They didn't.

She shut them off, then the engine. The mist pressed darkly against the Bronco's windows.

Getting out, she left her door ajar. "Cinch?" she called, not too loudly but loudly enough to be heard within the shack.

A match will flare, she kept thinking, *and I'll see him through the dusty panes lighting his lantern, his hair in cowlicks.*

But the shack remained dark.

She walked forward.

Near the corral gate she passed into a strong, coppery odor that made her halt. She meant to thumb on her flashlight for only a few seconds, but the beam came on and stayed on, riveted to the partially dried blood pooled on the ground. There were also reddish-brown stains and drippings on the fence rails.

She rushed up the steps to the door of the shack, but then forced herself to pause a moment, revolver drawn, listening.

Nothing.

She burst through and, clasping her flashlight and muzzle together, ran them over the small room.

Movement swiftly drew her eye to the floor—deer mice were scurrying for the spaces between the boards. Focusing on the cot, she saw blood on the cover, and almost cried out in horror before she saw that it was just red color woven into the Navajo blanket.

Cinch stirred and shielded his blinking eyes against the light. "Who . . . ?"

"Dee, godammit." She holstered. "You all right?"

He mumbled something she didn't catch.

She threw off the blanket, and his hands lowered to cover his crotch. All his clothes, she saw, were strewn over the floor, as was an empty pint of Cutty Sark and four crushed beer cans.

"Didn't think you liked Scotch." She tossed the blanket back over his nakedness.

"Don't. Figured I wouldn't drink so much that way."

"You figured wrong." She found the kitchen matches, then got the lantern going. "There's blood all over the corral."

"Just the gate," he said, his voice muffled by his jacket, which he was using to mask his eyes. "Finally had to slaughter that leppie. Just too weak. His mama stopped even tryin' to feed him. I skinned it off the gate crossbar. Put the carcass in the back of the truck under canvas." Then he added, "For Row and Cody."

She glanced over bottles and cans on the shelf. "Got any coffee?"

"Don't want no coffee."

"Yes, you do," she said somberly. "Olin's dead."

Dee could hear the mice scratching under the floorboards.

Cinch rolled over and looked at her for the first time. He seemed about to say something, but no words came, and eventually he just sat up. The last of his drunkenness seemed to desert his eyes. They were wide, unblinking now. He found his boxer shorts and threaded his chalk-white feet through them. He wriggled into his Levi's next, then bent over to pull his muddy boots on. His hair was thinning at the crown. It surprised her, although she then realized that it shouldn't have. His father and grandfather had been bald. "How?" he asked.

"Drowned in the canal."

"Shit, there ain't enough water in that ditch for a kid to go wadin'. How the fuck could a grown man drown?"

"Pancake investigated. He says Olin fell off his motorbike into it."

"Jesus," Cinch said, scratching his chest chair, "I just don't know about that."

"Neither do I."

He looked sharply at her.

"I think Augie Dietz killed him," she went on.

He stopped scratching. "Say what?"

"You heard me."

"Can you back that up?"

"No, not yet. I'll need your help for that."

Suddenly, he grasped the sides of his head in his splayed fingers as if he were trying to hold it together against inner pressure. "I don't believe it. Olie. *Olie*." He inhaled deeply, sat ramrod straight. She thought he was getting sick, but then he slouched at the shoulders again and asked, "How can you say these things, Dee?"

"You all right?"

"Comin' 'round, 'cept for the dynamite goin' off inside my skull. How could Dietz—?"

"Without knowing it, Dutch Gundry forced his hand. He was using Olin as an informant against the rest of you, and Augie just couldn't allow that. Not after what he'd done on his own."

"What's that?"

"Gunned down Reckling and Kwak."

Slowly, thoughtfully, Cinch buttoned his shirt. "He's a mean little shit, Dee, but he's learned how far he can go. The joint does that to a fella."

"Not always. . . ." She began telling him about Sidewinder Mining Company and the competition for Carlin Trend gold Milton Kwak had given him, but Cinch cut her off. "Whoa," he said. "Whose idea was it to use Olin as a snitch in the first place?"

She hesitated.

"Yours, Dee?"

"No."

"You tellin' me it was Gundry's?" Cinch said, his voice rising in anger. "He didn't know nothin' 'bout the horse kill. How could he, unless you told him?"

"Gundry got an anonymous call."

"Who?"

Caution, she told herself. She'd sensed the danger in this the moment Gundry told her about the caller's Basque accent. The last thing she wanted was to trip off a bloody chain reaction between the Hollands and their allies, and the Arraches.

But Cinch then misunderstood her silence. "Well,"

he said, standing, "that settles that. Good work, Dominica."

"Damn you—it wasn't me."

"You find that coffee? I got to clear this head and get down the mountain to Rowena. She'll go off her nut over this. You just see."

"It was Julian Arrache," she said, biting her tongue as soon as she'd said it.

He went quiet, but she could see his mind working behind his darting eyes. Then something fell into place for him. He nodded conclusively and mumbled, "Sure."

"Sure what?"

He smiled patronizingly at her. "Back off now, Dee. I'll handle it from here."

"*You?* Who the hell d'you think you are?"

"Somebody who's gotta make water bad."

He started out the door, but she grabbed him by the arm. "I need you helping me, Cinch—not working against me."

He gave her a kiss on the cheek. "You got it, lady. Get that coffee goin'. I'll be right back." But then he didn't move for a few moments longer, his gaze drawn to an empty spot on the floor. "After I agreed to marry Row," he said distantly, "Olin did the damndest thing. He was standin' 'bout there in his uniform"—Cinch pointed—"and he leant over and hugged me. Never before. And never since." He began to reach for his hat on a wall peg, but then decided against it and went bareheaded out into the growing light.

She found a can of Folger's, but the mice had chewed through the plastic lid. She was checking the coffee for droppings when she turned and stared pensively at the door. Cinch had come to a decision. She'd watched him make it, lock it in his heart, and now she wouldn't let him go until he told her what he meant to do.

But then she heard the GMC being fired up. She flew through the door in time to see Cinch drive through the outer gate, bail out, and hurriedly swing it shut.

"Don't you even think about it, Cinch Holland!" she warned.

But he gave her a wave, then locked the gate.

"You son of a bitch!"

There followed a clunk as he shifted gears and vanished behind the mist.

She ran to the gate and examined the big brass lock in her palm. This was the only opening in the fence surrounding the hollow. She drew her revolver again and squeezed the trigger twice. One of the bullets put a dent in the casing, but still the hasp refused to spring.

"Merde!"

On the shrouded hillside above, she could hear the pickup. Cinch was climbing toward the old sheep camp, which could only mean that the Arraches were there this morning and not at the hacienda. Doubtlessly, Cinch would've seen them coming and going from the high meadow.

Dee hurried back to the shack and ransacked it for wire cutters. But if Cinch had them, they were in the truck.

"Bastard!" She kicked the flimsy door until the hinges popped loose, then pried it off. She carried it across her back out to the Bronco, wedged it between the push bar and the grill.

Getting in behind the wheel, she revved the engine three times, then simultaneously dropped the shift lever into Low and jammed the accelerator to the floor.

The tires spun, mud thrummed against the flaps, but the Bronco sped forward.

She hunkered her head down into her shoulders just before the collision with the gate, cringed at the sound, but then peeked above the dash and saw that she was outside the hollow and still moving. *"Bon!"*

But suddenly the Bronco came to a mushy stop as if all four tires had gone flat at once. The line shack door had swept along the gate, its uprooted posts, and several hundred feet of five-strand fence, which had dragged the vehicle to a halt like a jet landing on an aircraft carrier.

Backing up, she watched the barbed wire go slack, then drove over it, through the brush, and onto the road again. The wooden door, shattered by the impact, fell away in pieces.

The Arraches would have their dogs with them up at the camp. She told herself that Cinch would never slip past their keen noses—at least not before she arrived to keep Holland and Julian apart. But still, inwardly, she had brief nightmarish glimpses of gunshot wounds, of men lying mangled in the meadow grass. Bittor gloating over Cinch's body.

She turned up the sheep camp spur. The mist dissipated, and first light broke over the northern face of Cayuse Mountain, making the feathery tails of the mountain mahogany fruit shine like gossamer. The road cut a long tunnel through this luminous woodland.

She could see water spangling where it had just oozed into the pickup's fresh tire tracks.

Cinch kept the slight breeze in his face as he hiked up a slope covered with wild rose. He wore his yellow slicker because packed over his left shoulder was the carcass of the leppie he'd slaughtered yesterday evening. In his right hand was his Winchester. He reached the wooded crest and quietly put down the calf, then lay down himself in the dead aspen leaves. They were limned with frost. It was a thousand feet higher here than at the line shack, and starting now, with summer fading, the freezing line would work lower down the mountain almost every night.

There'd been frost on Howard's headstone the first time Cinch's father had pointed it out to him. "See how it's different, son?" he'd said. "All the others have *died*, then the dates. But on Howard's we had to put *assassinated*. We owed him that much."

Tightly gripping his carbine, Cinch crawled forward until he was clear of the trees. From there, he could see the wall tents of the Arrache camp. A fire was going, bright yellow from kindling, and Nino Arrache, the youngest, was tending it.

No one else seemed to be up.

Two sheepdogs stood poised at the edge of the camp,

having already heard or smelled Cinch. Strung out across the bedding ground behind them was a large flock of sheep, some of them picking up on the dogs' alarm, baaing, shifting back and forth.

Cinch checked his pocket watch. Not much time before Dee showed up.

Rising to a crouch, he went back to the carcass, taking no care to keep quiet now, and stripped off his slicker and threw it down beside the calf. He inhaled, measuring the blood-rich smell. It was strong, despite the chill.

Nino's voice drifted up to him through the barking of the dogs. "Where you guys headed? What you got . . . coyote?"

Cinch then dropped below the crest and began circling the camp. The dogs, he was sure, would go no farther than the calf. When they failed to return soon, Nino would come up to see what had drawn them off the flock.

Five minutes later, Cinch crept down through some stunted aspen to the back side of the camp. A shadow flitted over him: a golden eagle taking off from the cliff behind.

Nino could be seen walking across the meadow. He stopped and whistled for his dogs.

Cinch could hear two men arguing indifferently in the nearest tent, sleep still in their voices—Bittor and Pello. That left the large tent in front of which the fire blazed. He went to it and ducked through the flaps.

Julian Arrache was seated on his cot, putting on a pair of gray woolen socks that were badly worn at the heels. He lowered them in surprise. "You mean to shoot me, Cordell?" he asked, yet without any fear Cinch could see.

"Maybe. Maybe not. But it's for sure, Julian, if you don't tell Bittor and Pello to get out in the middle of the meadow with Nino right now. I know you all got guns, but don't let me see 'em."

Cinch had parked his pickup at the foot of the last bluff before the meadow. The tailgate was down, the calf carcass gone from the bed. She pulled the Bronco up behind his truck, well off the single-lane road, and pocketed her keys. She sat a moment, wondering if she should take her shotgun. No, she soon decided. It might provoke one side or the other. Most anything could set them off.

She followed Cinch's tracks up the slope, the rose thickets snatching at her trousers. As she hiked, the sun broke through the aspens above, slanting down in a yellow shaft aswirl with gnats. Only the first hard frost would kill them. Beyond, the sheer north wall of Cayuse Mountain could be seen through the leaves, its last patch of snow preserved in deep shadow.

A dog barked. Another joined in with a long yowl.

Dee stopped, picked out the true sounds from the echoes, and then, shifting to the right slightly, continued upward toward the now incessant barking. The meadow lay in a cirque, a natural amphitheater gouged out by a glacier. It had the acoustical properties of a good concert hall. This was one of the reasons the old Bascos had chosen the site for the annual picnic, the way it amplified and carried their music.

Two of the Arraches' dogs were guarding the leppie's carcass, their neck fur raised and fangs exposed.

"Came in handy, didn't it, Cinch?" she whispered to herself, then told the dogs to back off with her own growl.

Still, one of them, a blue-eyed bitch, came at her low to the ground, snarling. Dee swatted her hard on the nose. A yelp, and then both dogs were streaking through the undergrowth back toward camp.

Dee took the game trail they'd showed her to an overlook, then quickly squatted behind a copse of snowberry. Julian's three sons were standing out in the knee-high grass, strangely idle, gazing back toward the tents. Bittor had drawn his knife and was clasping it threateningly in his fist. As a girl, she'd had no trouble discouraging his advances. He'd scared her.

One by one, the brothers turned and watched the noisy return of their dogs from the bluff. Above them in the meadow, the flock was stirring, sheep bells clanking.

Dee duckwalked to the edge of the copse, the point of her nightstick scraping the ground. From there she could see Julian seated at a table beneath a tent fly, his hands folded calmly in front of him, his back toward his sons. Cinch was sitting on the table itself. His carbine was trained on the old man's head, but his eyes kept shifting every few seconds to the young men only fifty yards away. Suddenly, he drew a bead on Bittor, who'd taken three defiant steps toward the tent before Cinch's Winchester made him stop short again.

"Sheathe that goddamn blade," Cinch ordered him.

Bittor refused.

"I won't shoot you first," Cinch went on to him, blinking against the risen sun, which had just found his face. "You'll go second, right after your daddy." He brought the muzzle to bear on Julian's head again.

The old man yawned, then lit a cigarette and slowly shook out the match. "Put your knife away," he then said, almost as if it were an afterthought. He would die before he'd reveal the slightest fear. In a perverse way, he was probably enjoying this trial. Yet, he put out his smoke after only a few puffs.

"Nobody moves." Cinch abruptly shaded his eyes with his free hand and peered up at the bluff. "That goes for you, too, Dee. You troop on down here and I got no choice but to shoot Julian. You hear me?"

Dee grimaced, but then called back, "I hear."

Pello spun around, his huge belly swaying, and tried to pick her out of the snowberry. "Kill him now, Dominica," he begged, "before he kills Papa."

Julian had to chuckle at that suggestion. But still he asked, "You got a rifle, Dominica?"

"Just my revolver."

"Don't use it no matter what. You'll wind up hittin' me, and blood shouldn't spill blood." Julian reached behind him for a wineskin hanging on one of the fly poles. It made Cinch startle a little. "Nervous, Cordell?"

Cinch didn't answer. He wiped his face on his shoulder. He was sweating profusely. Dee didn't like that.

She'd never seen him so agitated. His grip on the Winchester was spasmodic.

"Well, Cordell," Julian went on, grinning, "I know you wanna talk. Otherwise, I'd be mutton on the floor of my tent right now. Talk."

The flock began flowing around the three young men.

"Talk, man. You got my attention."

A shot rang out, and a puff of smoke drifted between Cinch and Julian. For an instant, she was sure that he had hit the old man, who was sitting rigidly, his eyelids clenched shut as he continued to grip the wineskin. But then Julian opened his eyes and scooted around on his bench to call out for his sons to show themselves. They were down in the grass. After several seconds, they all raised their heads, Bittor about ten feet distant from the others. She saw what had happened. He had tried to make the aspens, hoping to outflank Cinch through the confusion and dust of the sheep.

Incredibly, Bittor then started to crawl with the same intent, and Cinch roared, "This is for you, Uncle Howard!"

Dee heard the bullet sizzle through the grass, then thud into something. Bittor didn't move, the side of his face pressed against the earth. Dee drew her revolver, although for the first time ever it felt puny in her hand. "If he's hit, you're going down the hill with me, Cinch Holland!" she shouted.

But Bittor slowly sat up, and Julian laughed with boisterous relief. His laugh swiftly died. "Don't do that again," he cried to his sons. "All you stand up and stay together. This is a cattleman here. We're dealin' with a cattleman this mornin'!"

They obeyed.

"He shot one, Papa," Pello said, pointing at a bloodied ewe lying still in a patch of iris.

"You like mutton?" Julian asked Cinch.

"I don't even like lamb."

"Well, you just bought yourself a freezer full of mutton."

"Sold," Cinch said grimly, "as long as you tell me

what the deal was between Augie Dietz and you.''

Julian coaxed a long squirt of paisano into his open mouth, then swallowed. ''What's in it for me if I do?''

''For one thing, none of your boys winds up with a bullet in him.''

''You wouldn't kill like this. That'd be too cold even for a Holland.''

''Julian,'' Dee called down from the bluff, ''don't count on it.'' *A good man on the worst day of his life.* The sun might set this evening on Cinch Holland's worst day. He'd already come within a hairbreadth of shooting Bittor. She had no idea what he was thinking, and that scared her as much as anything.

The old man ran his eyes over the snowberry, trying to find her, but she decided to stay down. ''I see nothin' in it for me, my family, Dominica.''

''How about ending the feud?'' Dee said. ''That's something.''

Julian turned back to Cinch. ''This possible?''

''Christ, you old son of a bitch—you already offered that once, then set my ass up.''

Julian shrugged, then repeated, ''Is it possible? An end is all I ever wanted, one way or another.''

''Meanin' me destroyed or not destroyed?'' Cinch asked.

''Either's fine with me.''

''How fuckin' generous.'' Cinch paused to check on the whereabouts of Julian's sons, then said, ''I think there's a way we can make an end. But I want to hear some damn convincin' talk first.''

Julian had some more paisano, then said, his voice nearly expressionless, ''Nino and Pello were over in Gold Mountain a couple weeks ago, havin' a drink. They heard Augie Dietz talkin' against you.''

''He hates your guts, Holland,'' Nino said with immense satisfaction from the midst of the flock, which had finally settled down after the shooting and started grazing again. ''He told me you treat him like his darkey.''

Pello then piped up. ''Augie said that for ten bucks

he'd monkeywrench you and blame it on the tree-huggers."

That made sense of the disabling of Cinch's tractor, the cutting of his fence. Prepared to hit the nuclear testing site, Eric Brenner would have never risked arrest over something so niggling.

"So," Julian said, "I invited Dietz up to our place for a drink. It was true enough, what Nino and Pello heard. He had bad feelin's for you. Said he wouldn't mind seein' you brought down a peg. We drank, we chatted. Dietz said you ranchers were gettin' ready to cull the mustang herd. He said this was wrong."

Cinch shook his head, exasperated. "You shoulda seen him that night up at the spring. I couldn't stop him from shootin'."

"I asked if he was willin' to testify against you guys. He said no, he didn't want to do that. But he'd put together the evidence. For a price. You mind if I get myself some breakfast?"

Dee watched Julian rise and start to shuffle over to an ice chest, but then Cinch snapped for him to sit again. "How much?"

"Five thousand dollars."

"For doin' what?" Cinch asked.

"Stealin' your handgun and droppin' it near the dead horses up there on the mountain. You go to jail, lose your grazin' permits."

And the Arraches would recover the allotments they'd lost to the Hollands because of the Taylor Grazing Act, Dee surmised. It was the kind of thing Julian would do without batting an eye. He and every Basco in the West would consider it to be nothing less than poetic justice.

Cinch had been silent for some seconds. "So that's why you had me up to your place that evenin' after the horse killin'—so Pancake would have to verify in a court of law that I didn't have my service revolver no more."

Julian nonchalantly dipped his head.

"Christ, man," Cinch said, "if what you're sayin's

true, you knew from the get-go Augie kilt Reckling and the Chinaman.''

"It wasn't our affair.''

Cinch gestured with the butt of the Winchester toward the bluff. "Your own cousin works for the BLM.''

"If Dominica has hired out to the devil, that's her affair.''

Dee smirked. But then it sank in: Dietz had indeed dropped Cinch's revolver, but in a place that had better served his determination to stake out all of his Carlin Trend discovery without interference from Milton Kwak.

Cinch then said, "Augie'd never do that.''

"He did it,'' Julian said.

"Bullshit. He'd know how word gets 'round. He has to live here. If he crossed me, that'd be the end of Pinyon County for him. All the ranchin' folks would be against him.''

"Ah, but that's where you're wrong, Cordell. Dietz don't figure he has to live here. He says he has this big deal in the works that'll make him rich. He wants to go away as soon as he signs the papers, start a whole new life where people respect him. Montana, someplace.''

Cinch didn't ask what kind of deal, instead he gazed up toward Dee. He looked enraged, scarcely able to sit still. She thought that he was going to bolt for the valley, but instead he said to Julian's sons, "Okay—here's the only chance you got to free your daddy before I lose my goddamn temper. . . . ''

CHAPTER**EIGHTEEN**

Augie Dietz spent five restless minutes hovering over the jukebox in the back of the Snake Pit, searching for a title as jubilant as his mood. But he knew all the tunes, and they were too full of woe, wasted chances, and heartache to suit him, so he spun away and danced to his own inner music—fiddles and drums, he heard inside his head—all the way over to the bar, where he slid onto a stool and exulted, "Two million dollars, Charlie!"

"What?"

"It's walkin' through that door any minute with my name on it!"

"Sure, Aug," the bartender said, pouring him a draft.

"Don't 'sure' me like that, Charlie."

"Okay."

"You know why it's mine and not yours?"

"No, Aug."

" 'Cause you and every other stupid son of a bitch in this valley don't have a lick of imagination. You saw a wasteland, and I saw gold tricklin' out of a heap of earth. I saw the land as somethin' to utilize, fully, and you saw it as somethin' to let cows crap on."

"Don't own no cows myself, Aug," Charlie said, setting the glass in front of Augie.

"Then you're a cut above the rest of these ignorant grab-asses. I'll have this beer be my chaser."

"For what?"

"Chivas Regal. Make it a double."

When Charlie hesitated, Augie took out his wallet and slammed it on the bar top. "You wanna see my money first? There. Satisfied, Charlie—or you want me to show green? I got green. Had to pry it outta Cinch Holland's tight fuckin' fist, but I got it!"

"Stop it, Aug. I didn't mean nothin'."

"God, how I hate hearin' that. You meant everythin'. You meant oceans by it. Well, you watch yourself, man. You don't know who you're screwin' with. I'm so goddamn smart I can get away with the same trick twice, and that's the test of a clever man. A man who can cogitate his way out of a bad situation!"

His face blank, Charlie turned and reached for the jewel-shaped Chivas bottle.

"Oh, shit—I'm sorry," Augie said on a burst of good cheer. He couldn't stay mad. Not today. He swung his short legs around to the other side of the stool and squinted into the dimness. "Where the hell is everybody?"

"Don't know." Charlie gave him the whiskey in a snifter. "Sometimes it's just like this."

"That's a sissy glass. Give me another."

Charlie frowned but did what Augie had asked.

"Nothin' against you, Chuck. It's them sissies I hate, even the ones that don't act like sissies. They could make life miserable for a man up there in Carson." Augie accepted a big shot glass full of the rich amber liquid and quickly gulped it down. "Where the fuck *is* everybody? My day to party and there ain't a soul around to impress but you."

"I'm impressed, Aug."

"Go to hell." But then Augie grinned. "Two million. I'd like to dig up my daddy just to see the look on his face when I tell him. He always said I was different from my brothers and sisters, and he didn't mean it nice. He meant it like a cowbird left my egg in his and Mama's nest. But *two* million, Charlie. That'd change his tune, wouldn't it though?"

"You still in touch with any of 'em?"

"Who?"

"Your brothers and sisters?"

"No," Augie said, turning surly again. It felt like a dark stain creeping down over his happiness. "My older sister used to send me a card at Easter while I was up at Carson. No money for cigarettes. No words of her own, 'cept for her names. Both her first name and our stepdaddy's family name, like I was some kind of stranger. I wish my own daddy had lived to see that. All of 'em takin' that motherfucker's name. All 'cept me."

The door could be heard opening, and Augie sprang up from his stool in unbounded expectation. He was not disappointed: Coming toward him were Guillaume Lenoir and a round-faced man with a black, pencil-thin mustache, the mining law attorney he'd retained to handle his end of the negotiations. Both men were in business suits, and each carried an attaché case.

"Aug*ie*," Guillaume said, putting the stress on the second syllable, offering his hand, "how very nice to see you."

Shaking, Augie couldn't help but steal a glance over his shoulder at Charlie. The bartender's jaw had dropped. "Bring a bottle of champagne over to our booth," Augie told him. "Best you got. French."

"Oh no," the attorney said. His name was Jacobs. "Too early for me."

"Just a diet Coke please," Guillaume said.

"Make that two," Jacobs said.

"Be that way." Augie gestured at the booth he'd picked out for the meeting. There was an old Hamm's Beer sign over it that he especially liked, one that continuously scrolled a lake scene somewhere in the northern Rockies. Montana, he wanted to believe. In a few days he'd be there. Hell, he might even buy that very lake. He wanted to live in a green land, not scrub desert.

Then something unpleasant came to him. "You fellas pull up out front at the same time?"

"Uh—no," Jacobs said. "We rode down from Reno together, actually. More time to hammer out some of the details."

Guillaume added, "Yes, it was enjoyable to have company on the long drive for once."

Augie didn't like the two of them getting chummy. Jacobs was his man, and he wanted nothing to blur that distinction.

"There are a few changes we should consider before signing," the lawyer said, snapping open his case and grabbing a copy of the contract. Two inches thick. One inch per million. "Now, Guillaume here has prevailed upon me to look upon some of the compensation in a different light—"

"No," Augie said.

Both men gaped at him, then Jacobs took a sip of Coke and asked, "I beg your pardon, Mr. Dietz?"

"I want no changes this late. You take it in the ass when you agree to last-minute things."

Jacobs was clearly frustrated, but he glanced to Guillaume. The geologist finally put on a conciliatory smile and said, "I will have to advise my superiors at Thunder Bay. Perhaps we can meet again in the morning."

Augie could tell that the Canadian was nonplussed, but that only gave him greater pleasure in saying, "Today. We both sign today, or it's off."

Jacobs looked like he was going to faint, but Guillaume got up, excused himself, and went into the back hall for the phone. Before Jacobs could say anything, Augie splashed him full in the face with his Chivas.

The attorney sat petrified, the whiskey trickling off his chin.

Augie gave him the stare. "Don't you never buddy up to the other side. Not as long as you're workin' for me, mister. You understand?"

Jacobs's nod was almost imperceptible, but it was still a nod, and Augie chuckled amiably as the lawyer wiped himself with his handkerchief, "Sorry, but some things can really set me off. I kilt a man once just 'cause somethin' set me off. And yes, that's an old bullet hole you see under my eye. If I'm gonna get cut down, I want it in the face. Not behind my back."

Five minutes later, Guillaume returned and sat. He bit his lower lip, then said, "It's a deal."

"Yeah!" Dietz pumped his fist as if he were shooting dice.

"We will require a notary public."

Augie had anticipated this. Dixie Russell sold real estate part-time and was a notary on the side. "I'll have one here in no time." Then he ordered Charlie to call her for him. The bartender got right to it, which gave Augie a feeling of satisfaction so intense he giggled.

"She comin'," Charlie soon reported.

"Good," Augie said. "Bring that champagne even if these two bastards don't want some." He could tell that the Frenchman didn't like being called a bastard, which made the moment all the more fun. August Dietz was going to test every prerogative two millions dollars could buy. "Like hell I'm going to let this day pass without poppin' me a cork—"

Bittor and Pello Arrache had stepped inside. They waited at the entry, letting their eyes adjust to the gloom.

At last, Bittor led the way over to the booth. Both of the brothers smelled of sheep and wood smoke.

"Hello, boys," Augie said, "want you to meet some business associates of mine."

"Come with us," Bittor ordered.

Augie couldn't believe his ears. The tone. The Basque son of a bitch thought he was talking to the old Augie. "What—?"

"Stand up."

"You get the fuck outta here," Dietz said, jabbing his forefinger toward the door. "Tell your old man he can keep his lousy five grand." Nobody talked to him like that anymore.

Pello gripped Dietz's left forearm. He moved swiftly for a fat man.

"Damn you," Augie said, sliding his right hand down into his boot for the .25 automatic he'd concealed there ever since Olin Peters had seen him take it from his Levi's pocket. He wanted nobody to know what to expect from him. The little pistol was almost high enough to fire off a round when Bittor planted a sheep knife in the back of Augie's left hand, pinning it to the table.

He screamed, more from fright than pain, and his automatic flew into Jacobs's lap. The lawyer brushed it off him as if it were a rattlesnake.

Augie's vision began to gray as he focused on the big knife jutting from the back of his hand.

Bittor yanked it out.

Curiously, there was little blood, and Augie wanted to make a jest about it to Guillaume, who still sat white-faced across from him. But then he realized that his nose was bent against the table and he was gasping.

He'd passed out, not for long—for he felt the two brothers take hold of him and jostle him toward the door. He struggled once, flailing his legs at them, but the brothers just wrenched his arms farther up behind his back. The pain completely took his breath away for several seconds.

Lady Luck had him at last. But if given the chance, he'd gouge out her eyes and leave the whole world blind.

They met Dixie Russell in the parking lot, and Augie raised his slumped head long enough to laugh in her startled face and say, "Born to lose, Dixie Mae. But I'm goin' out shittin' on all you!"

After Bittor and Pello had started down the mountain in the Arraches' old Ford stake truck, Dee decided to make her presence weigh more heavily on Julian and Cinch. At first, she hadn't wanted to accidentally set them off, but over time she grew afraid of what they might do unless convinced that she was ready to jump in.

The waiting was taking its toll on the two men, Cinch especially.

She climbed down the bluff to a flat-topped boulder on the edge of the meadow. This perch was high enough to be out of the dust raised by the sheep but close enough for her to clearly see the expressions on the faces of the two men at the table—and for them to see hers. She sat with her legs swinging over the edge, her revolver holstered but the safety snap conspicuously undone.

Julian had insisted that Nino stay behind. The family was losing a day's work, and the old man ordered his youngest son to start inoculating. The change in weather had left some of the sheep with a form of pneumonia. Hacking coughs and snotty noses. They bleated pathetically at the stab of the needle. She was only glad that it was too late in the season for castrating the lambs. The most efficient means was for the sheepherder to bite off the testicles with his teeth, take a swallow from the wineskin, and go on to the next lamb.

Cinch and Julian had given up trying to talk to each other, except for an occasional exchange of grunts. At one point, the old man blamed cattle for all the deerflies this year. As if on cue, a buzzing, biting swarm found Dee, and she swatted and cursed until it drifted on.

By eleven-thirty, with still no sign of the Arraches' truck, she surmised that Bittor and Pello hadn't found Dietz at home.

A golden eagle flapped down into the aspens. To feast on the dead leppie, no doubt. The sunlight was hot, and she began to regret having given up the partial shade of the snowberry copse.

"Tine to eat," Julian announced. He was sounding more Basque by the minute. Probably just to goad Cinch. Another couple of hours and his accent would rival Gabrielle's. Cinch let the old man rise and go to the ice chest. "You wanna bite, Cordell?"

"What you got?"

"Homemade sausage."

"Hell no," Cinch said, shifting his carbine around to keep it trained on Julian. "God only knows what you put in it. What else?"

"Cheese."

"What kind?"

"The best—sheep's milk."

Cinch's mouth curled in distaste.

Over the last hour, Dee had sensed a gradual but steep plunge in his mood. He was morose and withdrawn. She almost preferred the bluster that had made him warn her to stay away from her Bronco and its radio, and then shout at Bittor and Pello, as they departed for Augie's shanty, that "bringin' any more law than what we already got up here will only earn your daddy a bullet."

The old man came back to the table with a sandwich. "Don't know what you're missin'," he said, chewing contentedly. "You don't eat, you don't shit. You don't shit, you die."

But Cinch didn't want to talk about health. "Don't try to be sociable, Julian. You set me up. You used my own hired hand to try to land me in the joint. You people would stop at nothin'."

"Same as you people."

"How can you say that?"

"You took the bread and meat out of our mouths by pushin' Congress to go with the Taylor Act."

"We were first on the land."

"No, the Shoshone were. You were second. We were third. What's the big difference between second and third? Except you drove the Indians off the springs."

Cinch laughed sardonically. "Since when'd a Basco give a shit about the warhoops? I heard how you beat ol' Dewey James half to death over takin' a sheep that hard winter. What was it? Sixty-nine, and the snow was chest-high everywheres."

"Dewey took without askin'," Julian said. "Had he asked, there woulda been no beatin'."

"And no meat in his springhouse neither."

Dee clapped her hands together at slow tempo and kept applauding until both men were staring up at her, questioningly. "Don't you two see what you're doing? What all you graziers in the valley are doing? You're playing the same old card of cowman against sheepman while Augie Dietz gets ready to trump you both. He's set to bring in mining before some tougher environmental laws go into effect. Big-scale stuff. Shovels the size of Volkswagens. Ore trucks as big as tugboats. And these'll scrape this range clean of vegetation for as far as you can see." She paused as the breeze rose, cooling her flushed skin and rattling the aspen leaves behind her.

"Oh, the mining company will promise to plant native species when they're all done. But you both know how that goes. Most plantings fail. And what ground moisture will those species have to get established? The miners will suck this valley bone-dry to soak their leach heaps. You'll both wind up hauling in water for your stock. Might as well pour Perrier in the trough for them, for what it'll cost."

The men, even Nino, who with syringe in hand had been gathering a breakaway gang of sheep, went silent. Out of this lull came the throaty sound of the stake truck laboring up the far side of the bluff.

Cinch and Julian stood, as did Dee a moment later.

The truck came into view through the trees, rocking over the rough road, leaving a pall of blue-gray exhaust among the white trunks. The Ford dipped down into the meadow, and Dee could see Augie Dietz slumped on the cab seat between Pello, who was driving, and Bittor.

Dietz glanced up as the Ford slowed to a stop near the tents. His face was ashen. Dee thought that he was sick until Bittor dragged him out the passenger door and she saw the red bandanna wrapped thickly around Dietz's left hand.

"What happened to you, Augie?" she asked, frowning.

He shifted woozily toward the sound of her voice, then smiled as he caught sight of her on the boulder. "Got my ass kidnapped, Miss Dee."

She jumped down off the boulder and went across the meadow, wading through the sheep. Dietz had a point, which his defense would latch on to—unless she quashed it now. "You're under arrest for the murders of Jack Reckling and Milton Kwak. . . . " He had no reaction. "Cinch Holland, as a reserve deputy, ordered Bittor and Pello to arrest you on the basis of posse comitatus. You know what that is?"

Dietz went on smiling in the same self-pitying way, but then nodded. Of course this jailhouse lawyer knew. The power of the sheriff or his officers to enlist any male adult to enforce the law, as needed. It was meaningless in urban areas, but a common-enough practice on the range that it might work. Might.

If Cinch had any problem with this tack, he kept it to himself. Dee saw that he'd lifted his Winchester off Julian and leveled it on Dietz.

There was still one huge fly in the ointment. "What happened to your hand, Augie?"

"Paper cut, Miss Dee. Off a two-million-dollar contract."

She tried to hold his moist, evasive gaze. "You sure that's how you want it reported?"

His eyes shifted to the two Arrache brothers flanking him, first Pello and then Bittor, who glared back at him, stone-faced. "Yeah. Poor, shit-ass loser like me oughta know better'n to put his hopes in contracts. If you're gonna get screwed, get screwed early. You suffer hope less that way."

"If you were abused," Dee pressed, "I want to hear about it now."

Augie didn't reply.

"Cinch," Dee then said, resting her hand on the backstrap of her revolver for emphasis as she stepped up to Julian, "start walking out into the meadow."

"I'll hang close to you, if you don't mind."

"I do mind. Start walking . . . *now*."

Cinch sighed, but then broke away from Julian and began ambling toward the grass, loosely holding the carbine by the barrel over his shoulder. He insisted on passing right between Bittor and Nino, but Julian growled for his sons to stay as they were. Cinch had just kicked at a ewe that was too slow getting out of his way when Julian called to him, "Does this mean the feud's ended, Holland?"

Cinch halted but didn't turn. "Christ, Julian—it's been over for years. We just been too stupid to see it."

"What d'you mean?"

"There's no profit left in what we do. I been survivin' on credit, and you on family charity. We got nothin' left to fight over." Then he walked on toward the bluff.

Julian stared at Dee's uniform a moment, then asked, "Isn't what Holland just done kidnappin', too?"

She nodded.

"Well, I won't ask for no charges. He's a son of a bitch, but I can understand a son of a bitch like him. He works with his hands. It's those people from 'Frisco you got stayin' at the Pyrennes who get me. They work with their tongues . . . like French *putas*." Julian turned to his sons. "You heard Holland. It's over. Everythin' what happened here stays here."

"See you later, Julian . . . boys."

"The hell you say, Dominica," Julian griped. "You never come 'round. You're sagebrushed, that's what I think. You spend too much time out alone."

"I like being alone."

"Isn't that just what I said? You're gone in the head. Ruined for men." Julian paused. "*Txarrie boda* is next week." Literally, this meant "pig wedding." The ritualized slaughter of swine for ham and sausage. Blood and wine again, as with the castrating of the lambs.

"I'll be there."

"You're just sayin'."

Dee firmly took hold of Dietz by the right arm, and he went along without a word. She wanted to handcuff and search him right away but figured the more urgent need was to put as much distance between Cinch and the Arraches as she could. If she knew Bittor, he'd work himself into a lather as soon as the danger faded. Cinch had sullied his father's dignity, if only slightly, and no doubt there were guns in the camp.

" 'Cuse me, Miss Dee," Augie said in a breathless whisper.

"What?"

"Gonna flash."

"Do it." She stood back from him in case it was a ruse, but then he proved that he really was. Vomiting improved his color and humor, and he grinned as he stood straight again. Dee could see where a trickle of blood had dried on his left wrist. Damn the Arraches—they'd cut him and that might throw the entire prosecution onto the trash heap. It seemed hopeless, trying to adhere to perfect justice in an imperfect world. "Did Bittor or Pello ask you anything?"

"No, Miss Dee. They didn't seem all that interested in me. Story of my life."

Cinch was waiting for them at the edge of the aspens. He shook his head at Augie, who laughed derisively, hatefully.

"I'll be there, Aug, the night you go out," Cinch said. "I'll be up there at the statehouse to watch. For Olin."

"It'll never go that far, Cinch. Believe me. It'll end right here with the west wind in my face."

That boast only increased Dee's worry over what a muddled and violent arrest would do to the case. Of course, had Bittor and Pello not taken Augie, Julian might now be slumped dead over that camp table. She needed to question Dietz as soon as possible on the off chance that he might confess. A confession would go a long way toward counterbalancing the legal mess she'd been handed once again.

She guided Dietz through the wild rose to a rock ledge, where she spread him against it and then frisked him as Cinch stood by.

"Just like them walls, Miss Dee," he muttered, gazing at the drab stone a few inches in front of his face. "Three walls of concrete. And then one wall of iron bars. I won't go back, you know."

"Is that a threat, Augie?" Dee asked, swinging his left hand behind his back and cuffing it. His right hand followed, and he was restrained. "I don't like being threatened."

"You know," Augie went on, "it's sad when everythin' you say is taken as a threat."

Each taking one of Dietz's arms, Cinch and she walked him down the north slope of the bluff. Through the foliage off to the east she could see the golden eagle hunkering over the calf's carcass, ready to fly, although the black eye fixed on her was piercingly hostile.

They deposited Augie in the backseat of the Bronco,

and Cinch said with a satisfied smile, "Well done, if I do say so myself."

"What d'you mean?"

"Bringin' in Augie like I did. Din't want you gettin' hurt. He's a rabid little piece of shit."

And then Dee realized what Cinch had been thinking from the moment he left the line shack that morning. "I'm twice as rabid as he is," she said, seething. He'd done all of this, jeopardizing the case against Augie, out of some misguided notion that she needed protecting. "Goddamn you, Cordell," she exploded, "don't you ever step in for me again!"

"Why not?"

"Because I'm *good* at this, you patronizing jerk!"

He looked shocked. "I was only tryin' to keep you safe and sound, lady. . . . " And then he increased her anger by trying to pass it all off as a joke. "And see maybe if Augie might not take a couple of Arraches along with him to hell."

"Get in the back," Dee snapped, swapping his carbine for her revolver, which would be less unwieldy for him in the backseat. "Sit directly behind me." So Dietz couldn't kick or spit at her, should his good humor evaporate.

"What about my pickup?" Cinch asked.

"I'll bring you back for it later."

She tucked the Winchester under the front seat, then turned the Bronco around and started down the mountain. Checking her rearview mirror twice in the same quarter mile, she was glad not to see the Ford stake truck following. Julian had prevailed over his eldest son. This time. God only knew what Bittor would become when the old man was gone.

"Augie, why don't you Mirandize yourself?" she said, taking out the small tape recorder she kept in the glove compartment and punching the On button.

Deitz chuckled. "You're somethin' else, Miss Dee. I wouldn'ta turned out so bad had I teamed up with a woman like you."

"Don't kid yourself. A couple years saddled with me

and you would've given Charlie Manson a run for it. Go ahead, read yourself your rights.''

''August Earl Deitz,'' he said in a mock-solemn voice, ''you have the right to remain silent. Anythin' you say can and will be used against you in a court of law. You have the right to an attorney—'' Then he giggled hysterically before suddenly turning quiet. Through the mirror she saw him staring sullenly out his window. His look made her throat tighten.

''Go ahead, Aug.''

''Oh, hell,'' he said, ''just tell me what you wanna know.''

''Why'd you kill Jack Reckling and Milton Kwak?''

Augie was quiet a few seconds more. She could see him smiling quizzically. ''You want to understand or just *know*, Miss Dee?''

''Understand, Augie,'' she said as gently as she could, given the disgust she felt for him.

He paused. ''All my life I been within an inch of makin' it. Almost had the family spread, but got jewed out of that. Almost won a poker tournament over Amarillo Slim, but my cards turned sour on the last big hand. And now I almost had the biggest gold mine in the world, but a Chinaman horned in and ruint it all for me. I'm not complainin', though. Not really.'' And then his voice turned dreamy, almost otherworldly. ''I guess I'm finally acceptin' who I am and what I gotta do. There's no good or bad. There's just where you are.''

Far down the mountain, Dee could see a plume of dust rising from where she knew the lower road to be.

''So Reckling died,'' she said, trying to sound matter-of-fact about it, not accusatory, ''because he was guilty of being at the wrong place at the wrong time.''

''That's right,'' Augie said, seizing on the idea with enthusiasm. ''Just like me. Story of my life, sister. Amen.''

''Why'd you drag me in on it?'' Cinch asked, clearly struggling with his anger. ''Why'd you have to drop my revolver on the flats?''

Augie shifted. Sitting on the handcuffs was giving

him some discomfort. "You know, I learned somethin' about the law when I was just a kid, Cinch. Got sent away to the youth authority camp for a burglary I din't even do. The law is just politics fancied up in a black robe. So, it needs a suspect right now. The real one'd be nice, but any suspect'll do in a pinch, 'specially if the public's puttin' the heat on."

Dee couldn't argue with that. Not entirely. "Why'd you kill Olin Peters?" she asked as blithely as if inquiring the name of the reform school he'd attended.

"Quit squirmin' and answer her," Cinch said hotly.

But Augie just laughed.

Then there was a smack, and Dee twisted around in time to see the side of Dietz's head bounce off the window, then sag so that his chin came to rest against his chest. Blood dribbled onto his shirtfront from his nose.

Dee hit the brakes so hard both men slid forward on the seat. She swung her nightstick around so that the point was almost touching Cinch's Adam's apple. "Don't you ever touch a prisoner of mine for something like that again!" she cried. "If he tries to kick me, smack him. If he tries to flee, shoot him. But don't touch him otherwise!"

"It's a hard country, Dominica," Cinch said after a bit.

"Yeah, but it's only the people who are cruel."

She drove on, checking her mirror as she accelerated, and Augie sneezed blood onto the glass of the side window. "It's all right, Miss Dee," he drawled, chuckling sadly. "I was born to this, and I'll go out to it. Hell, life'd make no sense if it treated me any other way. But I must confess—I'm sick and tired of swimmin' against the tide."

There was a faint snick from the backseat, and Dee realized that she'd failed to double-lock the cuffs, keeping them from slowly ratcheting tighter around Augie's wrists. "Cuffs hurting you, Augie?"

"Not bad. It's them little thumb cuffs that get to me."

"I refuse to use those."

"Appreciate it."

"What'd you do with the rifle you used on Jack and Milt?"

In the mirror, she saw Dietz glance toward Cinch.

"Augie?" she insisted.

"Buried it with the saddleguns what was used for the horse hunt."

"Where?"

"Cinch's gravel pit, Miss Dee. That's not all. It was his Weatherby magnum. I took it out of Olin's truck." Dietz hunched his shoulders slightly, as if still trying to get comfortable, then settled down again and yawned. "Sure, Cinch, I know I done you dirt. But you never done anythin' for me neither. Know what always got me 'bout you?"

Cinch refused to take the bait.

"You got everythin', and you don't even know it."

Cinch harrumphed.

"Right," Augie rattled on. "Never knew a rich man who din't talk a poor mouth. I'd sell my soul just to show you what nothin' feels like, Cordell Holland. The thirst and hunger of it. The gnawin' in the pit of your guts. But you'll never know 'cause you got it all. A ranch and several other holdin's with water. Best BLM allotment in the county. A boy to carry on your name, to keep the grave from erasin' your face . . ." Then, in a blink, his tone turned ugly, vicious. "A nice plump wife, plus a spare fuck for the line shack."

"Shut up."

"You both gotta forgive my language. I'm just poor white trash. I had ambitions, but I'm done with 'em now. There ain't nothin' I want from this world 'cept a shinin' path out. I'll make it shine, too, even if I got to light the fires myself."

"He's off his nut," Cinch said contemptuously.

Dee let up on the gas pedal. Ahead, dust billowed up from behind the next bend in the road, and then a BLM truck was coming toward her, Reckling's four-wheel drive. Out of habit, she momentarily saw Jack's face behind the wheel, but no—it was Dutch Gundry driving. He was holding the microphone to his mouth. At that instant his voice crackled over the Bronco's radio: "What's goin' on, Laguerre?"

Then Dee's vision went white. As from a far distance, she heard Cinch shout for her to hang on to the wheel. She held it tightly with both hands, strained to bring the road and approaching truck into focus. Something had clawed at the back of her head. Blood was dripping warmly down her collar.

Gundry was coming on fast, flashing his headlights at her.

She started to hit the brakes, but that only made the Bronco fishtail. She quickly eased up before the vehicle plunged off the steep bank.

Glancing in the mirror, she saw Augie flailing at Cinch with the cuffs, which were now attached only to his right wrist.

Something small and silvery clinked against the dashboard, then fell to the floor. A handcuff key.

Gundry's horn was blaring, but she looked back as Cinch drew her revolver from his waistband and tried to ward off the flying cuffs long enough to bring the muzzle to bear on Augie. Cinch's face and hands were nicked and bleeding.

Then Augie had a grip on the gun, too, and the two men were rocking back and forth, each trying to wrench it from the other.

Dee was swinging her nightstick over the back of her seat at Dietz's head when the Bronco was jarred violently. Metal screaked against metal, and the truck horn wailed past. She had sideswiped Gundry, but before she could see how he had fared a gun report deafened her and smoke was wafting around the inside of the cab.

She dropped her nightstick.

Cinch had let go of the revolver and was gripping his right shoulder. Blood showed between his fingers. Laughing, Augie reached over him and unlatched the door.

Dee jinked the wheel, trying to prevent what was coming. But it was no good. Augie grabbed the revolver

out of Cinch's limp hands, kicked the door all the way
open, and pushed Holland out.

Then, grinning in the rearview mirror, Augie took aim
at Dee. She reached for the Winchester on the floor. Too
late for the carbine. Another blast filled the cab, and
windshield glass crazed from the impact of the bullet.
She tumbled out her door and rolled. She kept expecting
to stop, but the downward force continued to somersault
her along. Then she was airborne, raking her hands
through the air. She landed a second later on scree, slid
all the way around on the loose rock, and came to rest.

CHAPTER**NINETEEN**

Dee raised her head, hoping to see the Bronco tumbling down the slope. But the dust from her fall cleared, and she glimpsed the vehicle far below on a hairpin curve, speeding down the road toward the valley and freedom. Dietz had managed to scramble between the bucket seats and take the wheel.

Her elbows were badly skinned. The inside of her mouth tasted as if she'd been sucking on pennies. She ran a dusty forefinger over her tongue and came away with blood.

Dutch Gundry leered over the edge of the roadbed, his revolver down at his side. "You all right, Laguerre?"

She braced herself, then slowly stood. Pain shot up her spine from her knees, but she could walk. Haltingly, she began trudging up the talus, the loose rock flowing against her with each step. "Where's Holland?"

Gundry half turned to look. "Sittin' on the bank back there, holdin' his shoulder."

"He's been shot."

"Oh, for chrissake," Gundry said, running heavily off to help.

Dee reached the road and plodded up to Reckling's truck, then rested a minute with her hands on her sore knees.

Gundry had somehow kept it from going off the side but had overcompensated and bashed the left front against the cut in the hillside. Still, the engine was running. Taking a deep breath, she got inside and drove up to the two men. Gundry was kneeling beside Cinch, helping him stem the flow of blood from the bullet wound with direct pressure. The hands of both men were stained a rich, arterial red.

"Stay here," Dee said through the open side window. "I'll turn around and come back for you."

Gundry nodded, but Cinch's expression remained blank, his face the color of lemon peel.

There was an alarming screak from the power steering as Dee made a U-turn in the first wide spot she came to. Driving back to the men, she made up her mind that she'd smack Gundry if he tossed off anything sarcastic in her direction. She was probably fired anyway.

But Gundry seemed more concerned than angry. "Scoot on over, Laguerre," he said as he helped Cinch inside. "You're in no shape to drive." She started to protest, but he went on, "I mean it. You're shaken up, even if you don't feel it yet."

She slid across the seat and pressed her clean handkerchief to Cinch's shoulder. The bleeding had almost stopped, but it scared her how he now looked: His skin was nearly colorless and his eyes were dull. But when Gundry, setting off again, said that he was bound directly for the hospital in Tonopah, Cinch stirred and said in a dazed voice, "No—follow Dietz."

"We'll get him sooner or later, Holland," Gundry said, "and that bleedin' could start anytime again."

Cinch shook his head weakly but adamantly. "Make sure he don't go up to the ranch."

"We'll see," Gundry said, then grabbed the radio microphone and advised the sheriff's dispatcher of the situation.

But when they reached a valley overlook near Highway 95, it was obvious by the long skein of dust rising in the south that a vehicle was racing up Cayuse Mountain Road. Dee found Jack Reckling's binoculars in the glove box and handed them to Gundry.

She held the wheel steady while he focused on the distant speck.

"Crap," he finally said.

Cinch realized as quickly as she did that it was the Bronco. Eyes squinched with fear, he moaned, "Dietz is over the edge. He'll hurt my people." Then his left hand reached unsteadily across Dee and grasped Gundry by the wrist. "Get me home, mister. Don't fuck 'round and just get me home to my family."

The agent shook him off and took hold of the microphone again. "Pinyon S.O.," he transmitted, "this is BLM Gundry."

"Go ahead with your traffic."

"Get the Holland Ranch on the landline and—"

Cinch wrenched the mike from Gundry. "Tell Rowena to get everybody inside. Lock the doors and keep Augie Dietz out. No matter what, Marlene. Use Cody's twenty-two if she's gotta. Just keep the son of a bitch outta the house."

The dispatcher acknowledged, and Cinch slumped back in the seat, his eyes closed and his left hand tight on his wounded shoulder once more. Dee added the pressure of her hand to his, squeezed reassuringly. "How'd you know where to find us?" she asked Gundry.

"Actually, I was doin' a favor for the sheriff's office . . ." He passed a line of three tour buses, then swerved back into his lane as the horn of an onrushing truck blatted at him. "Pancake's out of the area today, and there was a report of a stabbin' in the Snake Pit. I was in Holland Station—lookin' for you, Laguerre," he added in a spurt of ill temper, "so I volunteered to help out. One thing led to another, and I learned from the locals that the Arraches probably took Dietz up to their sheep camp."

Dee asked, "Is the sheriff rolling a backup unit from Gold Mountain?"

"As soon as possible." Gundry checked the rearview mirror for the cruiser, which would be coming out of the north. "No sign of him yet."

"Augie Dietz did it," Dee said. Time to get this out of the way. "We got a confession."

Gundry chuckled incredulously. "Oh, come on, Laguerre."

"Just listen to the woman, goddammit," Cinch said. His eyes were still clenched, most likely to keep them from tearing up.

Then, briefly, she told the agent why Reckling, Kwak, and Olin Peters—doubtlessly—had died. Gundry took it in without comment. When Dee was done, he simply loosened his necktie.

As they started up Cayuse Mountain Road, the sheriff's dispatcher's voice came over the airwaves. "I can't raise the ranch on the landline," she advised, sounding apologetic. "Somethin's wrong with the circuit. Still tryin'."

"Goddamn!" Cinch howled. "The son of a bitch cut the wire on me!"

Dee recalled the place where the telephone line swayed low across the dirt road up to the ranch.

She found herself using both hands to pin Cinch back against the seat: Gundry was doing seventy miles an hour over the rutted surface, but Cinch was squirming as if he wanted to crawl out of his window and fly on ahead to his family. Tears had finally collected in the corners of his eyes. He was gnashing his teeth. "Don't let me pass out, Dee. Slap me if you gotta."

"I'll take it for you, Cinch."

"No," he argued, drunkenly almost, "keep me on my feet."

She could forgive his distrust when it came to Cody's safety. But she also sensed that part of this was for Rowena—and, despite herself, it hurt a little. Yet, she murmured some idiocy about everything turning out all right.

She didn't believe that it would. Augie had a big jump on them, and his twisted, jealous words kept coming back to her.

"Here!" Cinch barked. "Here, man!"

Gundry had almost missed the turnoff to the ranch.

Swearing, he skidded in a four-wheel drift, then accelerated up the dirt lane.

When he saw the severed telephone line, Cinch just dropped his head and went motionless.

For a terrifying split second, she thought that the artery had blown out and he was gone. His eyes were that lifeless. But he finally blinked and said, "How many guns you got, Dutch?"

"Just mine. And there's Laguerre's, of course." Gundry hadn't noticed her empty holster, then.

But Cinch volunteered, "I lost Dee's to Augie, guardin' him."

"Christ." Gundry shifted down for the last mile of grade up to the ranch. "We stick together then. The house first, to make sure your family's okay. You got any weapons up there?"

"Just Cody's little twenty-two," Cinch said. His carbine, of course, was now in Dietz's hands as well.

Dee was on the verge of telling Gundry to slow down in case Augie had decided to ambush them—when she saw a black strand of smoke rising from behind the cottonwoods that marked the ranch. "Rowena burning trash today?" Dee asked Cinch.

He gave a dazed shake of his head. "I can threaten to kill Augie, but it don't mean nothin' to him. That's the awful thing of this, Dominica."

Gundry sped through the gate and around to the back side of the house. He bailed out, but then stood staring off toward the barn in amazement. "Jesus!"

Exiting the vehicle on his side, Dee saw where Augie had crashed the Bronco through the corral fence and then into the side of the barn. Flames were wrapping completely around the vehicle. The white paint on the tailgate was bubbling.

Either the collision, with some drums of diesel fuel, or Dietz himself had ignited the fire. It was swiftly enveloping the structure and sending up a pillar of dark, oily smoke that cast the entire ranch into twilight. In the corral itself, Cinch's gelding and Cody's pony had both been shot dead, left to lie side by side.

Turning, Gundry suddenly stiffened and aimed his revolver at the figure in the second-story window.

"Don't!" Dee cried to be heard over the raucous
crackling of the flames. "It's his mother!" Then she
realized that Cinch was nowhere in sight. "Dutch—
Cinch went on inside."

Gundry nodded and led the way to the back door. It
was ajar, and through the crack Dee could see Rowena
sprawled on the linoleum, pieces of a broken chair
strewn all around her.

She was dead—Dee was sure of it, for her eyes were
unseeing slits and her jaw was slack.

Following Gundry inside the kitchen, she noticed that
the doorjamb had been splintered. Dietz had kicked the
latched bolt of the lock right through it.

"See if the woman has a pulse," Gundry said, then
started for the stairs. But Cinch came down them at that
instant, his hand crablike on his shoulder. The wound
had begun to bleed anew from his exertion.

"He's got my boy," he said, his voice disbelieving.
He seemed not to want to glance toward his wife. "Mama's all right, but Dietz got my boy."

Dee found a neck pulse on Rowena, although she
doubted that her breath would have stirred a feather. The
chair had caught her on the right forearm, visibly breaking it, and then, less forcefully, along the side of the
head, opening a shallow gash.

Cinch dropped to his knees and, perhaps not knowing
what he was doing, pushed Dee's ministering hands
away. He cradled his wife's head in his bloody palms.
"Oh, Row . . . Rowena . . ."

"Watch her neck," Dee said. "Easy."

But he ignored her.

"Stop it, Cordell—let go before you hurt her more!"

He stared emptily at her, but then slid his hands into
his armpits.

Dee withdrew to the window. She thought she
glimpsed movement in the willows near the spring, but
then a rising breeze rocked and swayed all the foliage.

Behind her, Gundry said low, "Keep everybody to-

gether in here. I'll have a quick look 'round the yard."
Then he went out, probing the hot, smoky air with his
revolver.

Dee had to touch Cinch's back to get his attention.
His face drifted around toward her, confused and pale.
"Where is Cody's twenty-two?" she asked.

"His bedroom," Cinch said distantly, taking so long
to answer she almost thought he hadn't heard her. But
mention of the boy's name seemed to stir up his panic
all over again.

Rising, he asked, "Where's Gundry?"

"Outside, searching. He wants us to—" But before
she could get out another word Cinch had gone through
the door. She decided not to try to argue him back inside. Instead, she hurried upstairs to Cody's room, hoping to find the rifle on a wall rack. It wasn't.

She reeled, running her eyes over the entire room.

The breeze had shifted, and the smoke from the barn
was gusting past the window screen in patches. It reeked
of burned hay and diesel.

She knelt behind the sill to scan the yard and pasture
below.

Cinch was nowhere to be seen, but Gundry was working carefully along the creek toward the spring-fed pond,
stooping on a knee every few paces to peer under the
dense growth for Dietz's legs. He was chewing furi-
ously. A dribble of tobacco juice spilled down his chin
and went unwiped.

Suddenly, a covey of quail streaked out of the willows
and past the agent. He flinched. Then the smoke closed
around him, and he was gone.

Dee went to the closet door, threw it open.

Standing on her toes, she searched the shelf, saw nothing long enough to hold the rifle except an old pair of
leather chinks that had been shortened to fit Cody.
Rolled up inside them was the single-shot .22.

Her excited hands grabbed it, snapped open the bolt.

Nothing in the chamber.

Holding the rifle between her thighs, she groped along
the shelf for a box of ammunition, then began flinging

the assortment of boxes onto the floor, where she kicked through the debris.

Then, from outside, Gundry's voice stilled her. "Freeze!" he bellowed.

She ran to the window again.

The agent was crouching on one knee at the edge of the pond, clenching his revolver in front of him with both hands. He was aiming into the willows. Miragelike ripples of heat and flying red cinders were flowing around him. "Drop it, man!"

Dietz said something, but she couldn't make out what over the roar of the burning barn.

She saw the hammer on Gundry's revolver creep toward full cock—before catching as he suddenly eased off the pressure.

For some reason, he hesitated.

A report followed, but it was the sharp crack of a carbine. Gundry seemed to fold unnaturally at the base of the spine, then topple backward into the pond, headfirst. He took his revolver under with him.

After a few long moments in which Dee watched, motionless and sickened, he floated up, his empty hands outstretched.

Staggering, she burst into the adjoining room.

Mother Holland was sitting in her chair, immobile as always, staring through the window. Yet, her washed-out eyes seemed to be shrieking, and she was sucking noisily on her underlip.

"Help me, old woman," Dee said, scarcely aware that she was speaking. "Where's Cinch lock up the ammo?"

Seemingly on the verge of saying something, Mother Holland let out a long, sour breath. Then her face lost all expression.

Dee's ears were ringing from shock, the blood pounding in her head. She tossed the rifle onto the old woman's bed and began dumping bureau drawers onto the braided rug. If anything, she'd meant to try to bluff Augie with the unloaded rifle, but that was out of the question now that even a loaded revolver hadn't worked for Gundry. Cody had been taken hostage, as Cinch had said. She could think of no other reason why Gundry would have hesitated. He'd died rather than open fire.

She fisted her hands to keep them from shaking so badly. The contents of the drawers—petticoats, scarves, and hosiery—reeked of moth crystals. Giving up, grabbing the rifle, she headed for the master bedroom.

She no sooner reached it than she heard Cinch saying from below, "You can have me, Aug. It's me you want."

Rushing to the side of the window, she showed as little of her face as needed to gaze down on the pond.

Near it stood Augie Dietz holding Cody under his left arm like a sack of oats. He was clasping the Winchester in his right hand. One of Dee's handcuffs was still attached to that same wrist: He hadn't recovered the key from the floor of the Bronco, then. The boy was gagged with a bandanna, probably the one Dietz had used to bind up his injured hand, and his arms and legs were bound with a rolled-up bedsheet.

"I want it all," Augie said with a twitching grin to Cinch, who at that instant stepped into view from the direction of the barn. Dee couldn't see his face, but his shoulders were rounded from exhaustion and loss of blood. He stopped about thirty feet shy of Dietz, then swayed as if the smoky breeze would push him over at any second.

"All what, Aug?" Cinch asked wearily.

"*This!*" Dietz cried, indicating the entire ranch with a wave of the carbine. He had pivoted toward Cinch, and Dee could now see the grips of her revolver jutting from his waistband.

"Take it," Cinch said as if flabbergasted anyone would want his burdens. "I'll sign over the deed right now."

That only further enraged Dietz. "You think you're bein' smart?"

"Aug—"

"Is this some kinda joke to you!" Augie jerked the butt of the carbine at the corpse behind him in the pond. Gundry was slowly sinking; only his heels, his buttocks, and the very top of his head were still showing above the water.

"God, no." Cinch held out his arms as if he ached to take hold of his son. Blood had now soaked his shirt-sleeve all the way down to the cuff. "I'm serious as I can be. This spread don't mean a thing. The herd neither."

A hard, victorious look came into Augie's face. "Then what does mean somethin', Cinch?" When Holland obviously sensed where this question might lead and kept quiet, Dietz dropped the Winchester to the ground. He whipped out the revolver and pressed the muzzle to Cody's temple. "Am I gettin' close?"

Cinch started to surge forward, but Augie backed him off by thumb-cocking the hammer. Now only the faintest bit of pressure would send the firing pin against the cartridge primer.

Suddenly, from across the corral, came a crash and then a blizzard of sparks as the barn roof collapsed. Dietz had startled, and Dee looked in horror at Cody's head, sure that the sound had made Dietz pull the trigger.

But the boy was unharmed for the moment.

The smoke returned, sifted over the spring in ragged waves.

She turned back into the master bedroom. It was small but had a fireplace. There was no gun cabinet, just a desk in the far corner piled high with what she recognized to be BLM and EPA documents. She leaned the rifle against the wall. The pencil drawer was locked, which gave her a small feeling of hope that this is where Cinch stored ammunition.

A moment ago, she'd come within a breath of asking him, but then had realized that this would be the last straw to set Augie off.

She hastened over to the brick hearth and returned to the desk with a brass fire poker trembling in her hand. While she pried, she could hear Dietz and Cinch talking outside. An eerie lack of anger marked their words, as if both men had made up their minds that this would not end well—and Dietz especially simply wanted it to run its violent course and be over.

"It's too late for gifts, Cinch," Augie said. "I'm sick and tired of this world. The deck's always been stacked against me, and I'm tired of that most of all. They'll put me away this time, then take years before executin' me. It's thinkin' on that long wait up at Carson what settles it for me."

"What do I have to do?" Cinch asked. Begging. Close to sobbing.

Then Augie said with a chilling affability, "Nothin', hoss. Not a goddamn thing. Just relax."

The entire front panel of the drawer gave with a groan of oak, and Dee stared down into a jumble of pens, paper clips, condoms, erasers, and past due notices. She dumped the entire mess onto the floor and began sifting through it with both hands.

"We come into the world to learn, Cinch," Augie drawled on. "That's why the land, the range, don't mean as much as they say. It's just a blank slate to be writ on. School supplies. Now, I was born to teach—and din't even realize it till today."

"Teach what, Aug?"

"Why, what it's like to have nothin'. To look forward to nothin'."

Dee found a cartridge. But it was too large. Winchester .30-.30.

"I do know what it's like, Augie," Cinch pled. "I've learnt these past years. Bein' in debt. That's less than nothin'."

"Oh bullshit, Cinch. The world never even gave me the chance to go into debt, and that's the honest truth. . . ."

She almost missed them, they were so small. Two .22 long rifle shells. Her hand flew to them.

"Augie," Cinch said, his voice breaking, "don't hurt my boy. That's no way to get back at me. It's me you want."

"It's the only way to get through to you, Cinch. I'm sorry, but you're just that far gone in your pride."

Dee crawled back to the window, jacking one of the two cartridges into the chamber as she went. The other she kept in her mouth so she wouldn't have to dig frantically in a pocket for it. Just as she began to rise into the opening, a bullet smacked through the screen, passing like a hot breath a few inches above her head.

"Damn you, Miss Dee!" Augie ranted. "Don't think I ain't seen and heard you up there!" He then grunted as if trying to adjust Cody's weight on his hip. "I tried to end this civilized, God help me—but you sons of bitches won't let me!"

"Stay down, Dee!" Cinch cried.

But she saw no reason to do that. The boy would ultimately die if she did that.

She sprang up and steadied the rifle on the sill.

Dietz was clutching Cody to his chest as a shield and glaring with one eye shut over the revolver barrel up at her window. "Goddamn you there, Miss Dee—I tried, but you just won't let me!"

He fired again, and shards of glass fell from the panes above her and danced on the sill around her face. Ignoring them, she rested the open sights on Augie's nose, but the top of Cody's head kept getting in the way.

Then smoke scudded past, blotting out everything.

When it was gone, Augie was bringing the muzzle of the revolver back toward Cody's head.

Dee squeezed the trigger. The report sounded tiny. She raised up to look below, but more smoke was rolling over the spring. Immediately, she spat her last cartridge into her palm and reloaded as she ran down the stairs.

Outside, the sunlight was dim and sulfurous. The fire sounded like a tornado, so intense were the flames. But still she quietly crossed the yard toward the pond.

She found Cinch first, prostrate on the ground.

For an insane moment, she thought that she'd somehow hit him. But she counted no wounds other than the shoulder one Augie had caused in the Bronco, which had finally overcome him.

She moved on through the smoke toward the pond, gazing with smarting eyes over the rifle barrel.

Cody was on the ground, too. Beyond him, there was no sign of Dietz.

She knelt, then hesitated, afraid of what she would see when she rolled him over. But then he flopped onto his back by himself and looked up at her, bug-eyed. She lowered the bandanna gag around his neck, pressed her fingers against his lips before he could cry out. "Go back to your daddy and hold this sheet against his hurt shoulder," she whispered, unbinding him. "As hard as you can, Cody."

He obeyed, and she rose to inspect the place she was sure Augie had stood. Gundry was still floating in the pond. Boot tracks came up to the spot from the willows, and then went back into them nearly along the same path.

She shook her head, angry with herself.

She'd missed.

But inching silently into the foliage, she found a blood spatter on a willow leaf. It was shaped like a tiny red comet. This meant that Augie had been running as he bled, and the pointed end indicated the direction of his flight. That he was fleeing encouraged her. But not much. Neither the carbine nor her revolver had been dropped back near the pond, so she still faced both weapons.

Coming to the far end of the willows, she looked out across the pasture. A dozen cows and their calves were bunched together along a distant fence, lowing at the inferno that had been the barn.

Dietz's boot tracks struck directly across the open ground toward the west.

She squinted against the declining sun to scan the sage-covered ridge rising above the grass. He could easily pick her off from there. Even a mediocre marksman could kill her from that distance, and Dietz had shown a grisly talent for sniping in how well he'd dropped Jack and Milt in the rain.

But she finally stepped out into the open.

An irrigation ditch ran along the edge of the pasture in front of her, flowing about a foot and a half deep.

Dietz's tracks went beyond it. He was on the ridge, she now believed. She hungered for the concealment she'd just left.

She was preparing to jump over the ditch when Dietz bolted up out of the manure-brown water and fired both guns at once at her. The muzzle flashes almost captivated her. Pretty blue-yellow stars. Twisting completely around, she lunged for the willows, crashing headlong into the branches and crawling back into the shadows.

Silence. Except for her own breaths, which sounded like little explosions to her.

She drew back the rifle bolt for a peek inside the chamber, then sighed in relief. She hadn't fired. And it had obviously been Augie's turn to miss. No wonder. Despite his grin—which she knew would haunt her if she survived this, he'd been choking and spluttering when he sat up out of the ditch. Water had been sheeting over his eyes from his hair. But he hadn't missed by much. She'd heard his misses whir by.

She had also seen the graze her bullet had left along his neck. But he'd had the presence of mind to walk backward to the ditch along his own tracks. He knew how to spring a trap.

Something clipped the leaves overhead. It was followed almost instantaneously by the sound of a shot coming from the direction of the barn.

Dee crept out to the pasture on her elbows and knees, the rifle laid across the crooks of her arms. She saw Augie rounding the tallest of the flames at a sprint. He'd stripped to the waist.

She got up and ran after him. She couldn't let him get out of sight again, although she decided to go around the other side of the collapsed barn. Jumping over the rail fence, she landed in the corral and stopped, the heat of the fire painful on the left half of her face. Dietz had vanished, which made no sense. He couldn't have cleared the pasture and reached the sage in the time it had taken her to approach the barnyard.

She shifted a few yards to make sure he wasn't crouched behind one of the dead horses.

The sound of gently lapping water came to her. There were ripples on the surface of the trough.

She knelt, thinking, calculating, then slowly aimed her rifle at the tin basin a few inches above the lip.

The trough could fill automatically, but she saw no last few drips from the spout. And Cinch, that first day she'd come up here, had said that the float valve was broken. Had he or Augie fixed it in the meantime?

Getting up, she started for the trough, but then halted again before she'd taken three strides.

Dietz had nearly had her once. She couldn't trust her luck to see her through a flurry of bullets twice. It'd take hours, even days of submersion for modern ammunition to get wet enough to misfire. And there was no place for her to hide this time, other than behind the widely spaced fence rails.

One cartridge.

She gazed all around, hoping to glimpse him on the nearby hills. Nothing. Not even spooked cattle.

A trickle of tiny bubbles broke the surface at the end opposite the spout.

"Stick your hands out of the water right now, Dietz," she said, close to shouting, "or I'll shoot you dead."

She waited three seconds, then fired.

The bullet penetrated the tin with a plink, and a narrow stream of water arced out. After a few seconds, it turned pink, and, finally, as she stepped up to look inside, a striking red.

CHAPTER **TWENTY**

The last week of December brought the first *pogonip*, or ice fog, to the valley. It stole in during the night, and by dawn the range, the sagebrush, even the strands of barbed wire, were glistening white. The pinyon on the mountain looked like clumps of coral. A pale sun eventually showed through the shroud, but shone too weakly to cast shadows.

Dee drove her new Bronco up the lane to the Holland Ranch. Rabe Pleasant sat beside her, his hands in his jacket pockets despite the near roar of the heater fan.

"Strange to see no cattle," he said, pulling his woolen muffler down away from his mouth.

Dee didn't feel the need to respond. But yes—it was strange. The Holland Ranch was now virtually surrounded by the newly designated Cayuse Mountain Wilderness Area. Cinch, if he chose, could continue to run his operation on his own land, but his grazing allotments were gone forever. In September, Rowena had moved to Reno with Cody. She was working as a keno runner at Harrah's. Jewell Farley didn't think she had the figure for it. At least for decent tips. Cinch had stayed behind with Mother Holland, who yesterday afternoon had finally put the finishing touch on her long, silent death.

"Well, it's done," Rabe prattled on in an obvious attempt to cheer her up, "and you're leaving something behind, Dee. Not many people can take that from their work. A bona fide wilderness."

She nodded.

Even the local livestock operators had wound up supporting the legislation. First, though, Dee had taken them up to Esmeralda County to see a Thunder Bay Mining Company heap leaching operation in full swing. A five-mile gash through the sage and pinyon had been deepened by giant shovels; hundred-ton trucks raised clouds of dust as they rumbled from the pit to the mustard-colored piles being sprinkled with cyanide solution. Flourlike dust coated everything for miles, including human lungs, and Thunder Bay, by sinking deep wells to supply the water-intensive process, had depleted the aquifer so severely that all the springs in the basin dried up. The Esmeralda livestock operators tried to get an injunction, but then learned the sad truth about an 1872 federal law still in effect: Mining has priority over any other use of public land.

Seeing all this firsthand, the Cayuse Valley ranchers—cattlemen and sheepmen alike—decided to spare their range the same fate, even if it meant reducing the acreage available for grazing. The creation of a wilderness area, however detestable to them, turned out to be the only way they had to guard their water resources against Thunder Bay.

In a final irony, Tyler Ravenshaw had been retained by the state cattlemen's association to help draft the legislation. T.R. had cut short his honeymoon with Elsbeth to get going on it.

Eric Brenner and his friends walked free from a federal detention center because, as expected, the search and seizure was held to be unwarranted and unreasonable. In late October, Dee was contacted at the Pyrennes by an ATF agent and an investigator from the sheriff's office in Meagher County, Montana. Eric and Karena had been arrested for monkeywrenching by explosive device, and they wanted everything the BLM had on the irrepressible Greens. Allegedly, they'd used dynamite to down a powerline tower across a bridge that served several ranches, which gave Dee some idea of how Brenner had intended to disrupt the test on the nuclear site.

Cinch, Wade Russell, and the Wheatley brothers were not prosecuted for the mustang slaughter. Lack of evidence was blamed, but it was a political decision. Yet, Dee saw the wisdom, especially with the wilderness bill hanging in the balance, not to dog the ranching community any more this season.

She now parked at the gate, which was locked. She hadn't seen Cinch since the shooting inquest, and only now, with the passing of his mother, did she feel that she had a reason to call on him.

"Want me to go with you, sweetness?" Rabe asked.

"No," she said, leaving the engine running, "stay inside where it's warm."

He winked gamely at her. "Love's a vapor."

"It's a pain in the ass."

"How would you ever know?"

She got out and jumped over the gate. Her holstered revolver bounced against her hip as she landed on the frozen ground. She started for the house, but then spotted Cinch up at the family plot.

He waved, which made her feel better about coming.

Slowly, she went up to him. A raven flapped off the fence ahead of her, black against the whitish fog. She passed Howard Holland's stone: "assassinated by a foreigner." As if for the first time, she realized that Cinch had taken his own risks in loving her back then.

He looked thinner than usual, nearly as thin as he'd been in high school. He was sitting on a saddle in his fleece-lined coat, gazing at the blanket of ice crystals on the fresh, unmarked grave.

Dee crossed herself, but kept quiet.

He finally smiled up at her, cleared his throat. "Got close to her again these past months, Dee," he said. "I guess the two of us changed places, and this time 'round she was the little baby to look after. I did everythin' for her, just as she did for me when I was small. She din't seem old. Just small. It was a nice way for things to finish 'tween us. Kinda peculiar, but nice. Know what I mean?"

She nodded.

"Hear they're gonna transfer you."

"That's right, California maybe," she said. "It hasn't been decided where exactly. They're still looking for a hole deep enough. I've caused all the trouble I can in Pinyon County."

"Well, I'm movin' on, too."

"When?"

"Right now." Rising, he hefted the saddle onto his shoulder, winced from his gunshot wound, and started walking toward the road.

Dumbstruck, turning to watch him go, Dee suddenly realized that flames were showing through the windows of the house. She caught up. "Cinch, your place is on fire!"

"Better be or I just wasted five gallons of good kerosene." A window blew out, and a big orange lick of fire squirmed up and flattened under the eaves. The roof shingles started smoldering. Yet, Cinch just sauntered on down the hill. He glanced at her face and chuckled. "Lighten up. It ain't insured, Row got the furniture, the water rights are in question, and with no grazin' allotments the whole homestead ain't worth the powder to blast it sky-high."

"What'll you do?"

"Don't know. Quit askin' myself that. You're free if you can keep from askin' yourself that question. Free as you're ever gonna be in this life. I'll make out. Just like you."

She threaded her arm through his.

Rabe was waiting anxiously for them at the gate. "I'm sure there's an explanation," he said to Cinch, "but your house is going up in flames. Fast."

Cinch balanced his saddle on the gate, then climbed over. "There is an explanation—you win."

"Me?"

"Hell, not you personally, Pleasant. The goddamn gov'mint. You got the last of the original Cayuse buckaroos off the land. That oughta be worth somethin'."

Rabe said, "I'm not chalking this up as a victory."

Cinch nodded. "I know. I was just lettin' off steam.

Got a ton of it to bleed off.'' He helped Dee over, then shouldered his saddle again.

''You want a ride to the Greyhound stop?'' she asked.

''Nope,'' Cinch said. ''Ridin' away don't sound the same as walkin' away. And I mean to get a few beers out of this story. So long.''

He veered off the road and out into the sage, his boots leaving tawny prints in the frost. He was striking cross-country to Highway 95, then. He wanted to be alone, leaving his place.

But once, before he disappeared, he half turned and shouted, ''Dominica . . . where you figure to live in California?''

''You'll find out, Cordell, if you need to.''

He laughed, his voice full of devilment. Just like the boy she remembered from the long bus ride to Tonopah.

Then the fog had him.

FAST-PACED MYSTERIES
BY J.A. JANCE

Featuring J.P. Beaumont

UNTIL PROVEN GUILTY 89638-9/$4.99 US/$5.99 CAN

INJUSTICE FOR ALL 89641-9/$4.50 US/$5.50 CAN

TRIAL BY FURY 75138-0/$4.99 US/$5.99 CAN

TAKING THE FIFTH 75139-9/$4.99 US/$5.99 CAN

IMPROBABLE CAUSE 75412-6/$4.99 US/$5.99 CAN

A MORE PERFECT UNION 75413-4/$4.99 US/$5.99 CAN

DISMISSED WITH PREJUDICE

75547-5/$4.99 US/$5.99 CAN

MINOR IN POSSESSION 75546-7/$4.99 US/$5.99 CAN

PAYMENT IN KIND 75836-9/$4.99 US/$5.99 CAN

WITHOUT DUE PROCESS 75837-7/$4.99 US/$5.99 CAN

FAILURE TO APPEAR 75839-3/$5.50 US/$6.50 CAN

Featuring Joanna Brady

DESERT HEAT 76545-4/$4.99 US/$5.99 CAN

TOMBSTONE COURAGE 76546-2/$5.99 US/$6.99 CAN